THE
HYDE PARK
HEADSMAN

Anne Perry

FAWCETT CREST • NEW YORK

A Fawcett Crest Book
Published by Ballantine Books
Copyright © 1994 by Anne Perry

All rights reserved under International and Pan-American Copyright Conventions. Published in the United States by Ballantine Books, a division of Random House, Inc., New York, and simultaneously in Canada by Random House of Canada Limited, Toronto.

Library of Congress Catalog Card Number: 93-22124

ISBN 0-449-22350-7

Printed in Canada

First Hardcover Edition: March 1994
First Mass Market Edition: March 1995

10 9 8 7 6 5 4 3 2 1

To Leona Nevler, with thanks.

1

"OH GEORGE." Millicent let out her breath in a sigh of happiness. "Isn't it beautiful? I've never been out in the park at this time of the morning before. The dawn is so romantic, don't you think? It's the beginning of everything!"

George said nothing, but tiptoed a little more rapidly over the wet grass.

"Look at the light on the water." Millicent went on ecstatically. "It's just like a great silver plate."

"Funny shape for a plate," George muttered, regarding the long, narrow snake of the Serpentine with less enthusiasm than she.

"It will be like fairyland out there." Millicent had no respect for the practical at a time like this. She had crept out through the park to sail on the dawn-lit water alone with George. What place had the literal at such a point? She picked up her skirts to keep them from getting soaked in the dew; this much was merely common sense, which was a totally different thing. No one wanted the wet, heavy fabric flapping around their ankles.

"There's someone already out," George said with disgust. And in the broadening light it was quite plain that there was indeed one of the small boats about three yards from the shore, but the figure in it was curiously bent over, as if looking for something in the bottom of the boat by his feet.

Millicent could hardly contain her disappointment. Where was the romance if someone else was present, someone not part of the idyll? One could pretend Hyde Park, in the middle of London, were a wood in some European archdukedom and

George a prince, or at least a knight, but some other mundane-minded oarsman would definitely spoil it; apart from the fact that she should not be here, unchaperoned, and a witness was not welcome.

"Maybe he'll go away," she said hopefully.

"He's not moving," George replied with annoyance. He raised his voice. "Excuse me, sir. Are you quite well?" He frowned. "I can't see the fellow's face at all," he added to Millicent. "Wait here. I shall see if he will be a gentleman and move a little away." And he strode down towards the bank regardless of getting his shoes soaked, hesitated on the verge, then stumbled to his knees and slid with a violent splash into the water.

"Oh!" Millicent was horrified, painfully embarrassed for him, and having difficulty stifling her intense desire to giggle. "Oh, George!" She ran down the grass to where he was thrashing around in the shallows making a fearful noise and stirring up mud without seeming to regain his feet. Extraordinarily, the man in the boat took no notice whatsoever.

Then in the fast strengthening light, Millicent saw why. She had assumed he was bent forward, as had George. It was not so. His head was absent. There was nothing above his shoulders but the blood-soaked stump of his neck.

Millicent crumpled into total oblivion and fell headlong onto the grass.

"Yes sir," the constable said smartly. "Captain the Honorable Oakley Winthrop, R.N. Found 'eadless in one o' them little rowboats on the Serpentine. This mornin' about dawn. Two young lovers off for a romantic trip." He invested the word *romantic* with infinite scorn. "Poor souls fainted clean away—got no stomach for the likes o' that."

"Not unnatural," Superintendent Thomas Pitt said reasonably. "I should find it a very worrying thought if they had."

The constable quite obviously did not understand him.

"Yes sir," he said with bland obedience. "The local bobby were called, when the gentleman pulled 'isself together and got out o' the water. I gather as 'e fell in wi' the shock o' the event, like." His lips twitched very slightly but his voice was carefully ironed of even the suspicion of humor. "Constable Withers, that was 'im what was called, 'is bein' on duty in the park, like. 'E took one look at the corpse an' knew as 'e'd got a real nasty one, so 'e sent for 'is sergeant, an' they looked a

2

bit closer, like." He drew in his breath, waiting for Pitt to say something.

"Yes?" Pitt prompted.

"That's when they found 'oo the dead man were," the constable continued. " 'Im being an important naval man, and an 'Honorable,' like, they thought as it should be someone o' your rank to 'andle it—sir." He looked at Pitt with satisfaction.

Pitt was newly promoted to superintendent. He had fought it long because he knew his real skill, which was very considerable, lay in working with people, both with the denizens of the semiunderworld, the poor or the truly criminal, and with the inhabitants of the servants' quarters, the front parlors, and the withdrawing rooms of the gentry.

Then in the late autumn of last year, 1889, his superior, Micah Drummond, had retired from office in order to marry the woman he had loved ever since the appalling scandal that had ruined her husband and finally taken his life. He had recommended Pitt to fill his place on the grounds that although Pitt was not a gentleman, as Drummond most certainly was, he had the experience of actual police work, at which he was undoubtedly gifted, and had proved himself able to solve even the most delicate cases involving the politically or socially powerful.

And after the fiasco of the Whitechapel murders, still unsolved and perhaps destined to remain so, and the fierce unpopularity of the police, the public lack of faith in them, it was time for a bold change.

So now in the spring of 1890, the dawn of a new decade, Pitt was in charge of the Bow Street station, with special responsibility for sensitive cases which threatened to become explosive if not handled with both tact and extreme dispatch. Hence P. C. Grover was standing in front of him in the beautiful office which he had inherited from Micah Drummond, telling him of the decapitation of Captain the Honorable Oakley Winthrop, knowing that Pitt would be obliged to handle the case.

"What else do you know about it?" Pitt asked, looking up at Grover and leaning back in his chair, although at times like this he still felt it to be Drummond's chair.

"Sir?" Grover raised his eyebrows.

"What did the medical officer say?" Pitt prompted.

"Died of 'avin' 'is 'ead cut orf," Grover replied, lifting his chin a little.

Pitt considered telling him not to be insolent, but he was still feeling his way with the men in his command. He had not worked with them closely before, always having had one sergeant with him at most, more often no one at all. He was regarded more as a rival than a colleague.

They had obeyed Micah Drummond because he was from a distinguished family with private means and had a career in the army behind him, and thus was of a class doubly used to command. Pitt was totally different, a gamekeeper's son who spoke well only because he had been educated, by grace, with the son of the estate. He had neither the manner nor the appearance of one born to lead. He was tall, but he frequently stood awkwardly. His hair was untidy, even on his best days. On his worst it looked as if he had been blown in by a gale. He dressed with abandon, and kept in his pockets a marvelous assortment of articles which he thought might one day prove handy.

The Bow Street men were slow to get used to him, and he was finding leadership alien to his nature. He was used to disregarding the rules, and being tolerated because he succeeded. Command placed quite different obligations on him and required a stiffer and less eccentric example to be set. Suddenly he was responsible for other men's orders, their successes and failures, even their physical safety.

Pitt fixed Grover with a cold eye. "Time of death, Constable," he said levelly. "That would be more instructive to know. And was he killed in the boat or brought there afterwards?"

Grover's face fell. "Oh, I don't think we know that, sir. Not yet. Bit of a risky thing to do, though, chop a man's 'ead orf right there in the park. Could 'ave bin seen by anyone out for a walk."

"And how many people were out for a walk at that hour, Grover?"

Grover shifted his feet.

"Oh, well, don't seem as if there were nobody but them two as found 'im. But your murderer couldn't 'ave counted on that, could 'e." It was a statement rather than a question. "Could've been anyone out for a morning ride," he went on reasonably. "Or even someone comin' home late from a party, or a night out, takin' the air ..."

"That is if it was done in daylight," Pitt pointed out. "Perhaps it was done long before that. Have you found anyone else who was in the park yet?"

4

"No sir, not yet. We came to report it to you, Mr. Pitt, as soon as we realized as it were someone important." It was his ultimate justification, and he knew it was sufficient.

"Right," Pitt agreed. "By the way, did you find the head?"

"Yes sir, it was right there in the boat beside 'im, like," Grover replied, blinking.

"I see. Thank you. Send Mr. Tellman up, will you."

"Yes, sir." Grover stood to attention momentarily. "Thank you, sir." And he turned on his heel and went out, closing the door softly behind him.

It was less than three minutes before Tellman knocked, and Pitt told him to enter. He was a lean man with a narrow aquiline face, hollow cheeks and a tight sarcastic mouth. He had come up through the ranks with hard work and ruthless application. Six months ago he had been Pitt's equal, now he was his junior, and resented it bitterly. He stood to attention in front of the large leather-inlaid desk, and Pitt sitting in the easy chair behind it.

"Yes, sir," he said coldly.

Pitt refused to acknowledge he had heard the tone in Tellman's voice. He looked across at him with innocent eyes. "There's been a murder in Hyde Park," he said calmly. "A man by the name of Oakley Winthrop, Captain the Honorable, R.N. Found a little after dawn in one of the pleasure boats on the Serpentine. Beheaded."

"Unpleasant," Tellman said laconically. "Important, was he, this Winthrop?"

"I don't know," Pitt said honestly. "But his parents are titled, so we can assume he was, at least in some people's eyes."

Tellman pulled a face. He despised those he considered passengers in society. Privilege stirred in him a raw, bitter anger that stretched far back into his childhood memories of hunger, cold, and endless weariness and anxiety, a father beaten by circumstances till he had no pride left, a mother who worked till she was too tired to talk to her children or laugh with them.

"I suppose we will all be trudging holes in our boots so we can get the beggar who did it," he said sourly. "Sounds like a madman to me. I mean, why would anyone do anything so—" He stopped, uncertain what word he wanted. "Was his head there? You didn't say."

"Yes it was. There was no attempt to hide his identity."

Tellman pulled a face. "Like I said, a madman. What the hell was a naval captain doing in a pleasure boat on the Ser-

5

pentine anyway?" A smile lit his face quite suddenly, showing a totally different side to his nature. "Bit of a comedown, isn't it? Fellow like that'd be more used to a battleship." He cleared his throat. "Wonder if he was there with a woman. Someone else's wife, maybe?"

"Possibly," Pitt agreed. "But keep such speculation to yourself for the time being. First of all find out all the physical facts you can." He saw Tellman wince at being told something he considered so obvious. He disregarded the man's expression and continued. "Get all the material details. I want to know when he was killed, what with, whether it took one blow or several, whether he was struck from the front or the back, left hand or right, and if he was conscious at the time or not . . ."

Tellman raised his eyebrows.

"And how will they know that, sir?" he inquired.

"They've got the head," Pitt replied. "They'll know if he was struck first—and they've got the body, they can find out if he was drugged or poisoned."

"Won't know if he was asleep," Tellman pointed out sententiously.

Pitt ignored him. "Tell me what he was wearing," he went on. "And the state of his shoes. Did he walk across the grass to the boat, or was he carried? And you certainly ought to be able to work out whether his head was chopped off there in the boat or somewhere else." He looked up at Tellman. "And then you can drag the Serpentine to see if you can find the weapon!"

Tellman's face darkened. "Yes, sir. Will that be all, sir?"

"No—but it's a start."

"Anyone in particular you want me to take on this job, sir? Being as it's so delicate?"

"Yes," Pitt said with satisfaction. "Take le Grange." Le Grange was a smooth-tongued, rather glib young man whose sycophantic manner irritated Tellman even more than it did Pitt. "He'll handle the possible witnesses very well."

Tellman's expression was vile, but he said nothing. He stiffened to attention for an instant, then turned on his heel and went out.

Pitt leaned back in his chair and thought deeply. It was the first major case he had been in charge of since taking over from Micah Drummond. Of course there had been other crimes, even serious ones, but none within the scope for which

6

he was particularly appointed: those which threatened scandal or tragedy of more than purely private proportions.

He had not heard the name Winthrop before, but then he did not move in society, nor was he familiar with the leading figures in the armed services. Members of Parliament he knew more closely, but Winthrop was not of that body, and if his father ever took his seat in the House of Lords, it had not so far been to sufficient effect for it to have reached public awareness.

Surely Micah Drummond would have reference books for such an occasion? Even he could not have stored in his memory all the pertinent facts of every important man or woman in London.

Pitt swiveled around in the chair and stared at the immaculate bookshelves. He was already familiar with many of the titles. It had been one of the first things he had done on moving in. There it was—*Who's Who*. He pulled it out with both hands and opened it on the desk. Captain the Honourable Oakley Winthrop was not present. However, Lord Marlborough Winthrop was written up at some length, more for his heritage than his achievements, but nonetheless the book gave a very fair picture of a proud, wealthy, rather humorless man of middle age whose interests were tediously predictable. He had had a host of respectable minor offices and was related to a wide variety of the great families in the land, some quite distantly, but nevertheless each connection was duly noted. Some forty years ago he had married one Evelyn Hurst, third daughter of an admiral, later ennobled.

Pitt closed the book with a feeling of foreboding. Lord and Lady Winthrop were not likely to be placated easily if answers were slow in coming, or displeasing in their nature. It was probably unfair, but already he had a picture of them in his mind.

Was Tellman right—was a madman loose in the park? Or had Oakley Winthrop in some way brought it upon himself by courting another man's wife, welshing on his debts, or cheating? Or was he privy to some dangerous secret? These were questions that would have to be asked with subtlety and extreme tact.

In the meantime he would like to have gone to the park and sought the material evidence himself, but it was Tellman's job, and it would be time wasting as well as impolitic to oversee him in its pursuance.

Charlotte Pitt was occupied as differently as possible. With Pitt's promotion had come the opportunity to move to a larger house, one with a garden offering not only a broad lawn and two large herbaceous borders but also a very considerable kitchen garden and three old apple trees, at the moment the gnarled boughs fat with buds for blossom. Charlotte had fallen in love with it the moment she stepped through the French doors of the withdrawing room onto the stone-flagged terrace and seen the garden in front of her.

The house itself needed much work before it was ready to move into, but she could imagine all sorts of wonderful possibilities for it. A hundred times in her mind she had decorated it, hung curtains, found carpets, arranged and rearranged the furniture.

Now the wallpaper was stripped off in many places and the plaster was so damaged as to need gouging out and replacing with new. There were other things missing or broken, large pieces out of cornices, friezes and moldings. The plaster ceiling rose in the dining room was so badly chipped as to need replacing. The hall lamp was missing all its glass, as were several of the gas brackets in other rooms. The mirror on the overmantel in the dining room was spotted across the center and cracked at the edges, and the fireplace in the main bedroom had lost several of its border tiles. There would be a great deal to do, but she was full of enthusiasm, and so far undaunted by the prospect.

She was completely unaware of the murder in Hyde Park. She stood in the middle of the withdrawing room visualizing how splendid it would be when it was all finished. In the house in Bloomsbury they had had only a front parlor, very pleasant in its fashion, but it was a poor thing by comparison with this; or to be more exact, with what this could become. Then she would be able to invite people to dinner—something she had not done before in her married life, with the exception, of course, of immediate family.

Her parents had been quite comfortable—although at the time she had felt it to be barely sufficient. There was never money in hand for as many dresses as she would have wished, or for more than one carriage. But when she had scandalized her friends by marrying a policeman, at the same time as her younger sister, Emily, had married a viscount, both their lives had changed beyond recognition and beyond their power to imagine beforehand.

Then George Ashworth had died, leaving Emily a very rich widow, and later she had married Jack Radley, charming, handsome and virtually penniless. She seemed totally happy, and that was all that mattered. Her seven-year-old son, Edward, now Lord Ashworth, had a baby sister, Evangeline, known as Evie, and Jack was again attempting to gain a seat in Parliament. Under Emily's cajoling, flattering and persuasion he had found a social conscience and determined to forge himself a career. His first attempt had ended in failure, although, both Emily and Charlotte conceded willingly, a moral victory.

"Excuse me, ma'am . . ." Charlotte's thoughts were interrupted by the voice of her maid, Gracie, a tiny waif of a girl who had been with her ever since her move to Bloomsbury. Now she was an intelligent and determined eighteen-year-old who had beyond question found her place in life as the confidante and, as of the last case, the assistant to the wife of a detective. The change in her from the child she had been was miraculous. She bristled confidence and appetite for adventure. She was still as thin as a ninepenny rabbit. All the clothes she was given were too long for her and had to be taken up, but her cheeks had color, and she was more than a match for the most impertinent delivery boy or the most uppity servant of anyone else. After all, she had adventures. All they ever did was housework.

"Yes, Gracie?" Charlotte said absently.

"The dustman's 'ere 'oo said as 'e'd take them broken tiles and get the linoleum up from the kitchen that's all scuffed and frayed at the edges," Gracie said busily. " 'E said that it'd only cost one and sixpence, an' 'e'd take the rubbish out o' the back yard too."

"A shilling," Charlotte said automatically. "And he can have the broken lamp brackets as well, if he'll take them down."

"Yes ma'am." Gracie whisked out to return less than a moment later with Emily at her heels. Charlotte's sister came in in a whirl of rose-pink skirts, marvelous sleeves and a fashionably slender waist, not quite as it was before Evie, but still most becoming. Her fair hair sat in an aureole of curls around her face, and her expression was one of amazement.

"Oh Charlotte!" She gazed around and swallowed hard. Charlotte glared at her.

"It could be . . . beautiful," Emily added, then burst into giggles, sinking in a heap of skirts into the old sofa pushed over towards the front windows.

Charlotte opened her mouth to say something furious, then realized how absurd that would be. The room was bare and drab. Old wallpaper hung in ribbons from broken plaster, the windows were dirty and one was cracked, the lamp brackets broken. The old sofa was covered in a dust sheet like a solitary ghost. The rest of the house was no better. The only way to cope was to laugh.

"It will be all right," she said at length when they had recovered themselves.

"It will have to be replastered, then repapered," Emily pointed out, "before you can begin to choose new fixtures and fittings."

"I know that." Charlotte sniffed, wiped the tears away with her hand. "That will be half the pleasure. I will have reclaimed a disaster and made it into something fine."

"How very feminine of you, my dear," Emily said with a broad smile. "So many women I know spend their lives trying to do that—and not only with houses: mostly with husbands. But the trouble with that is you cannot move if it doesn't work!" She stood up again, absently straightening her skirts. "Show me the rest of this catastrophe. I promise I will try to see what a noble thing it may become. By the way, there has been a fearful murder in Hyde Park, did you know?"

"No, when?" Charlotte led the way to what would become the dining room. "How do you know? Was it in the morning newspapers?"

"No." Emily shook her head. "I gather the body was only found this morning, on the Serpentine in one of those little boats." She gazed around her. "This room has nice proportions, except it needs a larger mantel. But you could replace that one quite easily, and put it in the bedroom perhaps? It is too narrow for here. I heard it as we stopped for traffic at the Tottenham Court Road. The newsboys were shouting about it. Some naval officer had his head cut off."

Charlotte had started towards the window and stopped abruptly, swinging around to face Emily. "His head cut off!"

"Yes. Unpleasant, isn't it? I suppose Thomas will be in charge of it, because he was a captain, and his parents are Lord and Lady Winthrop."

"Who are they?" Charlotte asked with sharper interest. She and Emily had first met Pitt when he had investigated the murder of their elder sister, Sarah, and ever since then they had both involved themselves in his more serious cases as much as opportunity permitted, and frequently a great deal more than Pitt would have allowed, had he been consulted before rather than informed when it was too late.

"Oh, neither old money nor new," Emily replied dismissively. "Not really very colorful, but connected to half the Home Counties in one way or another, and very aware of it." She shrugged. "You know the sort of person? Never achieved anything in particular, but always wanted to be important. No imagination, absolutely sure they know what they believe about everybody and everything, quite kind in their own way, as honest as the day, and no sense of humor whatsoever."

"Deadly," Charlotte said succinctly. "And all the harder because you cannot really dislike them, just be infuriated and bored."

"Exactly," Emily agreed, moving towards the door. "You know, I can't even remember quite what Lady Winthrop looks like. She might be fairish and a little stout, or else she might be that darkish woman who is too tall. Isn't it silly? Or she might even be the pigeon-chested one whose face I can't place at all. I'm not usually like that. I can't afford to be, with Jack hoping to be in Parliament." She pulled a face. "Just imagine if one addressed the wrong person as the Prime Minister's wife!" She pulled an even worse face. "Disaster! Even the Foreign Office wouldn't consider you after that."

They were in the hallway, and she stopped with a little sigh of appreciation. "I do like your stairs. Now that is really very elegant, Charlotte. This newel post is one of the handsomest I've seen. My goodness, it must have taken some carving." She tilted her head back and followed the line of the banister upwards to the newel at the top, and then along the landing. "Yes, very gracious. How many bedrooms are there?"

"I told you, five, and plenty of space in the attic for Gracie," Charlotte replied. "Really nice rooms. She can have two, and I'll keep the box room and a spare one, just in case."

Emily grinned. "In case what? Another resident servant?"

Charlotte shrugged. "Why not—one day? Do you know anything about the man who was murdered?" She was thinking of Pitt.

"No." Emily opened her eyes very wide and bright. "But I could find out."

"I don't think you should say anything to Thomas yet," Charlotte said cautiously.

"Oh, I know," Emily agreed, nodding her head and leading the way up the stairs, caressing the banister rail as she went. "That's really very nice." She stopped for a moment and looked up at the ceiling. "That's nice too. I do like coffering. None of that plasterwork is broken. All it needs is a little paint. Yes, I know to be careful, Thomas is so much more important these days." She turned and gave Charlotte a radiant smile. "I'm so glad. I like him enormously, I hope you know that."

"Of course I know that," Charlotte said warmly. "I'm glad you like the ceiling too. I thought it was rather fine. It gives the hall dignity, don't you think?"

They reached the landing at the top and began looking at the bedrooms. Emily was joining in the spirit and ignoring the broken tiles in the fireplaces and the peeling paper on the walls.

"Have they set the date for the by-election yet?" Charlotte inquired.

"No, but we know who is standing for the Tories," Emily replied with a frown. "Nigel Uttley. Highly respected and very powerful. I'm not sure just how much of a chance Jack has, realistically. Of course I don't tell Jack that." She smiled ruefully. "Especially after last time."

Charlotte said nothing. Last time had been so fraught with other pains and tragedies that political failure had seemed almost incidental. Jack had withdrawn, refusing to be compromised or to join the secret society known as the Inner Circle, which would have ensured his acceptance as candidate and the support of a vast hidden network of men with influence, money and an unbreakable bond. But there was also the covenant of secrecy, the preferments offered to members at the expense of outsiders, the promises of protection, lies to conceal, and ostracism and punishment for transgressors. Above all what appalled Jack and frightened Pitt was the secrecy—the doubt, suspicion and fear sown by not knowing who were members, whose loyalties were already spoken for in a dark covenant, which consciences were in bondage even before the choices were framed.

"I assume this is going to be your room?" Emily asked, gazing around the large bedroom with its wide window over the garden. "I like this. Is this the biggest room, or is the front one a trifle wider?"

"I think it is, but it doesn't matter. I'd sacrifice size for that

12

window," Charlotte replied without hesitation. "And that room"— she indicated the door to her left—"as a dressing room for Thomas. The front one will do well for a nursery for Daniel and Jemima, and they can have the smaller ones for bedrooms."

"What color?" Emily looked at the walls, by now totally ignoring the stains and tears.

"I'm not sure. Maybe blue, maybe green," Charlotte said thoughtfully.

"Blue will be cold," Emily answered. "Actually, so will green."

"I like it anyway."

"What direction are we facing?"

"Southwest," Charlotte replied. "The afternoon sun comes in the French doors below us in the dining room."

"Then I daresay it'll be all right. Charlotte . . ."

"Yes?"

Emily stood in the middle of the floor, her face puckered. "I know I was rather hard on you when I came back from the country, in fact possibly even unfair . . ."

"About Mama? You certainly were," Charlotte agreed. "I don't know what you expected me to do!"

"I wasn't there," Emily said reasonably. "I don't know what could have been done, but surely something. For heaven's sake, Charlotte, the man's not only an actor—and a Jew—but he's seventeen years younger than Mama!"

"She knows that," Charlotte agreed. "He's also charming, intelligent, funny, kind, loyal to his friends, and he seems to care for her very much."

"I expect all that's true," Emily conceded. "But to what end? She can't possibly marry him! Even supposing he asked her."

"I know that!"

"She'll ruin her reputation if she hasn't done so already," Emily went on. "Papa will be turning over in his grave." She swiveled around very slowly. "You could have blue in here if you didn't have dark furniture." She looked back at Charlotte. "What are we going to do about her now? Grandmama is beside herself."

"She's been in a rage for months," Charlotte said without concern. "If not years. She enjoys it. If it wasn't this, it would be something else."

"But this is different," Emily protested, her face puckered

13

with concern. "This time she's right! What Mama is doing is absurd and dangerous. She could find herself quite outside society when it's all over. Have you even thought about that?"

"Yes, of course I have. And I've told her till I'm blue in the face—but it doesn't make a ha'p'orth of difference. She knows it all, and she considers it worth the price."

"Then she isn't thinking clearly," Emily said tartly, hunching her shoulders a little. "She can't mean it."

"I think I would." Charlotte spoke not so much to Emily as to the view beyond the window. "I think I would rather have a brief time of real happiness, and take the chance, than an age of gray respectability."

"Respectability isn't gray!" Emily retorted. Then suddenly her face crumpled into a giggle. "It's—brown."

Charlotte shot her a look of swift appreciation.

"All the same," Emily went on, her eyes steady in spite of her laughter. "The lack of respectability can be very unpleasant, especially when you are older. It can be very lonely to be shut out, whatever color the inside is."

Charlotte knew it was true, and why Emily had said it. Perhaps in her mother's place she too would have opted for a brief, painful and glorious romance, but she was not unaware of the bitter price.

"I know," she said quietly. "And Grandmama will never let her forget it, even if everyone else does."

Emily gazed around the room thoughtfully.

Charlotte read her thought.

"Oh no!" she said decidedly. "Not here! We haven't room!"

"No, I suppose not," Emily agreed reluctantly, then suddenly she smiled again. "Were you thinking of Mama or Grandmama?"

"Grandmama, of course," Charlotte responded. "Mama would remain in Cater Street, naturally. It is her house. I'm not sure which would be worse, living with Grandmama goading and complaining all the time, or all by yourself with no one to talk to at all. Sitting every day wondering if anyone will call, and if you dare call on someone else, or if they will all send polite messages to the door that they are not at home, even when you can see the carriages in the drive and know perfectly well that they are—and they know you know."

"Don't." Emily winced as if she had been struck. "I can't bear to think of it. We'll simply have to do something!" She looked at Charlotte. "Have you tried appealing to him? If he

14

cares for her at all, he must realize what will happen. Is he a complete fool?"

"He's an actor." Charlotte shrugged in a sort of exasperation. "It's a different world. He may not understand . . ."

"Well, have you tried to explain to him?" Emily demanded. "For goodness sake, Charlotte!"

"No I haven't! Mother would never forgive me. Telling her is one thing; telling him is quite another. We have no business to do that."

"We have every business!" Emily argued heatedly. "For her own sake. Someone's got to look after her."

"Emily! Can you hear yourself?" Charlotte demanded. "How would you feel if someone else, whatever their motives or however much they thought it was for your good, stepped in and tried to warn Jack not to marry you for your well-being?"

"That's quite different." Emily's eyes were bright and sharp. "Jack married me. Joshua Fielding won't marry Mama."

"I know he did, but Emily, my dearest, Mama might have thought Jack married you for your very considerable fortune."

"That's not true!" The hot color burned up Emily's face.

"I never believed it was," Charlotte said quickly. "I think Jack is a charming and honest man, but if Mama had thought otherwise, would it have been right for her to interfere—believing it was for your sake?"

"Ah—oh." Emily stood motionless. "Well . . ."

"Precisely." Charlotte led the way to the second bedroom.

"It's not the same," Emily said behind her. "There isn't any possible happy outcome to Mama's romance."

"It's still not right for us to go to Joshua," Charlotte insisted. "We'll just have to keep on trying with her. Maybe she'll listen to you. She certainly took no notice at all of me." They stopped just inside the doorway. "I think I'll do this room in yellow. It would be nice and warm. Daniel and Jemima could play up here in the winter, and on wet days. What do you think?"

"Yellow would be very nice," Emily agreed. "You could put a little green with it to stop it being too sweet." She looked across the room. "That fireplace needs a lot of mending. In fact you should get rid of it altogether and get another one. Those tiles are dreadful."

"I told you, I agreed I will move the one up from the withdrawing room."

15

"Oh yes, so you did."

"You will find out about Captain Winthrop, won't you?"

"Of course." Emily smiled again with sudden optimism. "I wonder if it will be a case with which we can help. I have missed all the excitement. It seems like ages since we did anything important together."

By mid-afternoon Pitt could no longer bear being on the sidelines. He collected his hat from the elegant stand by the door. He adjusted his jacket without making it hang any better, and decided he should take out of his pockets at least a ball of string which he no longer needed, two pieces of sealing wax and a rather long pencil, then he went out onto the landing and down the stairs.

"I'm going to see the widow," he informed the desk sergeant. "What is the address?"

The sergeant did not need to ask him which widow he meant. The whole station had been buzzing with the news since morning.

"Twenty-four Curzon Street, sir," he said immediately. "Poor lady. I wouldn't like to 'ave bin the sergeant wot 'ad ter tell 'er. Any death is bad enough, but that's the kind o' shock no one should 'ave ter take."

"No," Pitt agreed, ashamed of himself for being so grateful he had not been the one to bring the news. That was one benefit of promotion. Now Tellman would do the wretched duties that had been his only a few months ago. Then he shuddered. Tellman's lantern face was not the one he would have wished bearing tidings of bereavement. He looked too much like an undertaker himself, at the best of times. Perhaps Pitt should have gone after all.

He went out onto the pavement of Bow Street and started north towards Drury Lane and a hansom cab. But whatever he thought of Tellman, unless he proved himself incompetent at the task, he must not rob him of his stewardship. He lengthened his stride with a haste he could not explain.

In Drury Lane he hailed a cab and gave the driver the Winthrops' address, then settled back for the ride. He was not sure what he could add to the information Tellman would already have gathered, except his own impressions. But sometimes personal judgment was the most valuable element, the one thing no one else could give you, the small voice in the back of the mind which warned to look beyond the obvious.

16

No one had reported back yet, which did not surprise him. Tellman would leave it till the last possible moment that bordered on insolence but avoided outright insubordination. And Pitt was obliged by honesty to admit he had reported to his own superiors only when he felt he could evade it no longer. He disliked being told how he should conduct his case by someone behind a desk, who had not seen the faces of the men and women involved and knew nothing of their emotions. Much as it annoyed him, he could not justly blame Tellman for doing the same.

So now he was going to do what Micah Drummond had never done; he was on his way to interview the widow on the first day of the case. But it was a sensitive matter. This was the very reason he had obtained preferment instead of Tellman or some other officer brought in from another station. He knew how to treat the gentry with courtesy, and yet still to read their emotions, detect their lies and persist until he found the truth hidden beneath the layers of politics, ritual, subterfuge and pride.

Not a little of his past success was due to Charlotte's help, and he admitted it freely to himself, if not to the assistant commissioner.

The hansom drew up in Curzon Street, Pitt alighted and paid the driver, then taking off his hat in preparatory courtesy, he mounted the front door steps to number twenty-four and pulled the brass bell knob.

It was several moments before a white-faced butler answered and looked at Pitt almost expressionlessly.

"Good afternoon," Pitt said very soberly. "Superintendent Thomas Pitt, from Bow Street. I should appreciate a short interview with Mrs. Winthrop." He produced his card, now with his rank engraved on it as well as his name, and dropped it on the butler's silver tray. "I understand this is a most distressing time, but she may be able to help find the man who has brought about this tragedy, and speed is of the essence."

"Yes, sir," the butler conceded reluctantly. He looked Pitt up and down from his untidy hair to his beautiful boots. At any other time, when not suffering from shock, he might have been harder to override, but today he was not himself. "If you will come to the library, sir, I shall see if it is possible. This way, sir, if you please."

Pitt followed him across the gracious flagstoned hallway into a very fine library, paneled in oak on one side, with book-

17

shelves on two, and the remaining wall facing the garden, where deep windows were presently partly obscured by a tangle of coral-pink roses richly in bloom. Pitt thought only for the briefest moment of the new house Charlotte was so happy with, its broken plaster and peeling paper, and her profusion of dreams for it. Then he returned to the present, the somber shelves of unread books and the brilliantly patterned carpet, unmarked by the passage of feet. The desk in the corner was immaculate. No dust and no signs of use marred its virgin surface.

What manner of man had Captain Winthrop been? He gazed around the room seeking some clue as to character, some touch of individuality. He saw nothing. It was essentially a masculine place, dark greens and wines, leather upholstery, books, prints of ships on the wall, a heavy carved mantel with bronze statuary of lions at one end and two hunting dogs at the other. There was a heavy Waterford crystal whiskey decanter, a quarter full, on the side table. He had the powerful feeling of being in a room prepared for a man, rather than one a man had chosen for himself.

The door opened and the butler stood in the entrance.

"Mrs. Winthrop will see you, sir, if you care to come to the withdrawing room."

Pitt left the library with a sense of incompleteness and followed the butler back across the hallway and towards the rear of the house, where the long withdrawing room stretched towards the open lawn and formal rose beds. He had time only to be aware of excellent architectural proportions, spoiled by curtains which were too ornate for the windows, and a heavy carved white-and-gray marble mantel. Wilhelmina Winthrop was dressed entirely in black, as was to be expected, but the totality of it startled him until he realized why. She was a very slender woman, in fact unkind judgment would have said thin. Her fairish hair was swept up in heavy coils, making her neck look even more fragile. Her black gown, swirling around the chair in which she sat, was adorned by a black lace fichu covering her throat up to her chin, and her long sleeves came down in lace points over the backs of her hands, almost to her knuckles. It was the most alarmingly somber garb he had ever seen, and it made her look vulnerable. He thought at first glance that she was much younger than he had supposed, perhaps in her twenties. Then as he approached her more closely

18

he saw the fine lines in her face and the skin around her eyes. He adjusted his judgment. She was nearer her mid-thirties.

Behind her stood a man of medium height, not heavy but of athletic build, thickly curling brown hair, and a subtly aquiline face, the skin of which had been burned to a warm, deep color as from a climate where summer followed summer unceasingly.

"Good afternoon, Mrs. Winthrop," Pitt said gravely. "May I offer you my deepest sympathies upon your loss."

"Thank you, Mr. Pitt," she answered; her voice was soft and her diction clear and most pleasing. Her smile was only the barest expression of good manners.

The man behind her frowned. "You must have some more profound purpose than expressing your condolences, Superintendent. I am sure you will understand if we ask that you make this as brief as possible. It is hardly a time when my sister wishes to receive people, however necessary or well-intentioned."

"Please, Bart." She put up a hand towards him. "Mr. Pitt, this is my brother, Bartholomew Mitchell. He has come to be with me at this most—most trying time. Please excuse his manner being a trifle abrupt, but he is solicitous for my welfare. He does not mean to be rude."

"Certainly I shall not trespass on your time any longer than need be, ma'am," Pitt agreed. There was no easy or pleasant way to do this, even if he came after Tellman and had no news, simply questions to ask. Still they were intrusive and painful when she would almost certainly rather be alone to allow her mind and her heart to absorb the shock and begin to realize her new situation, the reality of death, aloneness, the beginning of grief and the long road which from now on would be without companionship or support.

"Have you any further news for us?" Bart Mitchell asked, leaning forward over his sister's chair.

"No—I am afraid not." Pitt was still standing. "Inspector Tellman is busy asking people who were in the park and who might have seen something, and of course looking for material evidence."

Mina Winthrop swallowed hard, as if she had some obstruction in her throat. "Evidence?" she said awkwardly. "What do you mean?"

"You don't wish to hear, my dear," Bart Mitchell said

quickly. "The less you have to know about the details the better."

"I am not a child, Bart," she protested, but before she could add anything further, he rested both his hands on her shoulders and leaned a little over her, looking at Pitt.

"Of course you are not, my dear, but you are a woman newly bereaved, and it is my privilege to protect you from any further unnecessary pain, not to mention my duty." This last was to Pitt, and his clear, very blue eyes were level and held an air of challenge.

Mina straightened up a fraction, lifting her chin.

"In what way may we help, Mr. Pitt? If there is anything I can do to assist you to find out who did this to my husband, please be assured I shall do it to the utmost of my ability."

"What could you possibly know?" Bart said with a shake of his head. "You have already told Inspector Tellman what time you last saw Oakley." He looked at Pitt again. "Which was late yesterday evening after supper. He said he was going to take a short walk for the good of his health. He never returned."

Pitt ignored Bart Mitchell. "When did you become concerned by his absence, Mrs. Winthrop?"

She blinked. "When I awoke this morning and came down to breakfast. Oakley normally rises early—earlier than I. I saw that his place was still set at the table and had not been used." She ran the tip of her tongue nervously over her lips. "I asked Bunthorne if the master were not well, and Bunthorne said he had not seen him this morning. Naturally I sent him upstairs to check, and he returned saying that Captain Winthrop's bed had not been slept in." She stopped abruptly, her face suddenly very pale.

Bart's hand tightened on her shoulder.

Pitt was going to ask the obvious question, about her and her husband having separate rooms, but it seemed unnecessary. He knew that many families, who could afford to, had separate bedrooms for husband and wife, with connecting doors. It had never appealed to him; he was used to the closeness of smaller spaces, the gentle intimacy, and found in it one of his greatest pleasures. But then few people were as fortunate in their marriages as he, and he knew it. To share even the privacy and vulnerability of sleep with someone one did not love must be a refinement of misery which would destroy the best in either person. And to one accustomed to the freedom to choose

20

whether to have the window open or closed, the curtains drawn or wide, the counterpane this way or that, consideration for another must be a strange and uncomfortable restriction.

"Had that ever happened before?" he asked.

"No—not that I recall. I mean . . ." She looked at him anxiously. "I mean not without his saying where he would be and when he would be back. He was always most particular about keeping people informed. He was very exact, you know. I expect it comes from his naval training." She opened her eyes a little wider. "I daresay one cannot command a ship at sea if one allows mistakes, or people to wander off and come back as they please."

"I imagine not, although it is outside my experience," Pitt equivocated. "I take it, ma'am, that he was a very precise man, used to keeping an exact order in things?"

"Yes," Bart said rather quickly, and then closed his mouth in a thin line. "Yes he was."

"Please do not misunderstand us." Mina looked at Pitt. She had very fine blue eyes with dark brown lashes. "He was not without humor. I would not like you to think he was a martinet."

The idea had not occurred to Pitt, but the fact that she denied it raised the question in his mind.

"Did he have friends in the neighborhood upon whom he might have called?" He asked this not because he thought it helpful—Tellman would already have asked—but because he wanted some clue to Winthrop's character. Was he sociable or reclusive? Whom did he consider his equals?

Mina glanced up at her brother, then back at Pitt.

"We are not aware of any," Bart replied. "Oakley was a naval captain, Superintendent. He spent a great deal of his time aboard his ship. When he was ashore he preferred to be at home with his wife. Or so it seemed. If he had the sort of acquaintance upon whom he would call alone in the evening, then my sister was not aware of it."

"He said he was going to take a walk for his health," she repeated, looking anxiously at Pitt. "He had eaten rather well at dinner. I—I imagine he walked farther than he realized, and found himself in the park, and was set upon by . . ." She bit her lip. "I don't know—a madman!"

"That may indeed be the case," Pitt agreed, although already he was aware of an undercurrent of something else, a sense of fear with the shock and the grief, and other emotions more

21

complex, harder to define. "I expect Inspector Tellman already asked you if you were aware of anyone who might have quarreled with Captain Winthrop or held any grudge against him."

"Yes—yes, he did ask that." Mina's voice was husky and she was very pale. "It is a fearful question. It makes me quite ill to think anyone one knows could have felt so dreadful a hatred as to do such a thing."

"Superintendent, you are distressing my sister quite unnecessarily," Bart said in a hard voice. "If either of us knew of such a person, we would have said so. We have nothing we can add to what we have already told your inspector. Now I really think that is enough. We have tried to be civil and as helpful as lies within our power. I would—"

He got no further because there was a knock on the door and a moment later the butler appeared.

"Mrs. Garrick and Mr. Victor Garrick have called, ma'am," he said somberly. "Shall I tell them you are not receiving visitors?"

"Oh no," Mina responded with a look of relief. "It is only Thora. I will always see Thora, she is so—so—yes, Bunthorne, please ask them to come in."

"Really, my dear, do you not think you should rest?" Bart remonstrated.

"Rest? How on earth can I rest?" she demanded. "Oakley was murdered last night." Her voice choked. "His head—cut off! The last thing on earth I wish is to be left alone in a dark room with my eyes closed and my imagination free! I would immeasurably rather talk to Thora Garrick."

"If you are quite sure?"

"I have not a doubt in my mind!" she insisted with a rising note close to panic.

"Very well—yes, Bunthorne, ask her to come in," Bart acceded, a look of pain in his face.

"Very good sir." Bunthorne withdrew immediately.

A moment later the door opened again and a handsome woman with shining fair hair came in. She was followed immediately by a man in his early twenties with a broad-browed face which at first seemed blandly amiable but on closer regard was of unusual softness and imagination. And yet also there was a certain indiscipline in it, a vulnerability about the mouth, as if he might easily be hurt, and quick to anger. Perhaps he might also be as quick to laugh. It was an interesting face, and

Pitt found himself staring, and he had to withdraw his gaze for fear of being offensive.

The woman's attention went first to Mina Winthrop, full of sympathy, then after acknowledging Bart Mitchell she turned to Pitt, poised either to welcome him or to join battle, depending upon how he was introduced.

Bart seized the initiative. "Thora, this is Superintendent Pitt, from the Bow Street police station. He is in charge of the case." He looked at Pitt with raised eyebrows. "At least that is what I understand."

"Correctly," Pitt said as he inclined his head towards Thora Garrick. "How do you do, ma'am." He looked at Victor. "Mr. Garrick."

Victor stared at him out of very wide dark gray eyes. He seemed still to be suffering from shock at the events, or else he was embarrassed by the situation. Pitt thought it quite likely it was the latter. It was never easy to know what to say to the bereaved. When the death is violent and as fraught with darkness as this one, it was doubly so.

"How do you do, sir," Victor said stiffly, then retired a pace or two to stand a little behind his mother.

"How kind of you to come," Mina asserted herself, leaning forward with a fragile smile, first to Thora, then to Victor. "Please do sit down. It is a very warm day. May I offer you some refreshment? You will stay a little while, won't you?" It was more than a polite invitation, it was definitely a request.

"Of course, my dear, if you wish it." Thora arranged her skirts so as not to crush them, and perched graciously on one of the bright red overstuffed chairs. Victor remained standing behind her, but he adopted a pose in which he looked quite at ease.

"The superintendent was just asking us if Oakley could have called upon anyone in the neighborhood last night," Mina continued. "But of course we do not know the answer."

Thora looked at Pitt with wide sharp eyes. She was a very comely woman, fair-skinned, her features regular and full of intelligence and humor and, he thought, a very considerable underlying strength.

"You surely cannot imagine anyone Captain Winthrop knew could have done such a—an insane thing," she said critically. "That is inconceivable. If you had had even the merest acquaintance with him, such a thought would never enter your head. He was an entirely excellent man. . . ."

Mina smiled nervously. Her hand jerked up as if to her face, then instead touched the black lace at her throat.

Bart winced and his hand tightened on her shoulder, almost as if he were supporting her, even though she was seated.

Victor stood perfectly still, his expression unchanging.

"He was a naval officer," Thora went on, still looking at Pitt, and apparently unaware of the emotion in the room. "I think you cannot realize what sort of life such men lead, Superintendent. He was not unlike my late husband." She straightened her shoulders a fraction. "Victor's father. He was a lieutenant, and would certainly have reached captain had he not been taken from us in so untimely a fashion." Her face lit with an inner radiance. "Such men have great courage and are powerful both as to character and person. And of course you cannot command in dangerous situations, such as obtain at sea, if you are not an excellent judge of men." She shook her head to dismiss such a weakness. "Captain Winthrop would not have kept the acquaintance of anyone of such violence and instability as to attack another person in so heinous a fashion. He must have been set upon by lunatics, that is the only possible answer."

"I was not imagining it to be an acquaintance, ma'am," Pitt said, not entirely truthfully. "I was wondering if anyone else might have seen him, and thus know where he was and at what time he was last seen alive."

"Oh—I see," she conceded. Then she frowned. "Not that I understand how that would help. There can hardly be hordes of criminal lunatics in Hyde Park. I know London is in a fearful state." Her eyes did not move from Pitt's. "There is anarchy everywhere, talk of sedition and rebellion, and Lord knows, enough trouble in Ireland, what with the Fenians and the like, but one may still walk safely in the better streets of London! Or at least one had supposed so."

"I'm sure one can, my dear," Mina murmured. "This is all a nightmare. I still think it may have been some sort of hideous accident—or foreigners perhaps." She looked at Pitt. "I have heard that the Chinese take opium, and it does all sorts of—well . . ."

"It sends them to sleep," Bart contradicted. "It doesn't make them violent." He glanced at Pitt. "Is that not so, Superintendent?" He did not wait for an answer but continued to speak to Mina. "No, I think, quite frankly, that it is someone from Oakley's ship who has had a quarrel with him and has maybe

24

drunk too much and lost his temper and his self-control. I have known drink, particularly whiskey, to produce uncharacteristic violence."

Mina shivered. "I suppose you could be right." Her eyes did not leave Pitt's face. "I cannot help you, Superintendent. Oakley never discussed his professional life with me. He—he thought it would bore me, I suppose. Or that I would not understand." A shadow of regret or embarrassment crossed her face. "I daresay he was right. It is an area of life about which I know nothing."

Bart muttered something under his breath.

Victor flashed a sudden smile at Mina.

"You should not mourn that, Aunt Mina. My father talked about it incessantly, and believe me, it was only interesting the first time, and that was so long ago I cannot remember it anymore."

"Victor!" Thora's voice was full of surprise and reproach. "Your father was a great man! You should not speak lightly of him in that way. He set a fine example for all of us, in every kind of moral excellence."

"I'm sure we all know Lieutenant Garrick was a very fine man," Mina said soothingly, glancing up at Pitt. Then she smiled at Victor. "But I do understand even the finest people can now and again become tedious when one has heard a story before. And familiarity can occasion a certain loss of respect. It is one of the small crosses that families have to bear, my dear."

Victor's face tightened, the muscles in his smooth jaw setting hard and his eyes looking far away.

"You are quite right, Aunt Mina. Being boring is a very slight thing, hardly a sin at all, just a misfortune. If I'm going to criticize I should reserve it for the sins that really matter."

"Better still not to speak about them at all." Thora nodded, apparently satisfied.

Pitt would have liked to interpose, but there was no way he could ask Victor what sins he had in mind without being so obvious he would receive no useful answer. Anyway, Oakley Winthrop would hardly have been murdered because he was a bore—of whatever proportions. He turned to Mina.

"Perhaps, Mrs. Winthrop, you would give me the names and addresses of any of the naval men Captain Winthrop knew, and whom he might have seen recently; any, perhaps, who live in this part of London."

Bart Mitchell looked up keenly.

"A good idea. If there were a quarrel, some seaman who imagined a grievance, they may well know of it. There may even have been a court-martial or something of that sort. Someone dismissed, or punished severely, perhaps some event that seemed an injustice . . ."

"Do you think so?" Mina said quickly, moving around in her seat to look up at him rather than twist her neck. "Yes, that does seem a reasonable answer, doesn't it?" She looked back. "Mr. Pitt?"

"We shall certainly investigate it," he agreed.

Thora looked uncertain. "Do you really think naval officers would behave in such a way?" She shook her head. "I cannot imagine it. They are highly trained, used to command and to self-discipline."

"They can still lose their tempers like anyone else." Victor pushed out his lip and stared straight ahead of him. He opened his mouth as if to continue, then changed his mind and stood tight-lipped.

"Oh that's nonsense!" Thora said sharply. "They are not like anyone else. If they behaved in such a way, Victor, they would not be raised to command, far less retain it." Her voice gathered conviction. "You should have gone into the navy. I'm sure a fine career would have been open to you. You have all the skills, and your father's name was highly enough honored that they would have given you every chance."

Victor's expression closed over, his eyes fixed ahead of him.

"I think that's a little harsh, Thora," Bart said quietly. "Architecture is an honorable profession, and it is surely a sin to waste a real talent. And there is no doubt Victor is gifted. His drawings are very fine indeed."

"Thank you, Mr. Mitchell," Victor said with cold resentful calm. "But unfortunately that is not seen as a brave and magnificent thing to do."

"Don't be foolish, dear," Thora said with a forced smile, the patience in her voice dying before she reached the second sentence. "Of course it is. It is just . . . uncertain. And we have such a fine naval tradition in our family, it would have pleased your father so much. Tradition is important, you know. It is the backbone of our country. It is what makes us English."

Victor did not reply.

Mina looked from one to another of them. The others seemed momentarily to have forgotten Pitt.

"I expect he would have been just as pleased with a fine building," she offered tentatively. "And certainly he could only have been pleased, listening to you play. I wonder: Victor dear, would you play for us—when we have a service of remembrance for Oakley? I should find it so uplifting. And you are almost family—after all, poor Oakley was your godfather."

Victor's face softened immediately and his smile was beautiful, his eyes bright.

"Of course, Aunt Mina. I should love to. Tell me what you would like and I shall be honored to play it for you."

"Thank you, my dear. I shall think on the matter and let you know." She turned to Pitt, again moving her head at a curiously rigid angle. "Victor plays the cello quite marvelously, Mr. Pitt. You have never heard anything lovelier. He seems to make the strings laugh and cry like a human voice. He can wring any passion from them he wishes, and take your heart with it."

"That is indeed a talent that it would truly be a sin to waste," Pitt said sincerely. "I would a great deal rather make music than fight battles at sea."

Victor looked at him curiously, his broad brow slightly puckered with doubt and interest, but he said nothing.

Thora was gracious enough not to argue the point further. She took up the thread of her original purpose in coming.

"Is there anything we can do to help you, dear?" she asked Mina. "No doubt there will be lots of arrangements in due course. If I can assist, lend you my cook, or help with invitations or letters, please let me know."

"How kind of you," Mina said with a smile of gratitude. "Even your company would be most welcome. It is such a grim task to perform alone. I admit I have barely thought of such things yet. My mind is still quite stupid with shock."

"Of course, my dear," Thora said quickly. "Anyone's would be. How you àre bearing up at all is a miracle. You are extraordinarily brave. You are worthy of the great sisterhood of naval widows that stretches back through history. Oakley would be proud of you."

A look of profound, unreachable emotion crossed Bart Mitchell's dark face.

Victor let out his breath very slowly.

"Did Captain Winthrop have any other family, apart from his parents?" Pitt asked in the silence.

Mina's attention jolted back to the present.

27

"Oh no—no, just Lord and Lady Winthrop." She used their titles, and Pitt had the impression that was how she thought of them, rather than merely a formality she was pursuing because he was not of their social standing.

"There will be his ship, of course," Bart offered. "But I will take care of that. Although with the newspapers writing as they do, no doubt they will all know by now anyway. Still, a notification from the family would be a courtesy, I suppose." He pulled a small face. "Oh, I forgot, Superintendent, you wished a note of the other officers who live in the area. I believe he has some record of those with whom he kept in touch, somewhere in his desk in the library. If you wait a few moments I will fetch it for you." And excusing himself to Thora Garrick, he left the room.

"If you will forgive me, Superintendent." Thora turned to Pitt with a faint flush in her cheeks. "I do not wish to appear to tell you your business, but you will learn nothing of poor Captain Winthrop's death here. You should be out in the streets or asking in the asylums if anyone has broken out. Surely a person who has committed such an act must be plain to observe. He cannot be sane in any sense of the word." She raised her fair eyebrows. "You will be able quite easily to find at least one person who has seen him. Possibly several."

Victor bit his lip and stared at the ceiling.

Mina looked at Pitt.

"It is possible, ma'am, and we will certainly try," Pitt replied. "But I do not hold out a great deal of hope. Madmen do not all have wild hair and staring eyes. I am afraid many of them look as normal as you or I most of the time."

"Really?" Thora said with cool disbelief. "I would have thought after an act like this he must be quite easy to see. No one could do what has been done and look like an ordinary person."

Pitt did not argue, there was no point, and he was spared the necessity of an answer by Bart Mitchell's returning with an address book which he held out in his hand.

"There you are, Superintendent. I think it may prove very useful. There is a full list of his ship's company and their home addresses. The more I think of it, the more I agree you are right, and that it is probably some quarrel or fancied injustice which someone has brooded upon, perhaps drunk too much, and temporarily lost all reason." His face brightened. "And that would account for the weapon. After all, it is not inconceivable that a naval officer might have in his possession a cutlass or some such sword." He looked hopeful.

Mina put both her hands up to her face.

Victor let out his breath in a little gasp and straightened himself as if he had momentarily lost his balance.

"Really, Bart," Thora said reprovingly. "I am sure you did not mean to, but you are being rather indelicate, my dear. It is a most distressing thought, and one we do not need to pursue. I am sure the superintendent is much more used to this kind of matter, and we do not need to point the way for him."

"Oh—I'm sorry." Bart was contrite. He turned to his sister. "Mina, my dear, I do beg your pardon." Then he looked at Pitt. "I don't think there is anything else we can do for you, Superintendent. If you will be good enough to leave us, I would like to take care of my sister and begin whatever arrangements are most advisable in the circumstances."

"Of course," Pitt agreed. "Thank you for sparing me so much of your time. Good day, Mrs. Winthrop, Mrs. Garrick, Mr. Garrick." And he inclined his head very slightly and took his leave, collecting his hat from the pale-faced butler in the hallway before stepping out into the sharp spring sunshine. His mind whirled with impressions of grief, anxiety, close family pain, and something else he could not as yet grasp clearly enough to name.

Later Pitt performed that other necessary but most disagreeable task at the outset of any such investigation: he visited the mortuary to look for himself at the body of Oakley Winthrop. He did not expect it to tell him anything that he could not have deduced from Tellman's report. But there was always the remote chance that he would observe something, even gather some impression, however faint, which later would clarify into meaning.

He hated mortuaries, their very bareness smelled sour and sickly and there was always a chill, even in summer. He found himself shivering as he told the attendant his purpose. There had been no need to give his name, he was already only too familiar.

"Oh, yes sir," the attendant said cheerfully. "I bin expectin' yer. Thought as this one'd bring yer 'ere. Nasty, it is. Very nasty." And turning on his heel, he led Pitt briskly to the room where the body was laid out under a sheet, its form unfamiliar, inhuman without the bump where one looked for the head.

"There y'are, Mr. Pitt, sir!" He whipped off the sheet with the air of a conjurer producing flowers from a hat.

Pitt had seen many corpses before, and each time he tried to prepare himself, and as always, failed. He felt a sinking in his stomach and a strange, slightly dizzy sensation in his head and throat. The remains of Oakley Winthrop lay naked and very white on the marble slab of the table. Without a head, a face, he seemed without dignity, even without humanity.

"What have you done with his head?" Pitt said involuntarily, then wished he had not. It exposed the rawness of his emotion.

"Oh . . ." the attendant said absentmindedly. "I put it on the bench. I suppose I'd better put 'im all together." He went to the bench in question and carefully picked up a large object covered with a cloth, unwrapped it dextrously and brought it over to Pitt. "There y'are, sir. That's all of 'im."

Pitt swallowed. "Thank you."

He looked conscientiously, avoiding nothing, but he did not learn any more than he already knew from Tellman's report, and what the coroner would have said in time. Oakley Winthrop had been a big man, broad shouldered, deep chested, muscular but now running to softness and the beginning of fat. He looked well fed, smooth, his hands very clean. There were no marks or bruises on him at all, except the lividity Pitt had expected from the natural settling of blood in a corpse when its heart no longer pumped. There was no other discoloration, no breaking of the skin. His hands were immaculate, nails unbroken.

Then he looked at the head. The hair was sandy brown and clipped short. Across the top of the scalp there was hardly any at all. He did not try it, but he knew it would be impossible to pick it up that way. He turned to the features. They were unremarkable, and without expression or life it was hard to guess what character they had betrayed. He could not detect the marks of humor or imagination, but it was unfair to judge.

Finally he forced himself to look at the wound, if one could call a complete severing such a thing. It was fairly clean, done by a simple, very powerful blow with some very sharp weapon, possibly designed for the purpose. It might have been a person of great strength, or alternatively someone perfectly balanced and striking from a considerable height, and using the force of weight and a long swing, as with a broadax.

The smell of the place was catching in his throat, and he was very cold.

"Thank you. That's all, at least for now."

"Yes, Mr. Pitt. Want ter see 'is clothes? 'E were dressed very smart, like; naval captain, they say. Nice uniform. Pity about the blood. Never seen so much in all me life."

"Anything in his pockets?"

"Only what yer'd expect, a little money, letter from 'is wine merchant, that's 'ow we knew 'is name, I reckon. A few keys, reckon wine cupboard or desk or the like; domestic anyway. 'Andkerchief, couple o' callin' cards, cigar cutter. Nothing interestin', no threatening letters." He smiled sepulchrally. "Got another nasty one, Mr. Pitt. I reckon there's a madman loose somewhere."

"Do you," Pitt said dryly. "Well cover him up and let us know when the coroner has been."

"Yes sir. Good night sir!"

"Good night."

Pitt arrived home tired and still unable to shake from himself the smell of the mortuary. He let himself in the door and took his boots off before going along to the warmth and light of the kitchen.

Charlotte did not turn around immediately; she was busy stirring a steaming pan on the large black cooking range.

"Hungry?" she asked without looking at him.

He sat down wearily at the scrubbed wooden table, letting the warmth surround him and breathing in the odor of the clean linen, flour, cooking, the coal and heat of the range, the well-washed floor.

She swung around, opened her mouth to speak, then saw his face.

"What?" she said gently. "Something bad, I can see it."

"Murder," he replied. "A beheading, in Hyde Park."

"Oh." She took a deep breath, pushing her hair off her brow. It was bright like polished chestnuts in the lamplight. "Soup?"

"What?"

"Soup?" she repeated. "Some hot soup and bread? You look cold."

He smiled and nodded, beginning to relax.

She opened the lid of the pot on the range and ladled some broth out into a dish. She knew he was too overwrought, too clenched with chill and emotion to eat yet. She placed it in front of him, with fresh bread and a pat of butter, then sat down again and waited for him to tell her. It was not courtesy

31

or any form of kindness, he knew that. She would be intensely interested, she always was. No pretense was necessary.

Briefly, in between spoonfuls of broth, he told her.

"YES SIR?" Tellman stood in front of Pitt's desk early the next morning, his face was hard and bleak as stone, his eyes focusing somewhere over Pitt's left shoulder. "Didn't come back in time to report to you, sir. Half past ten, it was. You'd gone home."

"What have you learned?" Pitt asked. He had done this to Drummond too many times himself to be irritated by Tellman's implied criticism.

"Far as the doc can judge, he died some time before midnight," Tellman answered. "Not sure exactly. Maybe eleven or so. Not much blood in the boat, so it probably wasn't there. In fact, unless he washed it out, it couldn't have been."

"Shoes?" Pitt asked, imagining carrying a headless body across the grass to the Serpentine before midnight when there were still late partygoers returning home and several hansoms up and down Knightsbridge, any of them liable to let off a fare for a midnight walk.

"Grass on them, sir," Tellman said expressionlessly. "Several pieces."

"And when was the park grass last cut?" Pitt asked.

Tellman's nostrils flared very slightly and his mouth pinched in. "I'll find out. But it doesn't matter. He didn't walk across it without his head."

"Maybe he was brought in another boat," Pitt suggested, as much to annoy Tellman as because he thought it a serious possibility.

"What for?" Tellman's eyebrows rose a fraction. "Doesn't

make any sense. What's different about one boat from another? And not easy to lift a corpse in a boat. Turn yourself over as like as not." He smiled sourly, his eyes meeting Pitt's for the first time. "His clothes were quite dry, except a very slight damp in one or two places from the dew. But dry as a bone underneath . . . sir."

Pitt conceded all that without comment.

"How deep is the water at the edge of the Serpentine?" he asked contentiously.

Tellman took his point instantly. "Not more than just above the knee," he agreed, then the smile came back to his lips. "But kind of noticeable, don't you think, to walk back across the park soaked to the thighs? People might remember that—dangerous."

"People might remember seeing a man having his head cut off too," Pitt said with an answering smile. "Tends to suggest there was no one around. What do you think yourself?"

That was a question Tellman was not prepared for. He wanted to argue, to mock. His long face tightened and he looked at Pitt with dislike.

"Too early to say . . . sir."

"Well when you've ruled out the impossible, what's left?" Pitt insisted. "Specifically!"

Tellman took a deep breath and let it out with a sigh.

Pitt waited.

"He was killed somewhere farther along the Serpentine, which we haven't found yet," Tellman replied. "And taken to where we found him in the boat. I've got Bailey and le Grange looking all along the banks now. I suppose someone could have brought him over the grass in some way. A trap or a cart maybe, but it would be a dreadful risk, not thought out . . ." He stopped, waiting for Pitt to ask the question that had occurred to both of them.

"Any feeling as to whether it was planned or a sudden rage?" Pitt put it into words.

"Too early," Tellman replied with a faint gleam in his eyes. "Might be clever thinking, might be luck. Know more when we've covered all the bank, or nothing. Looks clever, so far. I'll tell you this, sir—it doesn't look like any chance madman to me. And we did check, there's been no maniacs escaped from Bedlam or anywhere else. And we've no record of a crime like it before."

"Have you got the medical examiner's report yet?"

"There's a wound on the head," Tellman answered. "He was probably hit to stun him before he was beheaded. Not hard enough to kill, just rob him of his senses for a while." He looked at Pitt candidly at last. "Looks careful and nasty, doesn't it . . . sir."

"Yes it does. Is that all?"

Tellman opened his eyes wide, waiting for Pitt to continue.

"There was nothing on the rest of the body, so far as I could see," Pitt said patiently. "No bruises, no scratches on his hands or knuckles. What about his clothes? I didn't see them. Are they torn or scuffed? Green stains, mud?"

"No," Tellman said flatly. "No. He didn't put up a fight. Nothing at all."

"How tall does he estimate him to have been—with his head? Six feet?"

"About that, as near as we can judge—and big, broad chested."

"I know. I saw him. And yes, it does look nasty," Pitt agreed. "I think we need to know a great deal more about Captain the Honorable Oakley Winthrop."

Tellman's face split into a grin.

"That's why it's your case, Mr. Pitt. The powers that be reckon as you're good at that sort of thing. You'd better go and mix with the Honorable Winthrops and their kin. See who hated the good captain, and why." He stood still in front of Pitt's desk, amused and sharp with resentment. "We'll get on with finding witnesses and that sort of regular police work. Will that be all, sir?"

"No it won't." Pitt kept the dislike out of his voice with intense difficulty. He must remember he was in command; he had no business indulging in personal irritations and pettiness. He forced it out of his mind. "What did the medical examiner say about a weapon? I assume you haven't found anything or you would have said so."

"No sir, nothing yet." He preempted Pitt's repeating the orders. "We'll drag the Serpentine, of course, but makes sense to look in the easier places first."

"What did the medical examiner tell you?"

"Clean cut. Must have been quite a heavy weapon to do that in one blow, and with a very sharp blade. Either an ax with a broad head, or more likely a sword of some sort, again a big one, a cutlass or the like."

With a wave of sickening memory Pitt saw again in his

35

mind the severed stump of neck, and smelled the overwhelming carbolic and wet stone.

"Or a meat cleaver?" he suggested with a husky voice.

Tellman had got Pitt's vision. A flicker of annoyance crossed his face for not having mentioned it himself. "Yes—or that. Anyway, we'll know if we find it."

"When were the latest witnesses you could trace, so far?" Pitt went on.

Tellman looked at him expressionlessly. "How would you suggest we go about that, sir? Not easy to know who crosses Hyde Park of an evening. Could be anyone in London—or out of it, for that matter. Visitors, foreigners . . ." He left all the possibilities trailing in the air.

"Cabbies," Pitt said dryly. "They have areas." He saw Tellman's face flush, but continued. "Post a man on the paths and on Rotten Row, and along Knightsbridge, and see who passes that way this evening. Some people do things regularly."

"Yes sir." Tellman stood very stiffly. It was common-sense police work, and he knew it. "Naturally that will be done, sir. Is that all?"

Pitt thought for a moment. It was his responsibility to set the tone of their relationship and to keep command of it, but he had never considered it could be so difficult. The man had a far more powerful personality than he had imagined. One could order his acts but his attitude was beyond reach, as was his ability to poison the minds of all the other men. Of course there were punishments available, but that would be clumsy, and in the end rebound on Pitt. Drummond had managed it. He had balanced all their differing natures and skills and made them an efficient whole. Pitt must not be beaten when he had little more than begun.

"For the moment," he replied levelly. "Let me know when you make any progress with witnesses."

"Yes sir," Tellman acceded, then turned on his heel and left, closing the door quietly behind him.

Pitt sat back in the chair and thought for a moment, hesitating before putting his feet up on the desk. It was not as comfortable as he had expected, but it was a feeling of command and self-indulgence which was very satisfying. He began to review their knowledge to date, and all of it suggested Winthrop had been murdered not by some chance madman, or by a robber, not that he had ever thought that likely. The only conclusion consistent with what had emerged was that he had been attacked by someone he knew, someone from whom he was expecting no threat. It might be a colleague or a social acquaintance. It was more likely to be a member of his close family or immediate friends. Until Tellman returned with more physical evidence, he should begin to look for motive.

He swung his feet off the desk and stood up. He could accomplish nothing here, and the sooner this was cleared up the better. Already the newspapers were publishing black headlines about the murder and Winthrop's name was on everyone's lips. In a day or two they would be demanding results and asking what the police were doing.

Two hours later Pitt was in the train to Portsmouth, sitting beside the window watching the countryside rush past him in vivid green with giant trees beginning to bud for heavy leaf and the bare branches of the hazels already veiled in a soft mist of color. Willows leaned over water trailing streamers of soft, gauzy, green like women bent forward with clouds of hair around them. Flocks of birds followed the slow plows, wheeling and diving after the worms in the turned earth.

Another three hours and he was standing in a small room close to the Royal Naval Dockyard, awaiting the arrival of Lieutenant Jones, second in command to the late Captain Winthrop. He had already spoken with the harbormaster and learned nothing of value. Everyone was shocked and could only repeat trite expressions of grief and outrage, and the sort of eulogizing remarks which they no doubt felt appropriate, but were what they would have said of anyone.

The door opened and a slender man in his late thirties came in. He was dressed in uniform and carried his hat in his hand.

"Good afternoon, sir. Lieutenant Jones. How may I be of service?" He stood to attention and looked at Pitt anxiously. He was clean-shaven with light eyebrows and fair hair receding considerably. It was a face where strength was not immediately apparent, and only after Pitt had spoken with him for several minutes did he gain any sense of his inner resolve.

"Superintendent Pitt," Pitt introduced himself. "I regret intruding at a time which must be very difficult for you, but I am sure you will appreciate that you may be able to give me information which will help us find who is responsible for Captain Winthrop's death."

"I cannot imagine how, but of course I will give you any assistance I can," Jones acquiesced, remaining at attention. "What is it you wish to know?" His blue eyes showed total confusion.

Deliberately Pitt sat down in the hard-backed, wooden-armed chair beside the table, and invited Jones to sit as well.

Lieutenant Jones looked a trifle surprised, recognizing that Pitt intended the interview to be of length.

"How long have you served with Captain Winthrop?"

"Nine years, altogether," Lieutenant Jones replied, taking the chair opposite Pitt and crossing his legs. "I—I suppose I knew him pretty well, if that is what you are going to ask."

Pitt smiled. "It is. Please bear in mind that your loyalty to Captain Winthrop lies not only in speaking well of him but in telling the truth so that whoever murdered him is caught—" He stopped, seeing the surprise in Jones's face.

"Surely it was robbery, wasn't it?" Jones's brow puckered in consternation. "I had assumed it was some criminal lunatic loose in the park. It is inconceivable it was anyone who knew him, which seems to be what you're suggesting. Forgive me if I have misunderstood you, Superintendent."

"No, your understanding is both exact and swift." Pitt smiled very slightly. "There is some evidence to suggest that he was taken completely by surprise." He waited for Jones's reaction.

It was what he had expected. Jones looked startled, then dubious, then very grave as the full implication reached him.

"I see. And you have come to ask me if I know of anyone who may have held a grudge against him." He shook his head. "I don't. That is the simple answer. He was a popular man, Superintendent, open, candid, of remarkably good humor, friendly without being overfamiliar, and he did not gamble or run up debts he could not pay. He was certainly not an unjust commander, as no doubt you will ask me. I know of no man who had a quarrel with him."

"Are you speaking of officers, Lieutenant, or do you include ordinary seamen as well?"

"What?" Jones's eyes widened. "Oh. Well, I suppose I did mean officers. He would hardly know seamen personally. But you mean some sort of a grudge?"

"An injustice, real or imagined," Pitt elaborated.

Jones looked very doubtful. He shifted a little in his chair. "Most ordinary seamen, Superintendent, take their punishment resolutely and with reasonably good grace." He smiled weakly.

38

"We don't keelhaul anymore you know. Discipline is not barbaric, nor is it resented on the whole. No, I really cannot imagine that any man would be—absurd—ill-balanced enough to pursue Captain Winthrop up to London and follow him to the park and do such a thing." Again he shook his head. "It really would be quite preposterous. No, I am sure beyond any doubt that that is not what happened. As to a fellow officer, I . . ." He lifted one shoulder fractionally. "I know of no quarrel whatsoever. I suppose jealousy is not inconceivable, but it is highly unlikely. The whole thing is a mystery to me."

"Jealousy?" Pitt asked. "Professional rivalry, you mean? Or personal jealousy, over a woman perhaps?"

Jones's face showed surprise. "Oh no, I didn't mean that. I really don't know, Superintendent. I am struggling in the dark. If you are correct and it was not a madman or a gang of robbers, then one has to assume it was someone he knew. Please understand, I knew Oakley Winthrop very well. I worked with him for nearly a decade. He was an exemplary officer and a fine man." He leaned forward. A gull swooped past the window, crying. "Not only honest but genuinely likable," Jones said earnestly. "He excelled in sports, he played the piano and had a beautiful voice and sang for everyone's pleasure. He had a rich sense of humor, and I've heard him set the whole mess rocking with laughter."

"Sometimes a dangerous weapon," Pitt said thoughtfully.

"Oh no." Jones shook his head. "He was not a wit, if that is what you are thinking. He didn't make mock of people. It was a very robust, simple sort of fun. Harmless. You are not picturing the man at all, Superintendent, if I may say so. He was uncomplicated, bluff even . . ." He stopped, seeing Pitt's expression. "You disagree?" He leaned back in his chair again. "You have been misinformed, I assure you."

"No one is uncomplicated," Pitt replied with a wry smile. "But I accept what you say. I have formed no impression of him at all yet."

Jones's lips twitched very slightly. "If Captain Winthrop had a secret life he hid it with a subtlety and brilliance he did not display in his ordinary way. Believe me, I do wish I could offer anything of assistance, but I don't know where to begin."

"Was he popular with women as well?" Pitt asked.

Jones hesitated. Again the sounds of the yard intruded, the clank of chains, the creak of straining ropes as the water rose and fell, timber against timber, men shouting, and always the mew of the gulls. "No, not as much as perhaps I might have suggested," Jones went on. "Inadvertently, I mean. The sort of party I was referring to was strictly officers, not women. He was a seaman. I don't think he found the company of women easy." He blushed a delicate pink and his eyes moved away from Pitt. "One has so little social life, one gets out of practice in the sort of light conversation suitable for women."

Pitt had a vivid picture in his mind of a broad, blunt-faced man, hearty, outwardly confident, totally in command, quick to laughter on the surface, but underneath the superficial bonhomie, perhaps filled with darker emotions, fears, self-doubts, even guilt, a man who spent most of his life in a totally masculine world.

Had he a mistress? He looked at the fair, earnest face opposite him. Lieutenant Jones would not tell him even if he knew. But if it were some love or hate here in Portsmouth, would they have followed him to London, rather than committing the crime here?

"Lieutenant Jones, when did Captain Winthrop leave for London?"

"Er—ten days ago," Jones replied, watching Pitt's face again.

It was not necessary for either of them to point out that a quarrel in Portsmouth ten days ago was not likely to have resulted in a violent murder in London nine days afterwards.

"All the same," Pitt went on. "I'd like you to tell me all you can of his last few days here, whom he saw, anything out of the ordinary that was said or done. Have there been any unusual disciplinary decisions in the last few months?"

"Nothing involving Captain Winthrop," Jones replied, still a small pucker between his brows. "You are mistaken, Superintendent. The answer to this tragedy does not lie in anything that happened here."

Pitt was inclined to believe him, and after he had pursued one or two more questions he thanked Lieutenant Jones and excused himself, but he still remained in Portsmouth for several more hours, asking more questions, seeing the local police, public house landlords, even a brothel keeper, before catching his train back to London.

The following morning he found Tellman waiting for him.

"Good morning, sir. Learn anything in Portsmouth?" he asked, his hard, bright eyes searching Pitt's face.

"A little," Pitt replied, going up the stairs with Tellman behind him. "He left there eleven days ago. Nine days before he was killed. Doesn't seem likely anyone from there followed him up. Most of his closest associates are accounted for that night anyway."

"Not surprising," Tellman said bluntly as Pitt opened his office door and went in. "Could have sent le Grange down to find that out." He closed the door and stood in front of Pitt's desk.

Pitt sat down and faced him. "Send him down to check on what everyone says," he agreed. "I wanted to find out about Winthrop himself."

"Cheerful sort of person, according to his neighbors," Tellman said with satisfaction. "Always got a good word. Kept to himself most of the time, family man. Liked his home when he was not at sea."

"Scandal?"

"Not a breath. Model gentleman in every way." Tellman looked faintly smug.

"And what have you learned?" Pitt asked, opening his eyes wide. "Where was he killed? Have you got the weapon?"

The satisfaction died in Tellman's face, and his lips tightened.

"Haven't found the place yet. Could have been anywhere. We've looked for the weapon. We'll drag the Serpentine tomorrow." He lifted his head a little. "But we have found several witnesses. Couple of lovers were walking down the path at half past ten. He wasn't there then. It was still light enough to see that much quite clearly. Cabby going along Knightsbridge towards Hyde Park corner at midnight empty, on his way home, and going pretty slow, saw two people walking along Rotten Row, and is certain both were men. He didn't see anybody on the water then, although of course it was dark and he was some way from the Serpentine, but there was a good moon."

"And . . ." Pitt prompted.

"And another gentleman came home in his own carriage at two in the morning and passed the same way, and saw what he took to be a boat drifting," Tellman said, staring at Pitt.

"Sober?" Pitt asked.

"He says so."

"And your judgment?"

"Well, he was certainly sober enough when I spoke to him."

41

"Did you find him, or did he come to you?"

Tellman's face tightened again. "He came to us. But he's a gentleman. I meant the word exact. Banker in the City."

"Where had he been that he was away from home at two in the morning?"

Tellman's shoulders tightened.

"I didn't ask, sir. I gathered it was private business, an assignation maybe. It isn't done to press gentlemen of that sort as to where they've been, Mr. Pitt. Gets their backs up to no purpose."

Pitt heard the insolence in his voice and saw the satisfaction of contempt in his face.

"I suppose you did check that he is who he said he is?" he asked.

"Can't see that it matters," Tellman replied. "He saw a boat on the water at two o'clock. It's not police business if he gives us the right name or not—or where he'd been. If gentlemen go around bedding other gentlemen's wives, that's their way, and nothing to do with our case. He was a gentleman, that I know. You don't have to be a detective to tell the difference."

"And of course a gentleman couldn't have killed Captain the Honorable Oakley Winthrop!" Pitt said sarcastically. "If this informant of yours had a good voice, good manners and clean shoes, then it couldn't have been he who committed murder. . . ."

Tellman's face flushed a dull red. He glared at Pitt and remained silent.

"We'll assume it's the truth unless we find otherwise," Pitt said pleasantly. "That's a step forward. What did you find in the boat?"

"No blood, except the bit from the bleeding after he was dead."

"Any signs of another person there?"

"Such as what? They're pleasure boats. There could have been a hundred other people in it at one time or another. Even this last week!"

"I am aware of that, Tellman. Maybe one of them killed Winthrop."

"Without leaving any blood, sir? The man's head was cut off!"

"What about over the side?"

"What?"

"What if he leaned over the side?" Pitt asked, his voice ris-

42

ing as the picture became clear in his mind. "What if they were in the boat together and the murderer dropped something in the water, drawing Winthrop's attention to it. Winthrop leaned over, the murderer hit him over the head, then struck his head off—into the water? The blood would all go over the side!"

"Possible," Tellman said grudgingly, but there was a certain admiration in his voice, and a lift of excitement. "Could have been done like that!"

"Was the hair wet? Think, man! You saw it!" Pitt said eagerly.

"Difficult to tell, sir. Wasn't much of it. Very thin, almost bald on top."

"Yes. I know that. But what there was of it. The sides—the whiskers?"

"Yes—yes I think there were. But I'm not sure if there was water in the bottom of the boat—bilges . . ." He was reluctant yet to grasp the full implications, but he could not keep the urgency and the lift out of his voice.

"In a pleasure boat? Nonsense," Pitt dismissed it.

"Then yes, sir, the whiskers were wet—I think."

"Blood?"

"No—not a lot." Tellman did not take his eyes from Pitt's.

"Wouldn't there have been a lot if the head had simply fallen where he was killed?" Pitt asked.

Still Tellman was cautious. "I don't know, sir. It's not something I ever experienced before. I would think so, yes. Unless one held the head up to kill him."

"How?"

"What?"

"How would one hold the head up? He had hardly any hair on top."

Tellman breathed out, his eyes bright. He gave in at last.

"Then I expect you're right. I daresay he was killed in the boat, leaning over the side, and his head fell in the water. We'll never prove it."

"Look at the boat carefully," Pitt ordered, leaning back in his seat. "There may be a mark in the wood somewhere, a nick or a scratch. It must have been a very powerful blow, not easy to control. It would prove our theory."

"Yes sir," Tellman said steadily. "Anything else, sir?"

"Not unless you have something further to report."

"No sir. What would you like after that, sir?"

"I'd like you to find that weapon, and continue to learn whatever you can about the man's movements that night. Someone may have seen him."

"Yes sir." The old insolence returned as if he could not help it. The resentment was too deep. The truce was over. "And what about Mrs. Winthrop? Are you going to look into her a lot more? See if she had a lover? Or would that be too offensive to the family?"

"If I find out anything relevant, I'll inform you," Pitt said coolly. "Offensive or not. Now go and drag the Serpentine."

"Yes sir."

Pitt would rather have dragged the Serpentine than do the job he knew he should do next. He had been turning it over in his mind since leaving Portsmouth, debating whether it was really necessary or not. It might well prove useless in that it would turn up no new information, but that was not the only aspect to consider. There was the professional courtesy, and the fact that if he did not, the omission could prove expensive. Above all, he questioned himself, would Micah Drummond have gone; and he knew the answer without hesitation. He would have.

Accordingly, in the late morning Pitt found himself in the library of Lord Marlborough Winthrop's house in Chelsea, not more than a stone's throw from the Thames. It was a solid, gracious house, but lacking in any individuality of style, and the library where Pitt was waiting was unimaginative in its use of leather, gold tooling, rich mahogany, and heavy, pillared mantel shelf. After barely one glance around it he could have closed his eyes and described the rest of what he would see, and he was not mistaken.

Lord Winthrop himself, when he closed the door silently behind him and stood facing Pitt, was a man of indeterminate features, sandy hair and an expression which was lugubrious in the extreme, although whether that was his nature or the present circumstances it was not possible to say. Pitt felt in his mind it was the former. There seemed no softening in his face, no mellower lines around the eyes. He looked as if laughter did not come easily to him. He reminded Pitt queasily of the bloodless face in the morgue, the same features, the same mottled coloring. Of course today he was dressed entirely in black.

"Good morning, Mr. . . ." He looked at Pitt, trying to gather

44

some impression of him, to place his social status to know how to treat him.

"Superintendent Pitt." He still liked the sound of the title, and then felt self-conscious for having spoken it. The man might prove to be pompous and superficial, but he had just lost a son in a fearful manner. His grief and his shock would be real. To judge him now would be a far greater offense than any he was likely to commit.

"Oh—yes," Winthrop agreed as if memory were returning. In spite of being a big man and broad shouldered, he was not imposing. His size seemed more of an encumbrance to him than an asset. "Good of you to come." But his voice suggested that it was merely Pitt's duty, and his own thanks were a question of courtesy, no more. "Of course Lady Winthrop and I are most anxious to know what progress you have made in this terrible affair." He looked at Pitt, waiting for him to reply.

Pitt swallowed the desire to explain that his errand was one of discovery. Then the thought occurred to him that perhaps it was he who was mistaken. Micah Drummond's job had included a large element of diplomacy. It was something he would have to learn if he were to fill his shoes. Odd, but now that he was more senior, he was also less his own master. He was accountable in a way he had not been before.

"We have witnesses, sir," he said aloud. "People who passed by the park at various times during the evening and certain parts of the night, and it would seem as if the crime must have been committed at about midnight—"

"You mean someone saw it?" Lord Winthrop was incredulous. "Good God, man! What is the world coming to when such an act can be perpetrated in a public place in London, and men see it and do nothing! What is happening to us?" His face was growing darker as the blood suffused his cheeks. "One expects barbarity in heathen countries, outposts of the Empire, but not here in the heart and soul of a civilized land!" There was both anger and fear in his voice. He stood in the middle of his familiar room with all its trappings of social and economic safety, a frightened man, confusion threatening him in spite of it all. "Brutal murders in Whitechapel eighteen months ago, and nobody even caught for it." His voice was rising. "Scandal about the Royal Family, whispers everywhere, moral decay setting in, vulgarity in everything." Self-control was fast escaping him. "Anarchists, Irishmen all over the place. The whole of society is on the brink of ruin." He took a deep, shaky breath, then another. "I apologize, sir. I should not allow my personal feelings to be so—outspoken . . ."

"I am sure you are not alone in believing we live in most trying times, Lord Winthrop," Pitt said tactfully. "But actually I did not mean that anyone saw a crime committed, only that there was no one on the Serpentine when a young couple passed at ten o'clock, that two men were seen walking in Rotten Row a little bit before midnight, and that at two in the morning there was a boat on the water, apparently drifting. Since Captain Winthrop died approximately between eleven and midnight, as an estimate, that would seem to suggest it was midnight."

Lord Winthrop's voice leveled with an effort. "Ah—yes, I see. Well, what does that prove? It hardly apprehends anyone!" His expression tightened as if he had smelled something distasteful. "Only too obviously there are gangs of murderous thieves at loose in the heart of London. What are you doing about it, I should like to know. I am not one to criticize the established authorities, but even the most lenient of us has to say that the police force has a great deal to do to justify itself." He was standing in front of the mantel shelf, with a very traditional Chelsea vase on it, and behind his shoulder, on the wall, a painting of a calm, ordered landscape. "You have much to do to redeem your reputation, sir, after the Whitechapel affair," he continued. "Jack the Ripper, indeed! What about madmen who would"—he swallowed—"decapitate a man for a few pounds?"

"It is not likely that he was robbed, sir," Pitt interposed.

Lord Winthrop's nostrils flared. "Not robbed? Rubbish, sir! Of course he was robbed! Why else would a gang of cutthroats set on a complete stranger who was merely taking an evening stroll in the park? My son was a man of excellent physique, Mr. Pitt, superb in sports, especially the noble arts of self-defense. 'A healthy mind and a healthy body' was his motto, and he was always as good as his word."

Pitt was reminded suddenly of Eustace March, Emily's uncle-in-law, insensitive, pompous, opinionated and insufferable—and in the end tragic. Had Oakley Winthrop been like that? If so, it was not surprising someone had murdered him.

"There must have been several of them, and well armed, to have overcome him," Lord Winthrop continued, his voice rising as his anger mounted. "What are you doing to permit the situation to have reached this monstrous proportion, I should like to know."

"As you say, sir." Pitt kept a picture of Micah Drummond in his mind's eye, the long, rather serious face with its aquiline nose and gray, innocent eyes. It was the only way he could control his temper. "Captain Winthrop was a fine man in the prime of life, in excellent health, and skilled in sport. He must have been attacked either by a greatly superior force, such as that of several people, possibly well armed, or else he was taken by surprise by someone he believed he had no cause to fear."

Lord Winthrop stood motionless. "What are you implying?"

"That there appears to have been no struggle, sir," Pitt explained, wishing he could move to ease the tension in himself, and yet the quiet room seemed to forbid anything but utter concentration on the tragedy in hand. "Captain Winthrop had no bruises upon his body or arms," he continued. "No scratches or other marks, no contusions on his knuckles, nor were his clothes torn or scuffed. Had there been any struggle—"

"Yes, yes, yes! I am not a fool, man," Lord Winthrop said impatiently. "I realize what you are saying." He moved suddenly away from the mantel to stare out of the window onto the overgrown patch of dark laurels, his shoulders high, back rigid. "Betrayed—that is what it amounts to. Poor Oakley was betrayed." He swung back again. "Well, Superintendent whatever-your-name-is, I expect you to find out who it was and see that he is brought to justice. I hope you understand me?"

Pitt bit back the response that rose to his lips.

"Yes, sir. Of course we will."

Lord Winthrop was only partially mollified. "Betrayed. Good God!"

"Who was betrayed?" The door had opened without either of them noticing, and a slender woman with dark hair and large, heavy-lidded blue eyes stood just inside the room. Her manner was imperious and her face was full of passion, intelligence and anger. "Who was betrayed, Marlborough?"

Lord Winthrop turned to look at her, his face suddenly ironed of emotion.

"You do not need to concern yourself with it, my dear. It is better that you do not know the details. I shall tell you, naturally, when there is any news."

47

"Nonsense!" She closed the door behind her. "If it has to do with Oakley, I have as much right to know as you." She looked at Pitt for the first time. "And who are you, young man? Has someone sent you to apprise us of the situation?"

Pitt took a deep breath. "No, Lady Winthrop, I am in charge of the case and I came to assure you of every effort we can make, and to inform you of what little information we have already."

"And is that indeed that my son was betrayed?" she asked. "Although if you have not caught the assassin, how can you possibly know that he was betrayed?"

"Evelyn, it would surely be much better . . ." Lord Winthrop began.

She ignored him completely. "How can you know anything of the sort?" she demanded of Pitt again, coming farther into the room and standing on the heavy ornate carpet. "If you are in charge of the case, why are you not out doing something? What are you doing here? We can tell you nothing."

"There are several men out searching and asking questions, ma'am," Pitt said patiently. "I came to inform you of our progress so far, and to see if you might be able to shed any light on certain aspects of the case—"

"Us? What on earth do you mean?" Her eyes were very large and deep set, a little too close together for true beauty. "Why do you say 'betrayed'? If you are thinking of his wife, then that is total nonsense." She gave a little shiver and her body moved, rustling the stiff silk of her gown. "She is devoted to him. The idea that she might have entertained notions about other men is quite absurd. I don't know what sort of people you imagine we are."

"He did not say—" Lord Winthrop began again.

"We are landed aristocracy," she went on, ignoring him and staring at Pitt. "We are not involved in trade, nor do we marry foreigners. We are not greedy nor are we ambitious. We do not seek position, but we serve with honor and diligence when called upon. We know how to behave, Mr. Pitt. We know our duty, and have done it to the full."

Pitt discarded most of the things he had been going to ask. They would either fail to understand him entirely or they would be insulted.

"I had no one in mind, ma'am," he said as soothingly as he could. "It is simply that Captain Winthrop made no struggle at all, which strongly suggests that he did not expect any attack from whoever it was. He was taken completely by surprise, therefore I am inclined to believe it was someone he knew."

"Are you!" There was challenge in her voice, in the stiff attitude of her body beneath its black silk.

"When a man is walking alone in the park after dark," Pitt explained, "he is inclined to be wary of any stranger approaching, to remain facing him if he stops, don't you think?"

"Me?" She was surprised. Then she considered it. "Yes, I suppose so." She moved closer to the window and stared out at the light on the leaves. "Perhaps one of his neighbors has taken leave of his wits. Or do you imagine it is someone from the ship, someone racked with envy or some such thing? Perhaps Oakley beat him at some contest or other, or made a fool of him in some other way. Whoever it is, I expect you to find him and see to it that he is hanged."

"Of course he will," Lord Winthrop said at last. "I have already discussed the matter with Mr. Pitt. He is aware of my feelings on the subject."

"He may not be aware that the Home Secretary is a relative of ours." She turned and looked back at Pitt with sharp eyes. "As indeed are many other people of great influence. It is vulgar to be ostentatious about one's family connections, nevertheless, I would have you keep in mind that we shall not rest until the matter is closed and justice is done for my poor son." She raised her chin a little. "Now, we appreciate your coming to inform us of your intentions, but you had better not waste any more time standing here. Please accept our thanks and continue about your business." She swiveled around to her husband, dismissing Pitt. "Marlborough, I have written to all the Walsingham side of the family. I think it would be better if you wrote to the Thurlows and the Sussex Mayburys."

"They will all be perfectly aware of it, my dear," he said irritably. "The newspapers are full of it! Goodness knows, every little clerk and washerwoman in London will be familiar with the details of it by now!"

"That is hardly the point," she said. "It is our duty to inform the family properly. They will be insulted if we do not. They will wish to write to us to offer their condolences. And one keeps notices of deaths in the family. It is important." She shook her head impatiently and the facets of her jet beads caught the light. "I have not written to the Gloucestershire Wardlaws yet, or to cousin Reginald. I shall have to order

49

some more black-edged paper. One can hardly use ordinary deckle for such a purpose."

"Did Captain Winthrop ever speak to you of a rivalry?" Pitt felt as if he were interrupting, their attention had so obviously gone from him.

"No." Lady Winthrop turned back with some surprise. "Never, that I can recall. He wrote to us regularly, of course, and came here each time he was ashore, for dinner at least once. But I do not recall his ever having mentioned any enmity with anyone at all. He was remarkably well liked." A frown creased her forehead. "I thought I had already told you so."

"People who are popular and successful can attract the envy of those who are less so," Pitt pointed out.

"Yes, of course. I am aware of that," she retorted. "I have no idea. Surely that is your job to find out. Is it not what you are employed for?"

"Oakley never mentioned anyone," Lord Winthrop answered, putting his hand out tentatively towards his wife, then thinking better of it.

"But then he was not given to speaking ill of others. I daresay he was not even aware of it."

"Of course he wasn't aware of it," she said brusquely, her brows drawn together. "The superintendent said he was taken by surprise. If it had been a man who hated him, he would have been on his guard. He was not a fool, Marlborough!"

"Dammit, he trusted someone he should not have!" he said with a sudden burst of anger.

She ignored him and looked at Pitt.

"Thank you, Mr. Pitt. I assume you will keep us informed. Good day to you."

"Good day, ma'am," Pitt answered obediently, and walked past her to open the door and let himself out.

Pitt had not mentioned to Lord and Lady Winthrop that it seemed the crime had actually been committed in the pleasure boat on the Serpentine, but the fact was confirmed to him the following day when Sergeant le Grange came to his office. He was a smallish, solid man with dark auburn hair and a good-looking face.

"Looks as if Mr. Tellman was right, sir," he said with satisfaction, standing in front of Pitt's desk with a smile. "Crime was done right there in the boat, over the side. Very neat. All the blood gone into the water. Nothing to show."

Pitt gritted his teeth. It had not been Tellman's idea and yet it would be ridiculously childish to point that out to le Grange, even if le Grange were to believe him. And if he did not, it would make Pitt look absurd.

"You found a fresh nick in the wood," he said very levelly.

Le Grange's brown eyes opened wide.

"Yes sir! Did Mr. Tellman say so to you? He told me as he wouldn't have time to come up and see you, as he had to go and talk with someone in Battersea."

"No, he did not tell me," Pitt replied. "It is what I should have looked for in the circumstances. I assumed you did the same."

"Oh, not me, sir, except because Mr. Tellman told me to," le Grange said modestly.

"What did he go to Battersea for?"

Le Grange stared straight ahead of him.

"Oh, you'd better ask him that, sir."

"Are you still looking for the weapon?" Pitt asked.

"Yes sir." Le Grange pulled a face. "Not found anything at all so far. Don't know where else to look. I think as he probably took it away with him. Ah well, he must have brought it. I suppose he would take it back the same way."

"You've dragged the Serpentine?" Pitt did not argue. It was unpleasantly likely the murderer still had the weapon, or had dropped it in any of a hundred other possible places. They could hardly drag the Thames for it. It would have sunk deep into the river mud ages ago.

"Ah yes sir. Mr. Tellman is very thorough, sir. He made sure we did that, and did it properly. There is nothing in there now, sir, not a thing. You'd never credit the stuff we found!" His eyes opened a little wider. "Two perfectly good boots, both for the left foot. Shame about them. Don't know how someone could lose them. Three different fishing poles. I suppose that's easy enough to understand. All kinds o' boxes and bags, and a hat that looked nearly new. You wouldn't believe it! No money, o' course."

"I will believe anything you tell me, Sergeant," Pitt said without a flicker, and watched le Grange's surprise with satisfaction. "Now what has Mr. Tellman told you to do next?"

"He said as I should come up to you, Mr. Pitt, and see what you said we should do, you being in charge, like." The expression in his face had altered somewhat since he came in, but it was still cautious, that of a man whose old prejudices die hard.

51

With an effort Pitt ignored it. "Have you spoken to all the neighbors yet?"

"Yes sir. No one said anything helpful. One elderly lady did see 'im start 'is walk in the evening, but since we already know from Mrs. Winthrop what time it was, it 'ardly adds to anything."

"Yes it does," Pitt contradicted. "It confirms that she is telling the truth."

"You didn't suspect 'er, did you, sir?" le Grange said with disbelief and a touch of sarcasm, all under the veneer of respect. "She's really quite a small woman, sir. Tall, an' all that, but must weigh like a feather. No flesh to her at all."

"Not of doing it herself, Sergeant, but it is not impossible she was involved. A great many crimes of violence are domestic in origin."

"Oh. Yes, well I suppose you're right about that," le Grange conceded graciously. "But I wouldn't have thought a lady like that . . . well—I suppose you know the gentry, sir."

"It is a possibility, le Grange, that's all. I assume nobody saw him approached by anyone else?"

"No sir."

"And all these neighbors and acquaintances, were they all at home themselves?"

"Sir?"

"Can they account for where they were all night until about three in the morning, Sergeant?"

"I dunno, sir."

"Then that's what you do next. Find out!"

"Yes sir. Will that be all, sir?"

"Until you can answer that, yes!"

"Sir!" And le Grange turned on his heel smartly and went out, leaving Pitt irritated and knowing there was nothing he could do about it.

There were other cases which required at least some of his attention, a major robbery, a fire which seemed like arson, an embezzlement from a company of stockbrokers. It was the afternoon of the next day when Pitt was told by a pale-faced and breathless sergeant that there was a gentleman from the Home Office to see him, and the moment after he stood back, with an anguished glance of apology, a tall, very distinguished man came into the room. The sergeant beat a hasty retreat.

"Landon Hurlwood," the man announced as Pitt rose to his

52

feet. "Good afternoon, Superintendent. Forgive my calling upon you unannounced, but the matter is somewhat urgent, and I had a few moments I could spare."

"Good afternoon, Mr. Hurlwood," Pitt replied levelly. "Please make yourself comfortable." He indicated the chair he had so often sat in himself when Micah Drummond had occupied this office. As Hurlwood accepted, Pitt sat in the easy chair and looked across at his visitor expectantly.

Hurlwood was tall, almost as tall as Pitt, of slender build and still trim, although Pitt would have judged him to be in his late fifties. His hair was unblemished pewter gray, thick, and curled up over his ears. He had excellent, very dark eyes, and patrician features. He sat back and crossed his legs, totally at ease.

"This appalling murder of poor Captain Winthrop, Superintendent," he began, regarding Pitt with a slight smile. "What do we know so far?"

Pitt outlined the facts, keeping all speculation and deduction to himself.

Hurlwood listened intently. "I see," he said at last. "I confess, this is worse than I had thought. One discounts a great deal that the newspapers have to say. I fear they are more interested in sensation than truth, and cater to the lowest of minds. But in this instance it seems they are not inaccurate, even if their choice of language is a trifle hysterical. Tell me frankly, Superintendent, what are your prospects of finding the lunatic who did this?"

"If it is some chance madman, probably very little," Pitt replied. "Unless he kills again and leaves more evidence next time."

"Good God! What a fearful thought! I assume that you do not think it was a band of robbers? No, I must say it seems unlikely. They would not have left anything on him, and you say there were coins in his waistcoat pocket, and a gold watch and the chain commonly known as an albert." He moved his elegant head in a motion of denial. "And anyway, why on earth would thieves take off the poor man's head? Thieves come armed with knives or cudgels, or even a garrote, but not an actual cutlass. So in your opinion it resolves to either a madman or someone he knew?" His lips tightened. "How very unpleasant."

"Less frightening to the public than a gang of thieves who behead their victims," Pitt observed.

"Oh true, quite true." Hurlwood gave a ghost of a smile. "Nevertheless we must clear it up as soon as possible. What I would like to know, if you can tell me, is if it has anything to do with the navy, in your opinion. It is not unnatural that the Admiralty should wish to know."

Pitt caught a whiff of fear, and could imagine the preparation for denial, and thence, the disclamation.

"There is no evidence to suggest it yet," he replied carefully. "I have been to Portsmouth and spoken to his lieutenant, who says that he had no quarrel there, and he was not killed until eight days after he came up to London."

"Indicative." Hurlwood nodded his head, relaxing a fraction. "A long time to wait if one has a murderous quarrel. Hardly the heat of the moment. Still, not enough to rule it out." He was easier; his long, elegant hands were no longer clenched, but he was not naive enough to accept escape so swiftly.

"I also checked as many as possible of his colleagues and friends to see if they were in Portsmouth on the night of his death," Pitt added. "So far they were all in Portsmouth at times close enough to midnight of that night that they could not have been in London, even on the fastest of trains."

"I see. Yes, that would be conclusive." Hurlwood rose to his feet in a single, graceful motion. His clothes were beautiful. He made Pitt feel shabby. Micah Drummond would not have felt so far short in the comparison. He was not a dandy, but he had the elegance that comes without effort to the true gentleman.

Pitt stood up also, his jacket bulging where his pockets were stuffed with notes the desk sergeant had given him and a ball of string from which he had recently tied up a parcel.

"So you are left with a personal motive," Hurlwood continued. "All the same, I imagine you will give it your fullest attention, Superintendent, in view of the nature of the crime and the distinguished family of the victim." It was not a question but an assumption.

"Naturally," Pitt agreed. "But it is not a matter in which haste will be appropriate."

Hurlwood flashed him a broad smile. His teeth were excellent, and no doubt he was aware of it, but there was genuine humor in him, an appreciation of all that Pitt had not said.

"Of course," he agreed. "I do not envy you, Superintendent. Very courteous of you to spare me your time. Good day, sir."

"Good day, Mr. Hurlwood," Pitt replied, smiling himself at the euphemism. The day could hardly be good for any of them.

Hurlwood had been gone only half an hour when the sergeant returned, eyes wide again, breath catching in his throat. This time it was Giles Farnsworth, the assistant commissioner, who was a step behind him. He was smooth-faced, clean-shaven and perhaps ten years younger than Hurlwood. Today he looked angry and harassed. His white shirt was immaculate, his winged collar high and a trifle tight, his fair brown hair was thick and brushed back off his broad brow, but there was anxiety in his expression and the beginnings of a ragged temper.

"Good afternoon, Pitt." He closed the door behind him and remained standing.

Pitt came around the desk. "Good afternoon, sir."

"This damned Winthrop business," Farnsworth said, his mouth pulled tight with distaste. "What have you done so far? We can't let this one stand around. Police reputation is bad enough. We've never recovered from the Ripper and all the harm that did us. We can't afford another episode like that!"

"No reason to suppose we will have one again—" Pitt began.

Farnsworth's temper was intent and savage. "Good God, man! Of course it will happen again if we've got a criminal lunatic loose in Hyde Park. Why on earth would he be satisfied with one dead body?" He jerked his head angrily. "And if it's a gang of robbers come from God knows where, they'd do it as long as they can get away with it! We'll have panic in the streets again, people terrified to go out of their own doors, half the city paralyzed . . ."

"Captain Winthrop was not robbed."

"Then it's a madman!"

"Neither did he put up any struggle." Pitt kept his tone calm with an effort. He understood why Farnsworth was afraid. The political situation was tense. The Whitechapel affair had shown ugly manifestations of anarchy, a violence simmering frighteningly close to the surface. There was unrest in many of the major cities, the old sore of the Irish question was as painful as ever. The popularity of the monarchy was at its lowest ebb. It would not take much to spark the underlying fear into a blaze of destruction which would carry many of them away with it. "He was killed in the pleasure boat while leaning over the side, and with one clean stroke," Pitt said aloud.

Farnsworth stood still, his face tight and bleak.

"What are you saying, Pitt? That it was someone he knew? He must have known him well. Why on earth does a naval captain get into a pleasure boat on the Serpentine, at midnight, with another man carrying an ax? It's absurd. It's very, very ugly, Pitt."

"I know that, sir."

"Who is it? What was the man's private life? What about the wife? If it's scandalous, you are going to have to cover this up, if you can. I trust you know that?" He fixed Pitt with a sharp stare.

"I never expose people's private griefs and sins voluntarily," Pitt replied, but it was an equivocation, and Farnsworth knew it.

"Winthrops are an important family, connections all over the place," Farnsworth went on, moving his weight restlessly from one foot to the other. "For Heaven's sake be discreet. And don't pull faces, man! I know you've got to solve the case!" He bit his lip, looking at Pitt hard and obviously turning over something in his mind.

Pitt waited.

"It's going to be difficult," Farnsworth said again.

The remark was so obvious Pitt did not reply.

Farnsworth looked Pitt up and down closely, still cogitating. "You'll need connections yourself," he said slowly. "Not impossible. Self-made man, but that doesn't rule out influence, you know."

Pitt felt a sudden stab of fear, but still he said nothing.

"Just a few friends can make the world of difference," Farnsworth went on. "If they are the right ones."

The fear subsided. It was not what Pitt had dreaded. He found himself smiling.

Farnsworth smiled as well.

"Good man," he said with a nod. "Opens a lot of doors for you, furthers your career. Drummond was, you know?"

Pitt went cold. It was the Inner Circle he was referring to after all, that secret society, outwardly benevolent, inwardly malign, which Drummond had joined in his innocence and regretted so bitterly afterwards. The price of brotherhood was the surrender of loyalties, the forfeit of conscience so that an unknown army helped you, and could call on your help, at whatever cost, whenever it chose. The price of betrayal was ruin, sometimes even death. One knew only a half dozen or so other members, as the need arose. There was no way to tell to whom your loyalty might be pledged, or in what cause.

"No." Pitt blurted out the word before realizing how foolish it would be, but he felt cornered, as if a darkness were trapping him and closing tight around him. "I . . ." He drew in his breath and let it out slowly.

Farnsworth's face was flushed with annoyance and there was a bright glitter in his eyes.

"You are making a mistake, Pitt," he said between his teeth.

"I don't belong." Pitt kept his voice as calm as he could.

"If you want to succeed, you had better make yourself belong." Farnsworth looked at him unsmilingly. "Otherwise the doors will be closed. And I know what I am talking about. You need to clear up this case quickly." He gestured towards the window and the street below. "Have you seen the newspapers? The public are beginning to panic already. You have no time to dither." He walked to the door. "I'll give you three days, Pitt, then you had better have something very decisive. And I expect you to reconsider that other matter. You need friends, believe me. You need them very much." And with that he went out, leaving the door open behind him, and Pitt heard his footsteps down the stairs.

3

CHARLOTTE HAD HEARD the newsboys crying out the latest speculation on the Hyde Park murder, but she had given it less of her attention than she usually gave to Pitt's more sensational cases because her mind was very fully occupied with the matter of plasterwork on the ceiling of the new house. At present she was in the middle of what was to be the withdrawing room, and staring upwards. The builder, a thin, lugubrious man in his thirties with sad eyes and a long nose, was standing in front of her shaking his head.

"Can't do it, ma'am. Wouldn't expect you to understand why, but it just in't possible. Too far gorn, it is. Much too far."

Charlotte looked up at the broken plaster on the cornice.

"But it's only about two feet altogether. Why can't you just replace that bit?" she asked, as she thought, very reasonably.

"Oh no." Again he shook his head. "It'll look like a patch, ma'am. Wouldn't be right. Can't turn out work like that. I've got my reputation to consider." He met her eyes with a clear, indignant gaze.

"No it wouldn't," she argued. "Not if you put in the same pattern."

"Can't patch old wine bottles with new skins, ma'am. Don't you read your Bible?" he said accusingly.

"Not when I'm looking for instruction on repairing the ceiling, I don't," she replied briskly. "Well, if you can't do that piece, what about the whole of that side?"

"Ah—well." He squinted up at it, head on one side. "I'm not sure about that. Might be a different pattern, mightn't it?"

58

"Can't you find the same one? It doesn't look very complicated to me."

"That's 'cause you in't a plasterer, ma'am. Why don't you ask your husband to explain it to you?"

"My husband is not a plasterer either," she said with rising irritation.

"No ma'am, I daresay not," he agreed. "But 'cos 'e's a man, yer see, and men understand these things better than ladies, if you don't mind my saying so?" He regarded her with a sententious smile. "Now I wouldn't understand how to stitch a seam, or bake a cake, but I do know about cornices and the like. And you'll be wanting a new rose too, to 'ang them good chandeliers from. Gotta watch that, or it'll spoil the 'ole thing."

"And how much will a new one be?"

"Well now, that'll depend on whether you want paper stucco, which is very light, like, and very cheap, and comes at anything from three shillings for one what's nineteen inches across, to one what's forty-nine inches across, and it'd be too big for this room, at thirty-two and seven pence ha'penny." He sucked in his breath noisily and continued. "Or you could have plaster, plain or perforated, which comes at one and sixpence or thereabouts for twelve inches across, right up to four and sixpence for thirty inches across. It all depends upon what you want."

"I see. Well, I'll think about it. Now what about the lamp in the hall?"

"Ah well now, that's different. You could have a real plain twisted-'eart pendant which comes at about four and sixpence each, or the bigger ones at seven and sixpence each." He shook his head. "That don't include the globe, o' course."

"But that won't be the one I wanted. I like the one with the engraved glass."

"Ah—well that'd be a great deal more, ma'am; that'd be fifty-one shillings each, bronzed or lacquered. And now if you want it polished, it'd be fifty-seven shillings." He sucked at what was apparently a hollow tooth and stared at her.

"I don't like the other one," she said adamantly. "It's vulgar."

"I just fitted one like that for the lady what lives opposite," he said with satisfaction. "Very nice it is too. Very nice lady. Her cousin is married to Lady Winslow's brother-in-law." He imparted this last piece of information as if it clinched the argument.

59 .

"Then she won't thank me for doing the same," Charlotte retorted. "What about the finial for the west gable? Can you match the others?"

"I don't know about that." He shook his head doubtfully. "You'd be better to replace them all—"

"Balderdash!" said a brisk voice from the doorway. "You find a finial that matches, young man, or my niece will employ somebody who will."

Charlotte spun around with surprise and delight to see Great-Aunt Vespasia advancing across the room. More strictly speaking, she was Emily's Great-Aunt-in-law from her first marriage. However, George's death had made no difference to the closeness of their affection, indeed they grew in each other's regard with each new turn in their relationship. Now she felt a sharp sense of pleasure that Vespasia had spoken of her as a niece, even though she had no claim to that title.

"Aunt Vespasia," she said immediately. "How very nice to see you! You have come at the very best moment to give me your advice. I cannot offer you any refreshment. I am so sorry. I can barely offer you a seat." She felt acutely apologetic, even though she had not invited Vespasia and therefore was not responsible for the situation.

Vespasia ignored her and looked at the builder, who had little idea who she was but had worked on enough houses of the quality to know that in this instance he was now totally out of his depth. This was a lady of a quite different order. She was tall, slender verging on gaunt, but with a face of exquisite bones which still retained much of the marvelous beauty which had made her famous throughout England in her youth. She looked at him as if he himself had been the offending piece of plaster.

"What are you doing about that?" she asked, staring up at the broken cornice.

"Repairing that side," Charlotte said quickly. "Isn't that right, Mr. Robinson?"

"If you say so, ma'am," he replied sullenly.

"Quite right," Vespasia approved. "And I'm sure if you look hard enough, you will discover a rose that will fit with it quite satisfactorily. What about the dado rail? That is in an awful state. You will need to replace all of it." She looked at Robinson. "You had better set about finding something suitable. Now be off with you and begin." She dismissed him without further thought and turned to Charlotte. "Now, my dear, where may we go to leave this man to his business? What about the garden? It looks charming."

"By all means," Charlotte agreed hastily, leading the way, opening the French door for Vespasia and then closing it behind her. Outside on the paved terrace the air was soft and there was a scent of bruised grass on the breeze and the smell of hyacinths somewhere just beyond sight.

Vespasia stood very straight, her hair brilliant in the light, her black silver-topped cane in her right hand, not leaning on it so much as resting her hand over it.

"You will need a gardener," she observed. "At least twice a week. Thomas will never have time to attend to it. How is he taking to his new position? It was past time he was promoted."

It would not have occurred to Charlotte to tell her anything but the truth.

"Very well, for the most part," she replied. "But some of his men can be trying. They resent the fact that he was preferred over others who consider themselves just as good. Micah Drummond they could understand. He was a gentleman and it was to be expected, but they find it hard to take orders from Thomas." She smiled briefly. "Not that he says a great deal to me, I just know it from the odd remark here and there, and sometimes from what he doesn't say. But no doubt it will mend . . . in time."

"Indeed." Vespasia took a few steps forward over the grass. "What of this latest matter—the wretched man who was beheaded in the park? The newspapers did not say so, but I assume Thomas is in charge of it?"

"Yes, yes he is." Charlotte looked at her questioningly, waiting for the explanation of her interest.

Vespasia continued to stare at the trees at the far end of the lawn.

"I daresay you remember Judge Quade?" She began quite casually, as if the matter were of no consequence.

"Yes," Charlotte replied equally nonchalantly. The judge's sensitive, ascetic face leapt to her mind, and all her emotions crowding in on her, the fierceness of his integrity in the Farriers' Lane case, the memories he brought with him of a past Charlotte had not even guessed at, and above all the change in Vespasia, her sudden vulnerability, the way she blushed (a thing Charlotte had never seen before), and the laughter and shadows in her eyes.

"Yes, of course I remember him," she said again. She was

61

about to ask how he was, then stopped just before the words were out. Vespasia was not one with whom she could play such trivial games. It was better to wait in silence for her to say what it was she wished.

"He is very well acquainted with Lord and Lady Winthrop," Vespasia explained, walking a little farther onto the grass, her skirts catching on the longer, uncut stems.

Charlotte was obliged to follow in order to continue the conversation.

"Is he?" She was surprised. Thelonius Quade was a man of high intelligence and quiet wit. From what Emily had said, Lord Winthrop was quite the opposite. "Socially?" she asked.

Vespasia smiled, her silver eyes light with amusement.

"Hardly professionally, my dear. Marlborough Winthrop does nothing useful whatsoever; but that is not a crime, or half the aristocracy would be up before the bench. Of course, socially, which I imagine was not of Thelonius's choosing. The man is a monumental bore, and his wife is worse. She has violent opinions, all of which she has borrowed from someone else. She contracts them as some people contract diseases."

"Did he know Captain Winthrop?" Charlotte asked with mounting interest.

"Only slightly." Vespasia was standing in the middle of the lawn now, the breeze ruffling the pale green silk of her skirt. Her blouse was of a delicate ivory in the light, and the heavy pearls around her neck hung low across the bosom. Charlotte wondered if she would ever look quite so effortlessly elegant herself.

"I'm sorry," Charlotte said quietly. "He must be distressed for them."

"Of course." Vespasia accepted and dismissed the subject with a small gesture of her head. She moved a few steps farther across the lawn. "The funeral was a family affair, but they will be holding a memorial service for him tomorrow. Thelonius will attend. I thought I would go with him." She turned and looked at Charlotte with the first gleam of a smile in her eyes. "I wondered if you would care to accompany us?"

It would be indelicate, and quite unnecessary, to ask Vespasia's purpose in such an invitation. It was not the Winthrops she was thinking of, nor Thelonius Quade, and certainly not herself. In the past she had been involved in many social crusades, and worked with tireless passion. She had several times exhibited the same energy and devotion to meddling in Pitt's cases, assisting Charlotte and Emily in places and with people they could not reach alone. It would be clumsy to say she enjoyed it; it was both different and more than that. But there was no mistaking the light in her eyes now.

"It is very ugly," Charlotte said tentatively, catching up with her and looking at the slender daffodil spears under the trees.

"There is a note of stridency in the newspapers," Vespasia added. "It is imperative that Thomas establish himself in his new position as early as possible. This is an extraordinary case, or at least it has all the appearance of being so. We must do what we can."

"The newspapers are speaking of a madman loose," Charlotte agreed unhappily.

"Balderdash!" Vespasia dismissed the idea. "If there was a lunatic capering around Hyde Park cutting people's heads off we should have heard more of him by now."

"Someone he knew?" Charlotte asked, her attention sharpening. She forgot the daffodils, and was only dimly aware of the wind in the branches and the brilliant sprays of forsythia in bloom.

"That seems an inevitable conclusion," Vespasia agreed. "Thelonius informs me he was not robbed. Or so Lord Winthrop says."

Charlotte's imagination began to race. She started with what seemed to be to her the obvious.

"His wife has a lover? Or he has a mistress, and her husband . . ."

"Oh really!" Vespasia said impatiently. "Oakley Winthrop might not have been an imaginative man, but neither was he a cretin. If you have the misfortune to be taking a midnight stroll in the park and to meet your wife's lover carrying a cutlass, you do not go and climb into a pleasure boat with him. To discuss what? The equitable division of her favors?"

Charlotte smothered a giggle but held her ground. "Perhaps he was an acquaintance anyway, and Winthrop did not know of the arrangement," she suggested. "If it was his wife's lover, she may have been discreet. After all, Captain Winthrop will have been away a good deal of the time. It may never have occurred to him that she could have considered any other man."

"Then if he was unaware of the situation, why on earth would the wretched man murder him?" Vespasia asked, her eyebrows arching even higher. "That seems absurd, and quite unnecessary."

"Then perhaps it was his mistress's husband?" Charlotte thought aloud. "He may have been a very jealous man."

"Then why should Winthrop sit down in a boat with him in the middle of the night?" Vespasia whisked a long stem of grass with her stick.

"Perhaps he didn't . . ." Charlotte started, then realized it was foolish before she finished.

"His mistress was an innocent?" Vespasia said with a smile both tolerant and amused. "I doubt it. Not so innocent as to be unaware of her husband's nature." She turned and began to walk back up the long lawn towards the house. "No, the more one looks at this, the more bizarre it appears. I think Thomas may need such assistance as we can give him." She kept her expression almost without enthusiasm, but not even her strength of will could entirely disguise the inner energy that burned at the thought.

"Then I shall most certainly come with you to the memorial service," Charlotte accepted without further hesitation. "At what time shall I be ready?"

"I shall send a carriage for you at a quarter past ten," Vespasia said immediately. "And my dear, the next time you buy a new outfit, I should make it black if I were you." Her eyes gleamed. "It seems to be de rigueur for your husband's occupation."

Actually Charlotte sent an urgent message to Emily to request that she might borrow something suitable. She really had no extra money above that which was needed for the house. With new plasterwork, new finials, and several new fire tiles to be purchased, among a number of other things, every halfpenny must be put to the best use.

Emily was very happy to oblige, on condition, not open to negotiation, that Charlotte tell her every single detail of the case and include her in all future efforts. For this she would be willing to lend her any garment she liked throughout the duration of the endeavor.

Therefore at ten o'clock the next morning Charlotte was looking radiant, her cheeks flushed and her eyes bright, when Caroline Ellison arrived in a whirl of chocolate-and-gold-colored silks and a hat reminiscent of a turban.

"Good morning, Mama!" Charlotte said in surprise, both at the hat and at Caroline's unheralded arrival. It would be quite needless to ask if there were anything wrong; Caroline's face was shining with well-being.

"Good morning, my dear," Caroline responded, looking around Charlotte's bedroom, where they were as Charlotte put the finishing touches to her hair. "You look very well, but I am afraid a little funereal. Could you not put a touch of something brighter, at least around your neck? All this somberness may be fashionable, but it is a little extreme, don't you think?"

"It's not in the least fashionable," Charlotte said with astonishment. "Total black—in April!"

Caroline brushed it aside with a wave of her hand. "I have quite lost touch with fashion lately. Anyway, it still needs a little color. What about something different, unexpected? When I think of it, red is rather ordinary." She glanced around. "What about—oh, what do people not put with black?" She held up her hand against interruption while she thought. "I know—saffron. I have never seen anyone with black and saffron."

"Not anyone with a looking glass, anyway," Charlotte agreed.

"Oh! You don't like it? I thought it would be rather different."

"Completely different, Mama. And as I am going to a memorial service, I think the family might well be offended. I hear they are rather conventional anyway."

Caroline's face fell. "Oh—I didn't know. Who is it? Do I know them? I hadn't heard . . ."

"You would have read the newspapers." Charlotte put the last pin in her hair and surveyed the effect.

"I don't read obituaries anymore." Caroline perched on the edge of the bed, her skirts draped beautifully.

"No, I expect you read the theater notices and reviews," Charlotte said with a shade of asperity. She was delighted to see her mother so brimming with life and so obviously happy, but she was never able to banish for long the fear of the misery when it all ended, as it would have to. What about trying to regain the old life then? But she had already said all these things before, as had Emily. This was not the time to pursue it again, especially when she was about to leave in a few moments and could not even try to see the subject to a decent end.

"They are a great deal more uplifting to begin the day than a list of the people one knows who are dead," Caroline said with a half apology. "And even more so than of those one did not know. Obituaries tend to be rather repetitive."

"This one wasn't." Charlotte enjoyed the drama. "He had his head cut off in Hyde Park."

Caroline let out her breath in a gasp.

"Captain Winthrop! But you didn't know him—did you?"

"No, of course not. But Great-Aunt Vespasia's friend, Mr. Justice Quade, did."

"You mean Thomas is on the case," Caroline interpreted.

"I mean that also," Charlotte admitted, standing up from her dressing table. "It really is very complicated and difficult. I might learn something of use. Anyway, I am going."

"Yes, I can see that."

"Why did you call, Mama? Was there some special reason?" She began looking through her top drawer for small things she might need, a lace handkerchief, perfume, a hat pin.

"None at all," Caroline replied. "I have not seen you for several weeks, and I thought you might care to come to luncheon. I thought we could dine out at Marcello's."

"A restaurant?" Charlotte looked around in amazement. "Not at home?"

"Certainly a restaurant. It is very good indeed. You should try Continental cuisine some time, Charlotte. It is most broadening to the mind to experience such things."

"And to the waist, I imagine," Charlotte agreed without looking at her mother's figure. She closed the drawer.

"Rubbish," Caroline said scornfully. "Not if you take the occasional ride or long walk in the park."

"You don't ride," Charlotte replied with a laugh.

"Yes I do! It is an excellent recreation."

"But you never . . ."

"I didn't while your father was alive. I do now!" Caroline rose to her feet. "Anyway, I can see that you are otherwise engaged today. I am not at all sure that a memorial service will be more entertaining, but you are committed to it and cannot possibly change your mind at this point." She smiled warmly. "We shall go to luncheon another day, when I am free." She kissed Charlotte lightly on the cheek. "In any case, my dear, at least put a piece of white lace on that dress, or lavender if you have it. You look as if you were the chief mourner. You must not outshine the widow— she has enough to put up with. She should be the center of attention today. People will forget quickly enough, and the poor soul will have to spend the rest of her life in weeds—unless she is pretty, and fortunate." And quite forgetting that she herself was a widow, she swept out with a smile on her face and a look of blissful optimism.

Charlotte arrived at the church in Vespasia's carriage and alighted with the assistance of the footman. She felt more than a little self-conscious, since she had not been invited and knew not a soul among the people milling around, greeting acquaintances, nodding gravely and making dire predictions about the state of society. The sooner she found Vespasia and Thelonius, the better. However, she looked extremely handsome in Emily's black silk, and she knew it. It gave her more confidence than she would otherwise have had in such surroundings. Even the hat, also Emily's, was extraordinarily becoming, a sweeping brim, wildly asymmetrical, and decorated with pluming black feathers. She saw several glances towards it, admiring from men, envious from women.

Where on earth was Great-Aunt Vespasia? She could not stand here indefinitely without speaking to someone and inevitably explaining herself. She began to look around curiously, partly out of genuine interest, but mostly to appear as if she were expecting someone. Some of these people would be the friends of the late Captain Winthrop, others would be here as a matter of social duty. Was one of them, dressed decently in black, carrying his hat in his hand, the one who had murdered him and left him so absurdly on the Serpentine?

She saw several naval officers in uniform, looking very splendid, their gold braid making them stand out from the plain black of civilians. One large, curiously nondescript elderly man seemed to be presiding over the matter of welcoming and acknowledging people. He must be Lord Marlborough Winthrop, the father. The woman beside him, heavily veiled, was slender and very upright, but that was all that could be distinguished of her. Charlotte fancied she detected an aura of anger, a watching with pent-up rage, uncertain yet in which direction to level itself. But it could as easily have been the self-control of grief and the knowledge of more anguish to come, and inevitably a very public resolution to a most personal loss.

She was still pondering this when Vespasia arrived on Thelonius's arm. It was not an occasion for smiling, but Charlotte found herself doing so at the sight of Vespasia so graciously accompanied. She had been a widow since long before Charlotte had first met her, years ago, during the grotesque affair in Resurrection Row. And later George's death had wounded her deeply. He was no more than a great-nephew, but one of the few family she had, and she had been extremely fond of him. And regardless of consanguinity, murder is a dreadful way to die, even without the fear and suspicion that had followed.

Now, on the arm of Thelonius, Vespasia looked serene and confident again, her back as ruler straight as it had been years ago, and there was an imperious lift to her chin as though once again she would defy the world in general, and society in particular, and be perfectly prepared to blaze a trail in whatever direction she chose to go. Those who cared to could follow, and those who did not could go whichever way they pleased.

Thelonius, slender, ascetic, dryly humorous, was at her elbow, his face rendered almost beautiful by the richness of memory which illuminated it as he guided her through the press of people. More and more were arriving, wishing not to be absent from such an occasion, reverent, sympathetic, self-important or hoping for scandal.

Vespasia looked at Charlotte approvingly, but without words. Thelonius smiled at her and inclined his head, and together the three of them made their way into the church, where the painfully slow organ music was already creating the atmosphere of death and something close to decay.

Charlotte shivered. As so often before, her thoughts turned to the anomaly of people who professed a belief in a joyous resurrection meeting together to mark the passing of one, whom most had known only slightly, from where they deemed a vale of tears and into a realm of light. It said little of their estimation of his deserts that they did it with such intense and irrational gloom. One day she would ask a vicar why it was so. An usher with heavy side-whiskers nodded busily and indicated his desire to move them towards their pews. He shifted unhappily from one foot to another.

"Sir! Madam—if I may?"

Thelonius handed him his card.

"Of course. Of course." The usher nodded. "This way, if you please?" And without waiting to see if they followed, he led the way towards the point where a pew had been kept for them. On the way Charlotte glanced to the right and saw Emily's fair face filled with surprise, and then swift and complete comprehension, not untouched by amusement.

Vespasia and Thelonius took their seats, and with rather more haste than grace, Charlotte took hers beside them.

The music changed key and a hush fell over the congregation. The service began.

It was not possible during its course for Charlotte to twist around in her seat and observe the faces of anyone behind, and those in front presented only their backs. Rather than draw unwelcome attention to herself, she bent her head in decent prayers and lifted her eyes only to watch the vicar and listen to his sepulchral tones as he eulogized Oakley Winthrop as if he were a departed saint, and exhorted all those present to live worthily of his excellent example. Charlotte dared not look at Vespasia in case she met her glance and read her thoughts, not only of the departed but of the mourners.

Afterwards was a different matter. Everyone rose and trooped out into the sunshine murmuring whatever they felt appropriate, and then she began to search in earnest. Lord and Lady Winthrop were easy to see from the movement of people, the slowing down as they reached them, and the sudden complete hush, momentary embarrassment, and then release as they moved away.

Another group, smaller and somehow less distinguished, was moving in no particular order around a slender, very upright figure. She was only lightly veiled, and looked oddly young and vulnerable. Charlotte took her to be the widow. She would dearly like to have seen her expression, but beneath the veil it was impossible.

"Is that Mrs. Winthrop?" she asked Vespasia.

"I believe so," Vespasia answered, looking to Thelonius.

"And the man behind her?" Charlotte asked with interest.

"Oh yes." Vespasia nodded fractionally. "A face to remember. A clarity of gaze, a considerable intelligence, I think. Who is he, Thelonius? A relation, or an admirer?"

Thelonius's mouth twitched with amusement.

"I'm sorry, my dear, the answer is very ordinary. He is her brother, Bartholomew Mitchell. A man of unblemished character, without pomposity or pretension, so I hear. Very recently returned from Matabeleland. A most unlikely suspect for the murder of his brother-in-law."

"Mmm." Vespasia remained thoughtful.

"Now there's a man about whom you could not possibly say that." Charlotte looked across at the large figure smiling and nodding as he acknowledged acquaintances on all sides. "There is a man with pretensions, if ever I saw one. Who is he?" Too late she realized he might have been a friend of

Thelonius. "I mean . . ." She stopped. There was nothing to say that would mend it.

Vespasia bit her lip to conceal her amusement.

"You deserve to be told he is a dear friend," she replied. "However, I believe he is a prospective member of Parliament, in fact standing against Jack in the by-election. His name is Nigel Uttley."

"Oh." Charlotte thought for a moment before continuing. She watched Uttley as he progressed through the crowd, still smiling, until he came to Emily and Jack, then his expression of affability became a mask. The core of it vanished, leaving only the outer semblance. It was impossible to say in what precise way it was different, except that it seemed without life. They were not close enough for Charlotte to hear what was said, but it appeared to be trivialities.

Emily was dressed as beautifully as ever. Black suited her fair coloring and she had an inner glow as though she were only waiting for the memorial service to be over in order to go on somewhere exciting. One felt as if she would shed the black any moment and burst into color.

"I think we should pay our respects to the widow," Vespasia said with determination. She turned and smiled at Thelonius. "Do you think, my dear, that you would be generous enough to introduce us?"

He hesitated, knowing perfectly well what she intended, even though he was not sure what she expected to achieve.

She preempted his decision with a charming smile of gratitude and set out across the flagged yard towards Mina Winthrop.

Thelonius offered Charlotte his arm, and they followed after.

Mina acknowledged their introduction and accepted their sympathies graciously. All the while Bart Mitchell stood at her elbow, silent but for the civilities of courtesy.

Closer to her, Charlotte's first impressions were reinforced. She was very fragile, and even through the veil of her widow's weeds it was possible to see a pallor to her skin.

"How kind of you to come," she said formally. "We all appreciate it. Oakley had so many friends." She smiled tentatively. "A great many I confess I never knew. It is most touching."

"I am sure you will learn of much feeling for him that you were not aware of before," Vespasia said with an ambiguity that perhaps she had not intended.

70

"Oh indeed," Charlotte added quickly. "Sometimes people only express their true regard at such times. It raises a great many emotions we may not fully have realized."

"Were you acquainted with Captain Winthrop?" Bart Mitchell asked, looking at her narrowly.

"No," Vespasia answered for her. "My niece came in order to be of support to me."

Bart drew in his breath, presumably to ask her the depth of her own acquaintance, then met her eyes and changed his mind. What was a reasonable inquiry of Charlotte, of Vespasia would have been an impertinence.

Charlotte was grateful for the rescue, and even more so for the implication of relationship. She found herself smiling, although it was quite inappropriate.

"We are having a small breakfast," Mina said warmly. "Perhaps you would care to join us, Lady Cumming-Gould?"

"I should be delighted," Vespasia accepted instantly. "Perhaps we shall have the opportunity to become a little better acquainted."

It was an invitation for which many debutantes and society hopefuls would have sold their pearls. Mina might not have understood its rarity, but she perceived something of its value instinctively.

"Thank you. I shall look forward to that."

Vespasia had achieved what she sought, and etiquette required she withdraw and allow time for others to pay their respects. They excused themselves and were barely a couple of yards away when they came face to face with Lady Winthrop. She murmured something about their graciousness in coming, and Thelonius replied that they would see her at the breakfast.

"Indeed?" she said with some surprise. Then she forced a chilly smile. "How nice of Wilhelmina to invite you. I am delighted you are able to come." But the look she shot her daughter-in-law held no approval at all.

Bart Mitchell moved a step closer to his sister, and his eyes, looking back to Evelyn Winthrop, were guarded and full of warning.

"How interesting," Vespasia said when they were alone in Thelonius's carriage on their way, not to Oakley Winthrop's house, but to his parents' house in Chelsea. "How often grief divides a family instead of uniting it. I wonder why, in this instance?"

"Very often a great deal of grief is anger, my dear," Thelonius observed, sitting opposite them, his back to the driver, his fingers locked over the top of his cane. "One feels loneliness, resentment for the pain of it, guilt for all the things one did not do or say, and fear of the enormity of death. There is nothing to be done, no appeal against it. That anger can turn against those to whom one should be the closest. People occasionally feel isolated in their loss, as if no one else grieves as they do, indeed as if they do not grieve enough."

Vespasia smiled at him, her eyes gentle and bright. "Of course you are right. But I cannot help it crossing my mind that perhaps Lady Winthrop knows or suspects something that we do not."

Thelonius's smile was full of amusement. He braced himself very slightly against the movement as the carriage turned a corner and straightened again.

"She may indeed know something, but I doubt even she could suspect anything that you have not imagined," he agreed.

Vespasia had the grace to blush, very faintly indeed, but her eyes did not waver.

"Indeed," she said dryly. "What do you know of the Winthrops' marriage? I confess, I had not ever heard of them. Who are the Mitchells?"

Charlotte looked from one to the other of them.

"Very ordinary, I believe," he replied. "Evelyn Winthrop regarded the marriage as less than satisfactory. Wilhelmina had nothing to offer but herself and a small dowry. As for Bartholomew Mitchell, he went out to Africa in the Zulu war of '79, I believe, and has spent most of the eleven years since then either in Southern Africa or north in Mashonaland or thereabouts. Soldier, of course, to begin with. Something of an adventurer, I suppose." A shadow of amusement crossed his face. "But none the worse for that. Certainly he did not add to his sister's value in marriage."

"Then Captain Winthrop was in love?" Vespasia said with warmth and a flicker of surprise.

He looked at her very steadily. "I wish I could say so, but I think it was more a matter of realism. He was not without pretensions, but they were to naval office and personal power rather than social distinction. The Winthrops are not really . . ." He stopped, uncertain what word to use without a certain crassness.

"Out of the top drawer?" Charlotte suggested.

"Not even out of the second," he conceded with humor.

"But aren't they supposed to be related to all sorts of people?"

"My dear, if a distinguished person has a dozen children, one will find, in a generation or two, that half the Home Counties are related to him," Vespasia pointed out. She turned again to Thelonius. "But you used the term 'realism.' Was it a fortunate marriage? Are there children?"

"I believe there are two or three, all daughters. One died young, the other two are recently married."

"Married!" Charlotte was amazed. "But she looks—so . . ."

"She was seventeen when she married Oakley, and her daughters also married at about that age."

"I see." She pictured a man disappointed without sons, although perhaps the judgment was unjust. Why had the daughters both married so young? Love? Or a desire to grasp the first opportunity that was remotely acceptable? What had that family been like when the doors were closed and the polite faces set aside?

There was no more time for speculation because they had arrived at the house of Lord and Lady Winthrop. They alighted and were welcomed in by servants in full mourning and shown into a large reception room with a table laden with rich food set out on exquisite linen. Silver gleamed discreetly under the chandeliers, fully lit even though the day was bright, because the curtains were half closed and the blinds lowered as a sign of death in the house. The most conspicuous ornamentation in the room were bowls and sheafs of white lilies, and the cloying perfume of them was redolent of the hothouse.

"Good heavens, it looks like an undertaker's," Vespasia said under her breath, at the same time smiling as she saw Emily and Jack Radley only a few yards away. "Heaven knows what the funeral must have been like! Hello, Emily, my dear. You look quite charming, and obviously in excellent health. How is Evangeline?"

"Growing, and really quite well behaved," Emily replied with pride. "She is very pretty."

"What a surprise!" Vespasia did not try to conceal her humor. "Jack, how is your campaign progressing? How long is it until the by-election?"

Jack gave her his entire attention. He had made his way in society on his good looks and very considerable charm before marrying Emily, but Vespasia was one person with whom he would never have dared anything but the utmost honesty. He knew she had been George's great-aunt, and although he entertained no doubts that Emily loved him, in his darker moments he still walked in George's shadow. George had been handsome too, and his charm was that of a man who was born to wealth, title and effortless grace. That he had achieved nothing personal was canceled by his early death.

"A little under five weeks, Lady Cumming-Gould," he replied gravely. "I think the government will announce it very soon. As for the campaign, I am still very uncertain about that. I have an extremely strong opponent."

"Indeed? I know little of him."

"Nigel Uttley," he replied, watching her face to see if she wished further information or if she was merely making polite conversation. He must have judged the former, because he went on to describe him. "A little over forty, younger son of a wealthy family, but not socially prominent. He has been a strong supporter of the government for a long time, and quite honestly they fully expect him to win." He pulled a rueful face. "I think they gave him the opportunity as a reward for loyalty in the past."

"What does he believe in?" she asked perfectly seriously.

He laughed, a spontaneous, infectious sound. "Himself!"

"Then upon what platform is he campaigning?" she amended with a smile.

"Restoring the old values which made us great, in general," he replied. "More specifically, on imposing law and order in the cities, altering the police force to make them more efficient, harsher sentences for crime . . ."

"The Irish question?" she interposed.

His amusement was quick again. "Oh no, he is not foolish enough to tackle that one! It brought Gladstone down, and it will probably ruin anyone else who advocates Home Rule, which is the only real solution."

They were passed by a group of elderly gentlemen murmuring in low voices who glanced at Thelonius and nodded, then proceeded on their way. A naval officer in uniform spoke overloudly in a sudden silence and blushed.

"You won't catch Uttley committing himself to any grand statements," Jack continued. "He'd execute a few Fenians with pleasure, and make speeches against anarchy in general, but we can all do that."

"He is very critical of the police," Emily said with a glance at Charlotte. "I loathe him for it," she added cheerfully.

"My darling, you would have to loathe him for something." Jack put his arm around her. "But I agree, that is an excellent cause. And it gives me some solid foundation on which to oppose him." He sighed. "Although this latest murder doesn't help. It appears to be the second grisly lunatic loose in London in two years, and they didn't catch the first one."

Emily looked at Charlotte, a question in her eyes.

"Yes," Charlotte acknowledged. "He is."

"Thomas is on the case?" Jack said quickly. "Is there any progress? One can hardly ask the family, although Lord Winthrop keeps making dark noises about what he will have done and who he knows."

"I don't think it's a madman at all," Charlotte replied, her voice sinking lower and lower. "From all that we know, it seems undeniable it was a personal crime. That is why we are here—to help Thomas."

"Does he know that?" Jack asked.

"Don't be foolish," Emily said quickly. "We'll tell him when we can offer something useful. That will be quite soon enough." In a single sentence she had included herself in whatever was to be done. Vespasia noted it with dry amusement, but made no comment.

Further discussion was prevented by Nigel Uttley himself joining them. He was not quite as tall as Charlotte had thought, seeing him in the distance, but his blue eyes were sharper and there was an inner energy in him which was initially belied by a casual manner and a self-confidence which masked effort.

"Good afternoon, Lady Cumming-Gould," he said with a slight bow. "My Lord," he acknowledged Thelonius, addressing him as if he had been in court. "Really—Mrs. Radley . . ." He waited to be introduced to Charlotte.

"My sister, Mrs. Pitt," Emily obliged.

"How do you do, Mrs. Pitt." He inclined his head in something which was not quite a bow. "How nice of you to support the Winthrops at this wretched time. I fear it is going to become even more unpleasant for them as the days go on. I wish I could believe the police were competent to catch the wretch, but the very fact that such a hideous crime could happen in the heart of London indicates the miserable state to which we have fallen. Still we shall improve on it after the by-election." He

75

looked at Jack with a smile, but the underlying seriousness of his meaning was quite plain.

"Oh, I am so glad," Charlotte said with a tart edge to her voice and an expression which was intended to be eager. "It would be wonderful if such things were never to happen again. All London would be grateful to you, Mr. Uttley, indeed all England."

He looked at her with surprise, his fair eyebrows high.

"Thank you, Mrs. Pitt."

"How are you going to do it?" she went on, almost without drawing breath, and staring at him with intense interest.

He looked back at her, momentarily appalled.

"Well—er . . ."

"Yes?" she encouraged. "More policemen? Perhaps a patrol through the parks all night? It would rather interfere with privacy, I'm afraid." She shrugged. "But then only those doing something which they would prefer not to have seen would have to worry about that."

"I don't think patrols through the parks would be the answer, Mrs. Pitt," he said, relief gushing through his voice at having some concrete proposal to deny. "What we need is better efficiency when a crime has occurred, so that people keep the law in the first place."

"Yes, perhaps you are right," she agreed. "Someone of your quality, your skill and intelligence, would be the answer."

"Thank you, Mrs. Pitt. That is most generous of you, but I already have a career."

"As a member of Parliament—should you win."

"Should I win," he said with a broad smile and a glance at Jack.

"But even before that moment, Mr. Uttley, you could give us the benefit of knowing what you would do. How does someone with skill and perspicacity, and knowledge of human nature and an understanding of society, how does such a person set about catching someone who commits so dreadful a crime?"

For a moment he looked uncomfortable again, then his face smoothed out. Emily glanced at Jack. Neither Vespasia nor Thelonius moved.

"Madmen are notoriously difficult to catch, Mrs. Pitt," Uttley said in the silence. "We simply need more police diligence, more men who will work hard and have a better knowledge of what is going on, what people in their areas are strange and dangerous."

"And if it is not a madman?" she said very quietly.

But this time he was prepared.

"Then we need men in charge who are strong and who have influence! We need men who can command the loyalty of those who have power in their own spheres." His voice was growing in certainty. "I am sure you can understand that, ma'am, without my having to elaborate what should surely remain discreet?"

Charlotte had a sudden cold feeling that she knew very well what he meant. She glanced at Jack and saw his face tighten. Thelonius Quade shifted from one foot to the other, his skin oddly a shade paler.

Nigel Uttley's smile beamed even more.

Perhaps she should have said nothing now, but she heard her own voice blindly continuing, filled with an assumed innocence.

"You mean you are uncertain of their loyalty now, Mr. Uttley?"

A flash of exasperation crossed his face, and he kept his voice civil with an effort. "No, Mrs. Pitt, of course not. I mean people who have . . ." He searched for a word and failed. "Other powers—influence which perhaps they had not thought to exercise in quite that way. A sense of civic and social responsibility a little deeper than mere duty." His face relaxed, pleased with the way he had described what he meant.

The hum of conversation in the room was rising. There was a clink of glass and the discreet murmur of servants offering food and wine.

"I see," Charlotte said with wide eyes. "A sort of tacit understanding to betray certain information which at present they would not. A change of loyalties?"

"No!" Uttley's face was pink. "Certainly not! You have quite misunderstood me, Mrs. Pitt."

"I'm so sorry." She tried to sound contrite and knew she had failed. "Perhaps you had better explain again. I seem to be slow of understanding."

"Maybe it is a subject you are not familiar with," he said between his teeth, his smile so slight as to be almost nonexistent. "It is not one that lends itself to explanation."

Charlotte lowered her eyes, then glanced at Jack.

Jack grinned, a charming easy expression without malice, but underneath his apparent ease his attention was total.

"Well, you will need to do better than that in the hustings, or you will confuse the voters as much as you have Mrs. Pitt," he observed lightly. "I'm sure you don't want anyone thinking you are advocating a sort of secret society."

The color spread up Uttley's broad cheeks and his mouth hardened into a thin line. Vespasia stared at him. Thelonius drew in his breath sharply. Emily waited in anticipation, looking from one to another.

At the far side of the room someone dropped a glass.

"Nonsense, Jack!" Charlotte said in ringing tones. "How can you possibly advocate a secret society in an electoral address? It would hardly be very secret, would it?" She turned to Uttley. "Isn't that true?"

"Yes," he said grudgingly. "Of course it is. This whole conversation has become absurd. I was simply saying that with the right people in charge in the police we would get greater respect from certain persons—and with it, cooperation. Surely even the most . . . naive . . . can understand that?"

"I can," Charlotte said with self-mockery, looking at Uttley.

He had the grace to blush, stammer for words to deny his intention, and then fall silent.

"What sort of person would do?" She was relentless. "The disadvantage of gentlemen is that they might not know how to detect, especially ordinary crimes like robbery and forgery and so on." She turned to Thelonius, Vespasia, and finally back to Uttley. "Or should we have two types of policeman, one for the ordinary criminals, another for the special ones? The difficulty is, how do we tell which crime has been committed by which sort?"

Uttley's face was tight and hard.

"If you will forgive me, ma'am, this is an excellent subject to illustrate why women are so naturally suited to making home the beautiful place both of art and of spirit, which raises fine children and gives a man the resources from which to fight the world's battles and deal with the spiritually draining matters of trade and finance. You have a different sort of brain, and that is as nature, and God, intended, for the good and the happiness of humanity." He smiled without a shred of humor, an automatic wrinkling of the lips. "And if you will excuse me, I must speak to one or two other people. I see Landon Hurlwood over there. It has been charming to meet you, Lady

Cumming-Gould, Mr. Quade, Mrs. Pitt." And without giving any of them a chance to reply, he bowed and turned on his heel.

Charlotte let out her breath in a little grunt of fury.

"There you are, dear," Emily said gratingly. "Go home and sew a fine seam, bake your bread and don't think too much. It is unwomanly, and your brain is not built for it."

"It most certainly is!" Jack said, giving Charlotte an impulsive hug. "Listening to you it is quite obvious that political debate is one of your natural gifts. If I do half as well I shall have him destroyed entirely."

"You will have made a powerful enemy of him," Thelonius said very quietly. "He is not a man who will be mocked lightly. But beating him at the polls will be a different matter. People will laugh with you, but not necessarily because they understand what you mean. And believe me, his threat was not idle. He is assuredly a member of the Inner Circle, and will call on it to defeat you if he thinks it necessary."

The smile died on Jack's face, and he moved away from Charlotte again.

"I know. But I wouldn't be Prime Minister if it were at the cost of joining them."

"You may not be anything without," Thelonius warned. "That is not to advocate that you do, simply realism." His eyes became suddenly very intent. "But I give you my word on this, if you do not, I will give you every assistance within my power, for whatever that is worth."

"Thank you, sir. I accept."

Emily clasped his arm and squeezed it tightly.

Vespasia moved a step closer to Thelonius, and there was a brilliance in her eyes which might have been pride, or possibly merely affection.

Charlotte turned to watch Nigel Uttley walk towards the tall elegant figure of Landon Hurlwood, who swung around and smiled as he recognized him, as if seeing an old friend. Uttley spoke, but of course she could not hear his words. Hurlwood smiled and nodded. They both greeted a passerby, then resumed their conversation. Uttley laughed, and Hurlwood put his hand on the other man's shoulder.

Further private speech was prevented by Lord Winthrop requesting silence and then giving a brief address of gratitude to those who had come to honor the memory of his son, and praise of that most excellent man and an expression of the deep loss his passing was to his family, his friends, and indeed he was not unwilling to say, to the country.

There were murmurs of assent, nodded heads, and several distinct looks of embarrassment.

Charlotte looked, as discreetly as she was able to, at the widow, now unveiled and standing white-faced, chin high, next to her brother. Her features were calm, almost beautiful in their repose, and quite devoid of expression. Was she still numbed by shock or grief? Was she a passionless woman, not moved even by this appalling death so intimately close to her? Did she have the most superb, almost superhuman mastery of the outward show of her inner self? Or was it that there were other emotions conflicting within her and canceling each other, frightening her so she dared not show anything at all for fear it betrayed her?

The only flicker Charlotte could see that indicated she had even heard her father-in-law was a slow movement of her pale hand against her black skirt where she reached to clasp Bart Mitchell's stronger, larger hand, and held it.

His face too was beyond Charlotte's skill to read. His eyes were very blue and clear on Lord Winthrop's, but there was no softness in them at all, and certainly nothing that could be taken for grief. His hand still held Mina's.

Then another very different woman caught Charlotte's eye; her smooth fair hair shone in the light and the expression on her handsome face was one of rapt attention. Lord Winthrop could not have desired a more admiring audience, or one who seemed more totally at one with him.

"Who is she?" Charlotte whispered to Emily.

"I've no idea," Emily whispered back. "I saw her with the widow earlier on and they seemed very affectionate and definitely quite familiar. I suppose she is a family friend."

"She doesn't seem to share the widow's emotions, or lack of them."

"Maybe she was fonder of him than the widow," Emily suggested. "Perhaps she is what you are looking for. Or at least what Thomas is looking for?"

"A mistress?"

"Ssh!" A thin woman in front of them turned around and glared.

Emily lifted one shoulder a little and stared back, eyebrows raised.

The woman snorted. "Some people have no idea how to behave!" she said loudly enough for Charlotte and Emily to hear.

"Ssh!" hissed a woman a little to the left of her.

"Well!" the thin woman gasped, filled with outrage.

Lord Winthrop finally wound to a close, and footmen began to pass among the guests again, carrying trays of glasses filled with Madeira wine, heavy and sweet. Others came with glasses of white wine for the ladies, or lemonade for those who preferred it.

Emily pulled a face and took white wine. Charlotte hesitated, then chose lemonade. This might call for a clear head. It was certainly not an occasion for enjoyment!

"I must meet the woman with the fair hair," Charlotte said seriously. "How can we contrive it?"

"I can't think of a decorous manner," Emily replied. "I could simply be blunt."

"In what way?"

Rather than explain, and give Charlotte a chance to refuse, Emily demonstrated exactly what she meant. Excusing herself to pass a group of sober men remembering their days at sea, and what they did or did not recall of Oakley Winthrop, she sailed towards Thora Garrick with Charlotte a yard behind.

"Mrs. Waters!" she exclaimed with delight. "I was so hoping we should have the chance to meet again, although not in these circumstances, of course! How are you?"

Thora looked startled. She regarded Emily with alarm, then, seeing her smiling face and bright eyes, it changed to confusion.

"I am afraid you are mistaken. My name is Garrick. My husband was the late Samuel Garrick, lieutenant in Her Majesty's Navy. You may have heard of him?"

"Oh dear, I'm so sorry." Emily apologized profusely. "What a dreadful mistake to have made. Really, I fear my eyesight must be quite at fault. Now that I am closer, I can see that you are not she at all." She dismissed it with an airy wave. "Indeed, she is shorter and much older than you are, although of course she would not thank me for saying so, so I hope you will never repeat it? It is just that she also has that wonderful coloring."

Thora blushed with pleasure and uncertainty.

"Do forgive me, Mrs. Garrick?" Emily begged, clasping Charlotte's arm. "Do you know my sister, Charlotte Pitt? No, of course you don't, or she would have prevented me from making such a ridiculous mistake."

"How do you do, Mrs. Pitt," Thora said nervously.

81

"Oh—of course, if you are not Mrs. Waters, then you do not know me either," Emily exclaimed. "I am Emily Radley. I am so delighted to make your acquaintance—that is if you will consider me an acquaintance?"

"Of course. I am very happy to." Thora gave the only possible answer.

Emily smiled radiantly. "How generous of you! Especially at a moment of grief. Did you know poor Captain Winthrop well? Or is it indelicate to inquire?"

"No, of course not," Thora denied. "Although I have known him a long time. He served with my dear husband, who was a most outstanding man, not at all unlike poor Captain Winthrop. They both excelled in all manner of fields of endeavor, of the body and of the mind. They both had such a sense of duty, of purpose. Do you know what I mean?"

"Oh, of course," Emily said quickly. "Some men are immovable from the course of what is right, no matter what temptations are set in their path."

Thora's face lit with an inner radiance.

"Exactly! You know it precisely," she agreed. "One has to be immovable at sea. Mistakes can cost lives. My dear Samuel was always saying that. He would have everything done just so, to the inch and to the minute. Dear Captain Winthrop was the same. I do so admire command in a man, don't you? Where would the world be if we were all haphazard, depending upon intuition and hoping for the best, as I am afraid I am inclined to do too much of the time."

"Artists, I expect," Emily replied with a tiny frown. "And terribly unreliable. I imagine you were very fond of Captain Winthrop, then, if he had so many fine qualities in common with your late husband?"

"I had the highest regard for him," Thora agreed warmly, but there was the slightest shadow of guilt in her answer. "In fact he was my son's godfather, you know?" She smiled and turned to her left to indicate a young man with the same fair hair as herself, but the superficial resemblance in feature was almost negated by the difference in expression. The visionary delicacy in her was a serene certainty, as if she could see beyond the masks of the present to some greater truth whose beauty she believed utterly. In him there was still a searching, the pain of guilt and disillusion were marked in his eyes and his lips. He was someone far from the haven of knowledge in which she rested. At the moment he was settling himself in a small cleared area with a cello held lovingly in one hand, his bow in the other. "That is he," Thora said quietly.

"Is he going to play?" Charlotte asked with interest. It seemed so far from the picture of a stiff, dogmatic naval officer which she had had well in her mind.

"Mina Winthrop asked him to," Thora agreed. "He does play very well, but I think perhaps she asked him because he was so fond of her, and I know it eased the sadness of this whole affair for him that he should be able to contribute in some way."

"How thoughtful of her," Emily agreed. "It is remarkable at such a time for her to show so much sensitivity to the feelings of someone else. I do admire that."

"So do I," Charlotte agreed. "I have barely met her, and yet I feel most warmly towards her."

"I must introduce you more properly," Thora said quickly. "After the music . . ." She stopped as a hush fell over the room and everyone turned towards Victor, perhaps more from courtesy than a real desire to listen. However, when he put the bow to the strings and drew it across, a shudder seemed to pass through the air, and a sound of such aching loneliness, that what had begun as good manners simply became total absorption. He did not play from a sheet of music but from memory, and seemed to draw it from the depths of some awful bereavement of his own.

Charlotte looked at the widow and saw a smile touch her lips as she watched him play. It was a heartrending piece, and yet it did not draw tears from her so much as a calm gratitude. Perhaps she had already wept all she could. Or on the other hand, maybe she was still numbed from the shock of her loss, and its manner.

Lord Winthrop stood very pale-faced and seemed to be keeping his emotions in check with difficulty. Lady Winthrop tried and failed. The tears filled her eyes and spilled over. One or two women moved a little closer as if to protect her, or give her some kind of support by sheer physical nearness.

Thora Garrick, next to Charlotte, stood very straight, her face shining with pride as if it were a military funeral. He might have been playing the Last Post, rather than a lyrical lament in solo voice.

"He is very gifted," Charlotte said when the last note died away. "He plays with true inspiration."

"I admit I have never heard him play so well before," Thora

said with some surprise. "Although I suppose what I often hear is simply practice. But he was very close to poor Captain Winthrop. Oakley was so like his own dear father, who passed away in the line of duty several years ago." Her voice was thick with emotion and her gaze was fixed far away.

"Poor Victor was only seventeen. It is terrible for a boy to grow up without a father, Mrs. Pitt." She shook her head slightly, frowning. "A terrible thing. The power of example is so great, do you not think? And with all the devotion in the world, a mother cannot give that to a boy. The manliness, the honor, selfless dedication to duty, above all the self-mastery."

Charlotte had not thought of it in that light. She had had no brothers, and her son, Daniel, was too young to think of such qualities.

Thora did not seem to require an answer. "Poor Oakley gave him that, as much as he could. He was always encouraging him, telling him stories of the navy, and of course he would have given him every assistance to obtain a commission, had Victor been willing." A shadow of hurt and annoyance passed over her face.

"You must have been very fond of Captain Winthrop," Charlotte murmured.

"Oh, indeed," Thora said frankly. "I could hardly help it, he was so like my poor Samuel in all his qualities. A woman has to admire such men, don't you think? And count herself fortunate to have obtained the esteem of two in her life. And Samuel was so devoted to us. I have to remind Victor of that, or I fear in time he will forget."

In anyone else Charlotte might have taken Thora's remarks to mean that her relationship with both men had been of a similar nature, but there was such fervid innocence in her eyes she could not believe it to be more than an idealistic admiration.

But did Mina Winthrop know that? Or was it conceivable she mistook this ardent emotion for love? Was she, beneath that cool, fragile exterior, a jealous woman? And what about her brother? Charlotte looked across the room searching for Bart Mitchell. It took only a moment to find him, standing alone almost in the shadows of one of the great pillars which supported a small minstrel gallery at the side of the room. His eyes were unwavering, and as well as she could judge, following the line of his vision, it was Thora Garrick at whom he was staring.

Was she mistaken in reading it as innocence? Had that

heady admiration been too intoxicating for Captain Winthrop's vanity to resist? And had Bart Mitchell seen it?

Her thoughts were interrupted by Thora Garrick touching her very lightly on the arm. "Now I must introduce you to Mina," she said quietly in the flutter of applause as Victor ceased playing a second piece. "I am sure you will find her most charming. So totally unselfish, you know."

And indeed Mina was very gracious, and seemed genuinely pleased to meet Charlotte in a less perfunctory fashion than their previous introduction. After only a few moments they were talking intently about furnishings and decor, a subject in which Mina seemed to have a considerable knowledge.

It was half an hour later, when they had partaken of the excellent food which loaded the heavy oak table and sideboard, that Charlotte rejoined Emily.

"Have you learned anything?" Emily asked immediately. "Of value, I mean."

"I don't think so," Charlotte replied. "More a matter of impressions. I could not help liking Mina Winthrop."

"Being likable, unfortunately, does not make one innocent," Emily replied. "And some of the most insufferably tedious people, full of humbug, can be as pure as the day. At least of the crime in which one is interested. Of course they may indirectly have brought about all sorts of disasters ..."

"I am not begging the issues of guilt and innocence," Charlotte responded. "Fascinating though they are. And I know perfectly well that she might be guilty, at least vicariously, through a lover. Oakley Winthrop sounds the sort of man from whom one might well have needed a little relief. Something of a hero, according to Mrs. Garrick." She moved aside to allow an elderly lady to pass, leaning heavily on her husband's arm. "Her eyes shine when she mentions his name," she continued. "Although always in conjunction with her dead husband and the fact that Captain Winthrop stood in for him where Victor is concerned. Doesn't he play the cello beautifully? I can't see him striding the quarterdeck shouting commands, can you?"

"If he commanded anything at all, I imagine it would be a musical quartet," Emily replied. "I don't think we have accomplished much." She glanced over her shoulder. "Really, I find Mr. Uttley completely odious. He is so certain of himself. I wish I knew a nice juicy piece of scandal about him, something really delicious which people would laugh about and repeat to everyone else."

"Well just don't you be the one to do it," Charlotte warned with alarm. "It will rebound on you!"

"I know. I know. But it is an awful shame. Now if it were Mr. Hurlwood, I know a lovely piece about him, although of course I have no idea if it is true!"

"Is that important? Since he is not running against Jack?"

"No of course it isn't, but apparently he has a mistress."

"How very ordinary," Charlotte said with disgust. "In fact it's perfectly tame. He is a very striking-looking man. I am not at all surprised. Do you suppose his wife would be surprised if she knew?"

"She died a short while ago," Emily replied with certainty. "I suppose it's not very interesting really."

"What is Mr. Uttley's wife like?"

"Really quite nice, in a sort of a way," Emily conceded grudgingly. "I suppose . . ."

"Be careful, Emily." Charlotte became serious. "Jack refused the Inner Circle once. They won't forgive him for it. I expect Mr. Uttley knows about it. Unless I have everything completely mistaken, Mr. Uttley is a member and will use his influence to beat Jack in any way he can. Don't do anything to give him a weapon with which to wound you."

"I won't," Emily said with equal gravity. "And believe me, Charlotte, Jack is not the only one in danger. They have no love for the police either, except those of them who are in the Circle themselves. They will make things as difficult as they can for Thomas. And this Winthrop murder will not be solved quickly, I think. If it was someone who knew him, a personal enemy of a very terrible kind, then Thomas has a mighty task ahead of him, and no forgiveness from the public or the government, who cannot afford another embarrassment, and no help from anyone who is of the Inner Circle, because he is not one of them."

"You are right," Charlotte said grimly. "Perhaps we had better try a little harder?"

"Well I am with you all the way," Emily promised. "Anything I can do, or any other help I can give, it is yours."

"Thank you, thank you, my dear. Now let us go and speak to people and see if we can learn anything further about the late Captain the Honorable Oakley Winthrop, and his family, and those who profess to have come here to mourn him." And she took Emily's arm as they moved forward together.

4

TOM ILES WAS a musician of very moderate ability but immense enthusiasm. There was hardly anything which dampened his natural delight, and as he strode through Hyde Park towards the bandstand, he was singing cheerfully to himself, his trumpet swinging in his hand in its leather case. His sheet music was in his pocket, folded up, which made it harder to read but so much easier to carry. It meant he could stride out with a swagger, expressive of his soaring spirits.

He fully expected to be the first to arrive; he frequently was. Although today he was even more previous than usual. The long early morning light was almost turquoise on the dew-laden grass and there were clouds of small birds chattering in the trees.

He saw the octagonal outline of the bandstand ahead and increased his pace, singing a little more loudly. Then he stopped, observing with surprise an odd sense of irritation that he was not the first after all. There was someone sitting in one of the seats, apparently asleep. Now that really was an offense! If the indigent had to sleep in the open, then they should do so somewhere else. Tom Iles would tell him so.

"Good morning, sir!" he called out from some dozen yards away. "I say—you really can't stay here, you know. This is a bandstand and we shall be practicing any moment. Sir! I say!"

The wretched fellow was slumped with his head so far forward it was invisible.

"I say!" Tom Iles leaped up the step and then tripped over nothing in particular as his legs gave way under him. He landed hard, bruising himself painfully. His heart was beating with such violence it sent the blood thumping in his ears, his mouth was dry and his stomach lurching.

Slowly he straightened up. Yes, it was still there. He really had seen the appalling thing that was imprinted on his mind. The man sitting in the bandstand had no head. But it was there—on the floor—a little to the left of his feet, the dark hair with its silver streaks still quite smooth, the face turned down into the floor. Thank God for that!

He stayed on his knees for several more minutes. It was ridiculous, but there was no strength in him. His arms wobbled as if he had just exerted himself lifting an enormous weight. He felt sick.

He must go and tell someone. There was bound to be a constable on the beat somewhere near here! He must find him. He must stand up—but not for a minute or two. Wait until his brain stopped spinning and his stomach calmed down.

"Arledge, sir," Tellman said, staring at Pitt. "Aidan Arledge." He stood in front of Pitt's desk. It was half past eight in the morning and already he looked tired. His long, thin face had a gauntness built into the bones and the lines of exhaustion around his mouth and eyes. "Found in the bandstand in Hyde Park this morning, about a quarter to seven. Trumpet player going to practice. Got there before anyone else—and found him."

"Beheaded, I assume?" Pitt said quietly. "From the fact you brought it to me immediately."

"Oh yes, sir, taken right off and left on the floor near his feet," Tellman said with something not unlike satisfaction. His lip twitched as he met Pitt's eyes.

"Who is he? What sort of a man, do you know?" Pitt asked.

"Tall, distinguished-looking, about fifty-five or so," Tellman replied. "Thin, very light, I should think. Gentleman. Soft hands. Never done a day's work with them."

"How do you know his name?"

"Cards on him. Nice little silver card case, with his name engraved and half a dozen cards inside."

"Address?" Pitt asked.

"No. Just his name. Oh, and a little musical note. Affected," Tellman said with contempt. "Why on earth would anyone put a musical note on their card?"

"Singer?" Pitt suggested. "Composer?"

88

"Well certainly not in the halls!" Tellman gave a dry laugh. "His clothes were expensive, best tailors, Savile Row, shirts from Gieves."

"Any money on him?" Pitt asked.

"Not a halfpenny."

"Nothing at all? Not even coppers?"

"Not a farthing. Just a handkerchief, a pencil, and two sets of house keys. He must have been robbed. No one goes out without even the price of a newspaper, a cab ride, or a packet of matches." Tellman met Pitt's eyes, challenging them. "Funny they left the card case, though. As if they wanted us to know who he was, don't you think? Come to that, his shirt studs were still in."

"Maybe they were interrupted," Pitt said thoughtfully. "More likely they didn't want the card case. Not easy to sell a thing like that."

"Sane," Tellman said with a twist of his mouth. "Very sane, this madman of ours. Knows what will do him good and what won't. But then it makes you wonder why he didn't take the money the first time, from Winthrop, doesn't it?"

"It makes me wonder a lot of things," Pitt replied. He looked at Tellman's dark, flat eyes, giving nothing. He decided to preempt the criticism he thought was in Tellman's mind and say it himself. "I thought Winthrop's murder was personal. Now it begins to look as if it was a lunatic after all."

"Does, doesn't it?" Tellman agreed. He lifted his chin a trifle, his face almost expressionless. "Maybe it isn't a society case after all, just ordinary police work? Unless, of course, our lunatic is a gentleman?" A flash of humor crossed his eyes and vanished again. He said nothing, staring at Pitt and waiting for him to continue.

"I suppose lunacy can afflict any walk of life," Pitt agreed, knowing that had nothing to do with what Tellman meant. "But less likely, simply because there are fewer of them. What does the medical examiner say? Any struggle?"

"No sir. No other injuries at all, or scratches. No bruises. Hit on the head, like Winthrop, that's all."

"And his clothes?" Pitt asked.

"Damp in a few places," Tellman replied. "As if he lay on the ground. Muddy here and there, but nothing torn, and nothing soiled with blood, except around the neck as you would expect."

"So he didn't fight either," Pitt said.

"Doesn't look like it. Will you be dropping the case yourself then, sir?" He assumed an air of innocent inquiry.

It was absurd. His words were ambiguous, but always sufficiently respectful to keep him from charges of insolence, and underneath them his expression, his true meaning, was challenging, resentful, itching for Pitt to make a mistake professionally serious enough to lose him his position. They both knew it, although Tellman would have denied it with a smile if he had been accused.

"I should be delighted," Pitt said, meeting Tellman's eyes with an equally hard stare. "Unfortunately, I doubt the assistant commissioner will allow me to. Lord and Lady Winthrop seem to be of some importance, in his estimation, and that requires our very best effort, not only factually but apparently as well. However . . ." He leaned back a little farther in his chair and looked up at Tellman standing before the desk. He slid his hands into his pockets deliberately. "I certainly shall not take you off the case. You are far too important to it." He smiled. "Not a good idea to take an officer off when it's a series of murders anyway. You might have seen something too small or too subtle to put into your notes, but nonetheless of importance. One never knows. You may see something else, one day, and it will all make sense."

Tellman glared at him.

"Yes sir," he said with an answering smile that was a baring of the teeth, which were oddly irregular in his symmetrical lantern face. "I'm sure I shall solve it, one way or another."

"Excellent. You'd better find out about this Aidan Arledge, who he was, if there's any possible connection between him and Oakley Winthrop . . ."

"Probably just the same place," Tellman said dismissively. "Lunatics don't ask if people know each other."

"I said a connection," Pitt corrected. "Not necessarily a relationship. Did they look alike? Dress alike? Pass in exactly the same spot at the same time? Did they have some habit or interest in common? There must be some reason why our lunatic killed those two, and not any of the other people who were regularly in the park at night."

"Give 'im time," Tellman said dryly. "That's two in two weeks. At this rate he could do fifty in a year. That is if fifty people go on walking in the park. Which doesn't seem very likely. I wouldn't cross the park alone at night now." He looked at Pitt steadily, and Pitt knew what he was thinking.

They both knew the atmosphere of fear that was rising, the whispers, the jumpiness, the ugly jokes and the beginning of accusation and persecution of anyone new in an area or a trifle different. Some had even awoken memories of Whitechapel and that other awful madman never found.

"How far away was the bandstand from the Serpentine where Winthrop was found?" Pitt asked aloud.

"Just under half a mile."

"Was he killed at the bandstand where your trumpeter found him?"

"No," Tellman said immediately. "No blood at all, worth speaking of, and it would have been all over the place with a beheading like that. No grass on his feet even, but then the grass in the park hasn't been cut for several days, from the look of it. None on my feet when I walked across it. But I'll see the park keeper of course," he added before Pitt could tell him.

"Clean wound, was it?" Pitt asked.

"No, much messier than the first. Took two or three strokes, from the look of it." Tellman's face crumpled in disgust in spite of himself. "Takes a pretty good blow to cut through a man's neck. Maybe he was lucky the first time."

"And he was hit on the head first as well?" Pitt pursued.

"Yes, looks like it. Bad bruise under the hair at the back."

"Enough to render him senseless?"

"Don't know. Have to see the medical examiner for that."

"Any guess as to what time he died?"

Tellman shrugged. "About the same, midnight or soon after."

"Witnesses?"

"Not yet, but I'll find them." There was a note of hard deliberation in Tellman's voice, and looking at his face, Pitt felt sorry for any hapless passerby who refused to swear to all he knew.

"You'd better put someone else onto that, to begin with," Pitt directed. "Find out who Aidan Arledge was, anything you can about him, where he lived, what he did, who he knew, if he owed money, had a mistress, anything you can."

"Yes sir. I'll put le Grange onto it."

"You'll do it yourself!"

"But that's simple, Mr. Pitt," he protested. "And probably doesn't matter. Our lunatic won't give a cuss who the man was. He probably never saw him before last night, and I daresay never knew his name anyway!"

"Maybe," Pitt agreed. "But I still want a senior officer to go and speak to the widow."

"Oh, I'll do that." Again Tellman bared his teeth. "Unless you think he may have been important enough you should do it yourself, sir?"

"I might. When you find out something about him!"

Tellman's face hardened again. "Yes sir." And without waiting to see if Pitt had any further instructions, he turned on his heel and went out, leaving Pitt angry and disturbed.

He sat still for some time, trying to absorb the impact of this new crime, the difference it made to all the conclusions he had come to, albeit tentatively. He had been so sure the murder of Winthrop was a personal crime, now this new development made nonsense of it. No sane lover, however vicious, murdered his rival, then some complete stranger as well. And if it were a grudge based on his professional life, no sailor, no matter how resentful of injustice, real or fancied, would kill an additional random victim also.

And why was Winthrop not robbed? Was it as simple as having been startled by something and fled?

But Arledge had not been murdered on the bandstand. Then where? And above all, why?

It was hard to think in the office. It was too quiet, too comfortable, and too prone to interruption.

He rose suddenly and without bothering to take his hat or jacket, strode out and down the stairs, calling over his shoulder to the desk sergeant, and went into the street.

Immediately the noise and clatter surrounded him and he felt a sudden overwhelming familiarity. This was the scene he was used to, the ordinary people pressing in on him, full of their own business, peddlers, costers, small tradesmen, women bound for markets to buy or to sell, running patterers calling out in their singsong voices the hasty rhymes of the latest news.

Around the corner out of Bow Street, along towards Drury Lane he passed pie sellers, sandwich men, and a woman with peppermint drinks, another with fresh flowers, all calling out after him, some even by name. He waved a hand in acknowledgment, but did not stop. Hansoms drove their way between slower carriages with tops open to show ladies out to see the sights, and to be seen.

He continued on southwards into the Strand. There hoardings advertised drama, music halls, concerts, and recitals. Magical names were written in giant letters: Ellen Terry, Marie Lloyd, Sarah Bernhardt, Eleanora Duse, Lillie Langtry.

Who was Aidan Arledge, and why had someone killed him so brutally? Was it really no more than the accident of having walked alone . . . He stopped. No, not in Hyde Park, not necessarily. They must find out where he had been killed. That was the most important thing. If it were really no more than a coincidence of place, then they must know what that place was.

Someone bumped into him, apologized icily and strode on.

" 'Ere guv—wanna newspaper?" a ragged youth shouted cheerfully. "Another 'orrible murder in 'Yde Park! Mutilated corpse found on the bandstand! 'Omicidal madman loose in London! Jack the Ripper come back again! What are the rozzers doin'? 'Ere guv, d'yer want it or not? Read all about it 'ere!"

"Thank you." Pitt took it absently and handed the boy a copper. He stood back from the fairway, leaning against the wall, and opened up the paper. The words were just as bad as the headlines: sensational horror, columns of speculation, and the inevitable criticism of the police. So far they had not mentioned the second victim's name. At least Tellman had been swift enough to take the card case and keep it to himself. The widow, if there were one, should not discover her loss because some friend or servant had seen the blaring headlines in the newspaper.

He folded it up again and continued along the Strand. If it were a madman, a chance lunatic with no connection with either Winthrop or Arledge, it would be steady police work which caught him, if anything did. Tellman was good at that. Dammit, he was good at it himself! He knew the underworld and the petty thieves and forgers, macers, kidsmen, cardsharps and tricksters who would have wind of such a creature loose.

Then memory jarred his confidence. No one had caught the Ripper, no one had come anywhere near. There had been suspicions of a few people, but in the end the Ripper had eluded them all. History would remember the name with a shudder, and the superintendent who had been in charge of the case was a byword for his failure. Even Commissioner Warren had had to resign.

He wished fervently that Micah Drummond were still in

charge. Promotion was a very double-sided coin. If he succeeded, Tellman could easily take the credit; if he failed, the assistant commissioner would blame him, and justly so. He gave the orders, he made the decisions.

He turned and walked back up towards Bow Street, passing a watch peddler he knew and nodding to him. Why on earth would Winthrop get into a pleasure boat with a stranger? It made no sense at all. There must have been a connection at least between Winthrop and his killer, even if not with Arledge. And he must find out more about Arledge.

He increased his pace, and reached the station with a sense of urgency.

The duty sergeant looked up, his face anxious.

"Mr. Pitt, sir, Mr. Farnsworth's here to see you, sir. And Mr. Pitt . . ."

"Yes."

"He looks proper put out, sir."

"I imagine he is," Pitt said wryly. "But thank you for telling me." And he stopped and took a moment to steady himself and try to prepare in his mind what he would say.

He arrived at his office with his head still a blank, and pushed the door open.

Farnsworth was sitting in the easy chair. He did not rise as Pitt came in, but merely looked up at him, his face dark.

"Good morning, sir." Pitt closed the door and walked over to the other chair.

"Hardly!" Farnsworth snapped. "Have you seen the newspapers? Headlines in every one of them, and not surprising. Two headless corpses in two weeks. We've got another Ripper, Pitt, and what are you doing about it? I'll tell you this, I don't intend to lose my position because you don't catch the lunatic who's running amok. For God's sake, sit down, man! I'm getting a crick in my neck looking at you."

Pitt sat down immediately.

"Well, what are you doing?" Farnsworth demanded again. "Who is Arledge anyway? What was he doing in the park in the middle of the night? Was he picking up a woman? Is that the link? Were both these men picking up prostitutes, and some insane creature with a puritanical mind got it into his head to execute a kind of mad vengeance on them?" He pulled a face, doubt and anger in his eyes. "Although usually men with that kind of fixation kill the women, not the men."

"I don't know," Pitt admitted. "I've got Tellman out trying

to find out who Arledge was, and everything we can about him."

Farnsworth's shoulders were stiff, pulling on the fine worsted of his coat.

"Tellman—Tellman? Is he good? I know that name . . ."

"Yes, he's excellent," Pitt said honestly.

"Ah—yes." Farnsworth's face lit with remembrance. "Drummond always spoke well of him. Bit rough, but intelligent, good at ordinary police work, knows his petty criminals. Good. Yes, use Tellman. What else?" He looked at Pitt with hard, accusing eyes, very clear light blue.

"I've got other men out searching the park, looking for any possible witnesses, although tonight will probably be better for that."

"Tonight?" Farnsworth demanded with a frown. "You can't afford to waste time until tonight, man. What's the matter with you? For God's sake, Pitt—can't you see we are on the edge of another explosion of violence in the city? People are frightened. There is talk of anarchy, unrest, even murmurs of a republic. It'll only take another string of unsolved murders like this and some revolutionary will strike a spark that will set London ablaze. You haven't time to waste waiting around for evidence to come to you." He thumped a tight fist into the arm of the chair, leaning forward in it uncomfortably. "We none of us have!"

"Yes sir, I am aware of that," Pitt answered patiently. "But the most likely way for us to find a witness who may have seen something is to try those who are creatures of habit. The odd passerby who was there last night, and not ever before or again, we have no chance of finding unless they come to us. But those who go there regularly at that time will in all likelihood be there again tonight."

"Yes, yes—I see." Farnsworth was unable to relax, he still sat forward, all his muscles tight. "What else? You've got to do better than that. I don't suppose anyone saw anything of value. This lunatic is certainly twisted, warped, mad—but that doesn't mean he's a fool. You've got to do a great deal more than hope, Pitt." His voice rose and became sharper. "Abilene hoped with the Ripper—and look what happened to him!"

"He worked dammed hard too," Pitt said defensively. He had not known Inspector Abilene personally, but he respected his efforts and knew he had done everything any man could to catch the Whitechapel murderer.

"And you had better work dammed hard too." Farnsworth stared at him. "And something more. If you want to keep this office, we've got to get him."

"I've also got men out trying to find out where the murder was committed," Pitt added. Farnsworth was unreasonable. Even though Pitt understood the knowledge and the fear which drove him, it still angered him, though he could not afford to show it. It was a position he resented bitterly. There was no honor in placing a man so you could abuse his courage or his intelligence and leave him no recourse to retaliate, or even to defend himself. Now that he had power, he must make sure he did not do it so easily, regardless though Tellman might tempt him.

Did Farnsworth find him as irksome?

"What do you mean?" Farnsworth demanded, staring at Pitt. "Wasn't he killed where he was found? How do you know?"

"No—no blood," Pitt replied. "At the moment we don't know if it was somewhere else in the park or a place entirely different, which could be anywhere."

Farnsworth rose to his feet and began pacing the floor.

"What about Winthrop?" he demanded. "Wasn't he killed in the boat? Isn't that what you said before?"

"Yes—with his head over the side. We can't prove that, but it seems extremely likely."

Farnsworth stopped abruptly.

"Why?"

"Because there was a fresh nick in the wood of the boat corresponding in size, position and depth with where a blade would have caught it if it had struck off someone's head over the side," Pitt answered. "Also he had a few pieces of cut grass on his shoes. He was quite dry himself, but his head was wet."

"Good—good. That's definite. So Winthrop was killed in the boat, and Arledge was killed somewhere else, but you don't know where. I still think it could be connected with a prostitute. You'd better bring in all those who work around that area—and don't tell me it's several hundred. I know there are well over eighty thousand prostitutes in London. One of them may have seen something, may even know who this lunatic is. Do that, Pitt!"

"Yes sir," Pit agreed immediately. Actually it was an extremely sensible idea. So far the connection did seem the most likely. Prostitutes had their own areas, and the number he would need to see was actually relatively small. Winthrop might indeed have gone to the park for that purpose, or even have thought of it afterwards, when an opportunity presented itself. That was an answer to the seemingly impossible question of why he would have got into a pleasure boat with anyone. He could have with a prostitute, if she had expressed the desire to do so as a preliminary to her favors. Winthrop would suspect nothing, especially since he was a sailor. It might seem to him an amusing thing to do.

"Well?" Farnsworth went on. "What else? What do we say to the newspapers? Can hardly tell them we suspect the late Captain Winthrop of soliciting a whore in the park. Apart from anything else, we'd be sued. Lord Winthrop has been onto the Home Secretary, saying too little has been done."

"Tell them the assistant commissioner has made a penetrating and lucid suggestion which the police on the case are following," Pitt suggested soberly. "Let the newspapers work out for themselves what it is. Tell them you cannot say until it is proved, in case you do someone an injustice."

Farnsworth glared at him, uncertain whether to suspect sarcasm or not.

Pitt was saved the necessity of explaining himself by a knock on the door, and as he answered, Police Constable Bailey came in. He was tall, sad-faced, with a sweet tooth for striped peppermint drops. He looked at the assistant commissioner apprehensively.

"What is it, Bailey?" Pitt asked.

"We have found out 'oo Arledge was, poor devil," he replied, turning from Pitt to Farnsworth and back again.

They both spoke at once. Bailey opted to answer Pitt.

"'E were a musician, sir. 'E conducted a small orchestra sometimes and guested with a lot o' other different people. Quite distinguished 'e were, in 'is own circle, like."

"That's quick." Pitt looked at Bailey carefully. "How did you find out so soon?"

Bailey blushed. "Well sir, 'is wife said as 'e didn't come 'ome last night. She didn't realize it until this morning, like, but when she 'eard about the body bein' found, she got upset an' sent for us. The local constable knew it were 'er 'usband, o' course, because 'er name's Arledge—Dulcie Arledge, poor creature."

Farnsworth was sitting upright in his chair.

"What else? What sort of woman is she, this Mrs. Arledge?

Where do they live? What did he do, apart from music? He must have had money."

"Don't know about that, sir, but seems like 'e were quite famous in 'is own fashion. 'E did 'is conducting very well, so they say. As for Mrs. Arledge, she seems like a real lady, very soft-spoken, nice sort o' manners, dressed very quiet like, although not in black yet, o' course."

"How old, in your estimate?" Farnsworth pressed.

Bailey looked awkward. " 'Ard to tell a lady's age, sir. . . ."

"Oh for Heaven's sake, man! Make a guess. You must have some idea. You're not saying it in front of her!" Farnsworth said impatiently. "Forty? Fifty? What?"

"More like forty, sir, I should say, but still very pretty. One o' them sort o' faces that you can live with, if you know what I mean?"

"I have no idea what you mean!" Farnsworth snapped.

Bailey blushed unhappily.

"Do you mean pleasing without being consciously beautiful?" Pitt asked him. "The sort that becomes more agreeable as you know the person better, rather than less so?"

Bailey's face lit. "Yes sir, that's exactly what I mean. The sort you wouldn't get tired of, 'cos that's all there is to 'er—sir."

"A most attractive woman," Farnsworth said sourly. "But that doesn't mean her husband didn't go out after whores all the same."

Bailey said nothing, but his unhappiness registered in his features.

Farnsworth ignored him. "Find out, Pitt!" he said grimly. "Find out this Arledge's habits, anything you can about him, where he went for his pleasures, how often he took walks in the park in the evenings, any"—he hesitated—"any peculiar tastes he might have had. Perhaps he abused women, went in for sadism or perverted behavior—something that might bring a pimp down on him."

Pitt pulled a face.

"Don't be squeamish," Farnsworth said abruptly. "Good God, man, you know the situation! There's close to hysteria over this second case. Banner headlines everywhere, and articles about police incompetence. There's a by-election coming up, and already the candidates are out to make capital of it."

"I'm not reluctant to do it," Pitt explained as soon as Farnsworth finished speaking. "I simply don't think peculiar tastes, or even sadism, would make a pimp behead a client. They don't care, as long as they get paid and the girl isn't marked too much to be useful anymore."

Farnsworth looked at him through heavy-lidded eyes. "Really? Well I suppose that is your field of expertise. It isn't something I know a great deal about." His lip curled in distaste. "All the same, I think you'll find that's the answer. Pursue it, Pitt. Do all the other things, of course. See where he was killed. Get your other witnesses, if there are any, but find those women!"

"Yes sir," Pitt agreed.

"Do it." Farnsworth stood up, still ignoring Bailey, and went to the door. He readjusted his jacket to make it hang more symmetrically, and went out without saying anything further.

"Shall I ask Mr. Tellman to do that, sir?" Bailey said helpfully now that Farnsworth was gone. He pulled a paper bag out of his pocket and put a peppermint in his mouth.

"No." Pitt had made up his mind. "No thank you. I'll do that myself. You can go on looking for where he was killed. There'll be a lot of blood somewhere. Oh—and how he was moved, if you can."

Bailey looked startled. " 'Ow he was moved? Well, I suppose someone carried 'im. Bit messy, like, but if you've just 'acked a fellow's 'ead orf, I suppose a bit o' blood on yer clothes in't goin' ter upset yer too much."

"Bit risky, carrying a headless corpse through the park," Pitt said thoughtfully. "And why move him? Why not leave him where he was? Unless that place would lead us to whoever killed him. Find it, Bailey."

"Yes sir," Bailey said dubiously. "Anything else, Mr. Pitt?"

"Not yet."

"Yes sir. Then I'll go and get started, sir."

By the middle of the afternoon Pitt had been back home to Bloomsbury and changed into his oldest clothes: an ill-fitting jacket, shirt with twice-turned collar and cuffs, and boots that were scuffed on top, their soles coming apart. His trousers were frayed at the bottoms and his battered hat hid half his face. He set out for the Edgware Road, to the north of Hyde Park, and some of the warrens behind the facades, where he knew he would find the men he was looking for and, more important, the women.

It was a wild late spring day and a warm wind blew the

clouds in white drifts across the sky. Late daffodils still shone gold against the grass. Nursemaids in stuff dresses pushed perambulators along the paths, and children followed after dutifully, some with horse heads on sticks or china-faced dolls. Two boys chased a hoop and a third brandished a wooden sword.

He should have loathed being dressed as he was and bound on a duty of finding pimps and prostitutes, and yet there was vitality in his step and a sense of freedom merely in being out of the station and in the open air, and even more of having no one looking over his shoulder with criticism poised on the tongue.

He turned off the Edgware Road left into Cambridge Street. Halfway along he went down the steps into an areaway and knocked on the basement door. He waited several moments, then knocked again, twice.

After a minute the door opened a crack and an eye and a nose appeared.

"Watcher want? 'Ere, it's Mr. Pitt. Come down in the world, ain't yer? I 'eard as yer've bin made up ter one o' the nobs. Threw yer out, did they? Serves yer right! Nobody should try ter get above their station wot they were born ter. Could 'ave told yer that. Yer weren't born a gentleman, and nothing'll make yer one. Not cleverness least of anything. Gentlemen 'ates them what's clever. Back on the grubby cases, are yer?" The door remained firmly where it was.

"Don't know," Pitt prevaricated. "I could be. And yes, I'm on the grubby cases."

The eye looked him up and down.

"I can see that. Yer looks awful. Watcher want wi' me? I ain't done nuffink. I don't go in fer your kind of things."

"Women," Pitt said succinctly. "Some of your women work the park."

"I ain't sayin' as they do or as they don't. But wot's it to you? They don't go cutting people's 'eads orf. Bad fer business, apart from why should they? It don't make no sense. If yer think they did it, then yer should be back on the beat." He laughed hollowly at his own joke.

"Are you going to let me in, or am I going to get every one of your girls down to the station and ask them?"

"You're an 'ard man, Mr. Pitt, and unjust," he complained, but the door opened and Pitt went into a pleasantly proportioned room, now appallingly overcrowded with all sorts of

100

furniture, chairs, sofas, desks, cheval glasses, upholstered stools and a chaise longue. Nearly all of it that was upholstered was either red or sharp pink. It was extraordinarily oppressive, giving Pitt the feeling that at any moment something would fall over, although actually everything seemed to be resting quite safely on its feet.

The man who now stood in the small space in the middle of the red-and-gold carpet was of medium height with a straggly fair beard and mustache. His thin face with its aquiline nose did not seem to belong with the rest of his features. His shoulders were bent over, and his right side seemed to be withered in some fashion; his right arm was several inches shorter than the left. He looked at Pitt guardedly out of shrewd eyes.

"Life is unjust," Pitt said without sympathy. "But make the best of it you can. I can always send Mr. Tellman here . . ."

The man spat and his eyes narrowed.

" 'E's a bastard, that one. I'd see 'im in the bottom o' the river and dance on 'is grave, I would."

Pitt forbore from pointing out the impossibility of such a feat.

"No doubt," he said dryly. "Which girls do you have working the park at the moment? And don't miss any out, because if I find out, I'll see you're dragged through every charge in the book."

"Promotion's gorn to yer 'ead," the man said with a sour twist of his mouth. "And yer always was a nasty piece o' work."

"Rubbish. I never did anything to you you didn't deserve. Nothing to what I could do, and will, if you don't tell me who was in the park. And while we're discussing this . . ." Pitt sat down on one of the overstuffed chairs. It was more comfortable than he had expected. He crossed his legs and leaned back. "Anyone new in the area?"

The man smiled and ran his long forefinger across his throat. Then as Pitt's grin broadened, he blanched. "Oh no yer don't. I never done it! I can run me rivals out without doin' anything so—so dangerous." He pulled a face. "Anyway, if I was goin' ter do summink like that, which to my way of thinkin' is pure vulgar and unnecessary, I wouldn't do it in the park, now would I? If gents get too scared to come in the park on their own, what 'appens to me business, eh? I ain't stupid. And if yer think I'd do summink like that—"

"I don't," Pitt interrupted impatiently. "But I think your girls

101

might have seen something. And more than that, they might know if there is someone strange around, someone with bizarre tastes, someone who carries a large blade."

"No. No one any odder than always. Gents what comes into the park looking fer a bit o' fun often 'as their own tastes."

"Which might go too far?" Pitt said with eyebrows raised questioningly. "Which a new girl might resent?"

"Oh yeah? So she chops 'is 'ead orf?"

"Not personally."

"Well I don't follow me girls around. Gents don't like it." He laughed in a soft, whispering falsetto. "Daft bastards, think no one knows about 'em, so they like to keep things private." He grimaced, showing dark teeth. "And 'ow would I do that anyway? I don't carry an ax wi' me." He struck an absurd pose. "Pardon me, sir, but me girls don't like that sort of thing and would yer mind just bending down on the grass, like, so I can chop yer 'ead orf—just ter teach other gents wi' nasty ideas as it don't pay."

"They were hit on the head first," Pitt said sourly, but he could see the reason in the man's words.

"If I'd knocked 'im senseless, why cut 'is 'ead orf?" The man curled his lip with contempt.

"Someone did!" Pitt said. "Tell me which of your girls was in the park on those nights?"

"Marie, Gert, Cissy and Kate," he answered readily enough.

"Fetch them," Pitt said tersely.

The man hesitated only a moment, then disappeared, and a few moments later four women came in looking tired and drab in the daylight. By moonlight or gaslight they may have had a certain glamour, but now their skins were pasty, their hair lusterless and full of knots, their teeth stained and chipped, several gaps showing when they opened their lips. Kate, seemingly the leader, was a tall thin woman with red hair, and looked at Pitt with dislike. She appeared about forty, but she may well have been no more than twenty-five.

"Bert says as yer looking for the geezer what done them murders in the park. Well we dunno nuffink about it."

The other three nodded in agreement, one pulling her soiled robe around herself, another pushing a mane of fair hair away from her eyes.

"But you were in the park those nights." Pitt made it a statement.

"Some o' the time, yeah," Kate conceded.

"Did you see anyone on the Serpentine around midnight?"

"No." Her face filled with amusement. Pitt had spoken to her several times before over one thing or another. She had been a seamstress until she became pregnant. Sewing coats at sevenpence ha'penny for a coat and by working a fifteen-hour day she could make two shillings and sixpence; but out of this she had to pay threepence for getting the buttonholes worked and fourpence for trimmings. Even eighteen hours a day was not enough to keep herself and her child. She had taken to the streets to earn a day's wages in an hour. Let the future take care of itself. As she had said to Pitt, what was the use of a future if you didn't live beyond today?

"Gents like ter be a bit more private, like, even if they've a fancy for the open an' in an 'urry. Yer ever tried it in one of them little boats? They tip over awful easy."

Pitt smiled back at her. "I had to ask. Have you ever seen Captain Winthrop?"

"Yer mean was 'e a customer?"

"If you like. Or even just seen him walking?"

"Yeah—I've seen 'im a couple o' times, but 'e weren't a customer."

Pitt grunted. He had no idea if she was telling the truth or not. She had looked at him with total candor, and that in itself made him vaguely dubious.

"Look, Mr. Pitt," she said, suddenly serious, "it weren't nothink to do with any o' us, and that's Gawd's truth. Yer might get the odd bloke what gets stuck wi' a shiv. Wee Georgie's good at that, but it ain't no good for business ter get violent. Puts people orf, and then we don't eat. This ain't one o' us, it's some geezer wot's a real nutter. An' it's no use asking us 'oo, 'cos we don't know." She looked at the other girls.

Cissy pushed her blond hair out of her eyes again and nodded in agreement.

"We don't like it no more'n you do," she said, sucking on a rotten tooth and wincing, putting her hand up to her jaw. "Makes people un'appy about goin' out, it does. They're all spooked. And that's our patch."

"Yeah," one of the other two agreed. "It in't as if we could just move uptown, like. Fat George'd do us if we got onto 'is girls' patch." She shivered. "I in't scared o' Fat George. 'E's just a bucket o' lard. But that Wee Georgie, 'e scares the 'ell out o' me. 'E's a real evil little swine. I reckon as 'e in't right in the 'ead. The way 'e looks at yer."

"Eeurgh." Cissy pulled a face and hugged herself.

"But it don't make no sense fer 'im to cut nobody's 'ead orf," Kate insisted. "An' 'onest, Mr. Pitt, we don't know nothink about anyone around what's a real nutter. There in't nobody sleeps out that we knows of. Is there?" She looked at the others.

They all shook their heads, eyes on Pitt.

"Sleeping rough in the park?" Pitt suggested.

"Nah. There's them as sleeps rough, or tries ter," Kate agreed. "But the park keeper is pretty 'ard. Comes and moves 'em on. And o' course there's rozzers 'round every now and again. That's another reason why most gents don't fancy doing their business in the park. Makes yer look a right fool ter get caught by a passin' rozzer. We just makes acquaintance there."

There was no point in asking if they had seen Aidan Arledge. His description was that of a hundred men who might have been in the park.

"See anything unusual the night of the second murder?" he asked, without any real hope of a useful answer.

Kate shrugged. "Some amateur tried to get on our patch and Cissy pulled 'er 'air out . . ."

"I did not!" Cissy protested. "I just give 'er a nice civil warning, like."

"Sure she was an amateur?" Pitt asked. "She wouldn't have had a pimp somewhere behind, who'd—" He stopped. It was too unlikely to be worth pursuing.

Kate gave him a wry glance.

"Seen no one else 'cept the usual gents," she said, pulling a face.

"No one else at all?" he insisted.

"A rozzer a couple o' times, but 'e don't bother us if we behave proper and don't accost"—she used the word with heavy sarcasm—"any gentlemen what's taking a quiet respectable stroll by 'isself. 'E in't a bad sort. 'E knows we gotter eat like anyone else. An' the gentlemen wot pays 'is wages wouldn't like to be driven out o' their bit o' pleasure."

"Who else? Think, Kate! There is someone—someone with an ax or a cutlass . . ."

"Gawd!" She shivered. "Will yer quit yappin' on about it! I jus' saw ordinary-lookin' gents, one or two wi' a skinful, the rozzer, the park keeper goin' 'ome wi' 'is machine, or somethink. It were real quiet."

"It'll be a bloody sight quieter now," Gert said angrily. She looked up at Pitt. "Why the 'ell can't yer catch the bleedin' lunatic wot's doin' this and let us get on wi' our business? It ain't safe for no one anymore. I thought that was what the bleedin' crushers were supposed to be for? To make the place safe!"

"I don't think making it safe for ladies of trade was what the gentlemen of the government had in mind at the time," Pitt said wryly. "Then—on the other hand . . ."

Kate gave a sharp laugh. Gert pulled a face.

"Were you anywhere near the bandstand?" Pitt asked, looking at them one at a time.

They all shook their heads. Again there was no way of telling whether they were speaking the truth, but he thought they probably were. If anyone had seen the corpse there would have been screams, a commotion. Word would have spread.

"I see."

He thanked them and left, walking out past a sour and uncharacteristically curious Bert. He was afraid for business, the only sensitive area in his soul. Pitt ignored him and went out into the street. He did not dislike the women. He knew too many of their stories, and even the knowledge of drink and disease, vulgarity, manipulation and greed did not alter the fact that for almost all of them, there was little other chance of survival in London. They were unemployable as domestic servants, although that was how many of them had begun. One had to have references. A charge of immorality, true or not, an accusation of thieving, even if the mistress had merely mislaid an ornament or a pin, a comb, an earring—any of a dozen tiny items, it made no difference; a girl without a character reference would get no other post. There was no redress, and seldom a second chance. More than one handsome parlormaid had found herself on the streets because the master would not keep his hands off her.

Others found the sweatshops, match factories or markets too hard, far too little reward. The risk of disease on the streets was high, but then it was high anyway. At least they were less likely to starve to death.

Men like Bert, or the other pimp, Fat George, he regarded in a totally different light. And the sadistic and perverted Wee Georgie he would have seen dead with pleasure.

But what the women said made sense. He thought about it as he went back down the Edgware Road, passing peddlers and costermongers and a woman selling peppermint drink. He

105

stopped and bought a sandwich from a stall, and a mug of tea. He walked on slowly, listening to the chatter, gossip, haggling and abuse that ebbed and flowed around him. Occasionally he was greeted by name, and he replied briefly.

Twice he heard someone say "The Headsman," and knew whom they meant. Already the horror was there, the sudden silence and the chill, even in the sun and the bustle of the streets. There was fear—cold, gray fear—underneath the banter and the attempts to make a joke of it.

Was there a madman loose? Or was there some connection between Captain the Honorable Oakley Winthrop, R.N., and the conductor Aidan Arledge, something personal and so dreadful it had brought them both to their deaths?

He increased his pace till he was striding along the footpath so swiftly people scattered in front of him, grumbling about his manners.

"Hey?" one man yelled indignantly. "They put out the fire in 1660! Yer too late!"

"It was 1666!" Pitt yelled back at him, correcting his history with satisfaction.

Back in the office in Bow Street, le Grange was waiting for him. As soon as he saw Pitt's attire his ingenuous face filled with surprise and incomprehension.

"Are you all right, sir? You look—well . . ."

"Yes I am quite all right, thank you," Pitt answered, going around him and sitting down at the desk. "Have you something to report?"

"Yes sir. At least, Mr. Tellman said as I should come and say as there isn't really anything new . . . sir."

"Did he?" Pitt was irritated. That was one slip of protocol he had never indulged in, sending a sergeant to Micah Drummond to report progress. Either he had ignored him completely or he had come himself. "So Mr. Tellman has achieved nothing at all?"

"Oh no, sir." Le Grange looked upset. "That ain't what I mean, sir, not at all. 'E's been very busy. Never stopped, in fact. 'E's seen the bandsman what found Arledge, but 'e don't know nothing. Just unfortunate, you might say. And o' course 'e did question the park keeper, same as before, but 'e don't know nothing either. Thoroughly scared he were."

"Of Tellman or the lunatic?" Pitt asked with only a thread of sarcasm.

Le Grange weighed his answer for several moments. "Of

Mr. Tellman, I think, sir," he said at last. "Mr. Tellman being there, like, and the lunatic not."

"Very pragmatic," Pitt remarked.

"What, sir?"

"A good choice. What else?"

Le Grange looked at Pitt carefully. He took a deep breath.

"If you don't mind me saying so, sir, you shouldn't 'a gone questioning the criminal element yerself. There ain't no need. And Mr. Tellman's got a real skill at it. 'E don't waste no time bein' nice, and nobody tells 'im lies. 'E won't stand fer it. There are ways, sir, and it ain't what a senior officer like yourself needs to be doing."

"Indeed?" Pitt felt both insulted and excluded. Le Grange was telling him plainly as he dared that Tellman was better at the job.

"Well sir." Le Grange was insensitive to danger. "It's beneath you now, sir, isn't it?"

"No it's not. I learned some very useful things from some of the prostitutes. They don't think it's a lunatic at all."

"No sir?" le Grange said politely, disbelief all through his bland face. "Well I wouldn't take much notice o' what them sorts o' people says. They ain't exactly noted for their truthfulness, are they? Mr. Tellman says as they'd sell their mothers fer a flatch I mean an 'a'penny to you, sir. And beggin' your pardon again, sir, but you're too much the gentleman with 'em. They'll run rings 'round you."

"Is that what Mr. Tellman says?" Pitt said quickly.

Le Grange blanched. "Well—yes sir—in a manner o' speaking. This is a real bad case, sir. We got no time to pussy around wi' people, especially that sort."

"And do you think they know who killed those men, le Grange?"

"Well . . ."

"Don't you think they'd be willing enough to help us if they could?"

Le Grange's face softened with amusement. "Oh no, sir. That's where you got them wrong. They 'ate us. They'd not give us the time of day, willing like."

"No, le Grange," Pitt corrected. "That's where you are wrong, and Tellman, if he agrees with you. They don't give a toss about us one way or the other. What they do care about is business. And believe me, the Hyde Park Headsman is bad for business—very bad."

Le Grange sucked in his breath sharply as realization dawned on him. Gradually the full understanding came to him of just what Pitt meant, and with it the dawning of respect.

"Oh—well. Yes, I see. I suppose so."

"Indisputably so," Pitt agreed. "And you may report that back to Mr. Tellman when you see him. Find any witnesses yet?"

"Nothing very good." Le Grange's face was pink and he moved from one foot to the other. "Arledge definitely weren't there at ten o'clock. We got a judy what took a customer there after then, and she swears there weren't no one anywhere near, or she'd not 'ave—well ...." He stopped, not sure what words to use.

"Quite. Is that all?"

"No sir. Mr. Tellman went to see the widow, poor soul."

"And?" Pitt demanded.

"Well sir, 'e says she's a very decent sort of lady—"

"For Heaven's sake, le Grange!" Pitt exploded. "What did you expect? That she'd come to the door in scarlet pantaloons and a feather in her hair?"

Le Grange stared at him in total consternation.

"Of course she's a decent woman," Pitt said in exasperation. "What did he learn? What time did Arledge go out? Did he go alone? Where did he say he was going, and what for? A walk, to meet someone, to visit someone?"

Le Grange looked aggrieved.

"She said 'e went out about a quarter past ten, sir, just for a breath of air. 'E did that sometimes. She weren't worried because it's the sort o' thing gentlemen do on a spring evening, especially if they live near the park."

"Where do they live? You didn't say."

"Mount Street."

"I see. What else did Mrs. Arledge say?"

"She weren't anxious when she didn't 'ear 'im come 'ome, because she were very tired that night, and she just went ter bed and fell asleep straight orf. It was only in the morning when 'e didn't come down for breakfast that she got worried."

"And did she know Captain Winthrop?"

Le Grange's face fell.

"Mr. Tellman didn't ask?" Pitt opened his eyes very wide.

"No sir, I don't recall as 'e said. But if it were a lunatic, sir, what difference would that make?"

108

"None at all. But if it wasn't, then it might make all the difference in the world."

"Must be, sir. Mightn't 'a bin, just the one. But two, that's the work of a madman, sir." Le Grange's smooth face shone with conviction.

"That's Tellman's opinion?"

"Yes sir." Le Grange was aware of Pitt's irritation, and for the first time it discomforted him. "Maybe Wee Georgie's gone too far at last," he suggested. " 'E's a proper nasty little creature. Mr. Tellman's always said that one day 'e'd swing."

"I hope so," Pitt said with feeling. "But not for beheading Captain Winthrop. Wait till we got a prostitute with a shiv in the back."

"Fat George could 'ave done it. 'E's as strong as an ox."

"He's probably as heavy as one, but why would he behead two perfectly ordinary gentlemen walking through the park?"

"Maybe they weren't ordinary?" le Grange offered. "Mr. Tellman says as some o' these fancy gents 'as very funny tastes. 'E knew o' one what liked 'is women ter—"

"And did they murder him?" Pitt interrupted.

"Well—no—they just charged 'im double."

"Precisely. Murder is bad for business, le Grange, and whatever else Fat George is, he's a businessman. Go and find out more about Aidan Arledge. I don't suppose you've discovered where he was killed yet, have you?"

"Well—no sir, not yet."

"Then get on with it!"

"Yes sir! Will that be all, sir?"

"Yes it will."

Le Grange beat a hasty retreat, leaving Pitt wondering if he were capable of changing his loyalties from Tellman to him. How many of the other men felt the same? The sense of well-being with which Pitt had strode across the park had now totally withered away. He felt hemmed in. Farnsworth on one side was frightened for the reputation of the police, and no doubt feeling the pressure of it through the public demanding an arrest; and on the other, Tellman was growing more and more resentful at Pitt's promotion, and his contempt for him was increasing by the day. He took no trouble to conceal it from the other men, in fact it seemed he enjoyed to take them along with him.

Whatever had made Pitt accept Micah Drummond's offer? It was not the right job for him. He had not the nature nor the social position. He was not a diplomat and he was certainly not a gentleman.

He would go and see Mrs. Arledge himself. There must be a connection between the two men somewhere, unless it really was a random lunatic.

He was outside in Bow Street walking along the pavement when two ladies skirted around him, moving at least two yards to the left. Then he remembered he was not dressed as a superintendent in charge of Bow Street police station, and certainly not in a fit state to visit the widow of a gentleman.

He returned home a little after six, tired and dispirited, longing to sit down in the warmth of the kitchen, have a good meal, tell Charlotte what had happened, what he knew, and above all to share his fears and doubts about himself and the job. She would encourage him, tell him he was perfectly equal to it. She might not know, and her words would spring more from loyalty than any understanding of what was really involved, but nonetheless he would feel immeasurably better for it.

But when he neared the kitchen door there was no one there except Gracie.

" 'Ello, sir," she said cheerfully, her bright little face lighting up with pleasure. She was very neatly dressed, her collar clean, her apron starched and immaculate, ribbons tied tightly behind her tiny waist. She looked freshly scrubbed and beaming with importance. "Yer supper's ready, sir, an' I can get yer a bowl of 'ot water right away, an' another for yer feet if you like?"

"Thank you," he accepted. "One will be enough."

She looked him up and down dubiously. "What about a tub, sir? You bin in them rookery kind o' places again, 'aven't yer?"

"Yes." He sat down on one of the hard chairs and without asking she bent in front of him and unlaced his boots. "Where's Mrs. Pitt?" he asked.

"Oh, she's still at the new 'ouse, sir. Like ter be there all evenin', I shouldn't wonder," she replied, standing up and going to fetch a basin of steaming water. "There's a terrible lot ter be done, sir, an' she said as I was to make your supper— that was if you came 'ome for supper, o' course. An' I done some lamb stew for yer, sir, wi' potatoes an' onions an' some 'erbs from the new garden." Her eyes were bright with pride in it.

He swallowed his disappointment with difficulty. Charlotte

had been away so often lately he was beginning to feel unreasonably resentful. And it was unreasonable, he knew that. She was working at the new house with builders, decorators, plumbers and so on, things he would have done himself had he the time, but none of those arguments stopped the feeling of having been let down.

"Thank you, Gracie," he said somberly. "It sounds excellent. Where are the children?"

"Upstairs, sir. I told 'em not to bother yer till you'd 'ad yer supper." She screwed up her face and regarded him narrowly. "Yer lookin' a little peaked, sir. Shall I get yer summat ter eat before yer change yer clothes? I'm sure it don't matter, not in the kitchen, like."

He smiled in spite of himself. "Thank you," he accepted. "That would be a good idea."

She looked relieved. It was a big responsibility Charlotte had left her with. She was not a cook, just a maid-of-all-work who was day by day growing into a mixture of housemaid, parlormaid and kitchen maid, with a good deal of nursery maid as well. She was desperately eager to please him, and not a little in awe. She had been even prouder of his promotion than some of his family.

Hastily she set about mashing potatoes and serving them with a thick, deliciously aromatic stew, then sat down at the end of the table to await his further needs or instructions. She regarded him steadily, still a small pucker between her brows.

"Would you like some pudding, sir?" she asked at length. "I got some treacle sponge."

"Yes, yes I would." Treacle sponge was one of his favorites, which he thought she knew.

Her face lit up again, and she forgot to behave with the new dignity she had assumed and scrambled off the seat to get it for him. She presented it with a flourish.

"Thank you," he accepted. Actually it was extremely good, and he told her so.

She blushed with pleasure.

"Yer gettin' closer ter catchin' the 'Eadsman?" she asked with concern.

"Not much." He continued eating, then thought that was a bit abrupt. "I have been asking the local prostitutes if they knew of anyone who has been abusing the girls and brought a pimp down on them, but they say not. They've none of them seen anything, no one living in the park or wandering around."

111

"D'yer believe 'em?" she asked skeptically.

He smiled at her. "I don't know. It would take a lot for a pimp to kill a customer, if he paid—let alone two."

"Maybe they would if the customer marked a girl, like?" she said thoughtfully. "That's damaging goods. If you break summat in a shop, yer 'as ter pay for it."

"Quite true," he agreed, his mouth full of sponge and treacle.

"Yer like a nice 'ot cup o' tea?" she offered.

"Yes—please."

She got up and went over to the kettle, apparently lost in contemplation. Several minutes later she returned with a mug full of tea and set it on the table. She did not even seem to have considered bringing the whole teapot.

"Gracie?" he said questioningly.

"Yes sir? Is that too strong?"

"No, it's just right. What are you thinking about, the girls in the park?"

Her face cleared and she looked at him out of innocent eyes.

"Oh, nuffink really. I 'spec they told yer the truth. Why not?"

It was a wholly unsatisfactory answer, but he did not know why. He drank the tea and thanked her again, then excused himself. He must go upstairs and change into his best clothes. Since Charlotte was not home, he would go and visit the widow of Aidan Arledge.

It was early evening when he finally passed his card to Dulcie Arledge's butler in Mount Street and then was shown into a charming withdrawing room facing onto a garden with a long lawn sloping down to an old wall. The corner of a conservatory was just visible around the edge of a clump of lilies, the last light gleaming on its glass panes. Dulcie Arledge herself was naturally dressed entirely in black, but it could not mar the delicacy of her skin or the softness of her brown hair. She was as Bailey had said: a woman full of grace and pleasantness, with the sort of features that were not ostentatiously beautiful, yet carried their own regularity. There was nothing in her to offend. In every detail she was comely and feminine.

"How courteous of you to come in person, Superintendent," she said with a gesture of acknowledgment. "However, I fear I can tell you little beyond what I have already said to your men."

112

She led him over to a chair upholstered in a pattern of damask roses, its wooden arms heavily carved. Another sat opposite it, complementing the deeper wine-red of the curtains and muted pink of the embossed wallpaper. The proportions of the room were perfect, and in the few moments in which he had to notice such things, the furniture appeared to be rosewood.

She indicated one of the chairs, and as he accepted, sat in the other herself.

"Nevertheless, Mrs. Arledge," he said gently, "I would appreciate it very much if you would recount the events of that evening to me, as you recall them."

"Of course. My poor husband went out for what he intended to be a short stroll for a breath of air—shortly after ten, as I recall. He did not intimate that he had expected to meet anyone, or indeed that he would be longer than twenty or thirty minutes. We do not always retire at the same time." She smiled apologetically. "You see, Aidan was frequently out in the evenings because he conducted at concerts and recitals. It could be after midnight before he returned home, or even later if the traffic were dense and he found it difficult to obtain a hansom." In spite of the horror of the circumstances there was a warmth about her that brought to mind instantly Bailey's words about her being a woman of beauty.

"Waiting for someone can be so frustrating, don't you find?" she asked quietly. "There were many occasions when I did not stay up for him. I was willing to of course, but ..." She caught her breath. "He was most considerate."

"I understand," Pitt said quickly, wishing he could find any way at all of lessening the hurt for her. "Mrs. Arledge, my sergeant tells me Inspector Tellman did not ask you if you were acquainted with Captain Oakley Winthrop."

"Oh dear." She looked at him with alarm and then comprehension. She had very fine eyes, clear and dark blue. "No he didn't, but it would not have helped if he had. I'm afraid I had never heard the name until the poor man was killed. Does that mean something, Superintendent?"

"I don't know, ma'am."

"Of course my husband knew a great number of people whom I never met, admirers of his work, musicians and so on. Could Captain Winthrop have been such a person?" she asked gravely.

"Possibly. We shall have to ask Mrs. Winthrop."

She looked away and her face was filled with pity.

"Poor soul," she said softly. "I know death can come at any age, but one does not look to be widowed when not yet forty. I believe that is her age. I am afraid I do not read newspapers myself—my husband did not care that I should—but one hears talk, even among servants."

"Yes, I would judge Mrs. Winthrop to be of that age. I believe she has two daughters very recently married. Mrs. Winthrop is still young."

"I'm so sorry." The hands in her lap tightened a little.

Pitt would have given a great deal to be able to avoid doing anything but asking her a few obvious questions and offering her what little sympathy he could. He admired her composure, her lack of bitterness, anger or self-pity, any of which would have been so easy to understand.

But duty compelled him to pursue the more personal lines of inquiry, and as soon as possible. It was an intrusion which he felt even more acutely than usual.

"Mrs. Arledge, we need to look closely at your husband's effects to see if we can find anything which will provide a connection between him and Captain Winthrop. I realize it is not pleasant for you, and I am deeply sorry, but it is unavoidable. I really have no alternative."

"Of course," she said quickly. "I understand. Please do not feel that you have to apologize, Superintendent." She frowned, her blue eyes clouded. "Was it not some madman who chose his victims at random? Surely such a person has no reason in his mind?"

"We don't know yet, Mrs. Arledge. At this point we must examine every possibility."

"I see." She looked away across the room at a vase of narcissi whose sharp, sweet perfume was noticeable even from where they sat. "Yes, of course you must. What would you like to see first? Your man, I forgot his name, has already looked, but perhaps he missed something."

"Inspector Tellman," Pitt supplied.

"Yes—yes I do recall now that you repeat it," she said briefly. "He did not take very long. I rather gathered from what he said that it was"—she swallowed—"a maniac, and he expected no sense."

"I should like to see his papers." Pitt rose to his feet. He felt like apologizing again, but it would only make the intrusion the more apparent. Her graciousness, her quiet courage, awoke in him both a deeper respect for her and an instinctive liking,

and made his official task the more unpleasant. "Does he have
a study?" he asked as she rose also, moving with remarkable
grace and balance, as if in her youth she might have been a
dancer. "And after that, perhaps his dressing room . . ."

"Of course. If you would come this way I shall show you
myself." She led him out of the withdrawing room, across the
parquet-floored hall and into a large, airy study with surprisingly few books, no more than fifty or sixty, and none of the
heavy ornamentation he had found in so many rooms which
were ostensibly studies, but actually places in which to receive
visitors and to impress them with one's wealth and taste. It
gave the immediate impression of actually being a place of
work.

"Here you are, Superintendent," she invited. "Please look at
anything you feel may be helpful."

He thanked her as she excused herself, and felt even more
intrusive. It was perfectly customary to examine the effects of
a murdered person, and yet if he were the victim of a lunatic,
merely the place and the time choosing him rather than any
other, this was a pointless affront. Still, now he was here he
must do it. The only thing that justified it in his mind was the
finding of Winthrop in the boat. Surely he would never have
got in there willingly with a stranger accosting him in the
dark? And from the evidence of his shoes, he had walked
there. And there had been no struggle.

And Arledge had not struggled either. He must have been
attacked from behind, and without warning, or he too knew his
assailant.

He began with the contents of the desk and read through
them systematically. It was surprisingly interesting. Arledge
had been a man of humor and sophisticated tastes, but without
pomposity. Certain letters showed him also to have been generous both with his means and with his praise for others in his
field. The more Pitt read, the more he felt the loss of a man he
would have both liked and respected, a feeling very different
from that woken in him by what he knew of the late Captain
Winthrop.

What could these two possibly have had in common?

There were many books on music, piles of rough notes for
composition, at least fifty scores from works varying from the
operas of Messrs. Gilbert and Sullivan to piano concerti by
Bach and the later chamber music of Beethoven. Nothing

whatever suggested an acquaintance with Oakley Winthrop or any of his family.

After the study, he was shown by the maid to Aidan Arledge's dressing room, and after asking if there was anything else he wanted, she left him to search.

On the tallboy he found a silver-backed hairbrush, shaving equipment and personal toiletries. In the top drawer there were a handful of collar studs, shirt studs, cuff links and a blood-stone ring. It was a very small collection for a man who made frequent public appearances in evening dress. It was modest in the extreme.

He turned away and looked in the wardrobe. There were rows of suits, and in the drawers at least twenty shirts, most of them for ordinary daytime wear. He continued to look at the rest of the room. There were a few mementos, a photograph of Dulcie in a silver frame. She was dressed in riding habit, not found as one might wear in Rotten Row, but with the timeless elegance of a countrywoman who rode to hounds. She was smiling out at the camera, confident and happy. There was a pleasing blur of trees behind her. In a chest of drawers there were personal linen, handkerchiefs, and socks, the items one might expect.

He had not found a diary either in the study or here. The pair to the silver-backed brush was absent. There were no evening studs for the shirts.

He reviewed everything carefully, closed the drawers, and went down the stairs to knock on the withdrawing room door.

"Come in, Superintendent," she invited.

"Did your husband have dressing rooms at the concert hall, Mrs. Arledge?" he asked, closing the doors behind him. He loathed this. Already there was a dark premonition in his mind and he was angry and hurt on her behalf.

"Oh, no, Superintendent." She smiled at him very slightly, a shadow in her eyes in spite of the calm still in her voice. "You see, he conducted in many different places. In fact, it was seldom the same hall two weeks in a row."

"Then where did he change into his evening clothes?" he said quietly.

"Why here, of course. He was most meticulous about his appearance. One has to be when one is watched by a whole audience." Her voice dropped to little more than a whisper. "Aidan always used to say it was a terrible discourtesy to be

116

improperly dressed, as if you did not consider your audience worthy of your best effort."

"I see."

"Why do you ask, Superintendent?" She looked at him with a deepening frown, her eyes searching his face.

He avoided a direct answer.

"If there were a late performance, did your husband always come home, or did he perhaps stay with friends, other musicians, maybe?"

"Well—I think he may have once or twice." Now she was hesitant, her expression touched with anxiety, even the beginning of fear. "As I mentioned before, I did not always wait up for him." She bit her lip. "You may think that less than dutiful of me, but I do not find it easy to keep late hours, and Aidan would be very tired when he came in, and simply wish to retire straightaway. He asked me not to trouble myself by waiting up. That is why I did not . . ." Now she was controlling herself only with an effort. "That is how I did not miss him that night."

He felt a pity for her so sharp it caught his breath. His mind was full of confusion. How could a man as sensitive as the one suggested by the letters in his study have betrayed a woman like this?

"I understand, ma'am. It seems very sensible to me," he said gently. "I do not expect my wife to wait up for me when I am late. Indeed I should feel extremely guilty if she did."

She smiled at him, but the fear in her eyes did not lessen, indeed if anything it increased. "How very sympathetic of you. Thank you so much for saying so."

"Was Mr. Arledge conducting a performance that evening?"

"No—no." She shook her head. "He spent the evening at home, working on a score, one he said was very difficult. I rather think that is why he wished to go for a walk, in order to clear his head before retiring."

"Does he have a valet, ma'am?"

"Oh yes, indeed. Do you wish to speak with him?"

"If you please."

She rose to her feet.

"Is there something wrong, Superintendent? Did you find something—something to do with the Winthrops?"

"No, not at all."

She turned away.

"I see. You prefer not to tell me. I beg your pardon for having asked. I am not—not used . . ."

He wished intensely that there was something gentle and comforting he could say, something even remotely true that would ease the present pain in her, and the additional, fearful wound he now was almost sure was to come.

"It may prove to be of no meaning at all, Mrs. Arledge. I would prefer not to leap to conclusions." It was futile, and he knew it even as the words were on his lips.

"Of course. The valet," she agreed, her words equally hollow, and she did not meet his eyes. She rang the bell, and when the maid appeared, sent for the valet to meet Pitt in the study.

But the valet's answers only clouded the issue the more. Either he had no idea where the other silver-backed brush was or he refused to say. Nor did he know where to find the evening studs. He looked confused and embarrassed, but Pitt had no sense that it was guilt.

Walking home slowly along Mount Street towards the park, Pitt had the sad empty feeling that for all his humor and courtesy, Aidan Arledge was far less uncomplicated than he had seemed at first. There was something hidden, something unexplained.

Where did he go after late performances? Where were the things that Pitt had expected to find, and had not? Why had he two sets of keys? Did Aidan Arledge keep a second establishment somewhere, a place his wife knew nothing of?

Why? Why would a man keep a secret establishment?

He could think of only one answer: obvious, glaring and painful. He had a mistress. Somewhere there was a second woman mourning his death, a woman who dared not show her grief, dared not even claim his acquaintance.

Gracie had made up her mind while she was sitting at the kitchen table watching Pitt eat his treacle pudding, but it was after midnight before she could put her plan into effect. She had to be quite sure everyone in the house was asleep. If they were to catch her sneaking out, there would be no acceptable excuse she could give, and her whole venture would be aborted. And after last time, Pitt would be furious and perhaps even dismiss her. That thought was unendurable. But so was the knowledge that he was being criticized in the newspapers

118

by people who did not know what they were talking about and were not fit to speak to him, let alone air their opinions.

So there was nothing for it but to do her best to find out something. Added to which, with the mistress too busy with the new house to do anything, and Miss Emily all caught up in the by-election, who else was there to help?

Outside on the pavement she walked smartly towards the main thoroughfare. She had enough money to get a hansom to the park, first, and back again, of course. She had borrowed it from the fish money. It was not strictly honest. But then if she did not have any of the fish herself tomorrow, it would not be stealing either.

She did not look the part of a prostitute. No girls were out for business dressed in a maid's stuff gown, high to the neck, long-sleeved, and cut in plain gray-blue. But then she did not want to succeed in attracting anyone. It was information she was seeking, not trade. Also there was the danger of being seen as a rival and driven off, perhaps violently, by a protective pimp. Like this she would hardly occasion any such feelings. Mockery, perhaps, laughter, even pity, but not fear.

It took her several minutes to find a cab and convince the driver she had the fare, and then another quarter hour to reach the park and be set down.

The cab drove away, the horse's hooves loud on the deserted road, the carriage lamp disappearing towards Knightsbridge. The darkness closed in and the night seemed huge around her and full of strange sounds, any of which could be someone coming, an idle passerby, someone taking a late stroll, a man looking for a prostitute, a woman looking for trade, a pimp guarding his territory, the Hyde Park Headsman . . .

"Stop it," she said aloud to herself. "Pull yourself together, you stupid girl." And with that admonition, also aloud, she started to walk briskly along the footpath, her sharp step ringing out till it sounded like a beating heart in the night, and she realized she appeared far too purposeful to attract the slightest attention from the people she wished.

Actually it took her nearly an hour, by which time she was cold, frightened and at the point of abandoning the whole venture, before a tall, angular woman with straw-colored hair and a cheap dress came up and looked at her with suspicion and contempt.

"Ain't no omnibuses pass 'ere, dearie," she said sarcastically. "And wi' a face like yours, it's about all yer gonna catch."

Gracie lifted her chin, looked around, then straight at the woman. "Like you done, eh?"

"I'll get my share, yer cheeky bitch," she said without malice. "But you won't get enough to feed a rabbit. Yer look like yer ain't 'ad a decent bite in years, there's no flesh on yer bones, poor little cow. Men don't want a starveling wi' no bosom and no 'ips." She pulled a face. "'Less they're bent in some way. Yer should be careful—them ones can turn nasty—'cos they ain't right in the first place." She shrugged. "Anyway, this is my patch, an' I don't take to poachin' kindly. Even if I didn't see yer orf, there's my pimp wot will."

Gracie felt a shiver of fear and excitement. She took a shaking breath and let it out slowly.

"I dunno about bent ones . . ." She put a heavy doubt in her voice. "I don't take nobody wot gets nasty. I mean"—she stared at the woman—"there's nasty—an' nasty, if yer gets wot I mean?"

"Oh." The woman looked ashen in the glimmer of distant gaslight anyway, so it was hard to tell if her color changed, but there was a slackness of fear in the hang of her mouth. "I don't mean nuffink like the 'Eadsman. Gawd 'elp us—'e ain't bothered any o' us. Guess it's geezers wot 'e's after."

"I don't want any part of 'im!" Gracie said with a dramatic shudder, which was not entirely assumed. Standing here on the path under the windswept trees in the dark, with the chill air eating through her shawl, and only the faint chain of gaslights in the distance, fear did not have to be imagined. "I don't want ter be with a geezer wot rubs 'im up the wrong way. 'E'd 'ave ter do us too, just 'cos we seen."

"Yer right," the woman agreed, moving a step nearer, as if somehow their sheer physical closeness could be some sort of protection against the violence.

"D'yer reckon as there's some sorts as'd be 'is meat?" Gracie asked with as much innocence as she could manage. Actually her voice was shaking anyway, so her expression was marred from the start.

"Like wot?" The woman stared along the path towards the shadows in the distance. "Maybe there's a spot o' trade comin' our way. Don't you mess me up, yer fourpenny scrap rabbit, or I'll mark yer so nobody'll want yer."

Gracie drew herself up to spit back that she would not demean herself, then remembered just in time her new role.

"I gotter live," she said plaintively. "You'll do all right. Yer pretty . . ."

The woman smiled mirthlessly, showing dark, stained teeth.

"Crawly cow," she said, but without rancor this time. "Well, one thing's fer sure, I got a lot more'n you'll ever 'ave, poor bitch. I'll do this for yer, if 'e fancies yer, which ain't likely, yer can 'ave this one. An' if I see yer on my patch again, I'll do yer."

"I'll get meself a man," Gracie said defiantly.

"A runner?" The woman laughed. " 'Oo'd wanter run yer, yer ain't worth nuffink."

"Yes I am. There's gents wot likes 'em little, like kids!" Gracie knew this from tales she'd heard from less reputable relatives when they had not realized her childish ears were so sharp, before she first went to work for Charlotte.

"There's all sorts," the woman agreed with disgust. "There's them as likes yer ter talk dirty to 'em, them as likes yer ter cuss summat rotten an' pretend as yer 'ates them, them as likes ter be told orf like they were kids 'emselves—an' there's them as likes ter 'urt yer. Yer wanter watch for them—some o' them gets real ugly. There's one around 'ere wot likes ter beat girls up pretty bad, real vicious bastard 'e is, big geezer, but speaks ever so soft like a real gent, minds all 'is manners, then beats yer black and blue. Real bad one, 'e is. Ain't no money worth that. Yer want ter stay clear o' the likes of 'im."

Gracie swallowed and found her throat so tight she could hardly speak. Maybe this was it? Maybe this was the clue Pitt was looking for? Perhaps this man had beaten a girl, her pimp had killed him, and the second victim had been killed because he knew something about it.

"Yer right," she said chokingly. " 'E sounds real bad. Mebbe I should try a lighted street or summat. I don't wanter run inter summat like 'im."

"Yer won't, you daft little piece. 'E likes women, not kids." The woman laughed. "Anyway, I can see business coming. This one's mine. Good luck, you poor little swine—you'll need it." And with a parting wave, she turned and sauntered towards the approaching shadows, swaying her hips as she went.

Gracie waited until she was indistinguishable in the darkness, then turned on her heels and ran.

5

E*MILY WAS DRESSED* magnificently, as befitted the occasion. Her gown was her favorite nile green, elegant as water in the sun, and stitched with silver beading and seed pearls. The waist was tiny and, she admitted, less than comfortable, the bodice crossed over at the front with the bosom low-cut. The bustle almost vanished completely, its fullness replaced by the new fullness at the top of the sleeve, decorated with feathers on the shoulder. The whole effect was quite breathtaking, and she was aware of it in the lingering looks of gentlemen and the sharp glances and fixed smiles of ladies, and then the immediate, muttered conversation.

The dinner had been lavish and served in the grandest manner. Now the guests were all sitting or standing around the reception rooms in small groups talking, laughing and passing on personal and political gossip, although of course the personal was probably the most political of all. The by-election was drawing near and emotions were running high.

Emily was standing, not because she wished to but because her stays, which had contrived her exquisite waist, were far too binding for her to sit down for long with any comfort at all. Dinner itself had been more than enough.

"How delightful to see you, my dear Mrs. Radley, and looking so very—well." Lady Malmsbury smiled brightly and regarded Emily with no pleasure at all. Lady Malmsbury was in her mid-forties, dark, rather large, and an ardent supporter of the Tory party, and thus of Jack's rival, Nigel Uttley. Her daughter Selina was of Emily's generation, and they had been friends in the past.

"I am in excellent health, thank you," Emily replied with an equally dazzling smile. "I hope I find you the same? You most certainly seem so."

"Indeed I am," Lady Malmsbury agreed, discreetly looking Emily up and down, and disliking what she saw. "And how is your dear Mama these days? I have not seen her for such a long time. Is she well? Of course widowhood is so hard on a woman, at whatever age it occurs."

"She is very well, thank you," Emily replied a trifle more guardedly. It was not a subject she wished to pursue.

"You know, I had the oddest experience the other evening," Lady Malmsbury continued, moving a step closer so her skirts rustled against Emily's. "I was leaving a recital, a most excellent violin recital. Are you fond of the violin?"

"Yes indeed," Emily said hastily, wondering what Lady Malmsbury was about to say in such eager confidence. The gleam in her eyes boded no good.

"I too. And this was delightful. Such charm and grace. A most elegant instrument," Lady Malmsbury continued, still smiling. "And as I was walking down the Strand for a breath of air before taking my carriage home, I saw a group of people leaving the Gaiety Theatre, and one of them reminded me so much of your Mama." She opened her eyes a little wider. "In fact I would have sworn it were she, were it not for her dress and the company in which she was." She looked at Emily directly.

Emily had no choice but pointedly to evade the subject, or else to ask the inevitable question.

"Indeed? How odd. A trick of the light, I suppose. Streetlights can give the strangest impressions sometimes."

"I beg your pardon?"

"I said that streetlights can give the strangest impressions on occasions," Emily repeated with an artificial smile. She refused to ask who the company had been.

Lady Malmsbury was not to be deflected.

"They could not have created an illusion like this. She was with a group of actors, my dear! And she was so obviously at ease with them, it was not an accident of chance that they left together. Anyway, the Gaiety. Your Mama would never have been in there, would she?" She laughed at the absurdity of it,

123

a hard, tinkling sound, like breaking glass. "And with such people!"

"I don't think I would know a group of actors if I saw one," Emily replied with a chill. "You have the advantage of me."

Lady Malmsbury's expression tightened and she raised her flat eyebrows very high. "I know you have been out of society in your confinement, my dear, but surely you would recognize Joshua Fielding? He is quite the darling at the moment. Such an interesting face, remarkable features. Not in the least what you could call regular, but quite full of expression."

"Oh, if it was Joshua Fielding then I assume he was visiting the Gaiety, not playing there," Emily observed with elaborate casualness. "Isn't he a more serious actor?"

"Yes, of course he is," Lady Malmsbury agreed. "But still hardly the company a lady would keep—not socially, I mean." Again she laughed, still staring at Emily.

"I really don't know," Emily said, staring back. "I have never met him." That was a lie, but the occasion had not been in public, so Lady Malmsbury would not know of it.

"He is an actor," Lady Malmsbury repeated. "He makes his living on the stage."

"So does Mrs. Langtry," Emily remarked. "And she seems to be quite good enough for the Prince of Wales, socially, I mean."

Lady Malmsbury's face hardened. "Not the same thing, my dear."

"No," Emily agreed. "I am not sure that one could really say Mrs. Langtry earned her chief remuneration on the stage—acting possibly, but in a different position, and a somewhat less public venue—at least most of the time."

Lady Malmsbury blushed to the roots of her hair. "Well really! I am afraid I must say I consider that remark in the worst possible taste, Emily. Since you have remarried, my dear, you have changed a great deal, and not for the better. I am not surprised your poor Mama does not show herself in society as much as she used to. Even in a silk turban and a dress with no discernible waist."

Emily contrived to look puzzled, although inside herself she was seething with alarm. "I cannot imagine why anyone should show themselves in society in such a garb."

"At the Gaiety Theatre," Lady Malmsbury said. "Really most peculiar."

"Most indeed," Emily agreed. She had nothing left to lose

now, so she said exactly what came into her mind. "I hope you had a thoroughly enjoyable evening beforehand? A good dinner—an excellent dinner?" She lifted her eyebrows. "And convivial . . ." She pronounced the word carefully, and looked at Lady Malmsbury with an unwavering gaze.

Another tide of color swept up Lady Malmsbury's face. The suggestion was delicate, but not so subtle that she had missed it. "Pleasant, but not indulgent," she said between her teeth.

Emily smiled as if she did not believe a word.

"So nice to have seen you, Lady Malmsbury, and looking so . . . robust."

Lady Malmsbury let out her breath sharply, searched for something to say that was equally cutting, failed to find it, and swirled away in a rustle of black-and-green taffeta.

Emily had won the verbal victory, but she was nevertheless seriously worried. She did not doubt for an instant that it had been Caroline whom Lady Malmsbury had seen, dressed bizarrely and in the company of Joshua Fielding and his friends. She was going to have to do something about it, but for the time being it eluded her as to what.

For the moment she must be charming and give everyone the impression she had not a worry in the world, except how best to be a help and support to Jack while he won his parliamentary seat, even though she was not at all sure that he would win. The Tories were strongly supported in the area, Jack was very new to politics, and Nigel Uttley had many friends with power and, no doubt at all, the secret and pervasive help of the Inner Circle.

She assumed an expression of intelligent interest and sailed forth to do battle.

The following day she prepared for conflict of a completely different kind. There was no need to dress especially, this time; the armament was entirely mental and emotional. Accordingly she was in a very casual spotted muslin gown when she alighted from her carriage and presented herself at her mother's front door in Cater Street.

"Good morning, Maddock," she said briskly when the butler answered. She had known him since childhood and stood on no formalities with him. "Is Mama in? Good. I wish to see her."

"I am afraid she is not down yet, Miss Emily." Maddock did

not refuse to let her in, but he effectively blocked her way to the foot of the stairs.

"Then perhaps you would tell her I am here and ask if I may come up?" Then a sudden and totally appalling thought seized her. Caroline must be alone! Surely? She could not have so far lost her wits as to—Oh, dear Heaven. Emily was cold all through, and her legs were weak.

"Are you all right, Miss Emily?" Maddock said with some concern. "May I bring you a little tea? Or a cool lemonade, perhaps?"

"No. No thank you, Maddock." She took a deep breath. This must be faced, whatever the truth. "Just tell Mama I wish to see her urgently."

"Is anything wrong, Miss Emily?"

"That remains to be seen. But yes, I fear there is at least one problem."

"Very well, if you care to be seated, I shall tell Mrs. Ellison you are here." And without further argument he went up the stairs and disappeared around the corner of the landing.

It seemed like a quite wretched age while Emily paced the hall waiting for him to return. Could Caroline really be having a full-blown affair with Joshua Fielding? It did not bear thinking of. She must have taken total leave of her wits. That was it. Papa's death had driven her mad. It was the only answer. Dependable, predictable, ordinary Mama had become unhinged.

"Miss Emily."

"Oh . . ." She whirled around.

Maddock had come down the stairs and she had not even heard him.

"Mrs. Ellison will see you, if you care to go up to the bedroom," Maddock said calmly.

"Thank you." Emily picked up her skirts by the fistful in hasty and unladylike manner and raced up the stairs, clattering her heels on the wood, whirled around the corner at the top of the landing, and with hardly a knock flung open the door to her mother's bedroom.

Then she stopped abruptly. It was all quite different. The old, sober coffee and cream tones were gone, as was the dark wood furniture. In its place was a riot of pinks and wines and peaches mixed together in florals, a brass bedstead with gleaming knobs and pale furniture made of who knew what. The room looked twice the size, and as if it had been bodily transported out of the house and set up in the middle of a garden. As if the rose floral curtains and bedspread and canopy were not enough, there was a huge crystal bowl full of roses on the dressing table, and since it was still only early May, they must have been grown in someone's hothouse.

Caroline was sitting up in bed in an apricot silk peignoir, her hair trailing over her shoulders, and looking very happy indeed.

"Do you like it?" she asked, regarding Emily's startled face.

Emily was horrified at the utter change, the unfamiliarity of it, but honesty compelled her to admit that she did find it pleasing. "It's—it's lovely," she said reluctantly. "But why? And it must have cost—I don't know—a fortune."

"Not really," Caroline said with a smile. "But anyway, I spend a great deal of time in here, probably almost half my life."

"Asleep," Emily protested with a sinking horror in her stomach.

"All the same, I like it like this." Caroline looked around with obvious happiness. "It is my room. I've always wanted one full of flowers. And it feels warm, even in the middle of winter."

"You don't know that," Emily argued. "I was here in March, and you hadn't done this then."

"Well it will do," Caroline said with certainty. "Anyway, March can feel like the middle of winter. We frequently get snow in March. And I shall spend my money how I please."

Emily sat down on the bed. Caroline did look extraordinarily well. Her skin was glowing and her eyes were brilliant with vitality and enthusiasm. It made Emily sick to think how it would all change when Joshua grew tired and went his way. Suddenly she hated him.

"What is it?" Caroline asked, frowning a little. "Maddock said you had something you wished to speak to me about urgently, and you do look a little anxious, my dear. Is it to do with Jack and the by-election?"

"Only in the remotest way—actually, no, not at all."

"You sound confused," Caroline pointed out. "Perhaps you'd better tell me what it is, and we can decide what it has to do with afterwards."

Emily stared sideways at the window with its wonderful festoons of flowers.

"I was at a dinner party yesterday evening," she began, then

127

stopped. Now that she came to tell it, it sounded so trivial. She searched for the right words.

"Yes?" Caroline prompted, sitting a little more upright against her pillows. "I assume you met someone of importance?"

"Oh several people. But this particular person was of no importance whatsoever."

Caroline frowned, but she kept her patience.

"It was what she said," Emily continued. "Actually it was Lady Malmsbury . . ."

"Selina Court's mother?" Caroline looked surprised. "By the way, have you seen Sir James lately? He used to be really quite agreeable, now he has become very portly and is losing his hair already. I always thought Selina could have done rather better, but Maria Malmsbury wouldn't wait."

"Yes, I never thought much of him," Emily agreed. "But Lady Malmsbury said to me that she saw you outside the Gaiety Theatre, dressed in a silk turban and a gown with no waist to speak of, with Joshua Fielding and some other actors. Or to be more correct, she said it couldn't possibly be you. But of course she meant that it was."

"Oh yes, we had a most excellent time," Caroline said enthusiastically, her eyes bright with the memory. "It was such fun. I never realized how catchy some of those songs can be. And I haven't laughed like that for years. It is very good for one to laugh, you know? It makes the face look so agreeable."

"But in a silk turban," Emily said in anguish.

"Why not? Silk is a delicious fabric—and turbans are most flattering."

"A turban, Mama! And a dress with no waist! If you had to go at all, couldn't you at least have worn something ordinary? Even the aesthetes gave those up years ago."

"My dear Emily, I have no intention of allowing Maria Malmsbury to dictate what I should wear—or where I should find my entertainment, or in whose company. And I don't give a fig about the aesthetes. And dearly as I love both you and Charlotte, I shall not allow you to dictate to me either." She put her hand over Emily's. "If it embarrasses you, I'm sorry; but there have been in the past a few times when you have sorely embarrassed me. Your involvement with Thomas's detecting, to begin with."

"You have involved yourself," Emily said indignantly. "Less than six months ago. How can you be so . . ."

"I know," Caroline said quickly. "And if circumstances should offer me the opportunity, I shall do so again. Experience has taught me I was quite mistaken to be embarrassed. Perhaps in time it will do the same for you."

Emily let out a wail of frustration.

"Is that the only thing that troubles you?" Caroline inquired pleasantly.

"For Heaven's sake, Mama, isn't it enough? My mother is keeping company with an actor half her age, and the fact that it will ruin her in society doesn't seem to bother her at all. She is seen in the Strand dressed like I don't know what!"

"Well, my dear, if it frightens your respectable voters, it may endear me to those less respectable," Caroline said cheerfully. "Let us hope they outnumber the prudes. But if you wish me to stay at home and dress in purple so Jack can be elected, I am afraid I am not going to oblige you, dearly as I hope he wins."

"I am not thinking of Jack. I am concerned for you," Emily protested, truthfully, because she did not think Jack would win anyway. "What will happen when all this is over? Have you thought of that?"

The joy went out of Caroline's face, leaving her so intensely vulnerable Emily wanted to clasp her in her arms and hold her, as she would have a child.

"I shall be older, alone, and have memories of a glorious time when I was happy, and loved, even if it could not be mine forever," Caroline replied very quietly, looking down at the rose-colored quilt. "I shall have had laughter, imagination and friendship such as few women ever have, and I shall keep my memories without bitterness." She raised her eyes to Emily's. "That is what will happen. I shall not go into a decline, or expect you or Charlotte to sit with me while I weep over it. Does that make you feel any better?"

Ridiculously, Emily found there were tears in her eyes.

"No—I shall—I shall hurt for you so terribly!" She sniffed and fished for a handkerchief unsuccessfully.

Caroline passed her one from under her pillow.

"That is the price of loving, my dear," she said softly. "Usually it is parents who agonize for their children, but sometimes it is the other way too. The only way to avoid that is not to love anyone enough for their pain to hurt you. But that is like having part of you that is dead."

Emily let out her breath in a long sigh. There was nothing to say to that, no argument.

"Tell me about the campaign," Caroline suggested, retrieving her handkerchief. "And about the new house of Charlotte's—have you seen it?"

"Yes. It's awful, at the moment. But it could be really very nice indeed, with a great deal of work, and at least a hundred pounds spent on it, possibly even two." And she proceeded to tell Caroline about it.

As she was leaving half an hour later she met her grandmother in the hallway. The old lady was dressed entirely in black, as was her custom; she believed widows should behave like widows. She leaned heavily on her stick and watched Emily come all the way down the stairs to the bottom before she spoke.

"Well," she said viciously, "so you have been to see your Mama. The place looks like a harlot's place of work! She's taken leave of her senses—not that she ever had much. It was my poor Edward who kept her in some sort of dignity while he was alive. He must be turning in his grave to see this." She banged her cane on the floor. "I don't think I can remain here any more. It is all beyond tolerating. I shall come and stay with you." She twitched angrily and turned to stare up the hall. "Staying with Charlotte is out of the question. Always was. She married beneath her. I couldn't abide that."

Emily was aghast.

"Because Mama has had her bedroom redecorated?" Her voice rose with incredulity. "If you don't care for it, don't go in there."

"Don't be ridiculous!" the old lady said, swinging back to face her. "Do you suppose she did it like that for herself? She intends having that man in there. It's as plain as the nose on your face."

Emily really did not think she could endure having Grandmama living with her. Even Ashworth House, enormous as it was, was not big enough to share with the old lady.

"I'm not living in a house of scandal and immorality," the old lady went on vehemently, her voice rising in both pitch and volume. "That my old age should have come to this!" Her boot-button eyes were brilliant. "I shall go down to my grave in sorrow."

"Rubbish!" Emily said tartly. "Nothing has happened yet,

and it probably never will." Although she did not entirely believe that, and she avoided the old woman's stare.

"Don't you 'rubbish' me, my girl!" Grandmama banged the stick again furiously, scarring the wooden floor with its metal ferrule. "I've seen what I've seen, and I know a loose woman when I have one under my roof."

"It's not your roof. It's Mama's. Anyway, you've never had a loose woman here so you wouldn't know one if you had."

"You remember who you are speaking to, my girl," the old woman snapped. And as Emily moved towards the front door, she added, "And stand still when I'm talking to you. Where are your nerves, I should like to know."

"There's nothing else to say, Grandmama. I must return home. I have social duties to perform."

The old lady let out a long rumble of disgust, banged her stick on the floor one more time, then turned on her heel and stumped off.

Emily escaped while the chance was good.

She did not mention the matter to Jack at all. There was no purpose to be served by it, and the thought of Grandmama coming to live in Ashworth House, no matter how unlikely, would be sufficient to distract his mind totally from the business in hand.

Instead she went straight upstairs and burst into the nursery quarters. She startled the elderly, comfortable nurse sitting in her rocking chair holding the baby, almost asleep. The nursery maid, Susie, dropped the linen she was folding, and Edward abandoned the last of his rice pudding and left the table without permission.

"Mama!" he cried, running to greet her. "Mama! I learned all about King Henry the Sixth today. Do you know he had eight wives and he cut all their heads off. Do you think the Queen will cut Prince Albert's head off if she gets tired of him?" He stopped in front of her, upright, slender, his face shining with enthusiasm, his fair hair so like hers, falling over his brow. He was dressed in a loose white shirt with a wide collar, and dark striped pants. He jiggled from one foot to the other in excitement. "Wouldn't that be thrilling?"

"No it wouldn't," Emily said in surprise, reaching out her hand to touch him gently. She wanted to take him in her arms and hold him close to her, but she knew he would hate it. He considered it babyish, and submitted to a good-night kiss only under protest. "And it was Henry the Eighth," she corrected: "He only had six wives, and he only took some of their heads off."

He looked disappointed. "Oh. What happened to the rest of them?"

"One died, he divorced one, or maybe two, and one outlived him."

"But—he beheaded the rest?"

"I expect so. What else have you done today?"

"Sums—and geography."

Miss Roberts, his governess, appeared in the schoolroom doorway. She was a clergyman's daughter, trim and plain and now nearly thirty years old, too old to hope for marriage. She was obliged to earn her living, and this was an acceptable way to do it. Emily liked her and looked forward to her caring for and teaching Evie in time.

"Good afternoon, Miss Roberts," she said cheerfully. "Is he learning well?"

"Yes, Mrs. Radley," Miss Roberts said with a small downward curl of her mouth. "Rather more interested in intrigues and battles than laws and treaties. But I suppose that is natural. I like Queen Elizabeth, myself."

"So do I," Emily agreed.

Edward looked from one to the other of them, but he was too well disciplined to interrupt.

"You have not finished your rice pudding," Miss Roberts told him.

He looked up at her through his eyelashes. "It'll be cold."

"And whose fault is that?" she asked.

He considered arguing, regarding her face for a moment, then thought better of it. It was undignified to argue and lose, especially to a woman, and as a young viscount he was very sensitive to his dignity, which was hard enough for a seven-year-old boy surrounded by women to maintain. He walked nonchalantly back to the table, climbed into his chair and picked up the spoon.

Emily met Miss Roberts's eyes, and they both hid smiles.

Miss Roberts returned to the schoolroom.

The nursery maid departed with the pile of laundry to put it in the night nursery.

Emily turned to the nurse and held out her arms to take the baby.

"She's just gone to sleep, poor little soul," the nurse protested. She was a big comfortable woman who had been a wet-nurse in her youth, frequently taking the infants of noble houses into her own home to care for them and breast-feed them for up to the first year of their lives, or even longer, before returning them to their stately nurseries and the care of nannies, nursery maids and eventually governesses and tutors. She liked them best up to the age of about three, although she was prone to getting fond of an individual child and finding it hard to hand over her responsibility. Emily was not going to be refused. She wanted to hold the baby in her arms, feel its weight resting against her, touch its silken skin and look at the tiny face. She remained with her arms held out.

The nurse also knew better than to argue. She rose and passed over her charge.

Evie did not stir as Emily took her and rocked her gently. After several moments during which the nurse turned away and busied herself, although in truth there was nothing to do, Emily began to stroke the baby's downy head, and finally succeeded in waking her up. She sat down in the rocking chair and started to talk to her, largely nonsense, and after about fifteen minutes—during which the nursery routine was set back, the nursery maid could not clear up, the nurse had nothing useful to do, and Edward finished his tea and became late for his bedtime story—eventually Evie began to cry.

This time the nurse's patience was at an end. She took Evie without a word, dipped a piece of cotton in sugar water and popped it in her mouth, and quite firmly told Emily that it was time everyone resumed their proper duties.

Obediently Emily bade Edward good-night, without kissing him, which at first pleased him enormously, then on second thought left him feeling a little uncertain. Perhaps so much dignity was not really necessary yet? However, having made the decision he was not going back on it, especially in front of Roberts, whose opinion he valued. Tomorrow he would offer his cheek to be kissed, and thus have taken the initiative himself. That was an excellent solution. He went to bed well satisfied. Besides, the present bedtime story, about King Arthur, was a particularly good one.

Emily watched him go with a touch of emotion inside her, then, with a brief word to the nursing staff, turned and went back downstairs to wait for Jack.

He came in at about seven o'clock, having spent the whole day pursuing political affairs of one sort or another, and was delighted to forget them even for the short while before dinner and the arrival of another group to be pursued or persuaded. The date for the by-election had been set, three weeks from then, and his mind was fully taken up with preparations.

The following morning Emily was in the breakfast room, one of her favorite places in the house, when Jack came in carrying two newspapers. The room was octagonal with three doors, one of them to the small shaded garden to the east of the house, and the morning sun shone through the glass of that door onto the warm parquet floor and cabinets of delicate, floral porcelain against two of the walls.

"It's all over the place," he said, putting the newspaper on the corner of the table and regarding her gravely. "It's still on the front pages of the *Times*."

She did not need to ask what he was referring to. The last subject they had discussed before going to bed had been the Hyde Park murders, and it required no explanation that he should continue now.

"What do they say?" she asked.

"The *Times* is largely trying to keep some sort of calm," he answered. "One of the columnists is talking about madness, and saying it is on the increase. According to one of their correspondents there is some Viennese school of medicine which explains it all in terms of what happened in infancy, and talks of dreams and repression and so on." He sat down at the table, reached for the bell, but before he could ring it the butler appeared. "Egg and bacon and potatoes, please, Jenkins," Jack said absently.

"Cook has some very fine deviled kidneys, sir," Jenkins suggested. "On a little fresh toast?"

"Does that mean you have no eggs?" Jack looked up at him.

"No sir, we have at least three dozen eggs." Jenkins kept a perfectly sober face. "Shall I bring eggs, sir?"

"No, the kidneys sound excellent," Jack replied. He looked across at Emily inquiringly.

"Fruit compote and toast," Emily answered.

"Don't you get bored with it?" He frowned, but his eyes were gentle.

"Not at all. Apricots, if Cook still has any left, Jenkins." She could not permit Jack to know, and even less the servants, but she had every intention of getting her figure back to the exquisite shape it had been before Evie's advent, and keeping it so.

"Yes, ma'am." Jenkins still had difficulty in not calling her "my lady," as he had when George had been alive and she was Lady Ashworth. He withdrew obediently about his errand.

"Probably no bacon," Emily said with a smile. "What else?"

Jack was used to her patterns of thought. He knew she meant the newspapers again. The subject was far from exhausted.

"An eminent doctor gives his opinion as to how the crimes were committed," he continued. "Not very helpful. One writer is convinced it is a woman—I don't know why. Someone else has written about the phases of the moon, and predicted when the next one will occur."

Emily shivered and pulled a face. "Poor Thomas!"

Jack looked at her gravely. "But mostly it is criticism of the police, their methods, their character, even their existence." He let out his breath with a sigh. "Uttley has written a long article which the *Times* has printed, and I am afraid he is extremely hard on Thomas, although he doesn't refer to him by name. Of course his purpose is to make political capital from his own ideas and he doesn't care whom he hurts on the way."

Emily reached for the paper, and had it in her hands when Jenkins returned with Jack's kidneys and her fruit compote. The butler glanced at her and smothered his disapproval with difficulty. In his day ladies did not read anything in the newspapers but that which their husbands gave them, which would be the court circular, the marriages and obituaries, and if they were fortunate, the theater criticisms and reviews. Political opinion and commentary was not suitable for women. It excited the blood and disturbed the imagination. He had once been so bold as to remark so to Lord Ashworth when he had been alive, but unfortunately he had been disregarded.

"Thank you, Jenkins," Jack said absently, and Emily echoed his words with even less attention. Jenkins withdrew with a sigh.

"I know it," Emily said, ignoring her breakfast and beginning to read. " 'There is no question that when Her Majesty's Government created a police force to serve the citizens of London, it made a brilliant and decisive step for the good of every person in this teeming heart of the Empire. But is this present-day force what these men had in mind?

" 'In the autumn of 1888 there was a series of gruesome and

terrifying murders in Whitechapel which has gone down in history as among the most savage in all human experience. They have also gone down in history as unsolved. The very best our police can do, after months of investigation, is say "We do not know."

" 'Is this what we deserve, is this what we are purchasing with our money?

" 'I think not.

" 'We need a more professional force, men with not only dedication but the skill and education to prevent this sort of crime from recurring.

" 'We have an empire which stretches round the world. We have conquered and subdued wild nations of warriors. We have settled lands in the frozen north, in the burning south, the plains of the west and the jungles and deserts of the east. We have planted the flag on every continent on earth, and taken law and government, religion and language, to every people. Can we really not control the unruly elements of our own capital city?

" 'Gentlemen, we must do better. We must change this sorry story of incompetence and failure. We must reorganize our forces of law and make sure they are the best in the world before we become a laughingstock, a byword for incompetence, and we will have every criminal in Europe descending upon us to make good his chances.

" 'We do not need the soft options of the Liberal party. We need strength and resolve.' "

Emily put it down with disgust. She should not have been surprised and indeed she was not, but it still made her angry. She looked up at Jack.

"It's so stupid," she said helplessly. "This is all just words. He doesn't make any actual suggestions. What else could Thomas do?"

"I don't know," he confessed. "If I did I would be the first to go to him and tell him. But it isn't only finding the solution." He bit into his deviled kidneys and savored them with pleasure. He waited till he had swallowed the first mouthful before he continued. "It's finding the solution that society wants," he finished.

"Which is what? Some lunatic escaped from Bedlam that we can all disown, and say it has nothing to do with us?" she retorted, stirring the compote viciously. "If it isn't, then we can hardly blame Thomas."

"Emily, my dearest, people have blamed the messenger for the contents of the message as long as history has been recorded. Of course they can—and they will."

"That's childish." She swallowed a mouthful and it went the wrong way. She nearly choked before recovering enough to glare at him.

"Of course it is," he agreed, pouring her a cup of tea and passing it. "What has that to do with it? You don't have to be in politics long to know that an awful lot of people's reactions can be childish, and we usually cater to the very worst of those once we begin trying to beat each other."

"What are you going to say against Uttley? You've got to say something. You can't let him get away with this."

"I don't think Thomas will thank me for defending him—" he began.

"Not Thomas," she interrupted. "You! You can't sit here and let Uttley bring the battle to you. You've got to attack."

He thought for several moments, and she waited with difficulty, eating the rest of her compote without tasting it.

"There is no point whatever in talking figures to people," he said thoughtfully, setting down his fork as his meal was finished. "It has no emotion."

"Don't defend," she argued. "You can't defend effectively anyway. All the criminals caught don't amount to anything compared with the ones that are still at large—not in people's minds." She swallowed. "Anyway, it's bad to look defensive. It isn't your fault that the police are inefficient. And don't let him push you into a position where people imagine it is." She reached for the silver teapot. "Would you care for some more?"

He pushed forward his cup and she poured for him.

"Attack him," she went on. "What are his weaknesses?"

"Fiscal affairs, the national economy . . ."

"That won't do." She dismissed it out of hand. "It's boring, and people don't understand it anyway. You can hardly talk about shillings and pence on the hustings. People won't listen."

"I know that," he agreed with a smile. "But you asked me what his weaknesses were."

"Why don't you do what Charlotte did?" she suggested at length. "Pretend to be naive and ask him to explain himself. You know he can't abide people laughing at him."

"That's very dangerous—"

"So is his present attack on the police, and through them on you. What do you have to lose?"

He looked at her thoughtfully for several moments, then slowly his face relaxed and his eyes lit with enthusiasm.

"Don't blame me if it explodes in my face," he warned.

"Of course I shan't. But let's go down with a real battle." She leaned forward and caught hold of his hand where it lay on the table. "Let's go in with all flags flying and all guns firing."

"I may have to retire to the country afterwards."

"Afterwards, perhaps," she conceded. "But not before."

Jack contrived the opportunity the next day. Uttley was addressing a considerable crowd at Hyde Park Corner and Jack sauntered up, Emily on his arm. People were drawing closer from all directions, many with pies, sandwiches or peppermint drinks in their hands. The Punch and Judy man abandoned his stall, knowing the real drama was more fun any day. A nursemaid with a perambulator slowed her step and a newsboy and an urchin sweeping the crossing both ceased their shouting and listened.

"Ladies and gentlemen!" Uttley began, although the address to ladies was purely a courtesy. No women could vote, so their opinion was superfluous. "Ladies and gentlemen! We are at a crossroads in the life of our great city. It is up to you to decide which way you wish to go. Do you like it as it is, or do you want something better?" He was dressed in a dark coat, double-breasted and with silk lapels, and lighter striped trousers. The sunlight gleamed on his browned face and fair hair.

"Better!" yelled at least a dozen voices.

"Of course you do," he agreed with enthusiasm. "You want money in your pockets, food on your tables, and you want to be able to walk the streets of your city in safety." He gave a meaningful gesture towards the green expanse of the park behind him and there was a murmur of agreement from the crowd.

"How's he going to manage the money?" Emily whispered to Jack. "Ask him."

"No point," he whispered back. "The poor don't have votes anyway."

Emily gave a grunt of irritation.

"Never mind the street!"

"What about the parks?" a fat man in a coster's apron called out. "Can we walk them in safety too?"

There was a bellow of laughter from the crowd and someone whistled.

"Not now!" Uttley looked at him. "Not now, my friend. But you ought to be able to—if the police were doing their job!"

There were one or two cries of agreement.

"Do you want patrols in the park?" Jack asked loudly.

"Good idea, Mr. Radley," Uttley answered, pointing his finger at him to draw everyone's attention. "Why didn't you say that in your last address? You didn't, you know—not a word!"

Everyone turned to stare at Jack.

Jack surveyed the faces now looking at him.

"Do you want police patrols through the park?" he asked innocently.

"Yeah!" a couple called out, but most were silent. No one spoke against.

"What should they do?" Jack pursued. "Stop you—ask you what your business is? Who it is you are with?"

There was a rumble of denial.

"Search you for weapons?" he went on. "Take your name and address?"

"How about stop you from being attacked, robbed or murdered?" Uttley asked. The crowd gave a shout of approval and then a quick burst of laughter.

"Oh. I hadn't thought of that," Jack said, still with bland innocence. "Follow you. Of course. And then when someone approaches, they should come close enough to prevent any sudden blow or lunge. And if the person should prove to be merely an acquaintance . . ." He stopped amid a few murmurs of anger and glowing faces. "Oh no—that wouldn't do—because we don't know that it wasn't an acquaintance that killed Captain Winthrop and Mr. Arledge. Whoever it is, the policemen had better remain close enough to intervene if it should seem necessary."

"Don't be absurd," Uttley began, but he was drowned out by catcalls and laughter.

"Wouldn't that require an awful lot of policemen?" Jack asked. "In fact, roughly one each for every person who wanted to take a stroll. Perhaps we should call up the police station and wait for an escort. It would be terribly expensive. Taxes would double or triple."

139

There were calls of disapproval and derision, and one man laughed uproariously.

"This is ridiculous!" Uttley shouted above the melee. "You have reduced it to an absurdity! There are perfectly sensible ways of doing it."

"Then tell us," Jack invited him, holding his hands wide.

"Yeah," the crowd called, turning their faces from one to the other. "Go on—tell us!"

Uttley struggled to define them, but it became obvious he had thought only in generalities, and when it came to a specific solution he could not name one. The crowd whistled and cat-called, and Jack had no need to aid in his rival's undoing. Eventually, red-faced and furious, Uttley turned on him.

"What will you do that's better, Radley? Give us your answer!"

As one the crowd swiveled to look at Jack, their eyes keen, their jeering as ready to strip him.

"I blame the Irish!" one woman called out, her face red with fury. "That's who it is—you'll see!"

"Rubbish!" a black-haired man contradicted her with contempt. "It's them Jews!"

"Hang 'em!" a man in green shouted, raising his arm. "Hang 'em all!"

"Bring back deportation!" someone else called. "Let Orstralia 'ave 'em! Should never 'ave got rid o' deportation—that's wot's wrong."

"Can't do anything until you catch them," Jack pointed out. "I say get more professional police, men who are trained to do the job, not gentlemen who speak nicely and have good clothes but couldn't catch a thief if they were locked in a room with him."

"Yeah! Yeah, that's right!" someone called out. A thin woman in gray waved her hand approvingly. A stout man with waxed mustaches jeered and whistled. "What you got agin' gentlemen? You an anarchist, eh? You one o' them wot wants ter get rid o' the Queen, are yer?"

"Certainly not," Jack replied, keeping his equanimity with difficulty. "I'm a loyal subject of Her Majesty. And I like gentlemen—some of my best friends are gentlemen. In fact, at times I am one myself."

There was a roar of laughter.

"But I'm not a policeman," he went on. "I don't have that skill—and I know it. Neither do most other gentlemen."

"Even some o' our policemen don't, an' all!" the pie seller shouted, to more laughter. "'Oo's the 'Yde Park 'Eadsman, then? Why don't they catch 'im?"

"They will do!" Jack called out impulsively. "There's a first-class professional policeman on the case—and if the Home Office helps instead of curbing him, he'll catch the Headsman!" As soon as he had said it, Emily knew he regretted it, but the words were out.

There was a roar of skepticism from the crowd, and one or two turned to look at Uttley.

"Superintendent Pitt," Uttley said with a jeering smile. "A gamekeeper's son. I know why Mr. Radley has such confidence in him—they are brothers-in-law! Do you know something the public have not been told, Radley? Something secret, perhaps? What are the police doing? What is Pitt doing?"

Now the crowd was looking at Jack with suspicion, and an ugliness shadowed their faces. The mood had changed again.

"I know he's a brilliant policeman, working as hard as any man can," Jack shouted back. "And if he isn't hobbled by the powers in the Home Office and the government, trying to protect their own, then he'll catch the Headsman."

There was a low, angry rumble and again the mood swung right around and directed the anger at Uttley.

"Yeah!" a fat man said loudly. "Give us real police, not some bleedin' toff in fancy clothes wot won't get his 'ands dirty."

"That's right," the woman with the peppermint drinks added. "Get rid of them wot's protecting their own. The 'Eadsman maybe ain't a poor lunatic at all. Maybe 'e's one o' them fancy gents wot's got something personal agin' other gents."

"Maybe they was perverts wot picked up women an' got done by their pimps for something real nasty?"

Uttley opened his mouth to deny it, then saw their faces and changed his mind.

"They are our police, and it's our city," Jack said finally. "Let's give them our support and they'll catch this monster—whoever he is: gentleman or lunatic—or both."

There was a cheer from the crowd, and one by one they began to drift away.

Uttley jumped down from the carriage steps where he had been standing and walked over to Jack and Emily, his eyes hard and narrow, the small muscle in his jaw pinched. "A little cheap laughter," he said between his teeth. "Half a dozen men who can vote—maybe. The rest is dross."

"If they were no use, what were you doing here?" Emily said before she thought.

Uttley glared at her. "There are issues here, madam, you know nothing about." He looked at Jack with a steady, unblinking stare. "But you do, Radley. You know who is on my side . . . and who on yours." His lips parted in a very slight smile. "You made a bad mistake last time, and it will tell against you. You've made enemies. It will be enough—you'll see." And with that he turned on his heel, strode back to his carriage and swung himself up into it in a single movement. He shouted at his coachman and without hesitation the horses threw themselves forward as the whip lashed over their backs.

"He means the Inner Circle, doesn't he?" Emily said with a shiver as though the sun had gone in, although actually it was as bright as the moment before. "Can it really make so much difference?"

"I don't know," Jack answered honestly. "But if it can, it's a very black day for England."

Charlotte was in the kitchen after Pitt had left for the day, and the breakfast dishes were cleared away. Daniel and Jemima were preparing to leave for school, and Gracie was at the sink.

Five-year-old Daniel coughed dramatically, then as no one paid him any attention, Charlotte being busy with seven-year-old Jemima's hair, he did it again.

"Daniel has a cough," Jemima said helpfully.

"Yes I have," Daniel agreed immediately, and went into a paroxysm to demonstrate it.

"Don't do that anymore, or you'll have a real sore throat," Charlotte said unsympathetically.

"I have," he agreed, nodding his head, his eyes on hers, bright and clear.

She smiled at him. "Yes, my dear, and it is my considered deduction that you also have arithmetic today, yes?"

He was too young to have learned successful evasion.

"I don't think I'm well enough for arithmetic," he said candidly. The sun through the windows shone on his bright hair, gleaming with the same auburn as hers.

"You'll get better," she said cheerfully.

His face fell.

"Or on the other hand," she went on, finishing Jemima's hair and tying a ribbon on it. "If you really are ill, then you had better stay at home . . ."

"Yes!" he said with instant enthusiasm.

"In bed," she concluded. "We'll see if you are well enough to get up tomorrow. Gracie can make you some eel broth, and maybe a little light gruel."

Daniel's face filled with dismay.

"Then you can catch up with your arithmetic when you are well again," Charlotte added heartlessly. "Jemima will help you."

"Yes I will," Jemima cut in. "I know how to do sums."

"I think maybe I'll be all right," Daniel said slowly, giving Jemima a filthy look. "I'll try hard."

Charlotte gave him a radiant smile and touched his head gently, feeling the soft hair under her fingers.

"I thought you would."

When they were gone and Gracie had finished the dishes Charlotte turned her attention to the duties of the day. There were various garments that needed special cleaning, in particular a shirt of Pitt's which had a couple of fine bloodstains where he had nicked himself shaving and even afterwards a drop had fallen and made a mark. A little paste of starch, put on and left to dry before being brushed off, would see to that. Strong alcohol saturated in camphor would take out the oil stain on his jacket sleeve. Chloroform was better for grease. She would have to ascertain which it was.

And the black lace from the dress she had worn for the memorial service looked a little mildewed, and she must attend to that before returning it. She would use alcohol and borax. She refused to send to the butcher for bullock's gall to put in warm water, which she had been advised was actually the best. There were also feathers to be recurled, which was a disaster done with curling tongs. It was far better to do them over an ivory knife handle. It was a tedious job, but necessary if she were to continue to borrow her relatives' expensive and highly fashionable clothes. And of course she should not forget the black leather gloves which should be rubbed over with orange slice, then salad oil.

"Gracie," she began, then realized that Gracie was not listening to her. "Gracie?"

"Yes, ma'am?" Gracie turned slowly from where she had been staring at the dresser, her face pink.

"What's the matter?" Charlotte asked.

"Nothing, ma'am," Gracie said quickly.

"Good. Then will you heat the irons and I'll start on the lace. I think you could do the master's shirts and attend to those little blood spots—you know how."

"Yes, ma'am." And Gracie began obediently to pull out the flatirons and set them on the hob.

Charlotte went upstairs to fetch the feathers, and on her return, took out an ivory-handled knife. She only had two, one a butter knife and too small, the other a cake knife and just right.

"Ma'am?" Gracie started.

"Yes?"

"Uh—oh—no, it doesn't matter." And she splashed out a liberal helping of alcohol to begin her task.

Charlotte started very carefully curling the feathers, then realized that Gracie was putting the alcohol on the bloodstains, not the grease, and had forgotten the camphor altogether.

"Gracie! What is the matter this morning? Something is wrong. Tell me what it is before you cause a disaster!"

Gracie's cheeks were bright pink and her eyes were full of fear, her whole face pinched with urgency. Still she could not find the words.

Charlotte felt a lurch of fear herself. She was extraordinarily fond of Gracie, perhaps she had not realized how much until this moment.

"What is it?" she said with more sharpness than she intended. "Are you ill?"

"No!" Gracie bit her lip. "I know summat about the gennelman wot goes inter the park arter girls." She swallowed hard. "I got ter talkin' ter one o' them tarts in there one day." Her eyes were brimming with misery. She was lying, at least in part, and she hated it. "An' she said as there was one gent wot liked ter beat women, beat 'em really 'ard, 'urt 'em bad. I reckon as mebbe that were Captain Winthrop. She said as 'e were big. An' mebbe it were a pimp as done fer 'im. An' the other gent knew it. Mebbe 'e saw it, or summat, an' that's why 'e got done too."

For a moment Charlotte could think only of the likelihood of what Gracie said, and her spirits soared upwards.

"It could be," she agreed quickly. "It could very well be!"

Gracie gave a sickly smile.

Then the further meaning struck Charlotte.

"Gracie! You've been out detecting again! Haven't you?"

Gracie's eyes lowered and she stared in silent misery at the floor, waiting for the blow to fall.

"You went to the park at night to find one of those women, didn't you?"

Gracie did not deny it.

"You stupid child!" Charlotte exploded. "Don't you realize what could have happened to you?"

"They're goin' ter throw the book at the master if 'e don't catch the 'Eadsman." Gracie still did not look up.

Charlotte felt a stab of alarm, if what Gracie said were true, and then of guilt for her own so frequent absences.

"I could beat you myself for taking such a risk," she said furiously, swallowing hard. "And I will do, I swear, if you ever do anything like it again! And how on earth am I going to tell the master what you know without telling him how you found out? Can you answer me that?"

Gracie shook her head.

"I shall have to think of something very clever indeed."

Gracie nodded.

"Don't just stand there waggling your head. You'd better try to think as well. And get those grease stains out of his sleeve while you're doing it. We'd better at least have his clothes clean for him."

"Yes ma'am!" Gracie lifted her head and gave her a tiny smile.

Charlotte smiled back. She intended it to be tiny also, but it ended up being a wide, conspiratorial grin.

Charlotte spent the afternoon in the new house. Every day it seemed to be some new disaster had been discovered or some major decision must be made. The builder wore a permanent expression of anxiety and shook his head in doubt, biting his lip, before she had even finished framing her questions to him.

However, with the purchase of an excellent catalog from Young & Marten, Builders Merchants and Suppliers, she was able to counter most of his arguments quite specifically, and very slowly was earning his exceedingly grudging respect.

The principal problem was that she was racing against time. The Bloomsbury house was sold, and they must leave it within four weeks, and the new house was very far from ready to move into. Most of the major work was accomplished. Aunt Vespasia's instructions had been followed to the letter, and there was now an immaculate plaster cornice where the old one had been. There was even a flawless new ceiling rose as well. But it was all innocent of paint or paper, and the whole question of carpets was not even touched upon. Decisions crowded in from every quarter.

When talking to Emily about it she had thought she knew precisely what color she wished for each room, but when it came to the details of purchasing paper and paint, she was not at all certain. And if she were honest, her attention was not totally upon the matter. She could not help but be aware of the newspaper headlines and the tone of the articles beneath them criticizing the police in general—and the man in charge of the Hyde Park case in particular. It was grossly unfair. Pitt was reaping the whirlwind sown by the Whitechapel murders and the Fenian outrages and a dozen other things. There was also the general unrest in terms of political change, teeming poverty, ideas of anarchy come over from Europe as well as native-bred dissension, the instability of the throne with an old, sour queen shut away in perpetual mourning, and an heir who squandered his time and money on cards, racehorses and women. Headless corpses in Hyde Park were simply the focus for the anger and the fear.

It ought to be some ease of conscience to know that, but it was no use whatsoever as a defense. Thomas was so new in his promotion. Micah Drummond would have understood it; he was a gentleman, a member of the Inner Circle, until he broke from them with all the risk that that entailed, and a personal friend of many of his equals and superiors. Thomas was none of these things, and would never be. He would have to earn every step of his way—and prove himself again and again.

She stared around the room, her mind refusing to concentrate. Would it really be a good idea to have it green? Or would it be too cold after all? Whose opinion could she ask? Caroline was busy with Joshua, and anyway Charlotte did not want to see her and be reminded of that particular problem.

Emily was busy with Jack and the political battle that was now so close.

Pitt was working so hard she hardly ever saw him for more than a few moments when he came home at night, hungry and exhausted. Although tonight she would have to make an exception, no matter what the circumstances, to pass on Gracie's news, when she had decided how to. But he certainly did not need to be troubled with domestic decisions—even if he had

146

had the faintest idea what color a room was. So far in their married life he had either liked a room or disliked it, beyond that he had never expressed any observation at all.

Then a snatch of conversation came back to her from the memorial service for Oakley Winthrop. She had discussed interiors with the widow, Mina. She had not really intended to, but it had seemed something in which she took pleasure and, to judge from her remarks, had some talent. She would ask Mina's opinion. It would serve two purposes, the relatively insignificant one of deciding whether to paper the room green or not, and the far larger, and more urgent, one of perhaps helping Thomas. With Gracie's discovery it had become ever more pressing that they learn a little more about the captain, and if possible his habits.

There was no need to consider the decision. It was made. She was hardly dressed for calling, but it would be a waste of time to go back to Bloomsbury and change, and then have to take the omnibus back to Curzon Street. It would be extravagant to call a hansom. She did at least wash her face and make some rapid repairs to her hair before going outside into the sun and walking briskly to the nearest omnibus stop.

She did not seriously consider the impertinence of what she was doing until she stood on the doorstop of the late Captain Winthrop's house, saw the drawn blinds and the dark wreath on the door, and wondered what on earth she would say.

"Yes ma'am?" the maid said in little more than a whisper.

"Good afternoon," Charlotte replied, aware that her face was suddenly very pink. "Mrs. Winthrop was kind enough to give me some most excellent advice a few days ago. I am now sorely in need of some more, and I wondered if she would spare me a few moments of her time. I shall surely understand if it is not convenient. I am abashed at having called without informing her first. Her kindness quite made me forget my manners."

"I'll ask 'er, ma'am," the maid said doubtfully. "But I'm sure as I can't say if she will, the 'ouse bein' in mournin' like."

"Of course," Charlotte agreed.

" 'Oo shall I say 'as called, ma'am?"

"Oh—Mrs. Pitt. We met at Captain Winthrop's memorial service. I was with Lady Vespasia Cumming-Gould."

"Yes ma'am. I'll ask, if you'll be good enough to wait 'ere."

And she left Charlotte standing in the hall while she scurried away.

It was not the maid who returned, but Mina herself, still dressed in what appeared to be the same black gown with its very high neck and lace-pointed cuffs. She was as tall as Charlotte but much slenderer, almost waiflike with her fair skin and impossibly fragile neck. She looked tired, bruised around the eyes, as if in the privacy of her own room she had wept herself to exhaustion, but her face was full of pleasure at the sight of Charlotte.

"How nice of you to call," she said immediately. "You have no idea how lonely it is sitting here day after day, no one coming except to pay respects, and it isn't seemly for me to go out anywhere." She smiled briefly, half embarrassment, half shame, seeking Charlotte's understanding. "Perhaps I shouldn't even think like that, let alone say it, but grief is not helped by being by oneself in a darkened house."

"I'm sure it isn't," Charlotte agreed with a wave of both sympathy and relief. "I wish society would allow people to cope with loss in whatever way is easiest for them, but I doubt it ever will."

"Oh that would be a miracle," Mina said hastily. "I wouldn't look for anything so—so incredibly unlikely. But I'm delighted you have called. Please come into the withdrawing room." She half turned, ready to lead the way. "The sun shines in there, and I refuse to lower the blinds—unless my mother-in-law should call. But that is not probable."

"I should be happy to. It sounds a delightful room," Charlotte accepted, following her across the hall and down a passageway. She noticed Mina walked very uprightly, almost as if she were too stiff to bend. "It is about just such a matter that I would appreciate your advice."

"Indeed?" Mina indicated a chair as soon as they were in the room, which was indeed most attractive, and at the moment filled with afternoon sunlight. "Please tell me how I am to be of service to you. Would you care for tea while we are talking?"

"Oh that would be most welcome," Charlotte agreed, both because she would very much like a drink after the omnibus ride and because it insured that she stay longer without having to seek an excuse.

Mina rang the bell with enthusiasm and ordered tea, sandwiches, pastries and cakes, then when the maid was gone, set-

148

tled herself to give Charlotte her entire attention. She sat on the forward edge of the chair, hands folded in her lap, half concealed by the lace, but her face was full of interest.

Charlotte was acutely aware of the underlying tragedy in the house, the unnatural silence, the strain in Mina so close under the surface of her composure. However, she explained that she was moving house, and all the things that had yet to be done before that could be accomplished satisfactorily. "I simply cannot decide whether the room would be too cold if I had it papered in green," she finished.

"What does your husband say?" Mina inquired.

"Oh nothing. I have not asked him," Charlotte replied. "I don't think he will have an opinion before it is done, only afterwards if it is not agreeable. Although I daresay he will not even know why he does not like it."

Mina shrugged very slightly. "My husband had most definite opinions. I had to be careful if I chose to change anything." A look of guilt filled her face, sudden and startlingly painful. "I am afraid my taste was sometimes vulgar."

"Oh surely not?" Charlotte said quickly. "Perhaps he merely meant that his own taste was exceedingly traditional. Some men hate any change, no matter how much it is actually an improvement."

"You are very kind, but I am sure I must have been in the wrong. I had the breakfast room repapered while he was at sea. I should not have done it without asking him. He was most vexed when he came home and saw it."

"Was it very different?" Charlotte inquired, uncertain whether she should pursue a subject which seemed to cause such distress. To look back on a quarrel, perhaps unsolved, when the other person was no longer alive and so beyond reconciliation, must be one of the most terribly painful aspects of bereavement. She longed to be of comfort, and had no idea how.

"Oh yes—I'm afraid so," Mina went on quietly, memory filling her voice, and there was pleasure in spite of the shivering pain. "I did everything in warm yellow. It looked as if it were entirely filled with sunlight. I loved it."

"It sounds very delightful," Charlotte said sincerely. "But you speak as though it were no longer so. Did he insist that you change it?"

"Yes." Mina turned away for a moment, averting her face. "That was what he said was vulgar, everything in tones and shades of the one color, apart from the furniture, of course. That remained mahogany. Actually"—she bit her lip as if even now it still needed some apology or explanation—"it has not yet been done. Oakley locked the door and said we should not use the room until it had been put back as it was before. Would you care to see it?"

"Oh indeed." Charlotte rose to her feet immediately. "I should like to very much." She meant it both for the sake of seeing what such a room would be like, and even more to find out what Oakley Winthrop had considered so offensive that he had been willing to initiate such a quarrel over it that it was still apparently unresolved.

Mina led her out of the withdrawing room, back along the passageway and out of the main hall in the opposite direction. The door to the breakfast room was apparently now unlocked, and Mina pushed it open and stood back.

Charlotte looked past her into one of the most charming rooms she had ever seen. As Mina had said, it appeared to be full of sunlight, but it was more than that which pleased, it was a sense of space and graciousness, a simplicity which was restful and yet totally welcoming.

"Oh you are most gifted," Charlotte said spontaneously. "It's quite lovely!" She turned to look at Mina, still standing in the doorway, but her face now filled with amazement.

"Is it?" she said with incredulity, and then a dawning pleasure. "Do you really think so?"

"Indeed I do," Charlotte answered her. "I should love to have such a room. If this is of your creation, then you have a kind of genius. I am so glad I met you while my entire house is still undecorated, because if you will give me your permission, I will most assuredly have a yellow room too. May I? Would you consider it a compliment and not an impertinence?"

Mina was glowing with pleasure like a child given an unexpected gift.

"I should be most flattered, Mrs. Pitt. Please do not think for a moment that I should mind. It is quite the nicest thing you could say." She backed out of the doorway in a kind of excitement, and swung around without noticing the maid crossing the hall behind her. Charlotte called out, but it was too late. Mina's hand caught the teapot. The maid shrieked and let go and the tray went clattering to the floor. The maid shrieked again and threw her apron over her face, and Mina let out a cry.

Charlotte could see immediately what had happened from the dark stain of wetness over Mina's wrist, where the scalding tea had run over her.

"Quickly!" Charlotte grasped her without explanation or apology. "Where is the kitchen?"

"There." Mina looked to her left, her face tight with pain.

The maid was still shrieking, but no one took any notice of her.

Charlotte half pushed Mina towards the passageway, then thought of a far better idea. There was a large bowl full of lilies on the hall table. She turned and dragged Mina towards it, then as soon as she could reach, seized the flowers and dumped them on the table and pushed Mina's hand into the bowl full of cold water.

"Ah!" Mina said in amazement, the pain easing out of her face. "Oh—how wonderful."

Charlotte smiled at her, then looked at the maid.

"Stop it," she commanded fiercely. "Nobody's blaming you. It was an accident. Now don't stand there making that horrible noise, go and do something useful. Go back to the kitchen and send the tweeny to clean up this mess, and you come back with a bag of ice, and a tea cloth wrung out of cold water and a solution of bicarbonate of soda, and another one that's clean and dry. Get on with you."

"Yes, miss. Right away, miss," the girl said, staring at Charlotte with a tear-stained face and not moving from the spot.

"Go on, Gwynneth," Mina urged her. "Do as you are told."

Charlotte pulled Mina's hand out of the flower bowl as the maid disappeared.

"We'd better go to the light and see how bad it is." She walked with Mina towards the central chandelier, lit in spite of the sun because of the drawn blinds. Without asking permission she undid the buttons on Mina's long cuffs and pushed back the black fabric.

"Oh!" Mina gasped.

Charlotte also drew in her breath sharply, not because of the red scald she expected to see, but the broad yellow-and-purple stain of bruising with its deeper blotches like finger marks over the flesh. There was also a certain irritated pinkness, from the burn, but nothing like as serious as she had feared, and there was no blistering.

Mina was absolutely motionless, paralyzed with horror.

Charlotte looked up and met her gaze.

Mina's cheeks burned hot and her eyes filled with a desperate shame, and then overwhelming guilt.

"Do you need any help?" Charlotte said simply. A dozen questions raced through her mind, none of them she could ask: Gracie's gossip in the park, Bart Mitchell's protectiveness and his anger, and the fear in Mina's eyes.

"Help! No ... no. I ... everything is ..." She stopped.

"Are you quite sure?" Charlotte was aching to ask if it had been Captain Winthrop who had done it, and did Bart know—when did he know, before Winthrop's death, or after?

"Yes." Mina swallowed and caught her breath, looking away. "Yes, I am perfectly all right, thank you. It really hurts very little now."

Charlotte did not know if she meant the burn or the bruising. She longed to look at the other wrist to see if it was the same, and even more to see under the black lace fichu at her throat, over her shoulders and back. Was that why she walked so stiffly? But there was no way she could do it without being unforgivably intrusive and breaking every tenuous thread of friendship she had built.

"Do you think you should see a doctor?" she asked with concern.

Mina's other hand went to her throat and she shook her head as she met Charlotte's eyes again. The pretense was back, at least on the surface. "Oh no. I think—I think it will heal quite well, thank you." She smiled wanly. "Your quick thought saved me so much. I really am most grateful to you."

"Had I not been here viewing your beautiful room it would not have happened," Charlotte replied, allowing the charade. "Do you think you should sit down for a little, and maybe have a tisane? You have had a most unpleasant experience."

"Yes—yes that would be an excellent idea," Mina agreed. "I hope you will stay too? I feel such a poor hostess to have been so clumsy."

"I should love to," Charlotte accepted immediately.

They were at the withdrawing room entrance when the front door opened and Bart Mitchell came in. He glanced, first at Mina, seeing her wrist with the black cuff open and trailing, then at Charlotte, his face suddenly tight with anxiety. Curiously, he said nothing.

"Mrs. Pitt came to visit me, Bart," Mina said in the sudden silence. "Wasn't that considerate of her?"

"Good afternoon, Mrs. Pitt." Bart's blue eyes were very

152

wide and direct, searching Charlotte's face. Then he looked back at Mina.

"I scalded myself," Mina said very slowly, as if she owed him some explanation. "Mrs. Pitt was very helpful, very quick . . ."

At that moment, as if in further support, Gwynneth reappeared with the towels. She looked over to Charlotte.

Mina held out her arm, which was beginning to look pink again where the bruise did not mar it.

"Here, allow me to help." Bart dropped his stick and hat on the settee and came forward, grasping the wet towel and holding it onto the burn while Charlotte wound dry cloth around it. His hands were sunburned brown, slender and strong, but he touched his sister's arm as if it were fragile enough to break at the merest pressure.

"Thank you, Mrs. Pitt," he said finally when it had been secured. "I think perhaps in view of the unpleasantness of the incident, Mrs. Winthrop should lie down for a while. She is not strong . . ."

"This is nothing," Mina began, then stopped again, her face filled with fear. She glanced at Bart, then at Charlotte. "I have not even given Mrs. Pitt any tea," she said helplessly, grasping at the trifling problem of etiquette when so obviously something of overwhelming magnitude filled her mind. "It was the tea I spilled."

"I will give Mrs. Pitt tea, my dear," Bart answered, staring at her with a penetrating gaze. "You go and lie down for a while. You will be far better able to keep that bandage upon your arm if you rest it on a pillow. If you insist upon sitting up for afternoon tea in the withdrawing room you are bound to loosen it."

"I—I suppose you are right," she agreed reluctantly, but still she did not leave. She looked at Bart, and then at Charlotte, anxiety deep in her face.

"Should you call a doctor?" Charlotte asked.

"No—no." Bart shook his head with complete decision. "I am sure that will not be necessary. You appear to have done extremely well." He flashed a smile, beautiful and sudden as April sun. "Now if Mina will lie down for a while, I shall be most happy to give you tea, Mrs. Pitt. Please come into the withdrawing room."

There was no civil alternative but to do as she was invited, while Mina, equally obediently, went upstairs.

Charlotte followed Bart into the withdrawing room and sat down where he indicated. Apparently Gwynneth had already gathered that she was supposed to bring tea, or else possibly she always did so at that time of day, but it was only a few moments before she appeared again, very carefully balancing a tray in front of her, and put it down on the table, bobbed a curtsy and withdrew with more haste than grace.

When the formalities of pouring and passing had been completed, Bart leaned back and regarded Charlotte with careful, intelligent eyes.

"It is an unusual kindness to call upon someone who is in mourning, Mrs. Pitt," he remarked.

She had been waiting for him to say something of the sort.

"I have been in mourning myself, Mr. Mitchell," she replied quite lightly. "And found it very hard to bear, even though I had my mother and my sister in the house at the time. I wished profoundly to have a little conversation that was not in hushed tones and had nothing whatever to do with the dead." She sipped her tea. "Of course I could not know if Mrs. Winthrop would feel the same, but it seemed very natural to give her the opportunity, should she wish to take it."

"You surprise me," he said candidly. His expression was casual and charming, but his eyes did not leave her face. "Mina was devoted to Oakley. I think some people do not realize quite what courage it requires to maintain such a calm exterior to the world."

How much was he lying? She had no doubt now that he had seen at least some of those bruises. How many more were there? Did he guess, or know?

"We each of us have our own way of dealing with grief." She smiled back at him, her easy words belying the tension she felt. "For some of us, to resume normality is helpful. Mrs. Winthrop showed me the beautiful breakfast room, which I found quite delightful. I think it is one of the loveliest I have ever seen."

His face tightened.

"Oh yes. Mina has a considerable gift with color and grace." He was watching her very closely, weighing her reaction, judging why she had raised the subject in the first place.

"I am sure Captain Winthrop would have seen how charming it was once he had become accustomed to it," she continued, watching him as frankly. Between them, unspoken but now almost palpable, lay the awful bruises, and Mina's humil-

154

iation and embarrassment. What had she told him? And immeasurably more important, when? Before Winthrop's death—or after?

He started to speak, and then changed his mind.

"I am in the process of moving house myself," Charlotte said to fill the silence. "It is one of the most exhausting things I have ever done. The detail that requires to be attended to seems never ending."

"Surely your builder is of assistance?" he asked, still watching her. The conversation was meaningless and they both knew it, but they had to speak of something. What thoughts were racing through his head?

She smiled. "Of course. But he leaves the matters of domestic decoration to me. Just at the moment I am torn between choosing one color because I think I care for it, and another because it may prove more practical."

"A dilemma," he agreed. "What is your decision?"

There was another silence between them. Ridiculous as it was, it seemed as if his question meant more than a trivial matter of color, as if he were also asking what she intended to do about the bruises—to carry the tale back, or to dismiss it.

She thought for several moments before replying. Then she met his remarkable eyes with total candor.

"I expect I shall consult my husband," she answered at length.

His face was bare of all expression.

"I suppose I should have expected that," he said levelly.

She was caught in a confusion of emotions, anger against Oakley Winthrop because it seemed he had been a bully, and if Gracie were correct, even a sadist; pity for Mina because she had first endured it, and now must walk in terror in case Bart had killed him, and were discovered; a fear both for Bart, and as he sat opposite her, even a twinge of fear for herself.

The silence was becoming oppressive.

"Since it is his home also, it would be only civil," she said hollowly.

A very slight amusement touched his lips.

"Do I gather from your choice of words that you will not necessarily abide by his decision, Mrs. Pitt?"

"Yes—I think that is so."

"You are a woman of remarkable self-will—and perhaps of courage."

She rose to her feet, forming a smile.

"Qualities of very dubious attraction," she said lightly. "But you have been most charming, Mr. Mitchell, and generous with your hospitality, especially in such trying circumstances. Thank you."

He stood up in a single movement and bowed very slightly.

"Thank you for your friendship to my sister—as thoughtful and considerate as it is at this particular time."

"I look forward to it," she replied noncommittedly, and inclined her head in acknowledgment. He saw her to the door, which the maid opened, handing her her cape, and she walked swiftly along Curzon Street towards the omnibus stop, her mind teeming with questions.

Pitt was late home, and Charlotte found it difficult waiting for him. Gracie had gone to bed and Daniel and Jemima were long asleep. Impatience consumed her so she could not sit down and do anything useful. There was mending waiting her attention, and it lay in her sewing box untouched. There were certainly letters to write.

Instead she pottered around the kitchen, picking up this, and poking at that, half cleaning the stove, emptying things from one jar into another, dropping the tea caddy and spilling its contents all over the floor. No one was there to see her sweep it up hastily and replace it all. The floor was perfectly clean, and it would be scalded with water anyway.

When at last she did hear his key in the door she straightened her skirts for the tenth time, pushed her hair out of her eyes, and ran down the hall to meet him.

His first reaction was alarm, in case there were something wrong, then when he saw her face he was delighted and held her tightly until after a few moments she pushed him away.

"Thomas, I have discovered something really important today."

"About the house?" He tried to sound interested, but she heard the weariness in his voice.

"No—that is not the same sort of important," she dismissed it totally. "I went to see Mina Winthrop—actually about papering the dining room."

"What?" He was incredulous. "What on earth do you mean? That's nonsense!"

"About what color to choose," she said impatiently, leading him back to the kitchen. "Not about doing it."

He was totally confused. "How would she know what color you should use?"

"She is very gifted at that sort of thing."

"How do you know?" He sat down at the kitchen table. "There are tea leaves on the floor here."

"I must have spilled a little," she said airily. "I discussed it with her at the memorial service for Oakley Winthrop. I went to see her today— Will you please listen, Thomas. This is important."

"I am listening. Can you put the kettle on at the same time? It's hours since I had a cup of tea."

"It is on. I'm about to make tea. Are you hungry too?"

"No, I think I'm too tired to eat."

She ran a bowl of water, putting something into it he did not see, and put it down on the floor in front of him. "Feet," she said absently.

"I'm not walking a beat," he answered with a smile. "Have you forgotten, I'm a superintendent now?" He bent forward and unlaced his boots, slipping his feet out with intense pleasure.

"Don't superintendents' feet get hot in boots?"

He smiled and put his feet gingerly into the cold water. "What's in it?"

"Epsom salts, same as always. Mrs. Winthrop has been beaten. And Oakley Winthrop may have been a sadist who liked to beat women anyway. I mean prostitutes—that sort of thing."

"What?" He looked up at her sharply. "How do you know? Did she tell you that?"

"No, of course not. She spilled hot water on her wrist, and I undid her cuffs to see it. She is purple and green with bruises."

"An accident . . ."

"No it wasn't. There were finger marks. And I'm almost sure her neck was bruised as well, and who knows what else on the rest of her body. That's why she wears long cuffs and high necks: to hide the bruises."

"You don't know that."

"Yes I do! And what is more, I am almost sure Bart Mitchell knows it too."

"How?"

"Because I spoke to her, and I watched her. She was bitterly ashamed, and embarrassed, and she didn't tell me how it happened. She would have, if it had been all right. Her husband did it, Thomas. The good Captain the Honorable Oakley Winthrop beat his wife."

"What makes you so sure Mitchell knows about it?"

"Because he saw the bruises as well, and said nothing, of course. If he'd not known he'd have been horrified and asked her what had happened!"

"Maybe he beat her?"

"Why would he? And anyway, she's afraid for him, Thomas, I'm sure of that. She is terrified he was the one who killed Winthrop."

"You mean you are not sure of it," he corrected. "People always say they are sure when what they mean is they think so, but they are not sure. Your kettle is boiling."

"It won't come to any harm." She waved a hand at it. "Thomas, Mina is afraid Bart killed Oakley Winthrop because of the way he treated her."

"I see," he said thoughtfully. "And how did you come upon the information about the man who beats prostitutes in the park? Mina Winthrop didn't tell you that, did she?"

"No of course not."

"I am waiting."

She took a deep breath. "Thomas, please don't be angry—she did it because she is afraid for you. If you don't forgive her, and say nothing whatever, I shall not forgive you."

"Forgive me for what?" His eyebrows rose.

"For not forgiving her, of course!"

"Who? Is it Emily?"

"Perhaps I had better not say." She had not even thought of blaming Emily, but it was an excellent idea. Emily was not Thomas's responsibility.

"However, she knew about it?" he said very carefully. "At least give me the truth of that."

"She went into the park at night, and one of the prostitutes told her. I mean, she got into a conversation—naturally . . ."

"Naturally," he agreed dryly. "Does Jack know about this? I doubt it will improve his parliamentary chances."

"Oh no. And you mustn't tell him!"

"I would not think of it."

"You promise?"

"I do." He smiled, although the amusement was very double edged.

"Thank you." She turned around and made the tea, giving it

158

a moment to brew, then poured him a steaming mugful and brought it back to him. She watched him carefully as he took his feet out of the water and she gave him the warm towel.

"Thank you," he said after several moments.

"For the tea," she said gravely, "or the towel?"

"For the information. Poor Mina."

"What are you going to do?"

"Have my tea and go to bed. I can't think any more tonight."

"I'm sorry. I should have waited."

He reached up and kissed her, and for some time Mina Winthrop and her troubles were forgotten.

At dawn the following morning, Billy Sowerbutts was driving his cart slowly along Knightsbridge towards Hyde Park Corner when he was forced to come to a stop because the traffic ahead of him was packed solid. He was put out; in fact come to think of it, he was definitely angry. What was the point in getting up early, when you ached to stay in bed and sink back into sleep, if you were going to spend half the bleeding morning sitting as still as Nelson's monument because some idiot ahead has stopped and is holding everything up?

For a hundred yards people were beginning to shout and curse. Someone's horse shied and backed, and two carts collided, locking wheels.

That was really the last straw. Billy Sowerbutts tied the reins of his animal to the rail and jumped down. He strode past everyone else right up to the offending vehicle, a gig, which extraordinarily had no animal between the shafts, as if someone had pushed it there by hand and then abandoned it, leaving it lying askew, its rear end sufficiently far into the line of traffic to have blocked the way.

"Idjut!" he said harshly. "What kind of a fool leaves a gig in a place like this. 'Ere! What the 'ell's the matter wif yer? This in't no place ter take a kip!" He strode around to the recumbent figure lolling in the back amid piles of old clothes. "Wake up, yer bleedin' idjut! Get out of 'ere! Yer 'oldin up the 'ole street!" He leaned forward and shook the man's shoulder, and felt his hand wet. He pulled it back, and in the broadening light saw his fingers dark with something. Then he leaned forward again and peered more closely at the man. He had no head.

"Jesus, Joseph and Mary!" he said, and fell over the shaft.

6

$P_{ITT\ SAT}$ at his desk staring at Tellman. He felt numb, as if he had been struck a physical blow and the flesh were still too newly bruised to hurt.

"Knightsbridge, just outside the park," Tellman repeated. "Headless, of course." His long face showed no inner triumph or superiority this morning. "He's still out there, Mr. Pitt; and we aren't any closer to the swine than we were in the beginning."

"Who was he?" Pitt asked slowly. "Anything else we know?"

"That's just it." Tellman screwed up his face. "He was a bus conductor."

Pitt was startled. "A bus conductor! Not a gentleman?"

"Definitely not. Just a very ordinary, very respectable little bus conductor," Tellman repeated. "On his way home from his last run—at least, not on his way home: that's the odd thing." He stared at Pitt. "He lives near the end of the line, which is out Shepherd's Bush way. That's what the omnibus company said."

"So what was he doing in Knightsbridge near the park?" Pitt asked the obvious question. "Is that where he was killed?"

Memory of past conversations flashed across Tellman's face, of Pitt's insistence, and then his own failure to find where Arledge had been killed.

"No—at least it doesn't look like it," he replied. "There's no way you can chop a man's head off without leaving rivers of blood around, and there's very little in the gig he was in."

"Gig? What gig?" Pitt demanded.

"Ordinary sort of gig, except no horse," Tellman replied.

"What do you mean a gig with no horse?" Pitt's voice was rising in spite of himself. "Either it's a vehicle to ride in or it's a cart to push!"

"I mean the horse wasn't there," Tellman said irritably. "Nobody's found it yet."

"The Headsman let it loose?"

"Apparently."

"What else?" Pitt leaned back, although no position was going to be comfortable today. "You have the head, I presume, since you know who he was and where he lived. Was he struck first? I don't suppose he had anything worth robbing him of?"

"Yes, he was hit first, pretty hard, then his head taken off cleanly. Much better job than Arledge, poor devil. He was coming home from work, still had his uniform on, and he had three and sixpence in his pockets, which was about right, and a watch worth about five pounds. But why would anyone pick a bus conductor to rob?"

"Nobody would," Pitt agreed unhappily. "Have you been to the family yet?"

Tellman's narrow mouth tightened. "It's still only half past eight." He omitted the "Sir." "Le Grange is on his way, just to inform her, like. Can't see as she'll be any help." He put his hands in his pockets and stood in front of the desk, staring down at Pitt. "We've got another lunatic. Seems he attacks anyone, as the fit takes him. No sense to it at all. I'm going to try Bedlam again. Maybe they refused someone, or let a maniac go a while back . . ." But his dark flat eyes registered no hope that it would produce anything. Then suddenly the emotion was there, raw and violent. "Someone's got to know him!" he said passionately. "All London's snapping at itself with suspicion, people are jumping at shadows, no one trusts anybody anymore—but someone knows him. Someone's seen his face afterwards, and known he wasn't right. Someone's seen a weapon, or knows about it—they've got to!"

Pitt frowned, ignoring the outburst. He knew it was true, he'd seen the fear in the eyes, heard the sharp edge to voices, the distrust, the defensiveness and the blame. "This gig, where did it come from? Whose is it?" He sat down.

Tellman looked slightly taken aback, but he hid it immediately.

161

"Don't know yet, sir. Not much in it, no easily identifiable marks."

"Well you'll know soon enough if it was his, although I can't see a bus conductor going home in a gig," Pitt said thoughtfully. "Which raises the question as to why he was in it at all."

"But it would be too much to hope it belonged to our lunatic." Tellman curled his lip. "He's far too fly for that!"

Pitt leaned farther back in his chair. Without thinking, he asked Tellman to sit down. "It raises the question of why use a gig at all," he went on. "Let us assume it was stolen, if it did not belong to either of them. What did he want a vehicle for?"

"To move the body," Tellman answered. "Which means he could have killed him anywhere—like Arledge."

"Yes, but more probably either somewhere which would in some fashion betray him or—or somewhere which would be inconvenient to leave him," Pitt said, thinking aloud.

"You mean where he would be found too soon, maybe?"

"Possibly. Where would this bus conductor have left the last bus?"

"Shepherd's Bush station, Silgate Lane."

"Long way from Hyde Park," Pitt observed. "Is that where he lived?"

"Quarter of a mile away."

"Well he certainly didn't need a gig for a quarter of a mile. See if someone had a gig stolen from that neighborhood. Shouldn't take long."

Tellman preempted his next question, leaning back a little in his chair.

"Don't know where he was killed yet, but should be somewhere around there. Unless he hit the poor fellow on the head and took him somewhere in the gig, so he could do the job in private. It's not actually so easy to cut a man's head off. Needs a swing and a lot of weight behind it." He shook his head unhappily. "Wasn't done in the gig. Could have taken him somewhere and tipped him out, cut off his head, then put the head and the body back in the gig and driven it to Hyde Park. But why? It doesn't make sense any way you look at it."

"Then there's something about it we don't know yet," Pitt reasoned. "Find out what it is, Tellman."

"Yes sir." Tellman rose to his feet, then hesitated.

Pitt was about to ask him what he wanted, then changed his mind.

"You know," Tellman said slowly, "I still don't know whether it's a lunatic or not. Even a madman's got to have some sort of sense to pick people—some place, a job, or an appearance—something that set him off. And it wasn't the same place, we know that. They didn't look much alike." He leaned a little on the back of his chair. "The first two, maybe, although Winthrop was a big man, Arledge was very thin, and probably ten or fifteen years older. But the bus conductor was a little bald fellow with wide shoulders and a potbelly. And he was still in his conductor's uniform, so anyone would know he wasn't a gentleman. In fact they couldn't have mistaken him for anyone but who he was." He frowned in irritation. "Why would anyone want to kill a bus conductor?"

"I don't know," Pitt confessed. "Unless he saw something to do with the murders. Although how our madman knew that is beyond me."

"Blackmail?" Tellman suggested.

"How?" Pitt tipped back in the chair again. "Even if he saw one of the murders, how would he know who the madman was, or where to find him?"

"Maybe he would," Tellman said slowly, his eyes widening. "Maybe our madman is somebody he would recognize—somebody anyone would recognize!"

Pitt sat up a little straighter. "Someone famous?"

"It would say why he had to kill a bus conductor!" Tellman's voice was firm and hard, his face bright with satisfaction.

"And the others?" Pitt asked. "Winthrop and Arledge?"

"There's a connection," Tellman said stubbornly. "I don't know what it is—but it's there. Somewhere in his black mind there's a reason for those two!"

"I'm damned if I know what it is," Pitt confessed.

"I'll find it," Tellman said between closed teeth. "And I'll see that bastard swing." Pitt forbore from comment.

The storm burst with the midday newspapers. The Hyde Park Headsman was on the front of every edition and there was a harsh note of panic in the screeds of print beneath. It was a little after one when Pitt's door was flung open and Assistant Commissioner Farnsworth strode in, leaving it swinging on its hinges behind him. His face was white except for two high spots of color in his cheeks.

"What the hell are you doing about it, Pitt?" he demanded.

163

"This lunatic is rampaging through London killing people at will. Three headless corpses, and you still haven't the faintest idea who he is or anything about him." He leaned over the desk towards Pitt, glaring at him. "You make the whole force look like incompetent fools. I've had Lord Winthrop in my office again, poor devil, asking me what we've done to find the man who murdered his son. And I've got nothing to tell him. Nothing! I have to stand there like a fool and make excuses. Everyone's talking about it—in the street, in the clubs, in houses, theaters, offices, they're even singing songs about it in the halls, so I'm told. We're a laughingstock, Pitt." His hands were clenching and unclenching in his emotion. "I trusted you, and you've let me down. I took Drummond's word for it that you were the man for the job, but it begins to look as if it is too big for you. You are not up to it!"

Pitt had no defense. The same doubts had begun to occur to him, although he could not think what anyone else could have done, least of all a man like Drummond, who had never been a detective himself. Nor, for that matter, had Farnsworth.

"If you wish to place the case with someone else, sir, then you had better do so," he said coldly. "I'll pass over all the information we have so far, and the leads we intend to follow."

Farnsworth looked taken aback. It was apparently not the answer he had expected.

"Don't be ridiculous, man. You cannot just abdicate your responsibility!" he said furiously, taking a step back. "What information do you have? Seems from what your inspector says that it's damned little."

It was little, but it galled Pitt that Tellman had discussed it with the assistant commissioner. Even if Farnsworth had asked him, Tellman should have referred him to Pitt. It was a bitter thought that he could not expect loyalty even from the foremost of his own men. That was a failure too.

"Winthrop was killed in a boat, which indicates he was not afraid of his killer." He began to list off the few facts they had. "He was hit from behind, then beheaded over the side, at around midnight. Arledge was also struck first, but he was killed somewhere other than the bandstand where he was found. He may or may not have known who killed him, but it is indicative that he was moved. If we can find where he was killed, it may tell us a great deal more. I have half a dozen men looking."

"Good God, man, it can't be far," Farnsworth exploded.

"How far can a madman carry a headless corpse around the heart of London, even in the middle of the night? How did he do it? Carriage, gig, horseback? Use your head, man!"

"There were no hoof marks or carriage tracks anywhere near the bandstand," Pitt said stiffly. "We searched the ground thoroughly, and there was nothing unusual whatever."

Farnsworth stood three paces away, then swung around.

"Well what was there, for Heaven's sake? He didn't carry him over his shoulder."

"Nothing unusual," Pitt repeated slowly, his thoughts racing. "Which means he was brought in something that passed that way in the normal course of events."

"Such as what?" Farnsworth demanded.

"The gardener's equipment . . ." Pitt said slowly.

"What? A lawn mower." Farnsworth's expression was filled with derision.

"Or a wheelbarrow." Pitt remembered le Grange saying something about seeing a man with a wheelbarrow. "Yes," he went on with increasing momentum. "A witness saw a wheelbarrow. That would have been it." He sat a little more upright as he said it. "He can't have been killed far away. You can't wheel a corpse 'round in a barrow through the streets . . ."

"Then find it," Farnsworth commanded. "What else? What about this wretched bus conductor this morning? What has he to do with the other two? What was he doing in the park?"

"We don't know that he was in the park."

"Of course he was in the park, man. Why else was he killed? He must have been in the park. Where was he last seen alive?"

"At the end of his route, in Shepherd's Bush."

"Shepherd's Bush?" Farnsworth's voice rose almost an octave. "That's miles from Hyde Park."

"Which raises the question of why the Headsman brought him back to the park to leave him," Pitt said.

"Because his madness has something to do with the park, of course," Farnsworth replied between his teeth, his patience fast wearing out. "He'll have knocked him senseless when he found him, and brought him to the park to take his head off there. That's obvious."

"If he didn't find him in the park, why kill him at all?" Pitt asked calmly, meeting Farnsworth's eyes.

"I don't know," Farnsworth said angrily, turning away. "For God's sake, man, that's your job to find out, and a dammed slow business you are making of it." He looked back, his expression controlled. "The public have a right to expect more of you, Pitt, and so do I. I took Drummond's counsel to promote you, against my own instincts, and I may say it looks as if I've made a mistake."

He seized the newspaper he had dropped on the desk. "Have you seen this? Look!" He opened it to show a large cartoon of two small policemen standing with their hands in their pockets and looking at the ground, while the giant figure of a masked man with an executioner's ax towered over a terrified London.

There was nothing to say. Farnsworth had no better ideas, but to point that out would be useless. He already knew it, which was part of what made him so angry. He too was helpless, and had to answer to the political pressures above him. This failure could end the hopes of his career. The men above him were not interested in excuses, or even reasons. They judged by results alone. They answered to the public, and the public was a fickle, frightened master who forgot quickly, forgave very little, and understood only what it wanted to.

He slammed the newspaper down on the desk.

"Get on with it, Pitt. I expect to hear something definite by tomorrow." And with that he turned and stalked out, leaving the door still open.

As soon as Farnsworth's footsteps had died away down the stairs, Bailey's head appeared around the door, pale and apologetic.

"What is it?" Pitt looked up.

Bailey pulled a face. "Don't take no notice of 'im," he said tentatively. " 'E couldn't do no better, an' we all know it."

"Thank you, Bailey," Pitt said sincerely. "But we'll have to do better if we're going to catch this—creature."

Bailey shivered very slightly. "D'yer reckon as 'e's mad, Mr. Pitt, or it's personal? What I don't understand is why that poor bleedin' little bus conductor? Gentlemen you can understand. They might 'ave done somethink."

Pitt smiled in spite of himself.

"I don't know, but I'm going to find out." He rose to his feet. "I'm going to find out what Arledge's keys open, for a start."

"Yes sir. Shall I tell Mr. Tellman, sir, or not—as I don't really know where you're goin'." He opened his eyes wide. "I can't say as I recall what you said."

"Then if I don't repeat it, you won't know, will you?" Pitt said with a smile.

"No sir, I won't," Bailey agreed happily.

Pitt took the two sets of keys and left for Mount Street. He hailed a cab and sat back to think while the driver eased his way through the traffic, stopping and starting, calling out encouragement and abuse.

Dulcie Arledge received him with courtesy, and if she were surprised to see him she concealed it with the sort of sensitivity he had come to expect of her.

"Good morning, Mr. Pitt." She did not rise from the sofa where she was seated. She was still dressed entirely in black, but it was gracefully slender in the new line, with little peaks at the point of the shoulder.

She wore an exquisite mourning brooch of jet and seed pearls at her throat and a mourning ring on her slender hand. Her face was composed and she managed to smile. "Is there something further I can help you with? I hear that there has been another death. Is that true?"

"Yes, ma'am, I am afraid it is."

"Oh dear. How very dreadful." She swallowed painfully. "Who—who was it?"

"An omnibus conductor, ma'am."

She was startled. "An omnibus conductor? But—but why would anyone—I mean. . ." She turned away as if embarrassed by her confusion. "Oh dear, I don't know what I mean. Was it in Hyde Park again?"

He hated having to tell her at all. It seemed such an added offense to a woman of such courage and sensibility.

"Just outside it," he said gently. "At least that is where he was found. We don't know where he was killed."

She looked up at him, her eyes dark and troubled. "Please sit down, Superintendent. Tell me what I can possibly do to help. I cannot think of any conceivable connection between my husband and an omnibus conductor. I have been searching my mind to think if Aidan ever mentioned Captain Winthrop, but I can think of nothing which would be of service. He knew a great many people, a large proportion of whom I never met."

"Concerned with his music?" he asked, accepting the invitation to sit.

"Indeed. He really was very gifted, and so in great demand."

Her eyes filled with tears. "He was a remarkable man, Superintendent. It is not only I who will miss him."

Pitt did not know what to say. Weeping, fainting, hysterics were embarrassing and left any man helpless, but there was a quality in this quiet, dignified grief which was uniquely moving, and in its own way left him feeling even more inadequate.

She must have seen his consternation.

"I'm so sorry," she apologized. "I have placed you in an impossible situation. What can you say? I should not have let my feelings intrude." She folded her hands. "What else could I help with?"

He produced the keys out of his pocket and passed them to her.

She took them and looked at one set first, then at the second with a frown on her face.

"These are our household keys," she said, holding aside the first set. "One is the front door. He used to come home late on occasions and would not keep the staff up to wait for him." She smiled very bleakly, looking at Pitt. "The small ones are desk drawers and so on. I think this is for the cellar. There were times when he wanted to go down and perhaps get himself a bottle of wine without asking Horton." She turned to the second set, a pucker between her brows. "But these I have no idea. I don't recognize any of them." She held up the two sets side by side. "They don't look alike, do they?"

"No ma'am," he agreed, and yet he saw in her eyes the same thought that occurred to him. They looked like another set of house keys.

She passed them back to him. "I'm sorry. I'm not being of any assistance."

"Of course you are," Pitt assured her quickly. "Your candor is invaluable. Few people would have the courage that you have in such fearful circumstances, let alone the clarity of mind to be of practical help. It distresses me to have to put it to you at all." He meant it profoundly.

She smiled at him, warmth filling her face.

"You are very generous, Superintendent. Although with someone as sympathetic as you have been, talking of Aidan, and the whole tragedy, is not as difficult as you may imagine. It is never far from my mind anyway, and to be able to be frank is something of a relief." She made a little gesture of rueful impatience. "People mean to be kind, but they will speak of anything else, skirting around the subject all the time, when we all know we are thinking of little else, whatever we may say."

He knew precisely what she meant, he had seen it countless times before, the embarrassment, the averted eyes, the hesitation, then the rush into meaningless, irrelevant speech.

"Please ask me whatever you wish," she invited.

"Thank you. On the possibility that Mr. Arledge actually met whoever killed him, or had some connection, however accidental or tenuous, I would like to follow his actions in the last week of his life."

"What a good idea," she agreed immediately. "I am sure I can help with that. I can bring you his diary of professional appointments. I kept it because I was looking ahead to see what he was doing, and of course I have since had to write a great many letters." She shrugged delicately and pulled a little face of distaste. "I expect everyone read about it in the newspapers, or heard, but that is not the same."

"I would appreciate it." He had not asked before because Arledge's professional engagements seemed so far removed from a violent murder by a madman.

"Of course." She rose to her feet and he stood also, without even thinking, and it seemed a natural gesture of courtesy toward her.

She went to a small, inlaid walnut escritoire and opened it, putting her hand to a dark green leather-bound book and bringing it out. She offered it to him.

He took it and opened it where it fell naturally and saw the entry for the day of Arledge's death. There was a notation of a rehearsal in the afternoon and nothing else. He looked up and met Dulcie's eyes.

"He had only the one appointment that day?" he asked.

"I am afraid I don't know," she answered. "There is only one written there, but he did sometimes, in fact really quite often, go out on the spur of the moment. That diary was largely for professional engagements."

"I see." He turned the pages back for a week, then started reading forwards. Rehearsals, performances and luncheon and dinner engagements for meeting with various people connected with future projects were all written in a neat, strong hand with bold capitals and clearly legible cursive script. It was an elegant hand, yet not florid. "If I may take this, I shall see what I can learn."

"Of course you may," she said eagerly. "I can give you the

names of certain people he worked with regularly. Sir James Lismore, for one; and Roderick Alberd. They would know many others, I am sure." She stood up again and turned back to the desk. "I have their addresses in here somewhere. Lady Lismore is a friend of long standing. I am sure she would give you every assistance."

"Thank you," he accepted, unsure if it would prove of any value at all, and torn between the desire to know Aidan Arledge better and the dislike of finding that he kept a mistress. It would be an appalling burden for this woman to bear, on top of bereavement. He decided at that moment that if it were not relevant to the case he would keep silent, forget it as if it had never happened. He would be quite prepared to return the keys to her and lie about it, say he had failed to find the doors they opened.

He thanked her again, stood facing her in the quiet room trying to think of something further to say, to offer comfort or hope, and nothing came to him. She smiled and bade him good-bye.

"You will tell me—what you find, won't you, Superintendent?" she said as he was almost at the door.

"If I find anything that leads to unraveling the mystery, I shall certainly tell you," he promised, and before she could decide whether that was the answer she sought, he allowed the maid to show him out.

He began with the names she had given him. Roderick Alberd proved to be an eccentric with flying hair and whiskers in the manner of the late Franz Liszt, and his study in which he received Pitt was dominated by a grand piano. Alberd wore a wine velvet jacket and a large, very floppy cravat. His voice when he spoke was rasping and unexpectedly high.

"Oh, grieved, Superintendent," he said with an expansive gesture. "In fact desolated. What a perfectly senseless way to die." He swiveled around to stare at Pitt with surprisingly intelligent blue eyes. "That is the sort of thing that should happen to rakes and bullies, unsophisticated men of violence without taste or culture, not to a man like Aidan Arledge. There was nothing uncouth or predatory in his nature. It is an affront to civilization itself. What have you done about it?" His look narrowed. "Why are you here?"

"I am trying to learn where he went and whom he saw in the last few days—" Pitt began, but was interrupted.

Alberd threw up his hands. "Good heavens, what for? Do you suppose this madman knew him personally?"

"I think their paths may have crossed," Pitt acceded. "I do not think he was chosen entirely at random. Can you help me? Your name was given me by his widow."

"Ah yes, poor soul. Well—" Alberd sat down on the piano stool and flexed his fingers, cracking the knuckles. His hands were extraordinarily wide with long, spatulate fingers. Pitt found himself fascinated watching them. Had anyone been strangled, those hands with their power would have haunted his dreams.

Pitt waited.

"He was killed on a Tuesday, as I recall. Found Wednesday morning, yes?" Alberd began, then apparently not requiring an answer, he continued. "Well on the Monday I saw him. Middle of the afternoon. We discussed a recital next month. I shall have to find someone else to conduct now. I confess, I had not even thought of that." He cracked his knuckles again. "When he left me he said he was going to visit a friend, I forget whom. It was of no concern to me, not anyone I knew—not a musical person, I believe."

"If you could remember . . ."

"Good heavens, Superintendent, surely you don't imagine . . . ? No, I assure you, it was a friend of long standing. I believe a close friend." He looked at Pitt with amusement.

"What else can you tell me about his work, who else may know his movements that week, Mr. Alberd?"

"Oh, let me see . . ." He thought for several moments, staring at the floor, then finally gave Pitt a list of his own engagements for the time, and all those occasions in which his path had crossed that of Aidan Arledge, or in many instances, places or functions he knew Arledge would have attended. When he had finished it was a surprisingly complete picture.

"Thank you." Pitt excused himself and took his leave with considerable hope.

He also visited Lady Lismore, and from her suggestion several others. Three days later he had learned where Aidan Arledge had been most of the last week of his life, and several places he visited regularly. Certain names occurred again and again. He determined to question them all.

171

In between he returned to Bow Street, often late in the evening, to learn what Tellman had found.

"Don't know where Arledge was killed," he admitted sourly, looking at Pitt with irritation. "I've had men searching the length and breadth of the park, and every man on the beat for a mile in every direction has been told to keep his eyes open. Nothing!"

"What about Yeats, the bus conductor?" Pitt looked up at him without expectation.

"Don't know where he was killed either." Tellman sat sideways in the chair. "But there are one or two likely places in Shepherd's Bush. At least we know where the gig came from. A man called Arburthnot reported it stolen from outside his house in Silgrave Road."

"I presume you looked in that immediate area for a murder site?" Pitt asked.

Tellman withered him with a glance. "Of course we did. One of the most likely was in the railway siding just off Silgrave Road. Ground is so soaked with oil and covered with cinders and the like, it's hard to tell if there's been blood there or not."

"Anyone see Yeats after he left the bus?"

Tellman shook his head.

"No one that'll say so. Driver saw him off, said good-night, and said Yeats started along Silgrave Road. He lives in Osman Gardens, about four or five streets away."

"Did anyone else get off the bus at the same time?"

"Half a dozen people." Tellman pulled a face. "Says he can't remember any of them because he had his back to them throughout the journey, and at the end all he could think of was getting home and putting his feet in a bowl of Epsom salts."

"What about regular passengers?" Pitt asked. "They will have noticed if there was anyone unusual. What do they say?"

"Could only find one regular," Tellman said grimly. "It's. not the sort of time for anyone who works, or goes to any place of trade or entertainment. It's later than the theaters. Anyway, who goes to the city theaters from Shepherd's Bush on a bus?"

Pitt was losing patience. "What did your one regular say? Have you learned anything at all, man?"

"As far as he could remember, there were six or seven people on the bus by the time it got to Shepherd's Bush. At least four of them were men, one young, three older, and as far as he could tell, biggish. He couldn't recall any of them. He was tired and had a toothache." Tellman's chin came up and his long face was tight. "And what have you learned . . . sir? Anything that would be of help to us?"

"I think Arledge kept a mistress, and I expect to find her within the next day or two," Pitt replied, rather rashly.

"Ah . . ." It was hard to know from Tellman's wince if he were interested or not. "Could explain Arledge's death, if the lady was married, but why Winthrop? Or was he her lover as well?"

"I won't know that until I have found her," Pitt answered, standing up and walking over towards the window. "And before you ask, I don't know what Yeats has to do with it either, unless in some way he knew something and was a blackmailer." Below him in the street a hansom had stopped and a large man was alighting with difficulty. An urchin with a broom did not bother to hide his amusement.

Tellman raised his eyebrows. "The lady lived in Shepherd's Bush?" he asked sarcastically.

"But a madman who kills without any pattern at all doesn't make sense either," Pitt replied.

"It has something to do with the park," Tellman said decisively. "Or why bring Yeats all the way back in a gig? Much safer simply to leave him in Shepherd's Bush. Why put him in the gig at all, for that matter?"

"Perhaps he didn't want him left where he was," Pitt suggested, leaving the window and sitting on the edge of the desk. "Maybe he brought him back to Hyde Park because that's where our murderer lives."

Tellman opened his mouth to argue, then changed his mind. "Maybe. Arledge's mistress and her husband, I suppose? Perhaps she's a very loose principled woman, and she was Winthrop's mistress too? But surely not the fat little conductor's?" His lantern face broke into a hard smile. "I'll be entertained to meet this woman."

Pitt stood up. "Then I had better get on and find her. You find out where Yeats and Arledge were killed."

"Yes sir." And still smiling to himself, Tellman stood up and went to the door.

But it was another two long days of painstaking work with petty details of discussions, meetings and partings, half-heard conversations and glimpses of people, before Pitt had traced a

173

dozen or so of Arledge's acquaintances and begun to eliminate them from any suspicion. He was losing heart. They were all very properly accounted for, and their relationships were above reproach.

Tired, sore footed and discouraged, Pitt presented himself at the door of a much respected businessman who had contributed funds to the small orchestra which Aidan Arledge had frequently conducted. Perhaps Mr. Jerome Carvell had a beautiful wife?

The door was opened by a tall butler with a long, curved nose and a supercilious mouth.

"Good evening, sir." He looked Pitt up and down questioningly. Apparently he was uncertain of what he saw. The weariness and confidence in Pitt's expression belied the rather sloppy abandon of his clothes and the dust covering his boots.

"Good evening," Pitt replied, fishing for his card and giving it to him. "I apologize for calling so late, and unannounced, but the matter is somewhat urgent. May I perhaps speak with Mr. or Mrs. Carvell?"

"I will ask Mr. Carvell if he will see you, sir," the butler replied.

"I should like to speak to Mrs. Carvell also," Pitt insisted.

"Impossible, sir."

"It is important."

The butler's eyebrows rose higher. "There is no Mrs. Carvell, sir."

"Oh." Pitt felt unreasonably disappointed. Even if Mr. Carvell were as good a friend to Arledge as he had been led to suppose, and knew of his personal life, he would not now betray it to the police.

"Did you wish to see Mr. Carvell, sir?" The butler looked a trifle impatient.

"Yes please," Pitt replied, more out of irritation than hope.

"Then if you will come this way, sir, I will inquire if that is possible." Turning on his heel, the butler led the way to a small, very gracious study, wood paneled and lined with shelves of leather-bound books which looked unusually well read, arranged in order of subject, not of appearance.

Pitt was left for barely five minutes, during which time he looked at the titles and noted such areas of interest as exploration, classical drama, entomology, medieval architecture and the raising of roses. Then the door opened and he saw a man of perhaps forty-five. His fairish hair was beginning to turn gray at the temples and his face was of marked individuality and extraordinary intelligence. No one would have called him handsome—his skin was marked by some past disease, perhaps smallpox, and his teeth were far from straight—and yet he had such humor and perception that Pitt found himself regarding him with immediate liking.

"Mr. Carvell?"

"Yes?" Carvell came in looking anxious. "Superintendent Pitt? Have I done something amiss? I was not aware of anything . . ."

"I doubt there is anything, sir," Pitt replied honestly. "I am calling only in case you may have some knowledge which could help . . ."

"Oh dear. With what?" Carvell came farther in and waved absently for Pitt to sit down. He perched on one of the other easy chairs. "I don't think I know anything remotely useful to the police. I am a man of business. I know of no crimes. Has someone embezzled money?"

He looked so transparently innocent Pitt almost abandoned the quest altogether. It was only the necessity of explaining his presence at all that made him continue.

"Not so far as I am aware, Mr. Carvell. It is in connection with the death of Mr. Aidan Arledge. I believe—" He stopped. Carvell's face had gone completely white and he looked so profoundly distressed Pitt was afraid for him. He seemed to be having difficulty breathing. Pitt had been about to say "I believe you knew him"; but such a remark now would have been absurd. "Can I fetch you a glass of water?" he offered, rising to his feet. "Or brandy?" He looked around for a decanter or a tantalus.

"No—no—I apologize," Carvell stammered. "I—I—" He came to a halt, not knowing what to say. There was no reasonable explanation. He blinked several times.

At last Pitt saw the decanter. It looked like Madeira in it, but it would be better than nothing. He could see no glasses, so he simply picked up the whole thing and held it to Carvell's lips.

"Really—I . . ." Carvell stuttered, then took a long gulp and sat back, breathing hard. His face regained some color and Pitt put the decanter down on the table next to him and went back to his own seat. "Thank you," Carvell said wretchedly. "I really do apologize. I—I cannot think what came over me. . . ." But the grief in his face made it tragically obvious what had so robbed him of composure.

175

"No apology is necessary," Pitt said with a strange, dull ache of pity inside him. "It is I who should seek pardon. I was extremely clumsy in broaching the subject so very bluntly. I take it you were extremely fond of Mr. Arledge?"

"Yes—yes, we have been friends for a great number of years. In fact since youth. It is such a—a terrible way to die. . . ." His voice was husky with the crowding emotions he felt.

"It is," Pitt agreed. "But I think you can be assured that he knew nothing of it. One quick blow, and he would have lost sensibility. It is only terrible for those of us who now know the full details."

"You are very considerate. I wish—" Carvell stopped abruptly. "I have no idea what I can tell you, Superintendent." He looked at Pitt earnestly. "I know nothing about it at all. And I have naturally searched my brains to see if there is anything I could have done to prevent it, to foresee such—such an abominable thing, but I cannot. It was a bolt from nowhere! There was no"—he pulled his lips back in a ghastly caricature of a smile—" 'cloud bigger than a man's hand' on the horizon. One day everything was as usual, all the pleasures one takes for granted, the sun, the earth brimming with returning life, young people everywhere full of hopes and ambitions, old men full of memories, good food, good wine, good companionship, fine books and exquisite music." He sighed. "The world in its ordered course. Then suddenly . . ." His eyes filled with tears and he turned away, ashamed, blinking to cover his embarrassment.

Pitt felt acutely for him.

"We are all very shaken by it," he said quietly. "And very afraid. That is why I am obliged to intrude upon people in this fashion. Any help you can give, anything at all, may assist us to catch whoever is doing this. Did you know Captain Winthrop? Did Mr. Arledge ever speak of him to you?" He was evading the real issue, and he knew it, but he wanted to give Carvell time to regain his composure. Even while he was doing it, he knew it was tactically a mistake. Tellman would not have hesitated.

"Captain Winthrop?" Carvell looked totally confused. "Oh, yes, the first man who was . . . murdered. No. No, I cannot say I had heard of him before that. Oh—just a moment. Yes, I had heard his name mentioned, by a Mr. Bartholomew Mitchell, with whom I have had slight dealings. About a matter of business. I believe it was Mrs. Winthrop's name, in fact. Mrs. Winthrop is his sister, I think."

"May I ask what business, sir?"

"He purchased some shares on her behalf. I cannot think it could possibly have any connection."

"No, I cannot think of any either. When was the last time you saw Mr. Arledge?"

Again his face paled. "The evening of the day before he died, Superintendent. We had supper together after a performance. It was late and he knew his own household would have retired . . ."

"I see." Pitt pulled the set of keys out of his pocket and held them up. He was about to ask if Carvell knew what they were when the expression in his face made the question unnecessary.

"Where—" he began, then fell silent, staring helplessly at Pitt.

"Do they fit doors in this house, Mr. Carvell?" Pitt asked.

Carvell gulped. "Yes," he said huskily.

Pitt took the largest. "The front door?"

"The back," Carvell corrected. "It—it seems . . ."

"Of course. And these?" He held up the other two.

Carvell said nothing.

"Please, sir. It would be most undignified to have to obtain a warrant and search through all the doors and cupboards and drawers in the house."

Carvell paled even more and he looked desperately unhappy.

"Do you—do you have to . . . go through his—his things?" he stammered.

"What did he keep here?" Pitt asked with wrenching distaste. It was grossly intrusive, and yet he dared not avoid it.

"Personal toiletries." Carvell spoke jerkily, as if he had to wrench each item from his memory. "A little clean linen, evening dress, some cuff links and collar studs. Nothing that can possibly be of use to you, Superintendent."

"A silver-backed hairbrush?"

"Yes—I think so."

"I see."

"Do you? I loved him, Superintendent. I have no idea whether you can understand what that means. All my adult life I . . ." He bent his head and covered his face with his hands. "What's the use? I thought it would be a relief if I could share it with someone. At least be able to admit to being bereaved." His voice choked with pain. "I had to keep it secret, pretend

177

I was merely a friend, that he meant no more to me than that. Have you any idea what it is like to lose the person you love most in the world, and have to behave as if it were a mere acquaintance? Have you?" He looked up suddenly, his face stained with tears, his emotion naked.

"No," Pitt said honestly. "It would be impertinent of me to say I know how you must hurt. But I can imagine it must be unbearably deep. I offer you my condolences, which I know are worth nothing."

"Not nothing, Superintendent. It is something to have at least one person understand you."

"Did Mrs. Arledge know of your—your regard?"

Carvell looked appalled.

"Dear Heaven, no!"

"You are sure?"

He shook his head vehemently. "Aidan was sure. I have never actually met her except for a few moments at a concert, quite by accident. I did not wish . . . Can you understand?"

"I see." Pitt could only guess at the emotions of jealousy, guilt and fear which might have stormed through his mind.

"Do you?" Carvell said with only a thread of bitterness.

He looked utterly wretched. Pitt was acutely aware of his isolation. There was no one to comfort him in his grief, no one even to be aware of it.

Carvell looked up. "Who did this terrible thing, Superintendent? Is there really some demented soul loose in London with a lust for—for blood? Why should he have killed Aidan? He harmed no one. . . ."

"I don't know Mr. Carvell," Pitt confessed. "The more I learn of the facts, the less I feel I grasp the elements of it." There was nothing more to add, no questions he could think of that would have any meaning, even if he received an honest answer. He had come looking for a mistress, a cause for jealousy, a link with Winthrop. He had found instead a gentle, articulate man devastated with a very private and personal grief.

He excused himself and went out into the spring evening under a calm sky where an early moon had risen even before the sun had set.

"You've found her!" Farnsworth said the following morning, sitting bolt upright in the chair in Pitt's office. "What about the husband? What is he like? What did he say? Did he admit any connection with Winthrop? Never mind, you'll find it. Have

178

you arrested him yet? When shall we have something to tell the public?"

"His name is Jerome Carvell, and he's a quiet, respectable businessman," Pitt began.

"For Heaven's sake, Pitt!" Farnsworth exploded, his cheeks suffusing with color. "I don't care if he's an archdeacon of the church! His wife was having an affair with Arledge, and he found out about it and took his revenge. You'll find the proof if you look for it."

"There is no Mrs. Carvell."

Farnsworth's face fell. "Then what on earth are you telling me for? I thought you said you found the place where these alternative keys fitted? If he wasn't having an affair, what on earth did he have keys to the house for?"

"He *was* having an affair," Pitt said slowly, hating having to try to explain this to Farnsworth.

"Make sense, Pitt," Farnsworth said between his teeth. "Was he having an affair with Carvell's wife, or sister or whatever she is, or was he not? You are trying my patience too far."

"He was having an affair with Carvell himself," Pitt replied quietly. "If *affair* is the right word. It seemed they have loved each other for over thirty years."

Farnsworth was dumbfounded, then as the full meaning of what Pitt had said dawned on him, he was filled with anger and outrage.

"Good God, man, you're talking about it as if—as if it were . . ."

Pitt said nothing, but stared at Farnsworth with cold eyes, his mind filled with the tortured face of Jerome Carvell.

Farnsworth stopped, the words dying on his lips without his knowing why.

"Well you'd better get on and arrest him!" he said, rising to his feet. "I don't know what you're doing sitting around here."

"I can't arrest him," Pitt replied. "There's no evidence that he killed Arledge, and none at all that he even knew Winthrop."

"For God's sake, man, he was having an illegal relationship with Arledge." He leaned over the desk, glaring at Pitt. "What more do you want? They quarreled and this man—what's his name—killed him. You can't need me to remind you how many murders are domestic—or spring from lovers' quarrels. You've got your man. Arrest him before he kills again." He straightened up as if preparing to leave, the matter settled.

"I can't," Pitt repeated. "There is no evidence."

"What do you want, an eyewitness?" Farnsworth demanded, his face darkening with anger. "He probably killed him in his house, which is why you couldn't find the site of the crime before. You have searched his premises, Pitt?"

"No."

"You blithering incompetent!" Farnsworth exploded. "What's the matter with you, man? Are you ill? I feared you were promoted beyond your ability, but this is absurd. Get Tellman to search the place immediately, and then arrest the man."

Pitt felt his face burn with anger and a kind of embarrassment for both Farnsworth's ignorance and assumption, and for Carvell's crippling and so obvious emotion.

"I have no grounds for searching his house," he said coldly. "Arledge stayed there sometimes. That is not a crime. And there is nothing whatever to connect Carvell with Winthrop or the omnibus conductor."

Farnsworth's lip curled.

"If the man is a sodomite he probably approached Winthrop, and when Winthrop rebuffed him he flew into a rage and killed him," he said with conviction. "And as for Yeats, perhaps he knew something. He might have been in the park and witnessed the quarrel. He tried blackmail and was killed for his pains. Lose no sleep over that. Filthy crime, blackmail."

"There's no proof of any of it," Pitt protested as Farnsworth took another step towards the door. "We don't know where Carvell was the night Winthrop was killed. He may have been dining with the local vicar."

"Well find out, Pitt!" Farnsworth spat between clenched teeth, his voice sharp with his own fear. "That's your job. I expect you to report an arrest within forty-eight hours at the outside. I shall tell the Home Secretary we have our man, it is just a matter of collecting irrefutable evidence."

"It's a matter of collecting any evidence at all," Pitt retorted. "All we know so far is that Carvell loved Arledge. For Heaven's sake, if that were evidence of a murder, we should have to arrest the husband or wife of every victim in the country."

"That is hardly the same," Farnsworth said viciously. "We are talking about unnatural relations, not a normal marriage between husband and wife!"

"I thought you said most murders were domestic anyway?" Pitt said with a sharp note of sarcasm.

"Get out and do your job." Farnsworth pointed his finger at Pitt. "Now." And without waiting for any further debate he went out of the door and left it wide open.

Pitt went to the top of the stairs after him.

"Tellman!" he shouted, more violently than he had intended.

Le Grange appeared in the passageway at the bottom just as Farnsworth went out into the street.

"Yes sir? Did you want Mr. Tellman, sir?" he asked with elaborate innocence.

"Of course I did! What in the hell do you suppose I called him for?" Pitt retorted.

"Yes sir. He's working on some papers—I think. I'll ask him to come up, sir."

"Don't ask him, le Grange, tell him!" Pitt said.

Le Grange disappeared instantly, but it was another full ten minutes with Pitt pacing the floor before Tellman came in the door and closed it, his face registering bland complacency. No doubt Farnsworth's exchange with Pitt had been heard, and reported over half the station.

"Yes sir?" Tellman said inquiringly, and Pitt was positive he knew perfectly well what he was wanted for.

"Go and get a warrant to search the house and grounds of number twelve Green Street."

"Green Street?"

"Off Park Lane, two south of Oxford Street. It is the residence of a Mr. Jerome Carvell."

"Yes sir. What am I looking for, sir?"

"Evidence that Aidan Arledge was murdered there, or that the owner, Jerome Carvell, knew Winthrop or the bus conductor, Yeats."

"Yes sir." Tellman went to the door, then turned and looked at Pitt with wide eyes. "What would be evidence of knowing a bus conductor, sir?"

"A letter with his name on it—or a note of his address, any reference to him," Pitt replied levelly.

"Yes sir. I'll get a warrant." Before Pitt could add anything else, and make the remark that was on his tongue, Tellman was gone. Pitt strode to the door after him and stood on the landing.

"Tellman!"

Tellman turned on the stairs and looked up. "Yes, Mr. Pitt?"

"You'd better be civil to him. Mr. Carvell is a respected

businessman and has not committed any offense so far as we know. Don't forget that!"

"No sir, of course not, sir," Tellman said with a smile, then went on down the stairs.

Pitt went on the next errand he was loathing. He spent ten minutes in front of the mirror retying his cravat and adjusting his coat and rearranging the things in his pockets, trying to put off the moment. Eventually it became unavoidable, and he took his hat from the stand and went out and down the stairs. He stopped at the desk and the sergeant looked at his tidy appearance with surprise and some respect.

"I'm going to see Mrs. Arledge," Pitt said huskily. "If Inspector Tellman comes back before I do, have him wait for me. I want to know what he found."

"Yes sir! Sir . . ."

"Yes, Sergeant?"

"Do you think this Mr. Carvell did it, Mr. Pitt, sir?"

"No—no I don't think so, but I suppose it's possible."

"Yes sir. Forgive me, sir, but I had to ask."

Pitt smiled at him, and went out to find a hansom.

"Yes, Superintendent?" Dulcie Arledge said with her characteristic courtesy, and no apparent surprise. She was still dressed in total black, and as before it was beautifully cut, this time the full sleeves were decorated with black velvet bows at the shoulders, flat and neat and unostentatious. Her face pinched a little as she recognized him, a shadow crossing her eyes. "Have you learned something?"

He hated having to tell her, but there were questions he had to ask, and from their nature she would know there was ugliness and suspicion behind them. The fact that she had already guessed, at least in part, made it easier. They were in the withdrawing room and he waited for her to resume her seat, then sat on the elegant overstuffed sofa opposite her.

"I have found the doors for the keys, Mrs. Arledge," he began.

She took a deep breath. "Yes?" she said huskily.

"I am sorry, it is another house."

She looked at him without blinking. Her eyes were very steady and very blue. In her lap her hands were clasped together till the knuckles were white.

182

"A woman?" she asked very quietly, her voice little more than a whisper.

He wished he could have said that it was. It would have been better than what he had to say. He would like to have avoided telling her altogether but there was every possibility it was going to become public, and very soon, if Farnsworth had his way.

"Did you think that your husband might have been—might have cared for someone else?" he asked.

She was very pale and she avoided his eyes, staring down at the bright pattern of the carpet.

"It is something a woman has to learn to resign herself to, Mr. Pitt. One tries not to believe it, but . . ." She looked up at him suddenly. "Yes, if I am honest, it had occurred to me. There were small things, absences that he did not explain, gifts, things I had not given him. I wondered . . ."

There was no need to tell her it had lasted thirty years. He could at least spare her that.

"Superintendent."

"Yes, ma'am?"

She was searching his face. "Is she—married?"

The reason for her question was obvious; it was the same thought which had driven Farnsworth.

"Why do you hesitate, Superintendent?" she asked, anxiety in her voice now. "Is she—very young?" She stumbled over the word. "She has a father, perhaps? Or a brother . . ." She trailed off.

"The house belongs to a man, Mrs. Arledge."

Her brow puckered.

"I don't understand. I thought you said—" She stopped.

He could no longer evade the issue.

"The person your husband loved is a man."

She was totally confounded.

"A—a man . . . ?"

"I am sorry." He felt brutal and guilty of a terrible intrusion.

"But that's—impossible!" Suddenly her face flushed scarlet and her eyes were wide, stunned. "It cannot be. You made a mistake. It's—no—no!"

"I wish I had, ma'am, but I have not."

"You must have," she repeated foolishly. "It cannot be. . . ."

"He admitted it readily, and your husband's belongings, among them a silver-backed hairbrush, a pair to the one upstairs, were in the dressing room."

"It's—horrible," she said, shaking her head repeatedly, fiercely. "Why have you told me this—this—monstrosity?"

"I would much rather not have, Mrs. Arledge," he said with intense feeling. "If I could have allowed his secret to die with him, I would have done so. But I need to ask a great many more questions, and from them you would have known that there was something." He looked at her earnestly, willing her to believe him. "You would have been left with all the horror and the fears, until perhaps you would have read about it in the newspapers instead."

She stared at him helplessly, her face still full of denial.

"What questions?" she said at last. Her voice caught in her throat, but it was obvious that at last her intelligence was reasserting itself, in spite of the horror and her new, unimagined pain.

"Any other friends to whom your husband was extremely close?" he said gently. "Perhaps you could show me all the gifts he received that you did not give him, or know where they came from. Can you recall any occasions on which he was distressed in the last three or four weeks? When you think perhaps he may have been involved in a quarrel or a situation of high emotional anxiety or trouble."

"You mean—you mean he may have quarreled with this man . . . over some other person?" She was quick to seize the point and all its implications.

"It is possible, Mrs. Arledge."

She was very pale. "Yes—yes I suppose it is. And when I look back, how dreadfully it makes sense." She covered her face with her hands and sat motionless. He saw her shoulders rise and fall as she breathed deeply, in and out, in an effort to retain control of herself.

He stood up and went to the chiffonnier to see if he could find a decanter of sherry or Madeira to pour for her. It took him only a moment to see it and return with a glass. He waited until she looked up.

"Thank you," she said very quietly, accepting it with trembling hands. "You are most considerate, Superintendent. I am sorry to have so little mastery of myself. I have had a shock I could never have imagined—in my wildest and most fearful dreams. It will take me some little time to—to believe it." She looked down at the glass in her hands and sipped the sherry, and then her face crumpled. "I suppose I do have to believe it?"

He was still standing close to her.

"I am afraid it is true, Mrs. Arledge. But it does not invalidate all that was good in him, his generosity, his love and reverence for what was beautiful, his humor . . ."

"How can you . . ." she began, then bit back the words. "Poor Aidan." She lifted her eyes. "Superintendent, will this have to be made public? Couldn't he be allowed to rest in peace? It is not his crime that he was murdered. If he had died in his sleep no one would ever have known."

"I wish I could promise it to you," he said honestly. "But if this man is implicated in his death, then it will become public in all probability as soon as he is arrested. Certainly at his trial."

She looked as if he had struck her. It was several moments before she could master concentration to form her next question, and he stood by helplessly, wishing there were anything at all he could do to ease her burden.

"Do you believe this—this man—killed Aidan, Superintendent?" she said at last, her voice tight with the effort of control.

"I don't know," he said honestly. "I am inclined to think not. There is no evidence that he did, but it seems very likely that it is somehow concerned with their friendship."

Her brows furrowed with her effort to grasp the incomprehensible.

"I don't understand. What has Captain Winthrop to do with it? Or this other person—the omnibus conductor?"

"I don't know," he confessed. "I think there may be someone else involved whose name we do not yet know."

She looked away, towards the window and the sunlight in the garden beyond.

"How hideous. I am afraid it is all beyond my understanding." Suddenly she shivered convulsively. "But of course I will give you any help I can. I am trying to realize I did not know Aidan nearly as well as I imagined I did. But what I do know, you have only to ask me, and I will tell you."

"Thank you. I appreciate your candor, ma'am, and your courage."

She looked at him, smiling weakly. "Ask what you wish, Superintendent."

He spent three more hours asking her gently every detail of Arledge's life that he could think of and going through his belongings again, taking with him all those few personal items which she said she had not given him, nor, to her knowledge, had he bought for himself.

She showed him everything he asked to see, and answered all his questions with a simple candor, as if she were too stunned by the fearful revelation he had brought even to protect those few memories which normally would have been dearest and most private.

"We were married twenty years," she said thoughtfully, staring at an old theater program. "I didn't know he had kept this. It was the first concert he took me to. I was very unsophisticated then. I had just come from the country, where I grew up." She turned the worn piece of paper over and over in her hands. "You would have thought me very naive then, Superintendent."

"I doubt it, ma'am," he said gently. "I grew up in the country also."

She looked at him quickly, warmth in her face for the first time. "Did you? Where? Oh, I'm sorry, that is . . ."

"Not at all. Hertfordshire, on a large estate. My father was the gamekeeper." Why had he told her that? It was something he never mentioned, part of a past which included pain and a loss which still hurt, an injustice never remedied.

"Was he?" Her eyes, clear and dark blue, were full of uncritical interest. "Then you love the land too; you understand its beauty, and sometimes its cruelty, its economy of survival? Of course you do." She turned away, looking beyond the richly curtained windows to the rooftops and sky. "It seems so much . . . cleaner . . . doesn't it? More honest."

He thought how she must feel, the rage and confusion inside her over all the years which now must seem wasted, filled with betrayal, even memories twisted upon themselves and gone sour. She would recover from his death, it was a clean wound, but his deceit would hurt forever, it took away not only the future but the past also. Her whole adult life, twenty years, made a sham.

"Yes," he said with profound feeling. "Much more honest. The quick kill of one animal by another is the necessity of nature and an honorable thing."

She looked at him with amazement and admiration.

"You are a remarkable man, Superintendent. I am deeply grateful that it is you who are in command of this . . . this terrible affair. I would not have thought anyone could make this easier, but you have."

186

He did not know what to say. Any words seemed trite, so he smiled in silence and turned to the next piece of paper, an invitation to a hunt ball, and slowly, with stumbling memory, she recalled the time and the event.

He left early in the evening feeling weary and profoundly saddened. From what he had learned, there were numerous opportunities for further entanglements. Oakley Winthrop could have been one of them, or Bart Mitchell, or almost anyone else.

He arrived at Bow Street to find Tellman waiting on the landing outside his office, his long, clever face creased with anger and concern. He had obviously been waiting some time.

"What did you find?" Pitt asked, reaching the top of the stairs.

"Not a damn thing," Tellman answered, following him across the short space of the landing to the office door, then inside without waiting to be invited. "Nothing! He and Arledge were obviously lovers, but although that's a crime, we couldn't prosecute without seeing them doing it, unless someone complained. And since Arledge is dead, that's not likely."

"Arledge wasn't killed there?"

"No."

"You're sure?"

"Not unless he put his head over the bath and Carvell mopped the whole thing down afterwards," Tellman said sarcastically. "He stayed there all right, half lived there, I shouldn't wonder. But he wasn't killed there."

"I presume you looked in the garden as well?"

"Of course I did! And before you ask, it's all covered with paving and flower beds or grass, and none of it has been dug up in years. I even looked in the coal cellar and the gardener's shed. He wasn't killed there." He stared at Pitt, his brows drawn down in thought, his lips pursed. "Are you going to arrest him?"

"No."

Tellman breathed in and out slowly. "Good," he said at last. "Because I'm not sure as he didn't do it. But I am damn sure we haven't got a thing to prove that he did." He winced as if he had been hurt. "I hate arresting someone and then not getting a conviction."

Pitt looked at him, trying to read his face.

Tellman smiled bleakly. "Nor do I want to get the wrong

187

man," he added grudgingly. "Though God knows who the right one is."

Emily's concentration was torn in two directions. It was of primary importance that she give every possible help to Jack, even if all their efforts were almost certainly in vain. But she was also deeply concerned for Pitt. She had heard the remarks of various people with connections in government and political circles, and she knew the climate of fear and blame that prevailed. No one had any ideas to offer, and certainly no assistance, but the incessant public clamor had made them frightened for their own positions, and consequently quick to blame others.

Now that the by-election date had been announced there were speeches and articles to be delivered, and now and then a public appearance of a more social nature at a ball or a concert. Some of these were very formal, such as receptions for foreign ambassadors or visiting dignitaries, some of a more casual kind, such as the soiree this evening. Since Mina Winthrop was obviously in mourning, she could not be invited, similarly Dulcie Arledge, but Emily had done the next best thing by asking Victor Garrick to play the cello as part of the entertainment for her guests, and then naturally as he was there, Thora Garrick was invited as well. Emily was not sure what that might accomplish, but one did not require to see an end in order for it to be achieved.

The guests were almost all included for political purposes, people of influence of one sort or another, and the whole event would be hard work. There would be no time for the pleasant indulgence of gossip. Every word must be watched and weighed. Emily stood at the top of the stairs and gazed across the sea of heads, the men's smooth, the women's all manner of elaborate coiffeur, many of them bristling with feathers, tiaras and jeweled pins. She tried to compose her mind. There were at least as many enemies here as friends—not only Jack's enemies, but Pitt's as well. Many of them would be members of the Inner Circle, some peripheral, as Micah Drummond had been, hardly even knowing what it really meant. Others would be high in its rungs of power, able to call on debts and loyalties of staggering proportions, even of career or future if need be, and able to pronounce terrible punishments if disobedience or treachery were suspected. But no outsider knew which was which; it could be any innocent, smiling face, any courteous gentleman passing polite inanities, any harmless-seeming man with white hair and benign smile.

Involuntarily she shivered, not only with fear but with anger. She saw the fair hair of Victor Garrick shining under the chandeliers and began her way down to greet him.

"Good evening, Mr. Garrick," she said as she reached the bottom and approached him, standing with his cello held very carefully. It was a beautiful instrument, warm polished wood the color of sherry in sunlight, and richly shaped. Its curves made her want to reach out and touch it, but she knew it would be an intrusion. He held the instrument almost as if it were a woman he loved. "I am so grateful to you for consenting to come," she went on. "After hearing you play at Captain Winthrop's memorial service I could not think of anyone else."

"Thank you, Mrs. Radley." He smiled, meeting her eyes with unusual frankness. He seemed to search beneath the easy surface to know if she meant what she said, if she had any understanding of music and its meaning, its textures and values, or if she were simply being polite. He was apparently satisfied. A slow smile curved his lips. "I love to play."

She sought for something further to say; the situation seemed to invite it.

"It is a very beautiful instrument you have. Is it very old?"

His face darkened immediately and a look of acute pain filled his eyes. "Yes. It's not a Guanerius, of course; but it is Italian, and about the same period."

She was confused. "Is that not good?"

"It's exquisite," he said in a soft, fierce whisper. "It's priceless; money is nothing, meaningless beside this sort of beauty. Money is just so much paper—this is passion, eloquence, love, grief, everything of meaning. This is the voice of man's soul."

She was about to ask him if someone had insulted him by giving it a monetary value when her eye caught a blemish on the perfect smoothness of the wood, a bruise. She felt a sudden distress herself. The instrument had so many of the qualities of a living thing, and yet not the great gift of healing itself. That mark would remain forever.

She lifted her eyes and met his and saw them full of a blistering rage. There was no need to say anything. For that moment she shared with him all the helplessness and the loathing of the artist face to face with the vandal, the senseless damaging of irretrievable loveliness.

189

"Does it affect the sound?" she asked, almost certain in her heart that it did not.

He shook his head.

They were joined by Thora, looking extremely handsome with cascades of ivory lace from her shoulder to elbow, and swathed across a deep décolletage. The skirt was smooth and boasted only the smallest bustle. Altogether it was highly fashionable and most becoming. She looked at Victor with a slight frown.

"You are not distressing Mrs. Radley with that miserable accident, are you, dear? Really it is best forgotten. We cannot undo it, you know."

He stared at her with an unwavering gaze.

"Of course I know, Mama. When a blow is struck, it can never be undone." He turned to Emily. "Can it, Mrs. Radley? The flesh is bruised, and the soul."

Thora opened her mouth to say something, and then changed her mind. She looked at the cello, and then at her son.

Victor seemed to be waiting for a reply.

"No," Emily said hastily. "Of course it can never be undone."

"Do you think we should pretend it didn't happen?" Victor asked, still looking at Emily. "When friends inquire, we should smile bravely and say everything is well—even tell ourselves it does not really hurt, it will all mend soon, and doubtless it was an accident and no one intended any harm." His voice had been growing harsher and there was a note of something like an inner panic in it.

"I am not sure I agree," Emily replied, weighing her answer for something between honesty and tact. "An inordinate fuss helps no one, but I do think that whoever damaged your cello, accident or not, owes you a considerable debt and I can see no reason at all why you should pretend otherwise."

Victor looked startled.

Thora colored uncomfortably and frowned at her as if she had not totally understood.

"Sometimes accidents are caused by carelessness," Emily explained. "And regardless of that, we do need to be responsible for what we do. Do you not agree? We cannot expect others to bear the brunt."

"It is not always so easy . . ." Thora began, then stopped.

Victor shot Emily a charming smile. "Thank you, Mrs.

Radley. I think you have said it exactly. A lack of care, that is it. One must be responsible. Honesty, that is the key to it all."

"Do you not know who bruised your cello?" she asked.

"Oh yes, I know."

Thora looked puzzled. "Victor . . ."

But before he could answer, they were interrupted by a stout woman with remarkably black hair.

"Excuse me, Mrs. Radley, I simply had to say how much I appreciated Mr. Radley's speech yesterday. He was so very correct about the present situation in Africa. It is years since I listened to anyone with such a grasp of the essentials." She ignored Victor as if he had been a domestic servant, and apparently did not even realize Thora was part of the group. "We need more men like that in government, as I was just saying to my husband." She waved an arm airily towards a tall, thin man with a prominent nose. He reminded Emily of pictures she had seen of vultures. He was dressed in military uniform. "Brigadier Gibson-Jones, you know?" The woman seemed to assume that the name would be familiar.

Actually Emily had no recollection of either the brigadier or his wife, and therefore was most grateful to be reminded of their name. She was about to say something suitably agreeable, and to introduce Victor and Thora, but as if suddenly aware of a breach of good manners, Mrs. Gibson-Jones turned to Victor.

"Are you going to play for us? How jolly. I think music always lifts an occasion, don't you?" And without waiting for an answer, she moved away, having caught sight of someone else with whom she wished to confer.

Emily turned to Victor.

"I'm sorry," she said in little more than a whisper.

Victor smiled; it was sweet and dazzling, like a broad beam of sunlight. "What does she think I'm going to play—a jig?"

"Can you see her dancing to a jig?" Emily asked almost under her breath.

Victor's smile became a grin. He seemed at least temporarily to have forgotten the subject of the cello and the bruise.

Emily excused herself to both of them and set about the business of being charming. She moved from group to group, exchanging greetings, inquiries after health, small chatter of fashion, children, the weather, court and society, matters of the usual exchange in civilized conversation. She saw Jack speaking with men of wealth, good family, connections of every sort, both open and discreet. For a moment she wondered

191

again how many of them were members of the Inner Circle, which of them knew who else was, who walked in fear or guilt, who owed dark loyalties, who was prepared to betray. Then she dismissed it from her mind. There was no purpose in it.

"We need change," she overheard a thin man say, adjusting his spectacles on his nose. "This police force is simply not good enough. Good heavens, when a man of the distinction of Oakley Winthrop can be hacked to death in Hyde Park, we are sinking into anarchy. Complete anarchy."

"Incompetent officer in charge," his thickset companion agreed, looping his thumbs into the armholes of his waistcoat, leaving his jacket flapping. "I shall table a question in the House. Something must be done. It is getting so a decent man cannot take a walk after dark. Murmur and whispers everywhere, talk of anarchists, bombs, the Irish, everyone suspicious of his neighbor. Whole world in turmoil."

"I blame the asylums," a third man put in vehemently. "What kind of a lunatic is it who can do such things and remain at large? That is what I should like to know. Nobody's doing a damned thing about it."

"Have you heard Uttley on the subject?" the first man asked, looking from one to the other of his companions. "He's right, you know. We need some changes. Although I cannot agree about the lunatic. I rather think it is a purposely sane and very evil man. Mark my words, there is some connection between the victims, whatever anyone says."

"Really, Ponsonby?" The thickset man looked surprised. "I thought this second feller was a musician? Rather good. Did you know Winthrop? Naval feller, what?"

"Odd chap," Ponsonby said, pulling a face. "Decent enough family, though. Father's making a fuss, poor devil. Taken it hard. Can't blame him."

"Did you know him?"

"Marlborough Winthrop?"

"No, no, Oakley, man. The son!"

"Met him once or twice. Why? Didn't care for the chap greatly. Bit overbearing, you know."

"What, very naval, and all that? Still thinks he's on the quarterdeck?"

Ponsonby hesitated. "Not really, just had to be the center of things, always talking, always expressing his opinions. Only met him two or three times. Met the brother-in-law, actually.

Name of Mitchell, as I recall. Interesting feller. Deep. Been in Africa until very lately, so I believe."

"Deep? What do you mean deep?"

"Thought a lot more than he said, if you know what I mean. Couldn't abide his brother-in-law. Gave me some good financial advice, though! Put me onto an excellent man in the city, feller by the name of Carvell. Bought me some very good shares. Done well."

"Very useful, that—what."

"What?"

"Useful. Very useful to have a good financial adviser."

"Oh, yes. Talking about finance, what do you think of . . ."

Emily moved away, her mind whirling with snatches of words, half ideas, thoughts to report to Charlotte.

7

"YES OF COURSE I've been reading the newspapers every day," Micah Drummond said grimly. He was standing by the window in the library of the small house he had bought about six months ago, immediately prior to his marriage, not finding his apartment adequate for his new status. The home he had shared with his first wife, and where his daughters had grown up, he had sold on becoming a widower. His daughters were by then married, and he felt haunted by memories and uncharacteristically lonely.

Now everything was different. He had resigned his position in order to marry Eleanor Byam, a woman touched by tragedy, and unwittingly by scandal. He had loved her deeply enough to consider his resulting retirement from office a trifling price to pay for the constant pleasure of her companionship.

He looked at Pitt with a frown of concern in his long, sensitive face with its grave eyes and ascetic mouth.

"I wish I could think of something helpful to say, but with every new event I become more confused." He pushed his hands deeper into his pockets. "Have you found any connection between Winthrop, Arledge and the poor bus conductor?"

"No. It's possible Winthrop and Arledge knew each other, or more exactly that Winthrop's brother-in-law, Mitchell, knew both of them," Pitt replied, sitting comfortably in the large green chair. "But the bus conductor is a complete mystery. Men like Winthrop don't take omnibuses. Arledge might have, but I think it's unlikely."

Drummond was standing with his back to the fireplace. He

looked at Pitt anxiously. "Why? What makes you think Arledge might have used an omnibus? Why would a man of his standing do such a thing?"

"Only a remote possibility," Pitt replied. "He had a—a lover."

"A what?" The ghost of a smile touched Drummond's lips. "You mean a mistress?"

"No." Pitt sighed. "I don't. I mean what I said. Not a liaison he could afford to have known. He might have used an omnibus . . ."

"But you don't believe it," Drummond finished for him. "A quarrel?" He searched Pitt's face curiously, his brows puckered. "You are not satisfied with that?"

Pitt had thought about it deeply, and the easy answer troubled him.

"I might have been, if I had not met the man," he said slowly. "But he was desolated. Oh I know that doesn't preclude his having done it himself—people have killed those they loved before and then been destroyed by grief and remorse afterwards. I just don't believe he is one of those."

Drummond bit his lip. "I shall be surprised if Farnsworth sees it that way."

"Oh, he doesn't," Pitt agreed with a harsh little laugh. "But so far there is no evidence whatever to connect Carvell with either Winthrop or Yeats, so I can refuse to act for the time being."

Drummond looked at him closely and Pitt felt increasingly uncomfortable.

"So far there is no real connection between any of them," Pitt continued. "Only a very tenuous business matter. I cannot believe all this is over money."

"Nor I," Drummond admitted. "There is a passion in it, an insanity that springs from something which, thank God, is far less ordinary than greed. But I cannot imagine what." He hesitated, looking at Pitt.

"Yes?" Pitt prompted.

"Perhaps it is—bizarre . . ." Drummond said reluctantly, then stopped again.

Pitt did not interrupt again, knowing he would continue. He could see the struggle in his face, the attempt to find the words for the thought that previously troubled him profoundly.

"Could it be something to do with the Inner Circle?" Drummond looked at him narrowly. "I know the bus conductor is unlikely, but not impossible."

"A betrayal?" Pitt said with surprise. "You mean some sort of internal punishment? Isn't it a bit . . ."

"Extreme?" Drummond finished for him. "Perhaps. But sometimes, Pitt, I don't think you understand just how powerful they are—and certainly not how ruthless."

"A kind of execution?" Pitt was still doubtful. He thought Drummond was letting his own entanglement crowd his vision out of proportion. "Isn't it more in their line simply to ruin someone, have them blackballed from all the clubs, cancel their credit, call in all the debts and loans? That is extremely effective. Men have shot themselves over less."

"Yes, I know," Drummond said grimly. "Some men. But Winthrop was in the navy. Perhaps they couldn't reach him."

Pitt knew his disbelief was in his face and he could not conceal it.

"Listen to me, Pitt." Drummond took a step forward, his expression tense, his eyes bleak. "I know a great deal more than you do about the Circle. You only know the lower rings, the men like me who were drawn in without realizing anything beyond the charities everyone can see, and a little of the superficial obligations. They are just the knights of the Green."

Drummond blushed very faintly, but he was far too serious to allow embarrassment to tie his tongue. "That is what I was, a knight of the Green, someone bound but, in any real sense, untried. Next are the knights of the Scarlet. They are the ones who have proved themselves: blooded, if you like, committed beyond retreat. Beyond them are the Lords of the Silver. They have the power of punishment and reward. But Pitt, behind them is one man, the Lord of the Purple." He saw Pitt's face. "All right!" he said with a sudden edge of anger to his voice Pitt had never heard before. "You can smile. It has its absurdity. But there is nothing even faintly ridiculous about the power that man holds. It's secret, and for those in the Circle it's total. If he pronounced sentence of ruin, or death, it would be carried out. And believe me, Pitt, the perpetrators would go to the gallows without betraying him."

In this gracious room with its Georgian simplicity, its simple warmth and familiar touches, such talk should have been no more than a fanciful and rather ghoulish entertainment. But looking at Drummond's face, the tight muscles of his body, the horror in his eyes, it woke an answering fear in Pitt, and suddenly he felt chilled inside. The warmth no longer touched him.

Drummond saw that he had at last conveyed what he meant. "It might not be," he said quietly. "It might have nothing to do with the Circle at all. But remember what I say, Pitt. Whoever he is, you have already crossed him once, when you exposed Lord Byam and Lord Anstiss. He won't have forgotten. Walk carefully, and make friends as well as enemies."

Pitt knew better than to wonder if Drummond were suggesting he retreat. It was not in his nature even to think of such a thing. He had sometimes thought Drummond stiff, a product of his army career and his aristocratic upbringing, even lacking in information and grasp of which poverty or despair might be. He had wondered if he were capable of real laughter or of consuming passion. But never for an instant had he doubted his courage or his honor. He was the sort of shy, sometimes inarticulate, painfully polite, easily embarrassed, elegant, dryly humorous sort of Englishman who will face impossible odds without complaint and die at his post, but never, ever, desert it even if he were the last man living.

"Thank you for your warning," Pitt said soberly. "I shall not dismiss the possibility, even though in this case, I think it is unlikely."

Drummond relaxed very slowly. He was about to speak on some other subject when there was a tap on the door and both men turned.

"Yes?" Drummond answered.

The door opened and Eleanor Drummond came in. Pitt had not seen her since the day of her marriage, which he and Charlotte had attended. She looked quite different. The happiness was deeper and calmer in her, as if at last she believed it and did not feel the compulsion to clasp it to her in case it vanished. She was dressed in deep, soft blue and it flattered her dark hair with its touches of gray, and her olive skin and clear gray eyes. There was a repose in her face which Pitt found immensely pleasing.

He rose to his feet.

"Good afternoon, Mrs. Drummond. Forgive me taking up your time, but I was looking for a little counsel—"

"Of course, Mr. Pitt," she said quickly, coming into the room and smiling first at Drummond, then at Pitt. "It is too long since we have seen you. I am sorry it is this wretched business in Hyde Park which has brought you. It is that—isn't it?"

"Yes. I'm afraid it is." He felt guilty, and yet he would never have called upon them socially. Drummond had been his superior, only in a certain sense a friend.

"Then perhaps you and Mrs. Pitt will come to dine when this is over?" she asked. "And we can discuss pleasanter things." She smiled suddenly with brimming pleasure. "I am so glad you are superintendent now, and this has nothing to do with Micah. It must be totally wretched. I was sorry to hear about Aidan Arledge. He was a charming man. Captain Winthrop I cannot grieve over as much as perhaps I should."

"Did you know him?" he asked in surprise.

"Oh no," she denied quickly. "Not really. But society is very small. I am acquainted with Lord and Lady Winthrop, of course, but I could not really say I knew them." She looked at him apologetically. "They are not the sort of people it is easy to form any relationship with, but the most superficial, a matter of pleasantries when one meets them at the same sort of function year after year. They are very—predictable, very correct. I am sure there must be more that is individual, if one—" She stopped. They both knew what she was going to say, and it was pointless to pursue it.

"And the captain?" he asked.

"I met him once or twice." She shook her head a little. "He was the sort of man who always made me feel condescended to, I am not sure why. Perhaps because there are no women in the navy. I rather formed the opinion all civilians were in his view a lesser species. He was perfectly polite." She searched Pitt's face. "But the sort of politeness one keeps for the inferior, if you understand me?"

"Do you think he might have known Arledge?" Pitt asked.

"No," she said immediately. "I cannot think of two men less likely to have found each other agreeable."

Drummond glanced at Pitt, his eyes dark.

Pitt smiled back at him. He understood the warning. He had no intention of discussing Arledge's love affair in front of Eleanor, least of all its nature.

Eleanor moved over to Drummond, and a trifle self-consciously he put his arm around her. The freedom to do so was still new to him, and acutely pleasurable.

"I wish I could be of assistance, Pitt," he said seriously. "But it may well be the work of a madman, and to find him

198

you will have to learn what it is these men had in common."
He looked steadily at Pitt and their previous conversation
about the Inner Circle hung unspoken in the air between them.
"It seems exceedingly unlikely it is an acquaintance with each
other," he continued. "But there may be someone they all
knew. I assume you have thought of blackmail?" His arm
tightened around Eleanor.

"I thought Yeats might have known something," Pitt replied,
equally carefully. "But how?"

"Does his omnibus route go past the park?" Drummond
asked. "He does a late run, or he would not have been getting
off at Shepherd's Bush in the middle of the night."

"Yes, but he does not go past Hyde Park," Pitt replied.
"Tellman checked that."

Drummond pulled a face. "How are you getting on with
Tellman?"

Pitt had already decided to keep his own counsel. "He's
quick," he replied. "And diligent. He doesn't want to arrest
Carvell either."

Eleanor looked from one to the other of them, but she did
not interrupt.

Drummond smiled. "He wouldn't," he agreed. "If there's
anything Tellman cannot bear, it is to arrest someone and then
have to let him go. He'll want evidence to hang him before
he'll commit himself. He's a hard enemy, Pitt, but he's a good
friend."

"I'm sure," Pitt agreed equivocally.

"He's also a natural leader," Drummond went on, his eyes
careful on Pitt's face, his expression both apologetic and
amused. "The other men will follow him, if you allow it."

"Yes I know," Pitt said dryly, thinking of le Grange.

Drummond's smile widened, but he said nothing.

"May I offer you something, Mr. Pitt?" Eleanor asked. "It is
too early for luncheon, but at least a glass of wine? Or lemonade, if you prefer?"

"Lemonade, thank you," Pitt accepted gratefully. He had already made up his mind where his next visit would be, and
anything to delay it, to fortify him a little, would be more than
welcome. "I should enjoy it."

When he left half an hour later he took a hansom over the
river south across the Lambeth Bridge, past Lambeth Palace,
where the Archbishop of Canterbury had his official residence,

and up the Lambeth Road to the huge, forbidding mass of the Bethlehem Lunatic Asylum, more usually known as Bedlam. He had been there before, more than once, and it brought back memories of fear, confusion and wrenching pity.

He alighted from the hansom, paid the driver and approached the main gates. He was greeted with caution, and only after showing his identification did he obtain entrance. He had to wait over a quarter of an hour in a dim office crowded with dark leather-bound books and smelling of dust and closed air before finally the superintendent sent for him and he was conducted to his rooms.

He was a short man with round eyes and muttonchop whiskers. A few strands of grayish hair covered the top of his head. He looked distinctly displeased.

"I have already informed your junior, Superintendent Pitt, that we have had no one escape from here," he said stiffly without rising from his leather chair. "It does not happen. We have the most excellent system, and even if anyone did leave without permission, it would be known instantly. And if they were of a dangerous nature, it would naturally have been reported immediately to the proper authorities. I don't know what else I can say to you. My efforts so far appear to have been a waste of time." His nostrils pinched and his right hand rested on the large pile of papers on the desk beside him, presumably unattended to and waiting his perusal.

With difficulty Pitt reminded himself why he was here. To answer the man equally brusquely would defeat his purpose.

"I do not doubt you, Dr. Melchett," he replied. "It is your advice I am here for."

"Indeed?" Melchett said skeptically, at last waving to the other chair for Pitt to sit down. "Well that is not the impression your inspector left. Far from it. He implied very strongly that our methods here were lax and that either some dangerous lunatic had escaped, or else we had released someone who should have been kept here, and in shackles."

"He has a rough tongue," Pitt admitted, without the regret that perhaps he should have felt. He accepted the seat. "It was an obvious question to ask," he went on. "Someone insane enough to cut off three people's heads might well have passed through here at some time."

Melchett rose to his feet, his cheeks pink.

"If he was deranged enough to decapitate three total strangers, Pitt, he would not have passed through here!" he said furiously. "I assure you, he would have remained! Just come with me." He marched around the desk. "I should have taken that damn fool man of yours, but I seriously doubt he would have the wits to apprehend what he saw anyway. Just come along and look at it." He went to the door and flung it open, leaving it swinging back on its hinges, and strode along the corridor, assuming that Pitt was behind him.

Pitt hated the place. He had hoped he would never be here again. Now he was following a deeply offended Melchett along these corridors with their long silences and sudden screams, the moaning and the sobs, the wild laughter, and then the silence again.

Melchett was far ahead. Pitt had to hurry to catch up with him. It even occurred to him not to, to turn around and go back out. But he did not. His feet increased their pace and Melchett was waiting for him at the door, holding it open.

"There!" he said through clenched teeth, his eyes round and angry.

Pitt walked past him into the long high-ceilinged room. Around the walls was a kind of narrow walkway slightly three feet above the floor, creating the impression of a wall full of people, most of them sitting on chairs or on the floor, many huddled over, hugging themselves, some rocking back and forth rhythmically, moaning and muttering unintelligibly, and it was along this that Melchett now led Pitt. Between them a man with matted hair picked at a scab on his leg till it bled. His arms were covered with similar wounds, some half healed, others obviously new. There were what looked like bite marks on his wrists and forearms. He did not even see Pitt standing close above him, so intent was he upon his own flesh.

A second stared into space, saliva running down his chin. A third reached up towards them, hands clasping at the air, throat straining, mind seeking words and failing to find them. A fourth sat with his wrists in leather-padded chains, banging against the restraint with sharp, jiggling movements as if he were sawing at something. He too was so absorbed in his pointless, painful task that he neither saw Pitt nor heard Melchett when he spoke.

"How many do you want to see?" Melchett asked quietly, his voice hard with a mixture of anger and offense. "We have scores, all much like this, all sad, unreachable by anything we know how to do. Do you think someone like this is your lunatic? Do you think we accidentally let one go, and he got hold of an ax and started decapitating people in Hyde Park?"

Pitt opened his mouth to deny it, but Melchett rushed on, his anger if anything increasing.

"Where are they, Pitt?" he demanded. "Living in the park somewhere? Where do they sleep? What do they eat? All your police swarming over the area, searching for clues, cannot find the poor devil?"

There was no answer. Looking at the fierce, pathetic, troubled souls all around him, beyond reason, beyond reach, the idea was ridiculous. If Tellman had come this far into Bedlam, he would have curbed his tongue before making such comments to Melchett, or anyone else.

Pitt's silence seemed to soften Melchett a fraction. He cleared his throat.

"Hm—if your man is insane, Pitt, his obsession has not reached the stage where he would be committed to a place like this. He'll appear much like anyone else most of the time— that is if he is mad at all." He lifted his shoulders and straightened them again. "Are you certain there is no sane reason for all this carnage?"

"No I'm not," Pitt replied. "But there seems to be no connection between the victims, not one that we can find so far." He turned away from the poor creature nearest him, who was reaching up to the full extent of his restraining jacket as if to pluck at him.

Melchett saw he had more than made his point. He turned and led the way out of the great room into the corridor and back down in the direction of his office.

"If he were mad," Pitt went on, "what sort of an obsession would I be looking for, Dr. Melchett? What sort of a past makes a man turn to such random violence?"

"Oh, it is not random," Melchett said immediately. "Not in his mind. There will be a connection: time, place, appearance, something said or done which prompted the rage, or the fear, or whatever emotion drives him. It may be a religious passion of some sort. Many lunatics have a profound sense of sin." He raised his shoulders again and let them fall. "Nasty question, I know, but is it possible your men were all committing some act he might have felt to be sinful? Soliciting women, for example? It's not an uncommon form of delusion—that sexual congress with women is evil, debilitating, a snare of the devil." He sniffed. "Sick, of course. Springs from some dark recesses

202

of the mind we have barely begun to realize is there, let alone what may be in it. Lot of most interesting work being done abroad, you know? No—why should you . . ." He shook his head and increased his pace a trifle.

Pitt did not attempt to press him further until they were back in his office and the door closed, surrounded by books and papers and the paraphernalia of administration. It looked impersonal, sanitized from the confusion and despair he had just seen, and which still clung to him, thick in his throat like a taste he could not get rid of.

"What sort of a man am I looking for, Dr. Melchett, if it is that kind of obsession?" he asked finally. "What sort of character? What manner of family? What past will he have that has driven him to this?" He stared at Melchett. "What event will have provoked him to do this now, not before, not after?"

Melchett hunched his shoulders again in his odd, characteristic gesture.

"God knows. It could be anything from a real tragedy, such as a death in the family, right down to something as trivial as an insult. It could spring from memory. Someone said or did something that reminded him violently of a past shock, and he was disconnected, so to speak, from reality." He waved his hand dismissively. "I'm sorry, there is really little use in my speculating. I should think some sort of moral or religious passion is your best line. When I asked if your victims could have been soliciting women you did not reply. Were you being discreet?"

"Possibly," Pitt conceded. "But it wouldn't be the answer. One of them at least had a long-standing relationship with a lover."

"You mean a mistress," Melchett corrected. "That doesn't prevent him from—"

"No—I mean what I said," Pitt reasserted.

Melchett's eyebrows rose.

"Oh. Oh I see. Yes, well that would make it excessively unlikely he was soliciting a woman. What about the others? Same thing?"

"No reason to think so. But I suppose that could set off the same sort of violent reactions." Pitt was dubious and it must have shown in his face.

"Could have been anything," Melchett said with a sharp little laugh. "Something they said, something they did, a trick or gesture, something they wore, a place, anything at all. I would look seriously into the possibility that your man is as sane as most and has a perfectly understandable reason. I'm sorry I can't help you." He held out his hand.

It was dismissal, and there was nothing Pitt could usefully do but accept it. It was pointless to go on pressing for information neither Melchett nor anyone else could give him.

"Thank you," he said, stepping back a pace. "Thank you for your time."

Melchett smiled, drawing his lips tightly over his teeth. He acknowledged the courtesy, and showed Pitt to the door.

Pitt was hardly back in Bow Street when Farnsworth came in, stared at the desk sergeant, who snapped to attention, then at Pitt, and then at Tellman and le Grange, who were standing just beyond him.

"Find something," he said eagerly, looking from one to another.

Le Grange shifted his feet and looked away. It was not his responsibility to answer.

The desk sergeant blushed.

"The superintendent is just back from Bedlam," Tellman said sourly.

Farnsworth's face darkened. "For Heaven's sake what for?" He turned back to Pitt irritably. "If this dammed lunatic was safely locked up in the asylum, we shouldn't be having all this mayhem!" He swiveled to Tellman. "Didn't you already go there to make sure they hadn't had an escape?"

"It was the first thing I did, sir," Tellman replied.

"Pitt?" Farnsworth's voice was rising with anger and there was a sharp note of anxiety in it.

"I wanted to see if Dr. Melchett could tell me what sort of a man we are looking for," Pitt replied, biting his lip to keep from losing his own temper.

"It's damned simple what we're looking for!" Farnsworth said tartly, beginning to move towards the hall and the stairs up to Pitt's office. "Jerome Carvell! The man has motive, can't account for his whereabouts, and we'll find the weapon sooner or later. What else do you need?"

"A reason for him to have killed Winthrop and the omnibus conductor," Pitt replied between his teeth. "There's no connection so far to suggest he even met either of them, let alone had any cause to hate or fear them."

"If he killed Arledge, of course he killed the other two."

Farnsworth stared at him. "We don't need to prove it. Perhaps he made some wretched advance to Winthrop and was rebuffed. Winthrop may even have threatened to make it public. That would be enough to send the fellow off his head." His voice gained in conviction. "Had to kill him to keep him quiet. Sodomy is not only a crime, man, it's social ruin." He snorted very slightly through his nose and looked at Tellman.

Tellman's lantern face was sardonic. He looked at Pitt with a smile, and for the first time Pitt could recall, there was no animosity in it at all. On the contrary, it was faintly conspiratorial.

"Well?" Farnsworth demanded.

"I don't think so, sir," Tellman replied, standing to attention.

"Don't you, indeed!" Farnsworth turned back at Pitt. "And why not? I assume you have a reason, some evidence you have not yet shared?"

Pitt concealed a smile with difficulty. There was nothing remotely amusing in the situation. It added to the tragedy that it should also be absurd.

"Place," he said simply.

"What?"

"If Winthrop was disinclined, why would he be in a pleasure boat on the Serpentine at midnight? And would Carvell really bring along an ax on the off chance he was rebuffed?"

Farnsworth's face flamed. "What in God's name was anybody doing on the Serpentine with an ax?" he said furiously. "You cannot explain that for anyone at all. In fact you haven't answered very much, have you? I assume you read the newspapers? Have you seen what this damned fellow Uttley is saying about you in particular, and by extension about all of us?" His voice was rising and there was a thread of panic in it now. "I resent it, Pitt! I resent it deeply, and I am not alone. Every policeman in London is being tarred by the same brush as you, and blamed for your incompetence. What's happened to you, Pitt? You used to be a damned good policeman." He abandoned his decision to go upstairs to the privacy of Pitt's office. He was aware of le Grange and the desk sergeant listening to his own humiliation, and now Bailey as well was standing on the edge of the group. He would retaliate equally in public. "There's enough evidence. For Heaven's sake use it! Before the bloody madman kills again." He stared at Pitt. "I shall hold you responsible if you don't arrest him and we have another murder."

There was a moment's bristling silence. Farnsworth stood defiantly, unwilling to withdraw a word. Le Grange looked acutely unhappy, but for once there was no indecision in him. The accusation was unfair, and he backed Pitt.

"We can't arrest him, sir," Tellman said distinctly. "He'd have us for false charges, because there's no proof. We'd have to let him go again straightaway, and we'd only look even stupider."

"That would be hard," Farnsworth said grimly. "What about this omnibus conductor? What do you know about him? Any criminal record? Does he owe money? Gamble? Drink? Fornicate? Keep bad company?"

"No criminal record," Tellman replied. "As far as anyone in the neighborhood knows, he is a perfectly ordinary, respectable, rather self-important little omnibus conductor."

"What's an omnibus conductor got to be important about?" Farnsworth asked derisively.

"Touch of authority, I suppose," Tellman replied. "Tell people whether they can get on or not, where they can sit or if they have to stand."

Farnsworth rolled his eyes and his face expressed his contempt.

"Indeed. No secret vices?"

"If he had, they are still secret," Tellman replied.

"Well, there was something! What does the local station say?"

"Nothing known. He was a regular churchgoer, sidesman, or something of the sort." Tellman pulled a lugubrious face, bitter humor in his eyes. "Obviously liked telling people where to sit," he finished. "Had to do it on Sundays as well."

Farnsworth looked at him. "Nobody's going to cut his head off just because he's an officious little swine," he said, then moved back towards the door out again. "I must do something about this Uttley chap." He looked at Pitt, dropping his voice. "You should have listened to me, Pitt. I made you a good offer, and if you had taken my advice you wouldn't be in this predicament now."

Tellman looked from Farnsworth to Pitt and back again; he had only caught half of what had been said, and obviously did not comprehend the meaning. Bailey was still as amused as he dared to be at the vision of Winthrop and Carvell in the boat, the oars and the ax between them. He disliked Farnsworth and

206

always had done. Le Grange was waiting for orders from someone and moved from one foot to the other in uncertainty.

Pitt knew precisely what Farnsworth was referring to. It was the Inner Circle again, this time torn in its loyalties. Micah Drummond's words came back to his mind with added chill. But surely Farnsworth knew Uttley was a member himself? And Jack was not?

Or perhaps with all the secrecy, the different levels and rings, he did not? And even if he attacked, and drew on those loyal to him, perhaps he could not predict the outcome of such a test of strength. And far more dangerous, the trial of loyalty, the blooded knights against the tyros. Who else was bought by covenant, committed to a battle in which they had no interest and no gain but would be punished mortally if they backed the losing side?

Farnsworth was waiting, as if he thought even at this point Pitt might have changed his mind.

Pitt faced him blankly. "Perhaps not," he said pleasantly, but with finality in his voice.

Farnsworth hesitated only a moment longer, then swung around and went out.

Bailey let his breath out in a sigh and le Grange relaxed visibly.

Tellman turned to Pitt.

"We can't arrest Carvell yet, sir, but if we pushed a little harder we would get a damned sight more out of him. As Mr. Farnsworth says, there's a connection somewhere, and I'll swear he knows what it is, or he can guess."

Le Grange looked attentive.

"What have you in mind?" Pitt asked very slowly.

Tellman's chin came up. "He's guilty of one crime, by his own admission. You can get several years for sodomy. He may not realize we can't prove it. We can pursue him on that." His lip curled very slightly in unspoken contempt. "Mr. Carvell isn't the sort to take well to a term in somewhere like Pentonville or the Coldbath Fields."

"That's right, sir," le Grange said hopefully.

Pitt ignored him. He looked at Tellman with dislike.

"You have no evidence."

"He admitted it," Tellman said reasonably.

"Not to you, Inspector."

Tellman's face hardened and he stood facing Pitt squarely. "Are you saying you would deny it, sir?"

Pitt smiled very slightly. "I should say nothing at all, Inspector. All he told me was that he loved Arledge. That may be interpreted as you please. The emotion is not a crime. I imagine Carvell will say precisely that, and have his lawyers sue you for harassment."

"You're too squeamish," Tellman said, disgust written large in his face. "If you pander to these people you'll never learn anything. They'll run rings 'round you."

Bailey coughed loudly.

Tellman ignored him, still staring at Pitt. "We can't afford your delicate conscience if we want to catch this bastard who's cutting people's heads off and terrifying half of London. People daren't go out after dark unless they're in twos or threes. There are cartoons all over the place. He's making a laughingstock of us. Doesn't that bother you?" He looked at Pitt with something close to loathing. "Doesn't it make you angry?"

Le Grange nodded his head up and down, his eyes on Tellman.

"That's just what it sounds like," Pitt replied coldly. "The reaction of anger—not of thought or judgment: the instinctive lashing out of someone who's afraid for his own reputation and works with one eye over his shoulder to see what others think of him."

"The 'others' pay our bloody wages!" Tellman said, still staring icily and undeviatingly at Pitt. Neither Bailey nor le Grange interested him in the slightest, and the desk sergeant had faded from his awareness completely. "Yours as much as mine," he went on. He had committed himself too far to turn back. "And they are not pleased with you." His voice was rising. "Nobody cares how brilliant you may have been in the past—it's now that matters. You are leaving their lordships' reputations in tatters. They look like fools, and they won't forgive you for that."

"If you want me to arrest Carvell, prove he had something to do with it," Pitt demanded, his own voice angry and hard. "Where was he when Yeats was killed?"

"At a concert, sir," le Grange chipped in. "But he can't find anyone who saw him there. He can tell us what the music was, but anyone could get that from a program."

"And when Arledge was killed?" Pitt went on.

"Home alone."

"Servants?"

"No point. There's a French door in the study. He could

have gone out that way and none of the servants would have known. Come back the same way."

"And Winthrop?"

"For a walk in the park, so he says," Tellman replied with heavy disbelief.

"Alone?"

"Yes."

"Pass anyone?"

"Not that he can recall. Anyway, he'd have to pass pretty close for anyone to recognize him at midnight. People don't hang around the park at night these days—not as they used to."

"Not even the women?" Pitt asked.

Tellman shrugged. "They've got to, poor cows. Can't afford to stay in. But they're scared."

"Well go and see if you can find anyone who saw Carvell," Pitt said. "Try some of the women. What about in the street on the way home? Someone might be able to place him at a particular time. Don't his servants remember his coming home?"

"No sir. He kept rather odd hours, and preferred the servants to go to bed and leave him to it." Tellman's lips lifted in a faint sneer of distaste. "Presumably he preferred they did not see Arledge coming and going. Caught him out last time—if he was really there."

"Try the other people in the park," Pitt repeated. "Try Fat George's girls. They work that end."

"What'd that prove?" Tellman said with open disgust. "If no one saw him, that doesn't prove he wasn't there. And we can't find anyone who will say they saw him in Shepherd's Bush. Tried all the passengers on that last bus."

"And I suppose you haven't yet found where Arledge was killed either?" Pitt asked sardonically. "Seems you have quite a lot to do. You'd better get on with it."

And with that he went up to his office and closed the door, but Tellman's charges lingered with him. Was he being too fastidious in his prosecution of this case? Was he allowing the fact that he liked Carvell to influence his judgment as to the weight of the evidence? Pity, no matter how real, was not a factor he should allow to blind him. If it were not Carvell, then who? Bart Mitchell, over Winthrop's abuse of his sister? But why kill Arledge? And why Yeats?

Or was it really some obsessed lunatic who killed seemingly at random from the dark chaos in his own mind?

He must learn more about Winthrop, and his marriage, and Bart Mitchell.

Emily looked at Charlotte's new house with growing approval. There was something acutely satisfying about finding a house in a dilapidated state, then repairing it and decorating it to suit your own tastes. When she had married George she had moved into Ashworth House and found it in perfect order, everything maintained as it had been for generations. Every room had been added to by each succeeding chatelaine until by 1882 there had been little room for improvement or individual expression in any part of it. Even her own bedroom was curtained and mirrored in the taste of the previous incumbent, and it would have been wasteful to have altered it. Indeed, it was so lavish and so beautiful it could not have been bettered, it would simply have been Emily's own choice rather than someone else's.

Now, of course, Ashworth House was hers, and she shared it with Jack, but it still contained little that was of her creation or taste, even though she could find no fault with any of it. She was delighted for Charlotte, and also just a very little bit envious.

They were in the bedroom which overlooked the garden. Charlotte had chosen green after all, and today with a bright sun and the trees in full leaf, the whole room had the feeling of a shaded bower, full of light and shadow and the soft sound of moving leaves. What it would be like in winter remained to be seen, but at this moment it could hardly have been lovelier.

"I like it," Emily said decisively. "In fact I think it is quite marvelous." She screwed up her face unhappily and her hands with their gorgeous rings were knotted in her muslin skirts.

"But . . ." Charlotte said, feeling a sharp disappointment. She was so happy with the room, it was exactly what she had most hoped for, but it hurt her that Emily should have reservations, and to judge from her expression, very serious ones.

Emily sighed. "But have you seen Mama's bedroom lately? I called there." She turned to face Charlotte, her blue eyes very wide. "I had a chance to go upstairs. Have you? It's—it's so—I don't know what to say. It's just not Mama! It's as if she were someone totally different. It's—it's worse than romantic—it's lush. Yes, that's the word, lush."

"You are still trying to pretend it is a passing thing," Charlotte said slowly, going to the window and leaning her elbows on it to stare out at the garden. The lawn, now neatly clipped, stretched away under the trees to the rose-covered wall at the end. "It isn't, you know. I think I have faced that now. She really loves him."

Emily came beside her, also looking down at the garden in the dappled sunlight. "It will still end in tragedy," she said quietly. "There's nothing else it can do."

"She could marry him."

Emily turned to face her. "And do what?" she demanded. "She could hardly remain in society, and she would never fit in with the theater people. She would be neither one thing nor another. And how long could it last—happiness, I mean?"

"How long does it ever last?" Charlotte replied.

"Oh come on! I am very happy, and don't tell me you are not, because I should not believe you."

"Certainly I am. And look how many people predicated I should end in disaster."

Emily looked back at the garden. "That is rather different."

"No it isn't," Charlotte argued. "I married someone nearly all my friends said was hopelessly beneath me, and had no money to speak of."

"But he is your age. Or at least he is only a few years older, which is precisely as it should be. And he is a Christian!"

"I admit that is a difficulty, Joshua's being a Jew," Charlotte conceded unhappily. "But Mr. Disraeli was a Jew. That didn't stop him becoming Prime Minister, and the Queen thought he was wonderful. She liked him very much."

"Because he flattered her shamelessly, and Mr. Gladstone wouldn't," Emily responded. "He was a miserable old man, always talking about virtue." Her face lightened. "Although I did hear he was actually very fond of women himself—very fond indeed. In fact I heard it from Eliza Harrogate." Her voice dropped to little above a whisper. "She said she knew for a fact that he could hardly contain himself when in the presence of a pretty woman, whatever her age or state. That makes him seem a little different, doesn't it?"

Charlotte stared at her, uncertain if she were serious or joking. Then she burst into laughter. The thought was delicious, and completely novel.

"Perhaps he made an intimate suggestion to the Queen?" Emily went on, beginning to giggle as well. "Maybe that is why she didn't care for him?"

"You are talking the most arrant rubbish," Charlotte said at last. "And it has nothing at all to do with what we were discussing."

"No, I suppose it doesn't." Emily was suddenly solemn again. "What can we do about it? I refuse simply to stand by and watch Mama walk straight into a disaster."

"I don't see that you have a choice," Charlotte said grimly. "The only thing we can hope for is that it should come to a natural end before irreparable harm has been done."

"That's hopeless. We can't be so—so ineffectual," Emily protested, turning away from the window again.

"It's not ineffectual; it's a matter of not interfering, and robbing Mama of the right to choose for herself." Charlotte turned away as well.

"But—" Emily began.

"How is the election progressing?" Charlotte cut across her deliberately, a smile on her face.

Emily shrugged. "All right, for the moment I give up. Actually, it's going surprisingly well." Her delicate eyebrows rose, her eyes wide. "There have been a few extremely good articles in the newspapers in the last two days. I don't understand it, but someone has obviously changed their views and is now entirely for Jack; or to be more exact, against Mr. Uttley."

"How odd," Charlotte said thoughtfully. "There must be some reason for it."

"Well Jack has not joined the Inner Circle, if that's what you are thinking," Emily said fiercely. "I will swear to that."

"Of course not, I had not doubted it," Charlotte said soothingly. "But it does not mean that this change has nothing to do with the Inner Circle. They may have their own reasons."

"Why? Jack won't give them anything."

"That is not what I meant." Charlotte drew a deep breath. "Uttley has been attacking the police. Do you not think it is possible that there are those in the police who are high in the Inner Circle too, and Uttley was foolish enough not to realize it?"

"Oh! Like the assistant commissioner, perhaps?" Emily looked startled and, just for a moment, disbelieving.

"Micah Drummond was," Charlotte reminded her.

"Yes, but that was different. He didn't use it." Emily stopped suddenly. "Yes I see. That was silly. It doesn't mean Giles Farnsworth wouldn't. He will call on the right people in order to defend himself. Of course he would."

"Quite apart from that," Charlotte went on, "we don't know who else is."

"What do you mean?" Emily demanded. "Who are you thinking of?"

"Anyone," Charlotte replied. "The Home Secretary, for all we know. That's the whole thing about the Inner Circle, we don't know. We don't know whose loyalties are where. There can be alliances you never even imagined."

Emily looked at her, now very grave. "So Uttley may have defeated himself by attacking the police? Wouldn't he have known the dangers of that?"

"Not if he didn't know Farnsworth was a member, assuming it is Farnsworth. And if they were in different rings. But it was stupid of him not to have considered the possibility."

Emily frowned. "He must have thought he was safe. Charlotte—could there be a—rivalry within the Circle? Do such things happen?"

"I suppose so. Or perhaps it is so secret Uttley really did not know," Charlotte said thoughtfully. "According to Micah Drummond, he knew only a few other members, those of his own ring. It's a sort of protection. Only the senior members know all the other names. Then no one who becomes disaffected can betray the others."

"Then how do they know who is and who isn't?" Emily asked reasonably.

"I think they have signs," Charlotte replied. "Secret ways to recognize each other if they have to."

"How incredibly silly," Emily said with a smile. Then suddenly she shivered. "I hate things like that. Imagine the power those at the heart must have. They have all that blind loyalty—hundreds, maybe thousands, of men in positions of authority all over the country, all promised to give their allegiance without question, often without knowing to whom or even in what cause."

"They can go for years without being asked to do anything," Charlotte pointed out. "I expect most of them never are. When Micah Drummond joined he thought it was only a nice, anonymous, benevolent society, giving time and money in charitable causes. It wasn't until the murder in Clerkenwell, when he was asked to help Lord Byam, that he began to understand just what the price was, or to wonder how much of his own preferment had come because of his membership. Maybe Uttley was the same."

"Innocent?" Emily said doubtfully. "I can believe it of Micah Drummond. He really is rather . . . naive. Men trust people no woman in her right mind would dream of trusting with a thing. But Uttley is devious himself, and brilliantly ambitious. People who use others expect them to try the same." Then as she considered the idea it became more and more likely in her mind. "Not a very pleasant man, ready enough to grasp at any advantage, but without understanding what a vast and dangerous thing he was playing with?" She shivered again, in spite of the sun that danced on the sill. "I could almost feel sorry for him—but not quite."

"I would save your pity until the end," Charlotte warned.

Emily looked at her. "Are you afraid?"

"Only a little. I wish I thought they were protecting the police for some honorable reason, but I think it is because someone higher in the Circle than Uttley is on the force—maybe the assistant commissioner, but it could be anyone."

Emily sighed. "And I suppose Thomas is no nearer to finding the Hyde Park Headsman?"

"Not so far as I know."

"And we are not doing very much, are we?" Emily said critically. "I wish I could think of something!"

"I don't even know where to begin." Charlotte was growing more despondent. "It isn't as if we had the faintest idea who it could be. It isn't really—" She stopped.

"Very interesting," Emily finished for her. "Because we don't know the people. Madness is frightening, and sad, but really not . . ."

"Interesting." Charlotte smiled bleakly.

Pitt redoubled his efforts to find some link, however tenuous, between Winthrop and Aidan Arledge. In this endeavor he went again to see Arledge's widow. She received him with the same charming courtesy as previously, but he was saddened to find her looking weary and anxious. In spite of the shock she must have been suffering when they first met, there had been a bloom in her face. It was gone now, as if the long days and nights had drained her. She was still dressed carefully, her sweeping, feminine black relieved by delicate touches of lace and the same beautiful mourning brooch and ring.

"Good afternoon, Mr. Pitt," she said with a wan smile. "Have you come to report some further discovery?" She said it without hope in her voice, but her eyes, hollowed with shock, searched his face.

"Nothing that we yet know the meaning of," he answered. Her distress hurt him far more than Farnsworth's abuse or the criticism written with such a free hand in the newspapers.

"Nothing at all?" she pressed. "You have no idea who is doing these terrible things?" They were in the withdrawing room, which was still warm and restful, a large bowl of flowers on the table by the far wall.

"We have still found no link to connect your husband with Captain Winthrop," he replied. "And even less with the bus conductor."

"Please sit down, Superintendent." She indicated the chair nearest to him, and sat in another opposite, folding her hands in her lap. It was a graceful pose and she looked almost at ease, but her back was perfectly straight, as she had probably been taught to sit since nursery days. Charlotte had told him how good governesses would pass by and poke a ruler, or some other such sharp, hard instrument, at the bent backs of their less diligent girls.

Pitt accepted and crossed his legs comfortably. In spite of the circumstances, and the errand on which he had come, there was something about her presence which was extraordinarily agreeable, at once sharpening perception and yet leaving him with a sense of well-being. The thoughts and confidences shared last time were like a warm memory between them.

"Is there something else I can tell you?" she inquired, watching his face. "I have been searching my mind for anything at all. You see, the trouble is there is so much of Aidan's life in which I had no part." She smiled, and then bit her lip suddenly. "Oh dear. Far more than I meant, even when I said that. What I was thinking of was his music. I am very fond of music, but I could not possibly go every evening there was a concert, and it would have been out of the question to attend all the meetings and rehearsals." She searched his eyes to see if he understood, and did not find her culpable for such an admission.

"No woman goes to his art or profession with her husband, Mrs. Arledge," Pitt assured her. "Many women are not even fully aware what business their husbands have, let alone where it is or who else is concerned."

She relaxed a little. "No, of course you are right," she said with a smile of gratitude. "Perhaps it was a foolish thing to say. I am sorry. I just find—oh dear—please excuse me, Mr. Pitt, I fear my mind is all at sixes and sevens. The Requiem is weighing very heavily with me. It is in two days' time, and I still hardly know what to do."

Pitt wished he could help, but the police would be inappropriate even as a presence, let alone assisting.

"Surely he had many friends who would be privileged to help in any way at all?" he asked earnestly.

"Oh yes, yes naturally," she agreed. "Lady Lismore is being marvelous. She is a pillar of strength. Sir James knows all the people who should be invited. And Mr. Alberd, too. He will deliver an address. He is very well respected, you know?"

"I imagine it will still be a harrowing time for you, though," he said gently, imagining the grief she would feel, the overwhelming emotion as she heard his beloved music and his friends paying tribute, still blindly ignorant of the terrible secret which might all too soon be in every newspaper and billboard.

She swallowed with difficulty, as if there were an obstruction in her throat. "Yes, I am afraid so. So many thoughts keep whirling through my mind." She looked at him with sudden candor. "I am ashamed of many of them, Superintendent, and yet no matter how hard I try, I don't seem to be able to control them." She rose to her feet and walked over towards the window. She spoke with her back to him. "I am ashamed of myself for my weakness, but I am dreading it. I do not know who the man is whom Aidan—I cannot bring myself to use the word *loved*—and I shall end in looking at everyone and wondering." She turned back to face him. "That is very wrong, isn't it?" She said nothing of the storm of ridicule and contempt which would break when someone was arrested and it became public, but the knowledge was silent between them.

"But very understandable, Mrs. Arledge," he said softly. "I think we might all of us feel the same."

"Do you think so?" she asked. The slightest of smiles touched her mouth. Bailey had been right, she had the sort of face that became more pleasing the longer one knew her. "You are most comforting. Will you be present, Mr. Pitt? I should like it very much if you were, as a friend—as my friend, if you feel you are able?"

"Most certainly I shall attend, Mrs. Arledge." He felt guilty as he said it, and yet deeply complimented. He was obliged by the case to be there. Perhaps she understood that. He thought she was quite capable of asking him simply to make him feel less intrusive, and yet the warmth inside him was not lessened by the knowledge.

"There is to be a small reception afterwards," she continued. "I shall not hold it here, I really don't feel able." She was staring at the flowers on the table. "Sir James suggested we should have it at the home of one of Aidan's friends who both admired his work and was fond of him. That would be convenient for everyone, and much less distressing for me. I shall not be responsible in the same way, and if I wish to leave earlier, I may do so, and return home to be alone with my thoughts and memories." A small, rueful smile crossed her face and vanished. "Although I am not sure that is entirely what I wish."

There was nothing for him to say that was not trite.

"It is to be at the home of Mr. Jerome Carvell, in Green Street," she continued. "Do you know that?"

For a moment he was robbed of words.

"I am familiar with Green Street," he replied at last, his breath catching in his throat so that he spoke with difficulty. He hoped profoundly that she saw nothing in his face. "I expect that will be very suitable," he went on. "And as you say, relieve you of the main responsibility." Did his answer sound as meaningless as he felt it?

She forced a smile. "They will take care of refreshments, and of course we shall have music at the Requiem itself. They have attended to all of that also." Absently she rearranged one or two of the flowers, putting one a trifle farther out, handling a leaf here or there, nipping off a stem that was out of place. "Aidan knew so many excellent musicians. There will be many to choose from. He particularly loved the cello. Such a sad instrument. The tones are darker than those of the violin. Appropriate for such an occasion, don't you agree?"

"Yes." His mind immediately conjured a picture of Victor Garrick playing after Oakley Winthrop's funeral. "Who will play? Do you know yet?"

She turned away from the flowers.

"Some young man Aidan was fond of, someone I believe he helped and encouraged," she replied, looking at him with quickened interest. "Do you care for the cello, Mr. Pitt?"

"Yes." It was more or less true. He enjoyed it profoundly on the rare occasions when he had the opportunity to listen.

"I believe the young man is most gifted. He is an amateur,

217

but has both technique and extraordinary emotion, so Sir James tells me. And he had a regard for Aidan, because of the time Aidan devoted to helping him."

"Indeed? What is his name?"

"Vincent Garrick. Yes, I think that is right. No—no it was not Vincent—Victor. Yes, I am sure that is right."

"Did Mr. Arledge know him well?" Pitt kept the sudden sharpness out of his voice as well as he could, but she stiffened. He could see the line of her shoulder taut against the thick silk of her gown.

"Do you know him, Mr. Pitt? Does it mean something?" she demanded. "Why do you ask me?"

"It may mean very little, ma'am. Victor Garrick was Captain Winthrop's godson."

"Captain Winthrop's godson?" She looked confused, and then disappointed. "Perhaps it was absurd, but I was hoping, from your sudden attention, that there was some—some clue?"

"Did Mr. Arledge know Victor Garrick well?" he asked again.

Her eyes did not leave his face.

"I am afraid I have no idea. You could ask Sir James. He would know. He actually encouraged the young musicians rather more than Aidan did. In fact, to be honest, Superintendent, I fear it may have been Sir James's suggestion because Mr. Garrick is something of a protégé of his."

"I see." Pitt was stupidly disappointed. Still he would go again to Sir James Lismore and pursue the connection, no matter how remote. And most certainly he would attend the Requiem. "Thank you, Mrs. Arledge. You have been most patient with me, and most gracious." It was an understatement. No bereaved person had earned his admiration more.

"You will tell me, Superintendent, when you find something, won't you?" she said with eagerness lighting her face.

"Of course," he said quickly. "As soon as there is anything that is more than speculation and idea." He rose to his feet.

She rose also and walked with him to the hallway and the front entrance, thanking him again. He took his leave and set out to find a hansom immediately and go to the home of Sir James Lismore. But her face was still in his mind's eye and a confusion of emotions was raised by Aidan Arledge. He pitied him because he had met a violent and untimely death, and because he had loved where he could not fulfill himself, and yet also felt an anger he could not quell for his having betrayed such a remarkable woman and left her with nothing but dignity and grief.

"Victor Garrick?" Sir James said with surprise. He was a very ordinary-looking man of medium height, and his hair receded so far it was barely visible as one faced him. But there was a quality of concentration in his eyes that held the attention, and all the lines in his face spoke of intelligence and good nature.

"A young amateur cellist," Pitt added.

"Oh yes, I know who you mean," Lismore said quickly. "Most gifted, extraordinary intensity. But why does he concern you, Superintendent?"

"Was he acquainted with the late Aidan Arledge?"

"Certainly. Poor Aidan knew a great number of musicians, both amateur and professional." He frowned, looking at Pitt more closely. "Surely you cannot suspect one of them of being involved in his death? That is absurd."

"Not necessarily culpable, Sir James," Pitt explained. "There are many possibilities of involvement. I am trying to find any link whatever between Captain Winthrop and Mr. Arledge."

Lismore looked surprised. "I perceive the difference, Superintendent. I apologize for leaping to an unjustified conclusion." He put his hands in his pockets and regarded Pitt with interest. "But are you sure that Captain Winthrop was acquainted with Victor Garrick? I believe Captain Winthrop had no fondness whatever for music, and Victor certainly had no desire to have anything to do with the navy. He is a very peaceable, artistic sort of young man, a dreamer, not a man of action. He hates all manner of violence or cruelty, let alone the life of physical discipline and ordered belligerences necessary for life on board a naval vessel."

"It was not a friendship of choice," Pitt explained, smiling to himself at Lismore's description of naval life . . . one with which Victor would have agreed. "A family relationship," he added.

"They were related?" Lismore was amazed. "I understood Victor's father was dead and his mother had no extended family, at least none with whom she is in touch."

"Not related by blood. Captain Winthrop was his godfather."

"Ah." Lismore's face cleared. "Yes, I see. That would be quite different. Yes, that makes ample sense."

"Forgive me, Sir James, but you speak as if you knew Captain Winthrop?"

"Again I apologize, Superintendent. I have unwittingly misled you. Actually I never met him. It was Mrs. Winthrop I knew—very slightly. A charming lady, and most fond of music."

"You know Mrs. Winthrop?" Pitt seized on it, uncertain if it had any meaning, but even the tiniest threads were precious, he had so little. "Was she acquainted with Mr. Arledge, do you know?"

Lismore was surprised.

"Oh yes, indeed. Mind, I cannot say whether it was an acquaintance of any duration or depth, or merely a natural affinity in the love of music and a spontaneous kindness on Aidan's part. He was very gentle, you know, very easily moved to compassion."

"Compassion? Was Mrs. Winthrop in some kind of distress?"

"Indeed." Lismore nodded, watching Pitt curiously. "I don't know what may have been the cause of it, but I recall seeing her on one occasion deeply distressed over something. She was weeping, and Aidan was endeavoring to comfort her. I don't believe he was entirely successful. She left with a young gentleman, of a somewhat sunburned appearance. I believe he was her brother. He also seemed most disturbed about the event, and quite angry."

"Her brother. Bartholomew Mitchell?" Pitt asked quickly.

"I regret I don't recall his name," Lismore apologized. "Indeed I am not sure if I ever met him. Aidan said something about it afterwards, I think that is how I gained the impression he was her brother. You look concerned, Superintendent. Does that have some meaning for you?"

"I'm not sure," Pitt said honestly, but he felt his pulse race with excitement in spite of himself. "Is it possible Mr. Arledge and Mrs. Winthrop had a disagreement about something? Or even that Mr. Mitchell could have assumed it was so?"

"Aidan and Mrs. Winthrop?" Lismore looked startled. "I cannot imagine what about."

"But is it possible?" Pitt insisted.

"I suppose so." Lismore was reluctant. "At least I suppose it is possible Mr. Mitchell misunderstood the situation. He was angry, as I recall, very angry indeed."

"Can you remember anything of it at all, Sir James?" Pitt pressed. "A word, a gesture even?"

Lismore looked uncomfortable, pursing his lips.

"Please!" Pitt could barely contain his impatience.

Lismore took a deep breath and chewed his lower lip before speaking.

"I did overhear a few snatches, Superintendent. I dislike intensely repeating what was most certainly an intensely private conversation, but I can see that you believe it may be of importance."

Pitt was breathless with impatience.

"I heard the man—I shall assume it was the brother—say quite vehemently, 'It is not your fault!' He emphasized the negative most fiercely. He went on, 'I will not have you say so. It is quite absurd and untrue. If Thora is foolish and misguided enough to think so, that is her misfortune, but I will not have it yours. You have done nothing. Do you hear me, nothing, to cause it. You must put it from your mind, totally, and start afresh.' That may not be his words precisely, Superintendent, but it is extremely close, and it is certainly his sense." Lismore looked at Pitt expectantly.

Pitt was confused. Was Bart Mitchell referring to Winthrop's death? And what did Thora Garrick know of this?

"Well?" Lismore asked.

Pitt recalled his attention. "Did you hear the reply?"

"Only in part. She was in some distress, and not entirely coherent."

"And the part you heard?"

"Oh—she insisted it was her fault, that she had caused whatever it had been by her foolishness, and that he really should not be so angry, it was not an uncommon event, or something of the sort. I am sorry, I really was most uncomfortable to have overheard any of it at all."

"Did you see Mr. Mitchell with Mr. Arledge?" Pitt persisted. "What was his manner?"

"No—no I did not." Lismore shook his head. "So far as I can remember, Aidan had left in order to conduct the second half of the performance when I saw Mr. Mitchell take Mrs. Winthrop out towards the door and, I presume, leave the premises. They seemed to have resolved whatever difference it had been by then. Apparently he had persuaded her he was right, and she seemed pleased about it."

"Thank you. You have been extremely helpful." Pitt rose to

his feet with his mind whirling. "Thank you for your time and your frankness." He turned towards the door. "Good day, Sir James."

"Good day, Superintendent," Lismore said with some confusion, and obvious curiosity.

Emily had enjoyed the party, in spite of its having been an entirely political affair. There were many aspects of the campaign she did not care for in the slightest. Speaking in the streets was sometimes fun, other times more tiring, dispiriting or even dangerous. Helping Jack to write articles and speeches for specific audiences was a chore, and one she entered into only because she was loyal to him and wished him to fight with every possible advantage she could give, even if it were a battle he had little realistic chance of winning.

Although in the last few days that had changed markedly. The signs were quite subtle to begin with, an altered tone from one of the principal columnists in the *Times*, a questioning of Uttley's motives for the criticisms he had made of the police, even the suggestion that perhaps Jack Radley's loyalties were more what was desired at the moment. A question of patriotism was raised.

But this evening had been fun. She had danced and chattered, seemingly artlessly, but in fact with the greatest imaginable art. She had flattered and laughed, been amusing and, once or twice, as fitted the moment, even been astute in her observations, politically wise, to the amazement and delight of several portly and middle-aged men of influence. Altogether the whole event had been a resounding success.

As she and Jack took their leave she was on the crest of a wave, and swept out on his arm to walk the short way home to Ashworth House in the balmy late spring evening. The moon was high like a silver lantern above the trees, and the air smelled of night-scented flowers. The shadows of carriages, lanterns gleaming, clattered past them and left them in the darkness between the lampposts almost as if the gentleness of the night were wrapped around them.

Jack was singing under his breath and walking with a very slight swagger. It was not the result of too much indulgence, simply elation and a tremendous sense of well-being.

Emily found herself smiling widely and humming along with him.

They turned the corner from the broad, well-lit avenue into

a quieter road, trees overhanging the high garden walls, shadowing the lamps on their slender posts.

Suddenly Jack let out a cry and lurched against her, catching her roughly and knocking her sideways into the gutter before he fell forward onto his hands, only saving himself at the last moment from injuring his face as he struck the pavement.

Emily let out a shriek of alarm and astonishment. Then it changed to real fear. There was a dark figure looming over Jack, his head covered so his face was unrecognizable, and something raised in his hand with an enormous, wedge-shaped blade.

She screamed with all the force of her lungs.

Jack was sprawled on the pavement and the figure towered above him.

Emily had no weapon, nothing at all with which to defend Jack or herself; not that she even thought of herself.

The figure raised his arms high in the air.

Jack rolled over onto his back and shot out his legs, kicking hard. One foot caught the assailant on the shin just above the ankle, sending him off balance. He staggered backwards.

Emily screamed again and again. For God's sake, somebody must hear!

The assailant was regaining himself, starting forward.

Jack was still not on his feet.

The assailant lifted the great blade.

Jack launched himself from his hands and knees and charged, catching the assailant in the solar plexus with his head. The man gasped, choked, and went backwards into the wall, hitting it hard with his shoulders. There was a clatter as the weapon fell to the ground.

Jack clambered shakily to his feet.

Farther along the pavement someone else was coming, calling out, footsteps loud on the stones.

The assailant turned and fled, limping raggedly, but with a startling speed, until he was around the corner and swallowed up in the darkness.

An elderly gentleman in a dressing robe came running up the pavement, his white nightshirt showing beneath his skirts.

"Oh dear! Oh my goodness!" he gasped. "What on earth . . . ? Madam! Sir—are you injured? Here!" He knelt down beside Jack, where he was again sprawled on the pavement, having overbalanced with the weight of his charge. "Sir!

Are you injured? Who was it? Thieves? Have you been robbed?"

"No, no, I don't think so." Jack answered both questions at once. Then with the man's assistance he scrambled up again and turned immediately to Emily.

"Ma'am?" the man said urgently. "Are you hurt? Did he . . . ?"

"No—no. I am unhurt," Emily said hastily. "Thank you for coming so swiftly, sir, and at such inconvenience. I fear if you had not—"

"We should indeed have been robbed," Jack interrupted.

Another man came running up and stopped abruptly.

"What's going on?" he demanded. "Who's hurt? Are you all right, ma'am? Were these men . . ." He looked at Jack, then at his helper. "Oh—are you sure?"

"Yes, thank you, sir," Emily assured him breathlessly. "My husband was attacked—but he saw the man off, and with this gentleman's prompt arrival the assailant fled."

"Thank God for that. I don't know what the country is coming to." The man's voice was choked with emotion. "There is evidence everywhere. Would you like to come to my house? It is a mere hundred yards, and my staff would be happy to get you some restorative. . . ."

"No thank you," Jack said a little shakily. "Our own home is not much farther. But it is most civil of you."

"Are you quite sure? Are you, madam?"

"Indeed. Thank you." Jack took Emily by the arm. She felt him awkward, his body shaking.

"Yes, thank you," she agreed quickly. "It was very good of you to come out. You have most certainly saved us from a terrible experience."

"If you are quite sure . . . ? Well, as you wish, of course. Good night, sir. Good night, ma'am."

Jack and Emily thanked them again and hurried away, their feet loud on the pavement, eager to escape.

"It wasn't a robber," Emily said huskily.

"I know," Jack replied, his breath catching in his throat. "He was trying to kill me!"

"He had an ax," Emily went on. "Jack—it was the Headsman! It was the Hyde Park Headsman!"

8

THE FOLLOWING MORNING Emily's fear had turned into furious anger. She was still shaking as she sat at the breakfast table opposite Jack, who had come in walking stiffly, and as she faced him he looked distinctly pale.

"What are you going to do about it?" she demanded. "It's monstrous! A member of Parliament attacked in the street by a homicidal lunatic!"

He sat down carefully, as if any twisting or jolting might cause him pain. "I am not a member of Parliament," he said slowly, his brow furrowed as if he had to search for the words. "And there is no reason why I should be exempt . . ."

"Of course there is," Emily rejoined. "You have nothing to do with Captain Winthrop or Mr. Arledge, or the bus conductor, and we weren't even in Hyde Park."

"That is what I was thinking." Jack stared at his plate. Beyond the door came the sound of footsteps as one of the servants crossed the hall.

"What do you mean?" Emily demanded. "You are not making a great deal of sense! Have you sent for the police? I still think you should have sent for them last night. I know they wouldn't have caught anyone by then, but they should still have been told as soon as possible."

"I want to think . . ." Before he could complete his sentence the parlormaid came in with hot tea and fresh toast for Emily, and inquired what Jack would like, offering him smoked haddock, eggs, sausages, bacon and potatoes, or chops. He thanked her and chose the fish.

225

"Think? What about?" Emily demanded as soon as the maid had gone. "The Headsman attacked you, for goodness sake! What is there to think about?" She leaned forward across the table, peering at him. "Jack? Are you ill? Did he injure you?"

He pulled a face of self-mockery, but his amusement was hollow.

"No, of course not. I am a trifle bruised, that's all."

"Are you sure?"

"Yes, I am quite sure." He smiled, but his face was still very pale. "I want to think about it before I decide what to do. . . ."

"I don't know what you mean, what to do! You must report it to the police—preferably to Thomas. He has to know." She leaned on her elbow, staring at him.

"Thomas, of course," he agreed. "But I don't think anyone else."

"I don't understand. Why not anyone else? It is hardly a private thing to be attacked in the street!" Absentmindedly she poured the tea for both of them and passed his across.

"I think it might be better if I didn't mention it," he replied, accepting the tea and taking a slice of toast.

"What? What on earth do you mean?" Her voice rose in incredulity. "No one is going to blame you for it! In fact quite the contrary, they will be highly sympathetic."

"To me, perhaps," he said thoughtfully. "Although there may be those who will wonder if I had some secret connection with the murdered men, and no doubt speculation would be rife. My enemies would—"

"You cannot keep silent in case someone speaks ill of you!" she said quickly. "Those that are of that bent will do so anyway. You cannot run away from it."

"I wasn't thinking of that," he argued. "I was thinking of Thomas."

"But it might help him," she protested reasonably. "The more information he gets, the better chance he will have of finding the Headsman."

The parlormaid returned with the haddock, inquired if there were anything else, and on being told there was not, took her leave.

"I'm not sure it was the Headsman," Jack said as soon as the door was closed.

Emily was stunned. "What do you mean? I saw him. He had an ax! Jack—I saw him!"

"I know that," he said gently. "You saw a man with an ax,

226

but that doesn't mean he was the Headsman. As you just said, I have no connection with Winthrop or Arledge or the bus conductor, nor was I near the park." He took a mouthful of the fish. "And he attacked me when I was in company with someone else. It is not the Headsman's pattern."

"He has no pattern!" Emily said vehemently, ignoring the food.

He looked at her very seriously. "I shall tell Thomas, of course, but I don't think I shall tell the local police. Can't you imagine what the newspapers will say with another attack? It will play right into Uttley's hands."

"Oh." She sat back in her chair, momentarily robbed of anger. "Yes, of course. I hadn't thought of that. We must not give him anything at all. He would use it as another weapon, wouldn't he?"

"I'll send a message to Thomas." Jack ignored the rest of his breakfast and rose, pushing his chair back.

The butler came in behind him, a bundle of newspapers over his arm. He looked very somber.

"I'll look at them later." Jack made as if to walk past him. "I must go and write a note to Superintendent Pitt."

"I think he may already be aware of your misadventure, sir," the butler said gravely.

"There is no way he could," Jack replied, continuing on towards the door. "I did not tell the man who came to help us anything except that I lived not far away. It was too dark for him to have recognized me, even if he were minded to tell anyone, which he wouldn't."

The butler cleared his throat and set the newspapers down on the edge of the table. "I am sorry to say, sir, but you are mistaken in him. It is headlined in several of the newspapers this morning, most especially the *Times*. Mr. Uttley has written a very critical piece about the police force, I am afraid."

"What?" Jack strode back and seized the top newspaper, holding it up to stare at it in horror. "This is absurd! How could Uttley possibly have known in time to have written this? In fact, how could he have known at all?"

"I'm sure I don't know, sir. Do you still wish to send a note to Superintendent Pitt, sir?"

"Yes—no." Jack sat down again hard, scratching his chair legs on the polished wooden floor. "This is damnable!"

Before Emily could reply there was a knock on the door and

the maid opened it. "Superintendent Pitt is here to see you, sir. Shall I tell him as you're in, sir?"

"Yes. Yes of course I'm in," Jack said angrily. "Get him another cup and some more tea. And some fish, if he wants it."

"Yes sir."

Pitt came in almost as soon as she had withdrawn. He looked tired and profoundly worried.

"Are you all right?" he said quickly, looking from one to the other of them. "What happened? Why in Hell's name didn't you tell me last night?"

Emily swallowed hard and looked away.

"Sit down." Jack pointed to a third chair not far from the table. "There's more tea coming. Would you like something to eat? Smoked haddock? Eggs?"

"No thank you," Pitt dismissed the offer totally, but accepted the seat.

Jack continued talking. "I didn't tell you because I didn't tell anyone last night," he explained. "We came straight home and went to bed. No one knows but the servants." He smiled in self-mockery. "One cannot keep much from them, especially when one is covered with bruises and limping around like the Ancient of Days. But I was going to send you a note just now, when Jenkins brought in the newspapers and said it was all over the front pages. I'm damned if I know how."

"What happened?" Pitt asked wearily.

In careful and very precise detail, and without interruption from Emily, Jack recounted the events of the previous evening from the time he and Emily had left the reception until they had reached their home and closed the door on the street, with its sudden, inexplicable violence and fear.

The maid had brought a further cup and Emily had poured the tea, which Pitt sipped as he listened. Finally he put it down and regarded Jack with furrowed brows.

"Are you sure you haven't forgotten anything?"

Jack looked at Emily.

"Nothing," she replied. "That is exactly what happened."

"Who was the man who came to your rescue?" Pitt looked from one to the other.

"I don't know," Emily said quickly. "I didn't ask his name, nor did I give him mine."

"Would you know him if you were to meet him again?"

"Possibly." This time it was Jack who answered. "I'm not certain. The street was very ill-lit and I was considerably

228

shaken. Added to which he was not dressed as one customarily meets someone."

"How were you dressed?"

"Evening clothes, black and white." Jack shrugged. "I did not have an overcoat because the evening was very mild." He glanced at Emily. "Emily was in a deep green gown, but she did have a cloak, one with a hood, which she had up over her head."

"Could he have recognized you?" Pitt asked her thoughtfully.

Emily shook her head. "I've never met him before, so far as I can think. Anyway, why should he recognize me? I'm not running for Parliament." She shook her head even more vehemently. "No, no, I was on the ground some of the time, and while he was helping Jack I did stand up, but my face was towards Jack. I don't think I ever really looked at the man."

Pitt was thoughtful. "Then how did he know who you were? You are quite sure there was no one else?"

"Another man did come up as we were leaving," Jack replied. "But all we said to him was that we were unhurt."

"There were other people approaching as well," Emily added. "I had screamed as loudly as I was able. I imagine it attracted the attention of several people—I surely hope so. I tried hard enough."

"But I was not within a mile of Hyde Park," Jack pointed out. "And I know nothing about Winthrop or Arledge. Why me?"

"I don't know." Pitt sounded thoroughly discouraged and Emily was so sorry for him that for a moment she forgot her own anger.

"Jack thinks it might not have been the Headsman," she said very gravely. "He did have an ax, though, because I saw it quite distinctly. Do you suppose it could have been political?"

Pitt stared at her.

She looked embarrassed. Perhaps it was a foolish question.

Pitt rose to his feet and thanked them for the tea.

"I want to find out how Uttley knew about it," he said with a frown. "It doesn't make sense."

He expected to have some trouble locating Nigel Uttley, considering that the political campaign was in full swing, but actually it turned out to be quite easy. Uttley was at his home just off Manchester Square and received Pitt without any pre-

229

varication, choosing to come out to the hall to meet him rather than invite him into a library or study.

"Good morning, Superintendent," he said briskly, smiling and putting his hands into his pockets. "What can I do for you? I am afraid my knowledge of last night's affray is very secondhand and I can think of nothing to tell you which you could not easily discover for yourself."

"Good morning, Mr. Uttley," Pitt said grimly. "That may be so. However, I should like to know directly from you the facts you wrote in the *Times* and seem to be so familiar with."

Uttley's eyebrows rose. "I detect a certain note of sarcasm in your tone, Superintendent." He smiled as he spoke, and rocked very slowly back and forth on the balls of his feet. The hall was handsome, very classical, with a Romanesque frieze around the walls just below the ceiling. The front door was still standing wide open and the sun streamed in. A young man stood on the steps outside, apparently awaiting Uttley's attention.

Pitt would very much rather have discussed the matter in private, but Uttley apparently chose not to. He was going to wring the last possible political advantage out of it.

Pitt ignored the jibe. "How did you know about it, Mr. Uttley?"

"How?" Uttley seemed amused. "The local constable mentioned it. Why? Surely that cannot matter, Superintendent?"

Pitt was furious. What irresponsible constable had spoken to a civilian about the case? To have discussed it with anyone at all would have been bad enough, but to have chosen a politician who was building his platform upon his accusations of police incompetence was a breach of loyalty and duty beyond excusing.

"What was his name, Mr. Uttley?"

"Who? The constable?" Uttley's eyes were very wide. "I have no idea. I didn't ask him. Really, Superintendent, aren't you wasting your time over quite the wrong thing? Perhaps he should not have confided in me, but it is just possible he is as concerned as the general public about the violence in our midst." He hunched his shoulders and drove his hands deeper into his pockets. His voice was loud and very distinct when he continued. "I don't think you seem to realize, Superintendent, just how deeply alarmed people are. Women are terrified to go out and many are ill with fear for their husbands and fathers, begging them not to leave home after nightfall. The parks are deserted. Even theaters are complaining that their patronage is falling off because no one wishes to have to return home in the dark."

There were all sorts of answers Pitt might have given, but none of them countered the fact that the fear was real, however exaggerated. There was a smell of panic in the streets and he had felt it himself.

"I am aware of it, Mr. Uttley," he replied as civilly as he could. It was not that Uttley was pointing it out to him that stirred his anger, but the pleasure that gleamed in the man's eyes as he did it. "We are doing everything we can to apprehend the man."

"Well it is patently not enough," Uttley said penetratingly.

Outside on the step the young man was joined by a second.

"What did the constable tell you, Mr. Uttley?" Pitt kept the temper out of his voice as well as he could, but was not completely successful.

"That Radley had been attacked by a man with an ax who tried to kill him," Uttley replied, looking beyond Pitt to the man on the step. "I shall be with you in a moment, gentlemen!" He looked back at Pitt, the smile on his lips broader. "Really, Superintendent, is this the best you can do? Surely a man of your rank can think of something more profitable to pursue than asking me for secondhand information, which I cannot help but think you want for the purpose of victimizing some wretched junior for having told me what you perhaps wish to keep secret."

The young men outside came closer.

"Certainly if I find him, Mr. Uttley," Pitt replied between his teeth, "I shall criticize him for having told you rather than me. That was a dereliction of duty which requires a good deal of explanation!"

"Not told you?" Uttley was amazed. "Good heavens!" His face filled with surprise, and then delighted amusement, so open as to be on the edge of laughter. "Do you mean you are here to find the facts, because your own police force has not told you? My God! Your incompetence exceeds all imagination. If you think I have criticized you so far, my dear man, I assure you, I have hardly begun."

"No, Mr. Uttley, I am not here to find out the facts," Pitt spat back. "I have those from Mr. Radley, including the fact that he gave no one his name and did not call the police."

"Didn't call the police?" Uttley's face fell and he looked totally confused. "What do you mean? He was attacked in the street and damn nearly killed. Of course he called the police."

"He was attacked." Pitt was now also raising his voice. "But he was in perfect health this morning, and I understand from Mrs. Radley that he saw off the assailant fairly quickly, sustaining nothing more than a few bruises."

"Is that what he says?" Uttley's expression changed again to one of derision. "How brave of him—and loyal to his rather eccentric position of defending the police."

"Is it not the truth?" Pitt inquired, suddenly softly.

"He was attacked by the Hyde Park Headsman, I heard," Uttley said, not quite so blandly now. "Surely any man with a shred of responsibility would report that instantly to the police, whether he was actually hurt or not?"

"He reported it to me," Pitt replied, stretching the truth very considerably—in fact, if not in spirit.

Uttley shrugged, pulling a face, and turned away. "Well then I assume you know all that you need to. That makes it rather unpleasantly obvious that you are asking me only in order to persecute this wretched constable, doesn't it?"

"If he was the officer at the scene of the crime, it is important that I speak to him," Pitt replied, gaining confidence every second. "Since Mr. Radley left immediately upon his escape from the attacker, waiting only long enough to assure his rescuer that he was unhurt, it is possible the constable may have found something of interest, for example the ax."

Uttley looked startled, then composed himself rapidly.

"Then you had better go and look for him. It should not be beyond the powers of an officer of your experience to detect where one of your men has got to." He laughed loudly. "What a farce! Gilbert and Sullivan could write a hilarious song about you, Superintendent, even funnier than the one in *Pirates*. Wait until the newspapers hear that the superintendent in charge of the case is busy combing London for one of his own constables. I imagine the cartoonists will have a marvelous time. What a gift!"

"You seem to think I shall have some difficulty, Mr. Uttley," Pitt said just as clearly and penetratingly as Uttley had spoken. "Will it not be simply a matter of going to the appropriate station and inquiring as to who was on duty that evening?"

"I have no idea," Uttley replied, but there was a very faint pinkness to his cheeks and his eyes did not meet Pitt's as squarely as they had before. He thrust his hands deeper into his pockets and turned away. "And now if there is nothing further I can do for you, I have a great deal of other business to attend. I am sorry I cannot do anything to help you when you so apparently need it."

"You have helped me a great deal," Pitt replied. Then he added with a touch of bravado, "In fact, you may have solved it for me entirely. Good day, sir." He walked out of the front door and passed the two young men on the steps, tipping his hat gently. "Good day, gentlemen."

They turned to stare after him as he went on down the steps to the pavement, then looked at each other with wide eyes.

Pitt intended going straight to the police station from where any patrolling constable would have come, but before he reached it he was crossing a broad thoroughfare, moving between a fishmonger's barrow and a cart filled with potatoes and cabbages, when he was accosted by a very fat man with grayish hair which fell in curls over his collar. His green eyes were bulbous in his bloated face. He was dressed immaculately with a long gold watch chain across his vast stomach. Beside him was another man, who barely came up to his elbow, his squat figure distorted, his sharp face vicious, lips open to show pointed, discolored teeth.

"Good morning, George," Pitt said to the huge man. He looked from Fat George to his companion. "Good morning, Georgie."

"Ah, Mr. Pitt," Fat George said in a soft, high-pitched voice, oddly sad and whispering. "You've let us down, sir, that you have. The park isn't safe for gentlemen anymore. It's awful hard for business, sir. Awful hard."

"You aren't doing right by us, Mr. Pitt," Wee Georgie added in a voice that was a hideous mimicry of his partner's, the same breathy softness, but with a sibilance which made it harsher and immeasurably uglier. "We don't like that. It's costing us a lot o' money, Mr. Pitt."

"If I knew who the Headsman was, I assure you I'd arrest him," Pitt answered as levelly as he could. "We are doing everything we can to find him."

"Not good enough, Mr. Pitt," Wee Georgie said, pulling a face. "Not good enough at all."

"There's a lot of gentlemen wot's too scared to take their pleasures, Mr. Pitt," Fat George added, poking his silver-handled stick at the ground. "They're not happy, not happy at all."

"Then you had better see what you can do to find out who the Headsman is," Pitt replied. "You have more eyes and ears in the park than I have."

"We don't know anyfink," Fat George said plaintively. "I thought we'd told you that already, one way and another. Do you suppose if we did we'd be standing here in this street between the carts reproaching you, Mr. Pitt? We'd have dealt with him ourselves. It isn't any of our people. If you imagine it is something to do with business, you are mistaken."

"Fool!" Wee Georgie spoke viciously. "Cretin! Do you think we like this kind o' thing going on? If one of our people started cutting gents' 'eads off, we'd stick a shiv in 'is back and put 'im in the river. We might teach the odd person a lesson wot gets above 'emselves and starts poachin', but never touch a toff. It's bad for business, and that's stupid!" He fingered something at the side of his leg, invisible under his coat. Pitt was sure it was a knife. The little man licked his lips with a pointed tongue and stared at Pitt without blinking.

"What Georgie says is true, Mr. Pitt," Fat George whispered, breathing in and out wheezily. "It's not us. It's somefink to do with gentlemen, you mark my words."

"A lunatic from some . . ." Pitt began.

Fat George shook his head. "You know better than that, Mr. Pitt. I'm surprised at you. You're wasting my time. There's no lunatic living in the park, we both know that."

Wee Georgie fidgeted from one foot to the other. A succession of carts and wagons was passing in the streets just beyond the two men.

Pitt did not argue. He had never thought it was a random madman.

"You'd better find 'im, Mr. Pitt," Fat George said again, shaking his head till his curls bounced on his Astrakhan collar. "Or we shall be very upset, Wee Georgie and me."

"I shall be upset myself," Pitt said sourly. "But if it really bothers you, you'd better start doing something about it yourself."

Wee Georgie looked at him venomously. Fat George smiled, but there was neither humor nor pleasantness in it.

"That's your job, Mr. Pitt," he said softly. "We would like it very much if you would attend to it." And without saying anything further he turned on his heel and in a moment had disappeared between the carts. Wee Georgie looked up at Pitt one more time, his eyes full of malice, then trotted after his companion. He was obliged to trot in order to keep up, and it infuriated him.

Pitt continued on his way without giving the matter a great deal more thought, but it was an indication of the public mood that even Fat George should have felt the pinch of fear touching his business.

At the police station he was met with blank incomprehension. The inspector who spoke to him was a tall, lean man with a lugubrious, ascetic face and an air of harrowed dignity.

"We don't know anything about it," he said wearily. "Incredible as it seems, it was not reported to us. I know little more than I read in the newspapers."

"Not reported?" Pitt was startled. "This is the right station?"

"Yes it is." The inspector sighed. "I checked all my men. I wanted to know for myself what irresponsible idiot spoke to Uttley about it, but no one was on patrol in that area. And I've checked, so you don't need to wonder if my men are telling the truth or if someone is trying to lie their way out of a stupid mistake. Every man can account for where he was. Uttley didn't get it from one of them."

"How very curious," Pitt said thoughtfully. He did not doubt the man, nor did he think his constables were lying; it would be too easy to check, and the man found in such a stupid act would lose his employment.

"It's a dammed sight more than that," the inspector said tartly. "I can only suppose it must have been one of the people who came to help. Radley himself would hardly have told the newspapers. He at least seems to be on our side. He's about the only one. Have you seen the papers, sir?"

"Yes—yes, that's how I heard of it, in spite of the fact that Radley's my brother-in-law."

The inspector's bushy eyebrows shot up. "Wasn't he going to report it?"

"To me, because the man had an ax, but not to you. Wanted to save us the publicity of another attack."

"Makes us look pretty stupid, doesn't it?" the inspector said grimly. "It has to come to a sad state when a member of Parliament rides to power on the tide of public disgust with the police." He pulled a face. "Bit of a coincidence, isn't it, that the Headsman should attack Uttley's rival in the by-election?"

"More than a bit," Pitt replied. "Thank you for your time, Inspector. I think I'll go and see these gentlemen who came to Mr. Radley's aid, see what they have to say for themselves."

"Can't think what for. They didn't see the wretched man," the inspector said lugubriously. "Still, if you think it's worth it?"

"Oh yes—yes, it may be."

"Most certainly not, sir," Mr. Milburn said in amazement. "That would be an inexcusable liberty, sir. Why in Heaven's name should I do such a thing, indeed?"

"It might have been how you saw your public duty," Pitt responded soothingly. "Or it is possible to let something slip in the heat of the moment."

Mr. Milburn stood very straight, his shoulders square.

"The only heated moment, sir, was at the time of the attack upon the poor gentleman. And the lady too, for Heaven's sake! Right in the middle of an exceptional area like this. A person is not safe anywhere these days." Mr. Milburn shook his head, then ran his short fingers through his hair. "I really don't know what things are coming to. I don't wish to appear critical, sir, but the police force ought to be able to do better than this. We are living in the largest city in the world, and many would say the most civilized, and yet we walk our own streets in fear of anarchists and lunatics. It is not good enough, sir!"

"I regret it," Pitt said sincerely. "But I know of nothing we could do that we are not doing."

"I daresay, I daresay." Milburn nodded and looked a trifle embarrassed. "Fear does not bring out the best in us. Perhaps I spoke hastily. Is there any way in which I can be of help?"

"Did you recognize anyone, sir?" Pitt asked.

"My dear fellow, I did not even see the attack. I was in my bedroom preparing to retire when I heard the good lady's screams. I immediately ran down the stairs and out into the street to see what assistance I could give."

"That is most commendable," Pitt said sincerely. "And I may say, very brave."

Milburn colored faintly.

"Thank you, sir, thank you. I freely admit I did not even think of the danger to myself at the time, or I might have reconsidered the matter. But that is as it may be. No, I cannot help you in the slightest in that regard, I am afraid."

"Actually, sir, I meant did you recognize the lady and gentleman who were the victims of the attack?"

"No sir, I did not. It was all extremely hasty and in the dark. And I confess, normally I wear spectacles. I did not have them on this occasion, of course. The gentleman appeared to be quite young. He certainly moved in the most agile manner. And robust, yes definitely robust. I cannot say more than that." He took a deep breath and regarded Pitt very soberly. "As for the lady, it was certain she had spirit, and very fine lungs, but I really did not notice beyond that, even if she were fair or dark, comely or plain. I am sorry, sir, it seems I can be of no use whatever. I begin to appreciate your difficulty."

"On the contrary, Mr. Milburn," Pitt replied. "You are of the utmost help possible. In fact I think you may have solved the entire problem for me. Thank you, sir, good day to you." And he excused himself and left Mr. Milburn standing open-mouthed, searching in vain for something appropriate to say.

But at Bow Street the reception was entirely different. Giles Farnsworth was in Pitt's office, pacing the floor. He swung around as soon as he heard Pitt's hand on the door and he was facing Pitt as he entered, a newspaper in his hand.

"I assume you have read this?" he said furiously. "How do you explain it? What are you doing about it?" He waved the paper in the air. "Now a prospective member of Parliament has been attacked in the heart of Mayfair! Do you know anything about this Headsman at all, Pitt? Any single damn thing!"

"I know this wasn't the Headsman," Pitt replied in a calm, precise voice.

"Not the Headsman?" Farnsworth said incredulously. "Are you telling me we have two homicidal lunatics running around London swinging axes at people?"

"No, we have one madman and one opportunist taking advantage of the situation."

"What? What are you talking about?" Farnsworth demanded. "What sort of advantage would a sane man possibly take of this nightmare?"

"Political," Pitt replied succinctly.

"Political?" Farnsworth's eyes opened and he stood perfectly still. "Are you saying what I think you are, Pitt? My God, if you make this accusation, you'd better be right. And you'd better be able to prove it."

"I can't prove it sufficiently to charge him," Pitt replied, walking into the room and across to his desk. "But I am satisfied it was he who attacked Mr. and Mrs. Radley last night."

Farnsworth stared at him, the newspaper forgotten. "Are you? Your word, Pitt?"

"My word," Pitt replied slowly.

"How do you know? He didn't admit it?"

"No, of course not; but it was he who wrote it up in the newspapers. He told me that he heard of it from a constable on duty, but there was no such constable, nor did he learn it from the man who came to Mr. Radley's rescue, because he was unaware of Radley's identity."

"Indeed," Farnsworth said thoughtfully. "The man's a complete fool." The contempt in his voice was stinging. Then he dismissed the matter and looked back at Pitt with a return of his anxiety. "What about the real Headsman? The whole city is under a pall of terror. There have been questions in the House of Commons, the Home Secretary has been severely embarrassed at the dispatch box. Her Majesty has expressed her concern. She is distressed, and has made it known." Suddenly his voice rose, harsh and furious, the fear rushing back in like a tide. "For God's sake, Pitt, what's the matter with you, man? There must be something you can do to find enough evidence to arrest him!"

"Are you talking about Carvell again, sir?" Pitt asked carefully.

"Of course I'm talking about Carvell," Farnsworth snapped. "The man had the motive, the means and the opportunity. You've got the ideal leverage to pressure him into a confession. Use it!"

"I don't have anything—" Pitt began, but Farnsworth interrupted him impatiently.

"Oh, for God's sake!" He slashed his hand through the air. "Tellman's right, you're too squeamish. This is not the time or the place to indulge your personal conscience, Pitt." He leaned forward across the corner of the desk, resting his hands on it, staring at Pitt eye to eye. "You have obligations, duties to your superiors and to the force. You've got to be above such things. They're for juniors, if you like, not for the men in charge. Face your responsibilities, Pitt—or resign!"

"I cannot arrest Carvell," Pitt said very quietly. "And I refuse to persecute the man over what I believe his private life to be."

"Dammit, Pitt!" Farnsworth smashed his fist down on the desk. "The man was having an illicit love affair with the victim of a murder. He can't account for where he was either then or when Winthrop was killed. Arledge may have known Winthrop—"

"How do you know that?" Pitt interrupted.

Farnsworth looked at him incredulously. "He knew Mrs. Winthrop. It's not a large leap from that to suppose he knew Winthrop himself. And if Carvell was a jealous man, then the conclusion is obvious."

"Tellman told you?"

"Of course Tellman told me! What's the matter with you? What are you hesitating for?"

"It could as easily have been Bartholomew Mitchell."

Now Farnsworth was confused.

"Mitchell? Winthrop's brother-in-law? Why, for Heaven's sake? What had he to do with Arledge?"

"Winthrop beat his wife," Pitt replied. "Mitchell knew it. Arledge was seen with Mrs. Winthrop when she was extremely distressed over something."

"And the omnibus conductor?" Farnsworth pursued, ignoring the issue of Winthrop and the beating. "What about him? Don't tell me he had anything to do with this domestic melodrama?"

"No idea. But then we have no idea what he has to do with Carvell either," Pitt argued.

Farnsworth bit his lip. "Blackmail," he said acidly. "It's the only answer. Somehow or other he was in the park and saw one of the murders. I still think it's Carvell. Go after him, Pitt. Press him into telling you the truth. You'll get a confession, if he's guilty."

There was a knock on the door before Pitt could reply, and without waiting for an answer, it opened and Tellman came in.

"Oh," he said with some surprise, as if he had not known Farnsworth was there. "Excuse me, sir." He looked at Pitt. "I thought you'd like to know, Mr. Pitt. The men have been following up Mr. Carvell's whereabouts at the times of the murders."

"Yes?" Pitt said sharply, a sinking feeling in his stomach.

Farnsworth stared at Tellman, his eyes wide.

"Haven't found anyone to substantiate it," Tellman replied. "Not for Captain Winthrop or Mr. Arledge. I don't know what else we can try."

"That's sufficient," Farnsworth said decisively. "Arrest him for the murder of Arledge. The other two don't matter for the charge. Once you've got him in custody, he'll break."

Pitt drew breath to argue, but Tellman cut across him.

"We don't know about Yeats yet, sir," he said quickly, looking at Farnsworth. "He might have been somewhere he can prove when that happened."

"Well what does he say?" Farnsworth demanded irritably.

"That he was at a concert, and we're still looking into it," Tellman replied, his eyes very wide open, his expression innocent. "We'd look stupid if we arrested him, then found someone who said that they'd seen him at the theater half a dozen miles away at, say, midnight."

"What time was Yeats killed?"

"Probably between midnight and half past," Pitt replied.

"Probably?" Farnsworth said sharply. "How accurate can the medical examiner be? Maybe it was later. Maybe it was a couple of hours later. That would give Carvell plenty of time to have taken a hansom to Shepherd's Bush." He looked from Tellman to Pitt, his face triumphant.

Tellman looked at him very deliberately.

"Wouldn't matter, sir. Yeats would hardly have been hanging around the Shepherd's Bush bus terminal a couple of hours after he came in. He'd set off home, the driver said that. And since it's only fifteen minutes or so at a good walk, that narrows down the time of his death rather fine."

Farnsworth's lips tightened. "Then you'd better get on with finding out who else was at that concert," he said. "If the man was there, someone must have seen him! He's a well-known figure. He didn't sit in a room alone. For God's sake, man, you're a detective. There must be a way of proving if he was there or not. What about the interval? Did he take refreshment? He must have spoken to someone. Concerts are social occasions as well as musical."

"He says he didn't," Tellman answered. "It was shortly after Arledge's death, and he wasn't feeling like speaking to anyone. He simply went for the music, because it carried memories for him. He went in without speaking to anyone, and came out the same way."

"Then arrest him," Farnsworth repeated. "He's our man."

"What if it turns out to be Mr. Mitchell, sir?" Tellman said ingenuously. "Seems he could have had cause as well, and he can't prove where he was either, except for Mrs. Winthrop's word, and that doesn't count for much."

Farnsworth turned towards the door.

"Well you'd better do something, and quickly." He ignored Tellman and faced Pitt. "Or you will have to be replaced by someone who will be more effective. The public have the right to expect something better than this. The Home Secretary is taking a personal interest in the case, and even Her Majesty is concerned. The end of the week, Pitt—no more."

As soon as he was gone Pitt looked at Tellman curiously.

Tellman affected a certain indifference.

"They would," he said casually. "Pity they can't think of some useful suggestions. Damned if I know what else to do. We've got two men trying to find out everything they can about the damned bus conductor. He's so ordinary he could be changed with ten thousand other ordinary little men and no one would know the difference with any of them. Pompous, bossy, lived with his wife and two dogs, fancied pigeons, drank ale at the Fox and Grapes on a Friday night, played dominoes badly, but was rather good at the odd game of darts. Why would anybody murder a man like that?"

"Because he saw something he shouldn't have," Pitt answered simply.

"But he was on his bus when Winthrop and Arledge were killed," Tellman answered in exasperation. "And it didn't run anywhere near the park. And even if Arledge was killed somewhere else, we know exactly where Winthrop was killed."

"Then put someone further onto searching for the place where Arledge was killed," Pitt said without hope. "Search all the area 'round Carvell's house. See if you can find an excuse to call on Mitchell, and search that house again too."

"Yes sir. What are you going to do?" For once it was asked without insolence.

"I am going to attend the Requiem service for Aidan Arledge."

There was never any question that Charlotte would accompany Pitt, first to the Requiem service itself, and then to the reception afterwards. The new house was very nearly completed and there were a score more minor things to be seen to: curtains to be hung, loose floorboards to be screwed down, a water tap replaced, tiles to be affixed in the kitchen and more in the pantry, and so on. However, they all paled to insignificance compared with the opportunity to meet probably all the main protagonists in the tragedies Pitt was investigating.

Deliberately they arrived early, discreetly dressed like the other mourners. Indeed Pitt had spent three times as long in front of the cheval glass as usual. It was still only a matter of minutes, but he had also allowed Charlotte to readjust his collar, his cravat and his jacket until they were to her satisfaction. Charlotte herself was dressed in the same black gown she had worn for the funeral reception for Captain Winthrop, but with a quite different hat, this time high crowned and smaller brimmed, and absolutely up to the moment, if not a trifle ahead of it. It was a gift from Great-Aunt Vespasia.

They had only just alighted from their hansom, around the corner so as not to be seen without a personal carriage, when they met Jack and Emily, also arrived early. Jack was as casually elegant as usual, even though he still walked a trifle stiffly. Charlotte knew all about the incident from the newspapers, from Pitt, and from Emily herself, upon whom she had quite naturally called very shortly after reading of it.

Emily was ravishing in black silk overlaid with lace and cut with wide sleeves and pleated shoulders. However, there was a flicker of appreciation when she saw Charlotte's hat, and something like surprise in her face.

"I'm so glad you are here," she said immediately, moving over to stand beside Charlotte, and saying nothing about the hat. "I feel terribly guilty. We haven't accomplished a thing to help Thomas, and if I am honest, we haven't really tried. What the newspapers are saying is quite unjust, but then justice never had anything to do with it. Do you know who is who?" She indicated the gathering around to explain the meaning of her last remark.

"Of course I don't," Charlotte replied under her breath. "Except that looks like Mina Winthrop. And that's her brother, Bart Mitchell. Thomas." She looked around to find Pitt. "Why are they here? Is it just sympathy, do you suppose? She looks very sad."

"She knew him," Pitt replied, moving close to them again and acknowledging Emily.

"She knew him?" Charlotte was aghast. "You didn't tell me!"

"I only just learned of it. . . ."

"How well? How did she know him?" she plunged on. "Could it have been . . . ? Oh, no, of course it couldn't—"

"Oh look at that poor soul," Emily interrupted as Jerome Carvell passed within a few yards of them. "The poor man looks appalling." And indeed he did; his face was sickly pale, his eyes red-rimmed as if he had been up half the night straining them to see something which, when he had finally perceived it, had shaken him to the core. He walked wearily and threaded his way between people without meeting anyone's eyes. He spoke only to acknowledge people's sympathies.

"He looks deeply troubled," Charlotte said softly. "Poor man. I wonder if he knows something, or if it is merely grief?"

"It could be both," Emily answered, looking not at Carvell's back as he disappeared but at Mina Winthrop. Mina was wearing black for her own mourning, of course, as well as this occasion, but now with trimmings of garnet and pearl jewelry, and no veil over her face. Her skin was clear, and flushed with faint color, and she looked around her with interest. Her brother stood close beside her, and it crossed Charlotte's mind that he wished to be aware if she moved from him, as one does in the company of a small child who might be in danger if unsupervised, or might even wander off and get lost. She had stood close to her own children like that, talking to someone, and yet half her mind attuned to their presence.

She turned to Pitt. "Thomas . . ."

"Yes?"

"Is Bart Mitchell a suspect?"

"Why?"

"Because Captain Winthrop beat her, of course. I mean, what about Aidan Arledge? Could he also have done something to hurt Mina?"

"I don't know. She was very distressed on the occasion they were seen together. It is possible."

"What about the bus conductor?"

"No idea. There seems to be no reason for him, whoever it was."

"He saw something," Emily said reasonably. "From his omnibus."

"It didn't run anywhere near Hyde Park."

"Oh."

More people were arriving, among them a man of most distinguished appearance. He was in his middle years, with a handsome head, thick hair, graying at the temples, and a fine mustache. He was dressed immaculately in the latest cut of suit and silk shirt. He walked with shoulders back and a casual confidence which drew many people's eyes towards him. Apparently he was accustomed to such attention, because it did not seem to cause him any concern, in fact he seemed hardly to be aware of it.

"Who is he?" Charlotte asked curiously. "Is he a cabinet minister, or something of that sort?"

"I don't recognize him." Pitt shook his head.

Emily stifled a giggle with her black-gloved hand over her mouth.

"Don't be absurd. It's Sullivan."

"Who is Sullivan?" Charlotte asked tartly.

"Sir Arthur Sullivan!" Emily hissed. "Gilbert and Sullivan!"

"Oh! Oh, I see. Yes of course. Mr. Arledge was a composer and conductor, wasn't he? I wonder if Mr. Gilbert will come."

"Oh no," Emily replied quickly. "Not if he knows Sir Arthur is here. They've quarreled, you know."

"Have they?" Charlotte was surprised and disappointed. "I didn't know that. How on earth do they write such gorgeous operas together, then?"

"I don't know. Maybe they don't do it anymore."

Charlotte felt unreasonably disappointed. She could still remember the color and excitement, the gaiety and irrepressible melody, of the few evenings she had spent at the Savoy Opera. Now just as Pitt was promoted and they might begin to afford such things more often, there were to be no more.

Her disappointment was interrupted by a second wave of interest from the rapidly expanding group by the church door. People moved aside, nudged each other and, without intending to, turned to stare.

"That's him!" Emily said with unconcealed delight.

"Who? Gilbert?" Charlotte whispered back.

"Yes, of course. W. S. Gilbert," Emily said urgently.

"Did they really quarrel?" Charlotte watched as Mr. Gilbert moved inexorably closer to where Sir Arthur Sullivan was standing at the top of the steps by the church door, apparently oblivious of new arrivals. "What about?"

"I don't know. That's what I heard." Emily took Charlotte's arm and propelled her closer to the church steps. "I am sure it is time we went in. It would be most inconsiderate to keep people waiting, don't you think? And ridiculous, after having come here early, to enter the church late."

Charlotte accepted without demur.

At the top of the steps Sir Arthur Sullivan became aware of a considerable stir in the crowd and turned to see W. S. Gilbert a few yards from him, mounting the stairs at a steady pace, talking to those on either side of him with earnestness, and they were listening with such apparently total attention that they did not look or slow their stride until it appeared as if they were going to bump into each other.

Sir Arthur stood his ground, continuing his own conversation as though it were the most important thing in the world.

Mr. Gilbert was forced to come to a halt on the top step.

"Sir, you are blocking the way," he said clearly, his voice carrying to all the assembled people.

A hush fell over them. One by one they turned to stare. Someone cleared his throat nervously. Someone else giggled and instantly stifled it.

Sir Arthur stopped his conversation with a large man with white hair, and very slowly turned to face Gilbert.

"Are you addressing me, sir?"

Gilbert looked around carefully to see if there were anyone else in his immediate path, then faced Sir Arthur again.

"You have an excellent grasp of the obvious, sir," he replied. "I see you have reduced the matter to its core in one leap of deduction. I am addressing you, sir. You are blocking the entrance to the church. Would you be so kind as to make way?"

"Can't you abide your turn, sir, like a civilized man?" Sir Arthur's eyebrows rose in an expression of disdain. "Must the whole of society stop its business and move aside so you may pass the instant you wish to?"

"I like a man with self-esteem, sir, but to regard yourself as the whole of society is to verge upon the ridiculous," Gilbert replied.

Sir Arthur flushed a dull pink. The exchange had now made it impossible for him to move aside without losing face. He remained precisely where he was, right in Gilbert's path.

It was Lady Lismore who saved the situation. She emerged from the shadow of the church doorway and addressed Sir Arthur.

"I do apologize for interrupting you, Sir Arthur, but I should greatly appreciate your assistance. We must have the music right for such an occasion, and I am not at all sure about the cellist."

Sir Arthur looked irritated, as if he had actually had the perfect riposte on the edge of his tongue, but he went with her with some alacrity. "Of course, Lady Lismore. Any assistance I can offer . . ."

Mr. Gilbert smiled to himself and glanced sideways at the watching and listening assembly. But there was only the very faintest satisfaction in him as he went through the church doors and disappeared into the shade of the dim interior.

Charlotte let out her breath in a sigh.

" 'With a twisted cue and a cloth untrue, and elliptical billiard balls,' " Emily said cheerfully. " 'My object all sublime, I shall achieve in time . . .' "

"Ssh!" Charlotte frowned. "You can't go into church for a Requiem service singing *The Mikado*!"

Emily fell silent immediately, at least until they were shown into a pew rather nearer the back than they had wished. Pitt and Jack were somewhere to their left, Pitt well in the shadows of the support pillars.

"There are a lot of people here," Emily said as soon as they were settled. "I suppose it is because he was murdered. I'll wager half of them have only come out of curiosity."

"So have you," Charlotte pointed out.

"Don't be spiteful. You know the campaigning is going very well. I really think Jack has a chance of being elected."

"Good. Now be quiet! We are in church."

"It hasn't started yet," Emily replied. "Aunt Vespasia said she was coming, but I haven't seen her. Have you?"

"No. But I haven't seen anyone else I recognize either."

"Have you seen Mama lately?"

"No, I've been too busy with the house."

Emily bent her head as if she were deep in prayer or contemplation.

"She is getting worse," she hissed into her prayer book. "She was out on the river till dawn the other night."

"How do you know?"

"I saw her."

"So you were out too."

"That's different!" Emily was indignant. "Quite different. Really, sometimes you are obtuse."

"No I'm not. I just don't think there is any purpose in being upset about it. You can't stop her."

"If I saw her, then Heaven knows who else did!"

The woman in the pew in front turned around and glared at Emily, fanning herself with her order paper for the service.

"Are you unwell?" she said crisply. "Perhaps you should take a little air before the service begins."

"How considerate of you," Emily replied with a saccharine smile. "But if I were to leave, I doubt I should ever find my seat again, and then my poor sister would have to sit all by herself."

Charlotte covered her face with her hands to hide her laughter and allow the woman to assume it was grief.

246

The woman turned back with a frown.

The organ music swelled and then suddenly fell silent. The vicar began to speak.

Charlotte and Emily devoted themselves to appearing to mourn.

The reception afterwards was a very different matter. Emily's carriage deposited all four of them on the pavement in Green Street outside Jerome Carvell's house, then drove away to allow a brougham to arrive and its passengers to alight also.

Emily took Jack's arm and went up the steps to the door, where a tall, very upright butler with a high-boned face and magnificent legs examined Jack's card and made his decision.

"Good morning, Mr. Radley, Mrs. Radley. Please come in." He turned to Pitt. "Good morning, sir?" His expression had changed subtly; one could not say precisely how it was different, but the respect had drained away, his eyes were arrogant and disinterested.

"Mr. and Mrs. Pitt," Pitt replied with corresponding chill.

"Indeed, sir."

Charlotte felt her stomach tighten. She ached for Pitt in the face of the butler's superciliousness, but she was horribly afraid he would retaliate and earn still further contempt. She forced herself to smile as if she were totally unaware of anything but the usual courtesy.

Pitt lifted his head a little higher, but before he could reply the butler spoke again.

"I regret, sir, but this is not a convenient time for you to see Mr. Carvell. As you may observe, this is a social occasion of some gravity, and sadness."

Charlotte drew in her breath to say something crushing.

"I have not called to see Mr. Carvell," Pitt said politely, "but Mrs. Arledge. She is expecting me, and I should be distressed if she thought I had declined her invitation."

"Oh." The butler was clearly taken aback. "I see, sir. Of course. If you would be pleased to come in."

"Thank you." Pitt invested his thanks with only the faintest touch of sarcasm, and giving Charlotte his arm, he led her inside to the large reception room where already there was a considerable crowd gathered.

The table was spread with all manner of delicacies and presumably Carvell had hired extra staff for the occasion, because there were at least half a dozen maids and footmen in livery that Charlotte could see, standing discreetly ready to attend to everyone's wishes.

There was a small group of men standing together in the doorway to the next room and as she and Pitt came in they turned. One of them took a step forward, his highly intelligent face filled with a mixture of pain, apprehension and hope. She did not need to ask Pitt if it were Carvell, the power of feeling in him could only belong to the man Pitt had described. It was the same man she had seen at the service, and whose grief had so moved her.

Pitt glanced at her, realized her perception, and smiled before going towards Carvell.

"Good day, Superintendent," Carvell said with his eyes searching Pitt's face. "Is there some . . ." He saw from Pitt's eyes that there was nothing. "Oh, I'm so sorry. How clumsy of me. I beg your pardon. Should I say how good of you to come, or is that naive?" He did not seem to have realized that Charlotte was with Pitt. Curiously, she felt in no way slighted. Closer to, his face was uglier, the pockmarks on his skin showed very clearly, and yet it was also more intensely alive. In spite of knowing his relationship with Arledge, and her imagination of what it must have cost Dulcie, and the very real possibility that he was guilty of murder, she found herself curiously partisan on his behalf. Perhaps it was the sheer depth of his feeling and its reality she could not doubt. There was nothing indifferent in him.

"It is not news in the slightest," Pitt replied sincerely. "I have come because Mrs. Arledge invited me, and I am grateful to be permitted to pay my respects to a man I believe I would have admired very much, had I had the opportunity to know him."

Carvell bit his lip and swallowed hard. "You are very gracious, Superintendent. No one could have said that more generously and still have told the absolute truth. You have learned nothing more so far, and your duty brings you here, as well as your natural inclination. I do understand."

"I would not say there is nothing further," Pitt argued. "But the little there is leads to no conclusion. Mr. Carvell, may I present you to my wife?"

"Oh!" Carvell was completely taken aback. "Oh, I am sorry, ma'am. I beg your pardon for my complete rudeness. I had assumed—really, I am not sure what I had assumed. Forgive me." He bowed very slightly. "How do you do, ma'am."

He made no movement towards her.

"How do you do, Mr. Carvell," she said with a smile. "Please accept my sympathies for your loss. It is an inexpressibly bitter thing to lose one's dearest friend."

He stared at her, surprise in his eyes, then a moment of embarrassment, and at last a spontaneous warmth.

"How kind of you." They were very formal words, and yet she knew he meant them.

Before any of them could pursue the matter further and search for some easier subject of conversation, there was a stirring of movement at the doorway behind them, a murmuring of voices, a slither and brush of fabric as people moved against one another. Then as Pitt and Charlotte turned they saw a solitary woman enter the room, dressed in pretty and feminine black decorated with exquisite discreet mourning jewelry, lace at her wrists and throat. She was not a large woman, nor yet a strikingly beautiful one, but she commanded an immediate attention. Her features were well proportioned, her mouth gently curved. The delicate color of her skin was not marred, nor was her hair dressed less than gracefully; only her blue eyes betrayed the sleeplessness and the anxiety.

Charlotte felt Pitt stiffen and looked up quickly at him. There was an admiration in his face, and a profound gentleness which she had not seen in a long time, not even for Jerome Carvell. She did not need Pitt to tell her that this was Dulcie Arledge.

Dulcie looked around the room for an instant, her eyes resting on one person, then another. She did not hesitate at Mina Winthrop; apparently she did not recognize her, nor, it would seem, Bart Mitchell standing beside her. She smiled at Sir James Lismore and at Roderick Alberd. Several others earned a slight movement of her head and a shadow of a smile. Her glance slid over the graceful figure of Landon Hurlwood, a fraction taller than those surrounding him, but she gave no sign of acknowledgment.

Victor Garrick was sitting in an alcove with his cello cradled in his arms, waiting for the time when he was asked to play. His fair hair gleamed in the light from the gas bracket above him, and there was a look of peace in his face, as if he dreamed of something remote and uniquely lovely.

Dulcie inclined her head towards him, and pleasure softened his concentration in acceptance, and then the distant gaze returned.

Dulcie's eyes finally came to rest on Pitt and a delicate smile curved her mouth. She moved forward, nodding, exchanging a word here and there, until she was only a few feet away from him.

Pitt waited and Charlotte did not speak. She was startled by the depth of feeling she sensed in Pitt, not only for Dulcie's loss, and the dreadful disillusion she must be suffering with such dignity, but also a regard for her which held a tenderness and a respect he would almost certainly remember long after the case was over.

Charlotte admired him for it. She would not have wanted him to be incapable of such emotions; and yet it also stirred a twinge of unease in her, a consciousness that they had not shared this case, a recollection of the number of times that she had been absent when he had come home tired and worried, confused and needing to speak. She had been so full of her plans to make the new house beautiful, and to do it within an acceptable cost, that she had had room for little else in her mind. Now she was touched by a whisper of jealousy, soft, but unmistakable.

"Good morning, Superintendent," Dulcie said, smiling up at Pitt. There was a distinct hesitation before she turned to Charlotte. "How do you do. You must be Mrs. Pitt. How gracious of you to have come as well. Most sensitive of you."

Charlotte had to struggle to keep her answering smile sweet and think of something equally pleasant to reply. The slightest slip would be perceived and understood. She had only to meet Dulcie's eyes to know that nothing passed her by.

"Thank you, Mrs. Arledge. I hope it is not an intrusion?"

"Of course not. Please don't think that for a second." Dulcie turned to Carvell. Charlotte held her breath, then suddenly realized that of course Dulcie had no idea that he was anything more than another grieving friend, simply generous enough to have lent her his home for the occasion. She let out her breath again in a silent thanksgiving.

"Thank you, Mr. Carvell," Dulcie said with a slight tilting of her head. "Your generous hospitality has made all the difference to me in what could well have been an almost unbearable situation. I assure you I appreciate it more than you can know."

Carvell's face flushed deep red and he stood as if transfixed to the spot. Charlotte could only dimly guess at the storm of emotions that must rage through him as he faced Arledge's wife. He opened his mouth to speak, and his voice failed him.

Pitt was standing almost as stiffly himself.

Dulcie waited expectantly.

Surely Carvell would say something before he betrayed himself. Any second the thought must surely enter her mind. It had to be someone. The choice was not wide.

Pitt drew in his breath sharply.

The sound of it seemed to force Carvell back to reality.

"I am glad it is of some service," he said awkwardly. "It seems such a—a small thing to do. Not enough—not at all enough—"

"I am sure it is a great help," Charlotte interrupted, unable to bear the tension any longer. "Simply not to have to worry about practicalities, and to be free to leave when one cannot endure company any longer and would prefer solitude, that is a great gift."

Dulcie looked at her. "How perceptive of you, Mrs. Pitt," she observed. "Of course you are quite right. Your gift is great, Mr. Carvell. Please do not allow your modesty to belittle it."

"Thank you—thank you," he said again, backing away a little. "If you will excuse me, ma'am, I will make sure that Scarborough is ready to serve when it is required." And turning on his heel, he escaped to find the butler.

Dulcie smiled at Pitt.

"I had no idea he was so shy. What a curious man. But he has been very kind, and surely that is all that can matter."

Any further private discussion was cut short by various people approaching to offer Dulcie their condolences and to say how fine the service had been, how they had enjoyed the music.

"Yes, young Mr. Garrick is most gifted," Dulcie agreed. "He plays with more true feeling than anyone else I can recall. Of course I am not equipped to judge his technical skill, but it seems very fine to me."

"Oh, it is," Sir James Lismore agreed, nodding, and glancing across the room towards Victor, still sitting with his cello and talking to Mina Winthrop. "It is a pity he does not see fit to take it up professionally," he continued. "But he is very young and may yet change his mind. He could go far, I think." He turned to Dulcie. "Aidan certainly thought well of him."

"Who is the lady with him?" she asked curiously.

He turned. "Oh, that is Mrs. Winthrop. Do you not know her?"

"I cannot recall that we have met. Poor woman. We have much in common, I am afraid. I must offer her my sympathies." She smiled with twisted amusement. "Mine will be particularly apt, I'm afraid."

But before she could move to fulfill her words, they were approached by more guests, and she was obliged to murmur polite acceptances and thanks for several more minutes. Charlotte and Pitt excused themselves and moved away to listen and watch from a discreet distance the faces of the other mourners.

They observed Lord and Lady Winthrop standing side by side, speaking very gravely to an elderly gentleman with rimless spectacles on his nose.

"I am most disappointed in the police," Lord Winthrop was saying with obvious displeasure. "I had thought, considering my son's reputation, and his service to his country, that they would have made more of an effort to apprehend the madman who committed such a crime!"

"Dastardly," the elderly gentleman agreed. "Quite dastardly. One expects such things among the lower orders, but when it begins to invade the lives of respectable, even honorable people, the country is in a sad state. I assume you have spoken to the Home Secretary?"

"Of course," Lord Winthrop said quickly. "Frequently! I have written to the Prime Minister."

"He has had no reply," Lady Winthrop said fiercely.

"That is not quite true, my dear," her husband corrected her, but before he could take it any further, she cut across him again.

"Meaningless," she said. "All he did was acknowledge that he had read your letters. That is not a reply! He did not tell you what he was going to do about it."

The elderly gentleman with the spectacles made a clicking sound with his teeth and muttered something inaudible.

Pitt smiled. At least the Prime Minister was not going to be rattled.

The food was served. Footmen and maids moved among the guests with trays of wine and delicacies. All the time the supercilious butler, Scarborough, ordered the proceedings and saw that everything to the minutest detail was perfect.

Charlotte moved away from Pitt and began to observe for

herself as much as she was able. She spoke for some minutes to Mina Winthrop, who was delighted to see her, and to Thora Garrick, who had apparently chosen to accompany Mina, perhaps to hear Victor play.

"How nice to see you, Mrs. Pitt," Mina said with a rather uncertain smile. "You remember Mrs. Garrick, don't you?"

"Of course," Charlotte said quickly. "How are you, Mrs. Garrick?"

"I am very well, thank you," Thora answered with a smile.

"I have heard your son play," Charlotte went on. "He is extremely gifted."

"Thank you," she accepted.

"How is your house progressing?" Mina asked.

"It is very nearly finished," Charlotte answered. "I have a yellow room, thanks to your brilliant creative sense."

Mina flushed with pleasure.

"How is your arm?" Charlotte looked at her as casually as she could and still express concern.

"Oh it is nothing," Mina said quickly. "It really didn't hurt at all. I think it is most foolish to make too much of accidents. I . . . I really bring it upon myself. . . ."

Thora looked at Charlotte with wide eyes full of incredulity, then at Mina, whose discomfort was now apparent.

Charlotte perceived the layers of meaning and misunderstanding.

"I thought it was a nasty burn," she said gently. "The tea was extremely hot. I admire your fortitude, but . . ."

Mina relaxed so visibly the color rushed back into her face and her whole body seemed easier.

Thora sucked in her breath in sudden relief.

"But I should not think you self-indulgent to have admitted it was acutely painful," Charlotte finished. "I don't think I would have put on such a brave face." Then she changed the subject, and they spoke of porcelain, and what manner of design was most pleasing for clocks and mirrors.

But when Charlotte excused herself she was still turning over in her mind the fact that Thora Garrick was aware of Mina's bruises, and presumably of their cause, and yet it stirred in her neither overwhelming pity, nor anger, nor fear that Mina or Bart Mitchell might be involved in Winthrop's death. She must impart this knowledge to Pitt at the first convenient opportunity.

Victor Garrick was asked to play again, and did so with

exquisite melancholy, to a vociferous appreciation from an audience with a deeper love and understanding of music than he was accustomed to.

Nearly three quarters of an hour later Charlotte was joined by a furious Emily.

"That man is a complete swine!" Emily said with suppressed rage shaking her voice and her cheeks flaming.

"Who?" Charlotte was astonished, and amused. "Who on earth has behaved so appallingly as to cause you to use a word like that? I thought you were far too much the lady to—"

"It's not amusing," Emily said between her teeth. "I'd like to see him out in the street, begging with a bowl in his hand!"

"Begging with a bowl in his hand. What on earth are you talking about? Who?"

"That arrogant pig of a butler Scarsdale, or whatever he's called," Emily replied, screwing up her face. "I found one of the maids weeping her heart out just now. He caught her singing and dismissed her—because this is a Requiem reception. She didn't know the wretched man. Why should she know the difference between Victor Garrick's playing the cello and her singing a sad little song? I've half a mind to tell Mr. Carvell and ask him to do something about it. Reinstate the girl and put that abysmal man out in the street."

"You can't," Charlotte protested. "He won't dismiss his butler because of a maid being disciplined." But even as she said it, her mind was crowded with other thoughts. Jerome Carvell's face filled her inner vision, the pain and the grief in it, and the imagination. Surely he would not wittingly have permitted any one of his servants to treat people in that manner?

Or was he too vulnerable to a manservant who lived in his house and knew him as only a servant can?

"Charlotte?" Emily said slowly. "What? What is it?"

"A thought," Charlotte replied. "Perhaps nothing. But you cannot speak to Scarborough. You wouldn't help the maid."

"Why not? I certainly can."

"No! Believe me, there are reasons."

"What reasons?"

"Good reasons, concerning Mr. Carvell. Please."

"Then I'll employ her myself," Emily said decisively. "You should have seen her, Charlotte. I'm not going to allow that to happen."

Charlotte was about to reply when Dulcie Arledge approached them, smiling, her face weary, her shoulders still straight, her smile fixed.

"Poor creature," Charlotte said softly to Emily, almost under her breath, her gaze still upon Dulcie.

"I think she looks better than I would do in the same circumstances," Emily replied, but there was an ambiguity, a hesitation in her voice which Charlotte did not understand. However, it was too late to ask her what she meant. Dulcie was almost upon them.

"It has been a most moving occasion," Charlotte said courteously.

"Thank you, Mrs. Pitt," Dulcie accepted.

Emily added some appropriate remark, and before Dulcie could continue with whatever formality came next, they were joined by Lady Lismore and Landon Hurlwood.

"Dulcie, my dear," Lady Lismore began with a warm smile, "do you know Mr. Landon Hurlwood? He greatly admired Aidan's work, and came to pay his respects and offer his sympathy." She turned to Hurlwood.

"No," Hurlwood said.

"Yes," Dulcie said at exactly the same moment.

Hurlwood blushed.

"I am so sorry," he said quickly. "Of course I have met Mrs. Arledge. I simply meant that our acquaintance is very slight. How do you do, Mrs. Arledge. I am flattered you remembered me. There must be so many who admired your husband's work."

"How do you do, Mr. Hurlwood," she answered, looking up at him with wide, dark blue eyes. "It is very kind of you to have come. I am gratified you admired my husband's work. I am sure his name will live on, and perhaps give pleasure and encouragement for years to come."

"I have no doubt." He bowed very slightly, searching her face, his expression full of concern. "Would it be impertinent to say how much I admire your dignity in the face of such a loss, Mrs. Arledge?"

She colored deeply and lowered her eyes.

"Thank you, Mr. Hurlwood, although I fear you flatter me. It is most generous."

"Not at all," Lady Lismore said quickly. "It is no more than the truth. Now I am sure you must be ready to retire after all this emotion. I shall be privileged to remain here and bid people good-bye, if you would like me to."

Dulcie took a very deep breath, not looking at Hurlwood anymore.

"I think I should appreciate that, my dear, if you really do not mind?" she accepted.

"May I see you to your carriage?" Hurlwood offered her his arm.

She hesitated for several moments, then with a nervous flicker of her tongue across her lips, her face showing the exhaustion she must have felt, she declined graciously and walked alone to the door, where Scarborough stepped forward and opened it for her, following her out to accept her cloak from the footman and call her carriage.

"A most remarkable person," Lady Lismore said with feeling.

Hurlwood's eyes were still on the doorway where she had departed. There was a faint color in his cheeks. "Indeed," he echoed. "Quite remarkable."

9

LADY AMANDA KILBRIDE rode out alone, very early, towards Rotten Row. She had quarreled with her husband the evening before and wished him to rise and find her absent. Of course he would not think she had left in any permanent sense. Such a thing would be out of the question, but he would be worried. He would be anxious in case she had done something foolish, just possibly even fulfilled her promise to run off and have a dramatic love affair with the first presentable man who asked her.

Although in the cold, pale light of morning she was obliged to admit that there were not so many presentable men at all, let alone ones who would invite married ladies to have affairs. The chance that one had come along between her threat, made at about nine o'clock, and the time she had retired and locked her bedroom door, a little before midnight, was very remote indeed.

Still, let him wonder!

She reached the end of the Row and saw its rather gravelly surface stretching out in front of her beneath the trees. A good sharp canter was precisely what she needed. She leaned a little forward and patted her horse, giving it a word of encouragement. Its ears pricked at the change in her tone. All morning so far she had regaled it with the injustices done her. Now she urged it into a trot, and then a canter.

She rode well and she knew it. It added to her enjoyment of the sharp spring sunshine, the long shadows across the Row and the sheen of dew on the park grass beyond. There was hardly anyone else around, even in Knightsbridge, which she could see beyond the edge of the park; there was only an occasional late reveler returning home, or very early risers like herself, enjoying the cold, bare sunlight and the virtual solitude.

At the far end she turned and cantered back towards Hyde Park Corner, feeling the wind in her face and at last beginning to smile.

Three quarters of the way down she slowed to a walk. She knew better than to offer her horse a drink at the trough while it was still warm, but she would dearly like to splash her own face with its coolness. She dismounted, leaving the reins loose, and took a couple of steps to the trough. She bent down absently, her mind still on her husband's offense, then with her hands in the water she turned her head and looked.

The water was red-brown.

She withdrew sharply with a cry of revulsion. The whole trough was cloudy with some dark fluid, far too dark to be water. There was also something else in it, something large which she could not see because of the murkiness.

"Oh really!" she said angrily. "This is too bad! Who would do such a stupid thing? Now it's filthy!" She stepped back, and it was only as she stood up that she saw the odd object on the far side of the trough. It was so odd in its appearance that she looked more closely.

For a breathless instant she did not believe it. Then when it sank on her incredulous brain that it was truly what it seemed, she slid with a splash into the trough, face first.

The cold water choked her and in an effort to get her breath she pulled herself up again, gasping and gagging; the whole of the top of her body was soaked, and now thoroughly cold. She was too horrified even to scream, but crouched in silence, half arched over the edge of the trough, shaking violently.

There was a thud of hooves behind her, a scatter of pebbles, and a man's voice spoke.

"I say, ma'am, are you all right? Had a fall? May I—" He stopped abruptly, having seen the object. "Oh my God!" He gulped and caught his breath in a choking cough.

"The rest of him is in there." Amanda gestured weakly towards the trough, where now a liveried knee was protruding from the bloody water.

* * *

Tellman looked down at Pitt in his chair with a dark, grim expression in his lantern face.

"Yes?" Pitt asked, his heart sinking.

"There's been another," Tellman said, staring back without wavering. "He's done it again. This time you'll have to arrest him."

"He . . . ?"

"Carvell. There's another headless corpse in the park."

Pitt's heart sank even further. "Who is it?"

"Albert Scarborough, Carvell's butler." A shadow of bitter humor touched Tellman's face. "Lady Kilbride found him in the horse trough. Or to be more accurate, all of him except his head," he amended. "His head was behind it."

"Horse trough where?"

"Rotten Row, a hundred yards or so short of Hyde Park Corner."

Pitt tried to force the horror of it from the front of his mind and concentrate on the practical elements of the case. "Some distance from Green Street," he observed. "Any idea how he got there?"

"Not yet. He was a big fellow, so there is no way Carvell could have carried him. Might have walked there."

Pitt opened his eyes very wide. "Midnight stroll with his employer? Doesn't seem like the sort of person one takes a walk with for pleasure. And as the assistant commissioner has been at pains to point out, no one is strolling around the park these nights."

"So he didn't walk there," Tellman corrected with a grimace. "Carvell killed him in his home and took him there in some sort of conveyance. Could even have been his own carriage. Do you want to arrest him, or shall I?"

Pitt rose to his feet, his limbs suddenly very tired, as though his body were of enormous weight. He should have been relieved there was an end to the mystery, if not the terror or the tragedy of it; but he felt no sense of ease at all.

"I'll go." He went to the hat stand and took his hat, even though it was a fine morning. "You'd better come with me."

"Yes sir."

It was still before nine when Pitt and Tellman presented themselves at the front door of the house in Green Street. Pitt rang the bell, but it was several moments before it was answered.

"Yes sir?" A footman with untidy fair hair looked at him with anxiety.

"I would like to speak with Mr. Carvell, if you please," Pitt said, but his voice was a command, not a request.

The footman was startled. "I'm sorry sir, I'm not sure Mr. Carvell has risen yet," he said apologetically. "Could you call again at about ten o'clock?"

Tellman made as if to speak, but Pitt cut across him.

"I'm afraid it will not wait. The matter is of the utmost gravity. Will you tell him that Superintendent Pitt and Inspector Tellman are here and require to see him immediately."

The footman paled. He opened his mouth as if to say something, then changed his mind and turned away without remembering to ask them to wait, or direct them to a more suitable place than the hall.

Within a few moments Carvell appeared in a dressing robe, his hair standing in spikes, his face pale and filled with fear.

"What has happened, Superintendent?" he said to Pitt, ignoring Tellman. "Is there something wrong? What brings you at this hour?"

Again Pitt felt the tug of reluctance and the familiar pity inside him.

"I am sorry, Mr. Carvell, but we require to search your premises and question your staff. I know it will inconvenience you, but it is necessary."

"Why?" Carvell was now extremely anxious, his hands opened and closed at his sides and his face was ashen. "What has happened? For God's sake, tell me what is wrong. Has—has there been another . . . ?"

"Yes. Your butler, Albert Scarborough." Pitt was obliged to step forward and steady Carvell as he swayed. He caught him by the elbow and steered him backwards to the fine oak settle a yard or so behind him. "You had better sit down." He turned to the footman standing helplessly. "Get your master a small glass of brandy," he ordered. Then, as the youth still stood rooted to the spot, eyes wide: "Jump to it!"

"Yes—yes, sir." And the unfortunate young man ran out of the hall and disappeared, calling for the housekeeper in a shaking voice.

Pitt looked at Tellman.

"Go and start your search."

Tellman had only been awaiting the order. He departed briskly, his face grim.

Pitt looked at Carvell, who appeared as if he might well be sick.

"You think I did it?" Carvell said huskily. "I can see it in your face, Superintendent. Why? Why in God's name should I murder my butler?"

"I'm afraid the answer to that is unfortunately obvious, sir. He is in a perfect position to be aware of your liaison with Mr. Arledge, and of your possible involvement in his death. If that were so, you might well have felt it imperative, for your own safety, to be rid of him."

Carvell struggled to speak, and failed. He stared up at Pitt for long, dreadful seconds, then with utter hopelessness, sank his head into his hands.

Pitt felt brutal. Tellman's voice was drumming in his head, his contempt for Pitt's squeamishness, Farnsworth's charge that he was running away from his responsibility, both to his superiors, who had believed in him and had given him promotion, and to his juniors, whose loyalty he expected, and above all to the public. They had a right to believe they were getting the best the police force could offer and that he would set aside personal likes and dislikes, individual quirks of conscience or pity. He had accepted the job, with its honor and its reward. To do less than it required of him was a betrayal.

He looked at the wretched figure of Carvell in front of him. What had happened? What torrent of emotion had roared through him so that he had killed the man he loved? It could only be some kind of rejection, whether simply that the affair had died or that Arledge had found someone else.

Why Winthrop first? Winthrop must have been the other man. Somehow or other the bus conductor knew of it, not that night, but at some other time. And of course the sneering Scarborough had known it too. He tried to imagine the scene when the butler faced his master with his knowledge, standing very stiff and tall in his livery, his magnificent legs in silken stockings, his buttons and braid gleaming, his lip curled. He would have had no shred of an idea that his master would kill him too.

But that was stupid. He had already killed three other people. How could Scarborough have been so blindly confident as to have turned his back on a man he had threatened, and whom he knew to have murdered three times already? There could not have been a struggle. Scarborough was half Carvell's weight again, and at least six inches taller. Any face-to-face combat he would have won easily. Pitt would have to ask the medical examiner if there were wounds on Scarborough's body, a stab to the heart or something of that nature.

Tellman would already be searching. Would he begin by asking questions, or by looking for the place where it had happened? Or for some conveyance in which Carvell had taken the inert body of the butler to the horse trough in the park? Or the weapon? Presumably he had kept the weapon right from the beginning. Dangerous. Was he supremely confident he had hidden it, or that it would never be searched for in the right place? Or that if it was found it would not implicate him?

"Mr. Carvell?"

Carvell sat motionless.

"Mr. Carvell?"

"Yes?"

"When did you last see Scarborough alive?"

"I don't know." Carvell lifted his face. "Dinner time? You should ask the other servants, they would have seen him after I did."

"Did he lock up last night?"

"I really don't know, Superintendent. Yesterday was Aidan's Requiem service. Do you imagine I cared who locked up the house? It could have been open all night for all I thought of it."

"How long had Scarborough been in your service?"

"Five years—no, six."

"Were you satisfied with him?"

Carvell looked bemused. "He was good at his job, if that's what you mean. If you want to know if I liked the man, no I didn't. He was an objectionable creature, but he ran the house excellently." He stared at Pitt with unfocused eyes. "I never had domestic trouble of any sort," he said hollowly. "Every meal was on time, well cooked, and the household accounts were in perfect order. If there was ever a crisis, I didn't hear about it. I have friends who were always having complaints of one sort or another. I never did. If he sneered occasionally I really didn't care." A self-mocking smile touched his mouth. "He was superb at arranging to entertain. He would see to any size or scale of dinner party or reception. I never had to see to anything myself."

A maid crossed the landing above them but Carvell did not seem to be aware of her, or of the sounds of movement now coming from beyond the green baize door at the end of the hall.

"I would simply say, 'Scarborough, I wish to have ten people to dinner next Thursday evening,' " he went on. " 'Will you see to it,' and he did, and supplied an elegant menu at very reasonable cost. He hired in extra staff if they were needed, and none of them were ever impertinent, slack or dishonest. Yes, he was a condescending devil, but he was good enough at his profession for me to overlook it. I don't know how I shall find anyone to replace him."

Pitt said nothing.

Carvell gulped and gave a choking little laugh that ended in a sob.

"Or perhaps I shall be hanged, and then I won't have to bother."

"Did you kill Scarborough?" Pitt said very gently.

"No I didn't," Carvell replied quite calmly. "And before you ask me, I haven't the slightest idea who did, or why."

He was wretchedly miserable and frightened. Pitt questioned him for a further ten minutes, but he learned nothing that added either to his knowledge or to his impression of the man. He left him sitting crumpled up in the hall and went to see what Tellman had discovered.

He found him in the servants' hall, a comparatively small place compared with some he had been in, but very comfortably furnished and with a pleasant smell of lavender and beeswax polish. The odor of luncheon cooking made him suddenly aware of hunger. The white-faced footman was standing to attention. An upstairs maid was in tears, a duster in her hand, a broom leaning against the wall. The housekeeper sat upright in a wooden-backed chair, her keys at her waist, ink, presumably from the household ledgers, on her fingers, her face looking as if she had just found something unspeakable on her plate. The scullery maid and the cook were absent. The kitchen maid was facing Tellman, a smudge of black lead on her sleeve from the stove, her expression tearful and obstinate.

Tellman looked around at Pitt. Seemingly his questioning of the maid was not worth pursuing.

"What have you learned?" Pitt asked quietly.

Tellman came over to him. "Very little," he said, his face showing some surprise. "After the reception the staff spent a great deal of the afternoon clearing up. The extra footmen and maids hired for the event were paid off and left. One of them had been dismissed earlier for unbecoming conduct, I don't know what it amounted to, some domestic misdemeanor. Nobody seemed to know exactly what. Carvell spent the afternoon out somewhere, the staff don't know where, but the footman thinks it was simply to be alone and grieve in his own way."

"Grieve?" Pitt said quickly.

Tellman looked at him without comprehension.

"Was the footman aware that Carvell had a profound feeling towards Arledge?" Pitt said under his breath, but with a sharpness to his voice.

Tellman shook his head. "Oh—no, I don't think so. Seems he regarded any death as a very somber affair, needing a space for recovery."

"Oh! What about Scarborough?"

"Spent the afternoon in his pantry, and checking the stock in the cellar," Tellman replied, drawing Pitt a little farther away from the servants, who were all staring expectantly. "Dinner was a light affair, a cold collation of some sort. Carvell read in the library for a while, then retired early. Staff were excused at about eight. Scarborough locked up at ten and no one saw him after that." Tellman's face was uncompromising in its conviction, his dark, deep-set eyes level, his mouth in a hard line. "No one rang the doorbell, or the other staff would have heard. It rings in the kitchen, and in here." He turned and gestured to the board with all the bells on, listed by room. The front door was plainly visible.

"And no break-in, I presume," Pitt said, not even making it a question.

"No sir, nothing at all. All the windows and doors were properly fastened—" Tellman stopped.

"Yes?" Pitt said sharply. "Except?"

Tellman pulled a face. "Except the French doors in the dining room. The housemaid says she thinks they were open when she went in there this morning. At least not open, but unlocked. Carvell probably went out that way, and when he came back, forgot to bolt them."

"Somebody did," Pitt agreed. "It is just conceivable Scarborough went out that way himself, alive and quite voluntarily."

Tellman's face showed disbelief, and contempt for Pitt's indecision. "What for?" His sneer was obvious. "Don't tell me you think the butler went out into the park at night to pick up a woman? I thought we'd abandoned the idea it had anything to do with prostitutes. We knew that was daft when the commissioner said it! This is not a lunatic with an obsession about fornication, it's a perfectly sane murderer who's been betrayed in love and was out to get revenge—and then kill anyone who knew about it and threatened him!"

Pitt said nothing.

"Are you still thinking about Mitchell?" Tellman went on. "It makes no sense. Maybe he had a reason for killing Winthrop, but not the others; and certainly not the butler. Why on earth would Mitchell have anything to do with Carvell's butler?"

"The only reason for anyone killing Scarborough is because he knew something," Pitt answered. "But no, I can't see any connection with Mitchell."

"Then you are going to arrest Carvell?"

"Have you searched the house yet?"

"No, of course I haven't. I've looked in Scarborough's pantry and I've been upstairs to his room. There's nothing there, but I didn't expect anything."

"Papers?"

Tellman looked surprised. "Papers? What sort of papers?"

"Record of money," Pitt replied. "If he was blackmailing Carvell there should be something to show for it."

"Over Arledge? Maybe he only just tried it after the murder, and met his payment last night."

"Why would he wait that long? It's been days since Arledge was killed."

"I didn't find anything, but I didn't have time to read all the letters and things. I've questioned the cook about her meat cleaver, and looked in the garden shed for an ax. There isn't one. They get their kindling wood ready cut."

"What about the cleaver?"

"Can't tell." Tellman dismissed it with his tone. "Cook says it is exactly where she left it. Turned a very funny color, but I think she was telling the truth. Seems a well-disciplined sort of woman, no screaming or outrage. Sensible kind of person." He shrugged. "I don't know what he did with the weapon. I expect we'll find it when we get a whole lot of men down here. My opinion, sir, Carvell will break when we get him in a cell and he realizes he can't get away with it anymore. He'll panic and tell us the bits we don't know."

"Possibly," Pitt said, but he did not believe it, and it was there in his voice.

Tellman looked sour. He was fed up with Pitt's prevarication and he took no trouble to conceal it.

"We've no reason not to now! We may not know all the details yet, but that's only a matter of time. Even if we can't get him for the bus conductor, we've got him for Arledge and Scarborough." He turned and moved a step away. "Shall I send for the wagon, or can we take him in a hansom? I don't think he'll give any trouble. Not the sort."

"Yes," Pitt agreed reluctantly. "Take him in a hansom." He was about to add not to force on him any unnecessary indignity, then realized how foolish that was, and how unlikely to affect Tellman in the way he acted.

"You're not coming?" Tellman said in surprise, already the sneer in his eyes that Pitt would not do it himself.

"I'll arrest him," Pitt said. "You take him to the station. I want to stay here and see what else I can find."

Carvell was not surprised when he saw them return. He was still sitting in the hall where they had left him, looking pale and sick. He raised his head when he recognized Pitt's step. He said nothing, but the question was plain in his eyes.

"Jerome Carvell." Pitt hated the sound of his voice as he said the familiar words. The change in tone, the sudden complete formality presaged what he was going to say, and Carvell's face suddenly took a numb, almost bruised look, all his fear become reality. "I am arresting you for the murder of Albert Scarborough."

"I didn't kill him," Carvell said quietly, without hope of being believed. He rose to his feet and held out his hands. He looked at Pitt. "Or any of the others."

There was nothing for Pitt to say. He wanted to believe him, and some small fraction of him did, but the evidence could no longer be ignored.

"Inspector Tellman will take you to the station. There is no need for manacles."

"Thank you," Carvell said almost under his breath, and dutifully, shoulders stooped, face white, he went across the hall with Tellman and out of the front door. He made no attempt to move suddenly, still less to loose himself from Tellman's grip. The passion, even the life, seemed to have gone out of him as if a long-awaited and inevitable blow had finally fallen.

Pitt went upstairs to the butler's room and searched it meticulously; he found no more than Tellman had. He came down again and looked through the house, the main reception rooms and the servants' hall, butler's pantry, housekeeper's sitting room and kitchen, laundry, scullery and still room, and found nothing of interest. Lastly he went out into the mews and stables, where the footmen told him Carvell kept one horse and a light two-seater gig which he sometimes used on a summer afternoon, driving himself with considerable skill and pleasure. The animal was looked after by the bootboy, who took delight in escaping from the house on any pretext, and really there were few enough boots to occupy his time. He also assisted the gardener when there was little to do outside, and the winter mud necessitated extra grooming and polishing.

"Yes sir?" he said in a businesslike fashion when Pitt approached him, his broad, good-natured face full of concern.

"May I look at your stable and carriage house?" Pitt asked, although it was a formality. He would not have accepted a refusal.

"Yes sir, if you want to." The boy looked surprised. "But there's nothing missing, sir. Gig's there, and all the harness, like."

"Nevertheless I'd like to look." Pitt walked past him and up to the stable door. It was a long time since he had been near horses. The warm smell of the animal, the paved yard under his feet, the odor of leather and polish brought back memories of long ago on the estate where he had grown up, of the stables and tack rooms there, and then of the feeling of a horse under him, its power and speed, matching its will to his, the art and the joy of being one with the animal. And then the work afterwards, the brushing and cleaning, the putting away, the aching muscles and the exhilaration, and then the peace. It all seemed a very long time ago now. Dulcie Arledge would have understood, with her love of horses, the long ride to hounds, the exhaustion of muscles, the ache that was half pleasure.

Absentmindedly he patted the animal's neck. The boy was just behind him.

"Have you brushed him this morning?" Pitt asked, looking at the horse's hooves and seeing a few smears of mud on them, a few dry grasses clinging to the hair of its fetlocks.

"No sir. What with Mr. Scarborough being gorn, like, and nobody knowing what 'ad happened to 'im, the 'ole kitchen is in a state."

"Did you brush him last night?"

"Oh, yes sir! Shone like a new penny, 'e did. 'E's got a real

267

good coat on 'im. 'Aven't yer, Sam?" he said, patting the animal and receiving a gentle nuzzle in reply.

Pitt pointed to the mud.

"Well that weren't 'ere last night!" the boy said indignantly. 'Ere!" His face paled and his eyes widened. "Yer mean someone 'ad 'im out? In the night, like?"

"Looks like it," Pitt answered, gazing around the stable floor just to make sure there was no mud tracked in and that the horse could have stood in it, but it was immaculate. Bootboy or not, he was a diligent groom. "Let's have a look at the gig." He turned towards the carriage house. Now the boy was almost treading on his heels.

He swung open the carriage house door and saw a smart gig propped up, its shafts gleaming in the sunlight, its paintwork spotless. He turned to the boy. "Look at it carefully. Look at the harness. Is it exactly how you left it?"

There was a long silence while the boy looked minutely at everything, every piece of leather or brass, without touching a thing. Finally he let out his breath in a long sigh and faced Pitt.

"I can't be sure, sir. It sort of looks the same, but I'm not certain about them straps up there. The harness was on that 'ook, but I don't think them bridles next to it was that way 'round. I couldn't swear to it, mind!"

Pitt said nothing but went over to the gig and peered inside. It was clean, polished, doors fastened, seats bare.

" 'As it bin used, sir?" the boy asked from just behind him.

"Not so far as I can see," Pitt replied, not sure if he was relieved or disappointed. He unlatched the door and opened it. It swung wide on well-greased hinges. He looked down at the step and saw a thread of fabric caught around the screw that held down the sill. He bent to catch it between his finger and thumb and ease it very gently away. He held it up towards the light. It was long, pale, coiled like a corkscrew.

"Watcha got?" the boy asked, his eyes fixed on it.

"I don't know yet," Pitt replied, but that was not true. He was almost sure it was a thread from a footman's livery stockings. "Thank you," he added. "I'll see if there's anything else. Does Mr. Scarborough ride in this gig, do you know?"

"No sir. Mr. Scarborough stayed in the 'ouse, sir. Mr. Carvell drove it 'isself, and if he sent anyone on an errand it were me."

"Do you ever wear livery?"

The boy's face split into a grin. "What, me! No sir. Mr.

Scarborough'd 'ave a fit if I got fancy ideas like that. Put me in me place right quick, 'e would."

"No stockings?"

"No! Why?" He looked at the thread again, suddenly serious. "Did that come from someone's stockings?"

"Probably." Pitt would rather not have had him realize that, but it was too late now, and the questions were unavoidable. It would have been proof of nothing if Scarborough had used the gig himself. He put the thread into a screw of paper and then into his inside pocket. There was little point in asking the boy not to repeat it to the rest of the household, but he did anyway.

"Oh no, sir," the boy replied solemnly, backing away, then following Pitt as he searched the rest of the gig and the carriage house before returning to the back door, unaccountably tired, as if the energy were drained out of him.

Pitt did not go back to Bow Street. He was angry, with no reason, and loath to go and see the formal charge against Carvell. Farnsworth would be oozing satisfaction and it would gall Pitt bitterly. He felt no sense of achievement at all. It was a tragedy of such proportions all he could think of was the darkness and the pain of it. When he closed his eyes he could see Dulcie's sweet, intelligent face, and the terrible shock in it when he had told her of her husband's love for another man. She had accepted that he had had some involvement with another person, but that it should have been a man had almost broken her courage.

And yet deeply as Pitt abhorred it, there was a part of him still suffering a kind of shock, not yet accepting that it was Carvell.

He gave the cabdriver Nigel Uttley's address. It would serve no purpose at all, but he wished to tell Uttley he knew it was he who had attacked Jack. It would be acutely satisfying to frighten the man, and he could not see how it would harm Jack. Anything Uttley was able to do in that line, he would do anyway, regardless of Pitt.

He arrived there to find Uttley out, which was infuriating, but he should not have been surprised. It was very close to the by-election now. He might well be absent all day.

"I really cannot say, sir," the footman replied coolly. "It is possible he may return before dinner. If you wish to wait you may sit in the morning room."

Pitt hesitated only a moment, then accepted. He would wait

exactly half an hour. If Uttley did not return by then he would leave his card with a cryptic message on it, and hope it unsettled Uttley as much as possible.

For over forty minutes he walked up and down the elegantly and economically furnished room, surprisingly comfortable in its simplicity. Then he heard Uttley's voice in the hall, sharp with surprise.

"Pitt? Whatever for now? Poor devil's hopeless, isn't he? I don't know what he imagines I can do. My God, there'll be some change in the police when I'm in office. Excuse me, Weldon. I'll only be a few moments." His step sounded briskly on the marble-inlaid floor until he opened the morning room door and stood just inside the entrance, big, square-shouldered, dressed in a pale suit and beautifully polished boots. He looked casual and supremely confident. "Good afternoon, Superintendent. What can I do for you this time?" His expression was full of amusement.

"Good afternoon, Mr. Uttley," Pitt replied. "I came to tell you that we know who attacked Mr. and Mrs. Radley the other evening, although precisely why is not clear." He raised his eyebrows. "It seemed such a pointless thing to have done."

"I would have thought that all crime of that sort was rather pointless," Uttley replied, leaning against the doorpost and smiling. "But it was civil of you to come and tell me you have solved it." He looked at Pitt, hesitated a moment, then went on. "Was it the Headsman after all, or some chance thief?"

"Neither," Pitt said, equally calmly. "It was a political opportunist hoping to make a little capital out of the present tragedies in order to gain office for himself. I don't imagine he intended actually to kill Mr. Radley . . ."

Uttley paled. He still leaned against the doorway, but now his pose was contrived and his body rigid.

"Indeed." He swallowed, his eyes on Pitt's face. "You mean someone wanted to get rid of Radley? Frighten him out of his—candidacy?"

"No, I don't." Pitt held his gaze. "I think he wanted to make Radley's position of defending the police seem absurd and cause him to be laughed at by the public."

Uttley said nothing.

"Which is not as feasible as it might have seemed," Pitt continued. "Because it angered a number of people with a great deal of power."

Uttley swallowed, his throat tight. His hands were clenched by his sides.

"In certain quarters," Pitt added with a smile. "People with influence more than one might suppose."

"You mean—" Uttley stopped short.

"Yes, that's what I mean," Pitt agreed.

Uttley cleared his throat. "What—what are you going to do about it? I . . . suppose you have no proof, or you would arrest the fellow, wouldn't you? After all, it's an offense—isn't it!"

"I don't know whether Mr. Radley will prefer charges or not," Pitt said offhandedly. "That is up to him. Since he didn't report it in the regular way, maybe he considers it will rebound upon the perpetrator sufficiently that justice will be served without his taking any hand in it."

"But you?" Uttley said, taking a step forward. "What about you? You . . . didn't say whether you had proof or not." He was watching Pitt very closely.

"No, I didn't, did I?" Pitt agreed.

Uttley was beginning to gain confidence. His shoulders straightened a little.

"Sounds rather like guesswork to me, Superintendent," he said, pushing his hands back into his pockets. "I imagine that is what you would like it to be. The assistant commissioner would be less . . . critical of your performance."

Pitt smiled. "Oh, Mr. Farnsworth had very strong feelings about it indeed," he agreed. "He was furious."

Uttley froze.

"But I rather think he would like to deal with it in his own way," Pitt continued lightly. "That is the one reason I have not bothered to make a case. The proof is there. I don't think Mr. Farnsworth would have accepted my word for it otherwise. After all, it is so incredibly . . . inept! Isn't it?"

Uttley forced a sickly smile, but words failed him.

"I thought you should know," Pitt concluded, smiling back at him. "The next time you write an article, I'm sure you will wish to be fair." And with that he put his own hands in his pockets. "Good day, Mr. Uttley." He walked past him and out of the front door into the sun.

Pitt arrived home with no sense of elation. The satisfaction of having bested Uttley had worn off, and all he could think of was Carvell's shocked and despairing face. Even with his eyes closed he could see his hunched shoulders as he walked out beside Tellman, and the slightly spiky hair at the back of his head when the light caught it as he went down the steps.

For once Charlotte was home. She had been away so often in the last few months, organizing one thing or another for the new house, he had fully expected to find the place silent and nothing but a message on the kitchen table. However, there was the cheerful noise of bustle, kettle hissing, pans bubbling and the clink of china and swish of skirts. When he pushed open the kitchen door the room was bright with late sun and filled with the aroma of fresh bread, clean linen on the rack above him hanging from the high ceiling, steam from the kettle, and a faint savor of cooking meat from the oven.

Gracie was finishing tidying away after the children's supper and she whisked the last dishes off the table and put them on the dresser before dropping him a hasty bob and fleeing upstairs. A passing thought occurred to him to wonder why, but Jemima launched herself at him with cries of delight and demands that he listen to her account of the day. Daniel pulled faces and tugged at his sleeve to show him a paper kite he had made.

Charlotte dried her hands on her apron and came over to him immediately, poking her hair back into its pins, then smiling as she kissed him. For several minutes he was involved in giving everyone due attention before Daniel and Jemima departed, satisfied, and they were left alone.

"You look very tired," Charlotte said, looking at him closely. "What's happened?"

He was glad not to have to find a way of cutting through her stories of the house and its triumphs and disasters in order to catch her attention and tell her. Too often if he had to seek for her to listen, there was no sense of sharing and no release in it.

"I arrested Jerome Carvell," he replied. He knew she was watching his face and would read the emotions in him. She knew him far too well to imagine it would please him or give him any sense of victory.

"Why?" she asked.

It was not the response he had expected, but it was a good one. He told her everything that had happened during the day, including his visit to Uttley. She listened in silence, but she did smile towards the end.

"You are not sure Carvell did it, are you?" she said at last.

"I suppose my head tells me he must have, at least Scarborough, even if not the others. It was certainly his gig that was used to take him from the house to the park, and he had an excellent reason if the man was blackmailing him."

"But?" she asked.

"But I find it so hard to think he would kill Arledge. I cannot help but believe he loved him."

"Is it possible he killed Scarborough but not Arledge?" she asked.

"No. His only reason would be if Scarborough knew something that would damn him. The relationship itself doesn't seem enough after all this time. He must have known about it before. And servants who betray confidences about their masters' private lives don't find another position. He would have to make enough out of his blackmail to live on for the rest of his life. No—it—" He fell silent. There was really nothing more to say.

She finished cooking the dinner and they ate it in companionable silence. He went up to see the children, and read a very short story, before saying good-night, then came back down again and sat in the parlor, thinking that for all the pleasure of moving to a larger house, a beautiful house with a garden in which he would take intense delight, if he ever had the time, still there had been so much of his happiness here in this house, rich memories, and he would not leave it without regret and a sense of tearing.

Charlotte sat on the floor beside him, her sewing idle, her thoughts who knew where, but the warmth of her close to him gave him a sense of peace so sweet he eventually fell asleep in his chair, and she had to waken him to go to bed.

At noon the following day Bailey came into the Bow Street station looking worried and out of breath, his long face flushed and his eyes filled with a strange mixture of anxiety and determination.

Pitt was downstairs with Tellman and le Grange, discussing the final details of evidence.

"You've still got to find the weapon, or at least—"

"He could have thrown it anywhere," Tellman argued.

"In the river," le Grange added with a glance of sympathy at Pitt. "We may never find it. It could be under the mud by now. It's tidal, you know?"

"Of course I know it's tidal!" Pitt said. "If you hadn't interrupted me I would have said, or at least the place where he was killed. He can't have thrown that away."

"He killed Scarborough right where he was found," Tellman replied, disregarding Bailey, who was moving from one foot to the other in impatience.

"And Arledge?" Pitt insisted. "Where did he kill him, and how did he get him to the bandstand?"

"In a wheelbarrow, or something of the sort," le Grange replied, attempting to be helpful.

"Whose wheelbarrow?" Pitt pressed. "Not his own. You looked at that: no blood anywhere. Not the park keeper's either. You looked at that."

"I don't know," Tellman admitted grudgingly. "But we'll find it."

"Good! Because without it you are giving the defense an excellent weapon to raise doubt. No wheelbarrow, no murder site, no weapon and no proof of a motive."

"A quarrel, jealousy. His gig was used for moving Scarborough, and his horse to pull it," Tellman responded. "Not to mention Scarborough was his butler."

"Tidy it up," Pitt commanded. "You aren't finished yet."

Bailey could not contain himself any longer.

" 'E didn't kill the bus conductor!" he burst out. " 'E was at the concert, just like 'e said!"

Tellman glared at him.

"I found someone 'oo saw 'im," Bailey said defiantly. "No mistake. Stood as close to 'im as I am to you, and knew 'im quite well."

"Who is he?" Tellman asked, doubt heavy in his voice.

"Manager o' Coutts Bank," Bailey said with profound satisfaction. "They're bankers to royalty, they are."

Tellman's face pinched. "Maybe the bus conductor was done by somebody else," he said irritably. "We couldn't work out how he fitted with anyone."

"Yes," le Grange agreed. "Perhaps we couldn't make any connection because there wasn't one. Maybe it was just a private revenge for something, and whoever did it made it look the same?"

"Maybe they're all different," Pitt said sarcastically. "But I doubt it. No, it looks as if Carvell is not the Headsman. Thank you Bailey. An excellent piece of work."

Bailey flushed with pleasure. "Thank you, sir."

"You're not going to let him go, are you?" le Grange asked with wide eyes, forgetting the "sir."

Tellman made a short, sneering sound, but it seemed to be anger in general, rather than directed specifically at Pitt.

"Yes I am," Pitt replied. "A good lawyer will force us to anyway. There are too many other possible explanations."

"It was his gig and his horse," Tellman said darkly. "He damned well has something to do with it."

"Scarborough could conceivably have taken it himself," Pitt replied. Then as Tellman's face showed quite plainly his total disbelief, he added, "A lawyer would point that out, and a jury might very well consider it reasonable doubt. It is not impossible to steal a gig, especially if you have the connivance of the butler, who might well have keys. Carvell has no stable boy."

"Oh yes?" Tellman said incredulously. "What for? Just to take a midnight spin after a long day ordering the other servants around?"

"Maybe he had a lady friend," Pitt suggested. "Nice and impressive to roll up in a handsome gig. Much better than an omnibus, and less expensive than a cab, as well as giving him more freedom. A romantic ride in the park, perhaps?"

"With the Headsman around?" Tellman said scornfully. "Very romantic."

"Or maybe he intended to pick up a prostitute," Pitt continued.

Tellman gave him a filthy look. "Are we back to that again? I thought we'd dismissed that."

"We have," Pitt agreed. "Doesn't mean to say any lawyer worth his fee couldn't make a case for it."

Tellman swung around to Bailey and le Grange.

"Then you'd better start all over again, hadn't you. God knows where, or with what!"

"With finding where Arledge was killed," Pitt answered him.

Tellman swore long and viciously and without repeating himself.

Pitt also went back to the beginning. It was a long time since he had thought of Oakley Winthrop and centered his deliberations on Winthrop's death instead of Arledge's. That had been the start of it, perhaps the one on which all the rest hung. Who had killed Winthrop, why, and why at that time? Whom had he met in the park that night that he would get into a plea-

275

sure boat with? He should have given that more thought. It was the key.

It was an absurd thing to do. It could only have been someone he knew, someone of whom he had had no fear. But even so, why? What possible reason could anyone have, even a friend, for such a ridiculous activity in the middle of the night?

Bart Mitchell?

Or Bart and Mina?

He alighted from the hansom and crossed the pavement to the Winthrops' front door, and rang the bell. It was answered almost immediately by the parlormaid.

"Good afternoon." He passed her his card. "Will you please ask Mrs. Winthrop if I may speak with her? It is a matter of some importance."

She took the card, and returned only a few moments later to conduct him to the withdrawing room, where Mina was standing by the window staring into the garden. She was dressed in deep green which was so dark it was almost black except for the sheen on it where the sunlight fell. It suited her marvelously, complementing her fair skin and long slender neck. Her soft hair was coiled on her head. She was smiling, and suddenly Pitt could see in her the girl she must have been twenty years before.

Bart Mitchell was standing by the mantel shelf watching Pitt with vivid blue eyes, his expression guarded.

"Good afternoon, Superintendent," Mina said warmly, coming towards him. "Is there something more I can tell you? I'm sure I don't know what. I have searched my mind over and over, but nothing seems to mean anything."

"It wasn't about your husband I was going to speak, Mrs. Winthrop," Pitt replied. He glanced at Bart Mitchell and acknowledged him, then looked back at Mina. "It was about Mr. Arledge I wished to ask you."

She looked startled.

"Mr. Arledge?"

"Yes ma'am. I believe you knew him?"

"I—not to say knew him. I . . ." She looked confused, and glanced at her brother.

"Why do you ask, Superintendent?" Bart stepped forward into the middle of the room. "Surely you don't imagine Mrs. Winthrop had anything to do with his death? That would be absurd."

"I am looking for information, Mr. Mitchell," Pitt replied

276

with a small gesture of courtesy towards Mina. "An observation, a word overheard, or a perception which only now seems relevant."

"I apologize," Bart said stiffly, and without moving back. "But why would Mina know anything pertinent about Arledge's death? She met him only very formally on the occasion of attending one or two of his concerts. That's hardly a personal friendship where she could know the sort of detail you imply."

Pitt ignored him and looked at Mina.

"You did know Mr. Arledge, ma'am?"

"Well." She hesitated. "I did meet him one or two times. I am very fond of music. He was such a good musician, you know."

"Yes, so I believe," Pitt conceded. "But surely you also knew him a little more personally, Mrs. Winthrop? You were not merely a member of the audience."

Bart's chin came up and his eyes were sharp.

"What are you suggesting, Superintendent? Normally such a question might be quite inoffensive, but since you are investigating why the man was murdered, your remarks take a quite different tone. My sister's acquaintance with Mr. Arledge was slight, and there was nothing whatsoever improper in it."

"Of course not, Bart," Mina said carefully and with apology in her voice. "I don't imagine that was what the superintendent was thinking. There would be no cause for such an idea." She turned back to Pitt. "A few pleasant words, that is all, I assure you. Had I been aware of anything at all which could help you, do you not think I would have sent word to you immediately? After all, he was killed by the same man who murdered my husband!"

"Mina!" Bart said quickly. "Of course there was nothing improper in it. That is not the superintendent's train of thought. He is supposing that, for that very reason, you may have known more than you are willing to tell."

"No it is not, Mr. Mitchell," Pitt said sharply, but not entirely truthfully. "There may be a connection Mrs. Winthrop is unaware of. As you have pointed out, there must be a connection of some sort."

Bart looked at him with his remarkable eyes hostile and guarded.

"Mrs. Winthrop?" Pitt pursued.

She looked at him with wide innocence and said nothing.

He was obliged to be specific. "You were observed to be in a state of distress at a reception after a concert, and Mr. Arledge spent some time comforting you. You appeared to confide in him."

"Oh." She drew in her breath in a gasp, then looked at Bart, her eyes full of fear and shame.

He came forward to stand beside her.

"Whoever reported that to you, Superintendent, did so in very poor taste," he said stiffly. "It was a small domestic matter, such as happens to all of us from time to time, and can have had nothing to do with why Mr. Arledge was killed. For Heaven's sake, man, how can"—he hesitated, only a second—"the death of a household pet be connected with a lunatic from God knows where who cuts people's heads off in Hyde Park? That is absurd. If you have no better clues to chase than that, no wonder the wretch is still at large!"

Mina gulped. "You are being unfair, Bart. The superintendent could not have known that it was . . . as—as you said. All he knew was that I was distressed and Mr. Arledge comforted me. It could have been of importance." She smiled at Pitt with embarrassment. "I'm sorry it is so totally useless to you. I am afraid you will have to look elsewhere. Mr. Arledge was merely being kind to me because the music had touched my emotions. He would no doubt have done the same for anyone. That is the depth of our acquaintance, I'm afraid. He said nothing to me that would throw any light on his death. In fact I cannot even remember what he did say. It was all rather general."

She hesitated as if about to add something, then looked nervously at her brother.

"Did you know Mr. Arledge, sir?" Pitt asked suddenly.

"No!" Mina said instantly, then blushed at her forwardness. "Oh! I am sorry, that was most rude of me. I simply meant that—that—Bart has only recently returned from abroad."

"When was this incident, ma'am, exactly?"

She paled. "I—I don't recall . . . exactly. Some time ago."

"Before the injury to your wrist?" he asked.

There was a moment's total silence. The clock on the table by the window sounded like twigs breaking it was so loud.

"That was only the other day," Bart said icily. "An accident with a pot of tea. A clumsy maid who did not look where she was going." His blue eyes bored into Pitt's with anger and challenge. "Surely you know that, Superintendent?"

278

"I was referring to the bruises, Mr. Mitchell," Pitt replied without flinching.

"That was my own fault too!" Mina said quickly. "Really it was. I—I . . ." She turned to face Pitt, away from her brother. All the confidence had drained away from her. She looked frightened and guilty. "I was being foolish, Superintendent, and my husband caught hold of me to . . . to prevent me from falling. I had already lost my footing and—and so . . ."

Bart was seething with some emotion he could barely suppress, and yet dared not reveal. He seemed on the verge of exploding into speech, and his face was dark with fury.

"And so his strength—my weight . . ." Mina stammered. "It was all very silly—and entirely of my own causing."

"It was not your fault!" Bart lost control at last; his voice was quivering and very low. "You must stop blaming yourself for—" He stopped, turning to glare at Pitt, both his hands around Mina, holding her as if she might fall if he let her go. "Superintendent, all this has really nothing whatever to do with your inquiry. It happened long before Mr. Arledge's death, and had no relevance to it whatever. I am afraid we neither of us had any personal acquaintance with him, and much as we would like to, we cannot help you. Good day, sir."

"I see." Pitt did not believe him, still less did he believe Mina, but there was nothing he could do to prove it. He was convinced Oakley Winthrop had beaten Mina; frequently and severely, and she was terrified that when Bart had seen it he had killed Winthrop, or that Pitt would think so. "Thank you for your time, Mrs. Winthrop," Pitt said politely. "Mr. Mitchell." And with a bow, but no pretense of accepting their words as truth, he excused himself and took his leave.

—————— 10 ——————

THE DAY FINALLY came for moving house. Since the Headsman was still at large and the mystery as deep as ever, Pitt was unable to offer more than an hour or two's help. Of course he had employed men to pack and move the furniture, and Charlotte had spent all the previous day rolling glasses and cups and plates in old newspaper and wedging them carefully in boxes. All clothes were packed up, and linen; carpets had been taken up in the morning, and now everything was on its way from the old Bloomsbury house to the new house, which was finally decorated. The tiles around the fires had been replaced, all the gas brackets mended and in working order, shades were whole, every tiny piece of coving and dado rail mended or replaced, and the wallpaper and paint were immaculate.

Now that the reality was here, the children had realized exactly what moving meant. A whole new world beckoned full of excitement, experience, possibly adventure. When he had first got up Daniel had jiggled up and down with exuberance without really knowing why, and his questions had been endless. It had not noticeably dampened his spirits that no one had answered most of them.

Jemima had been quieter. Being two years older, it had taken her less time to realize that accepting the new inevitably means relinquishing the old, and the pain and uncertainty that brought with it. She had bursts of enthusiasm and curiosity, then long silences when she gazed around the familiar places, saddened that they now looked bare and already abandoned without curtains, pictures or the family furniture. When the carpets were rolled up it was as if the floor itself had been removed, and she spent several minutes rather tearfully with Gracie chiding her and hugging her, and giving her a string of instructions how to be useful, none of which she was able to follow.

However, by half past ten, Gracie and both children had gone with Pitt in the hansom, squashed rather uncomfortably close together in its narrow confines. There was no way in which Charlotte could also have ridden, quite apart from the fact that they had gone first in order to open the house and be ready to receive the goods when they arrived. Charlotte, on the other hand, was waiting till every last thing was packed and she had made triply sure that nothing whatsoever was left behind, forgotten, or mislaid, and the door was latched for the last time.

When all was accomplished and she had given the removal men the new address yet again, she picked up her two very best cushions, hand embroidered in silks, which were far too good to entrust to the men and too big to put in the boxes. She wrapped them in an old sheet, closed the front door once more, and hesitated on the step, looking around.

Then she pulled herself together and walked down the path to the gate. There was no time to think of all the happiness she had had here, or of regrets. Memories could not be left behind. They were part of one, carried in the heart.

She went through the gate, closed it, and set out along the pavement towards the omnibus stop, carrying the sheet with its two cushions. They did look a trifle like laundry and she was glad not to pass anyone she knew.

The omnibus came within five minutes and gratefully she stepped up, lugging the cushions behind her.

"I'm sorry miss, yer can't bring 'em in 'ere," the conductor said sharply, his round face full of contempt. He stood squarely in front of her, chin jutting out, brass buttons gleaming, expression bright with authority.

Charlotte stared at him, taken completely by surprise.

"You'll 'ave to get orf!" he ordered. "There'd be no room for fare-payin' passengers if I let every washerwoman in Bloomsbury get on 'ere with—"

"It's not laundry," Charlotte said indignantly. "It's cushions."

"I don't care what it is," the conductor replied with a laugh.

"It could be the Queen's nightshirt for all I care. Yer can't bring it in 'ere. There ain't no room for it. Now be a good girl and get orf, so the rest of us can be on our way."

"I'm moving house!" Charlotte said desperately. "My husband and children have gone on ahead. I've got to catch up with them."

"That's as may be, but you ain't doing it on my bus—not with that bag full o' laundry! What d'yer think this is, a trades van?" He pointed his finger towards the pavement. "Now get orf, before I call the police and yer gets taken in custody for causing a disturbance."

Someone else inside the bus came forward, an elderly gentleman with a mustache and a black walking stick in his hand.

"Let the poor creature ride," he said to the conductor. "I'm sure there's room, if she holds it on her knee."

"You sit down, sir, and don't go interferin' in what ain't your business," the conductor commanded him. "I'll take care o' this."

"But . . ." the old gentleman began again.

"Sit down, you silly old duffer," a woman called out from the inside. "Don't interfere! 'E knows what 'e's doing. Goodness sakes, you can't 'ave people bringing on their laundry! Whatever next?"

"She said it's not laundry—" The man was interrupted brusquely by the conductor.

"You go and sit down, sir, else I'll 'ave to put yer orf too. We gotta keep to a time 'ere, yer know!" He turned back to Charlotte. "Now look 'ere, miss, are yer goin' to get orf on yer own, or do I 'ave ter call the rozzers and 'ave yer taken in charge fer disturbin' the peace?"

Charlotte was too furious to speak. She let out her breath in a gasp of rage and stepped back off the platform onto the pavement. She only thought to thank the old gentleman who had tried to help her when it was too late and the bus had jolted forward, overbalancing him until he fell against the conductor and had to pick himself up. The driver shouted at the horses again and cracked his whip in the air above their backs and they gathered speed, leaving Charlotte alone on the footpath with her cushions, and a monumental rage.

"Where on earth have you been?" Pitt said, staring at her when she finally arrived, hot, untidy, hair falling all over the place and her cheeks still burning with temper, the cushions clasped in her clenched fist.

"I have been in a hansom cab," she replied heatedly. "That driveling officious little ... swine wouldn't let me on the omnibus!"

"What?" Pitt was confused. "What are you talking about? Everything's here. The men have unpacked about half of it."

"The impertinent, condescending, arrogant little toad wouldn't let me on with the cushions ..." she went on furiously.

"Why not?" He frowned at her. He could see that she was bristling with rage, but he did not perceive the reason. "What do you mean? Wasn't it the ordinary omnibus?"

"Yes of course it was the ordinary omnibus!" she shouted. "The autocratic, bossy, self-opinionated little oaf thought the cushions were laundry, and he wouldn't let me get on. He even threatened to call the police and have me taken in charge for disturbing the peace!"

Pitt's mouth twitched and his eyes were very bright, but after a moment of total silence when her blazing expression dared him to be amused, he composed himself to suitable sympathy.

"I'm sorry. Let me take the cushions." He held out his hand.

She thrust them at him. "Where are the men now? I don't see them."

"Gone 'round the corner to the public house to have lunch. They'll be back in half an hour or so to unpack the rest. Gracie is in the kitchen." He gazed around the drawing room where they were standing. "This really is very nice indeed. You've done a magnificent work here."

"Don't humor me," she said tartly. But she was longing to smile and she sniffed and stared around also. He was right, it was looking very good indeed. "Where are the children?"

"In the garden. The last I saw of them, Daniel was up the apple tree and Jemima had found a hedgehog and was talking to it."

"Good." She smiled in spite of herself. "Do you think they'll like it?"

His expression answered her question without the necessity of words.

"Have you seen the green room upstairs? That's going to be our bedroom. Here, let me show you."

He considered saying he really had not time, and changed

his mind. And as soon as they were upstairs he was glad he had changed his mind. The room had a peace about it, a sense of apartness from the haste and the bustle of the streets. The wind was rustling the leaves and the light flickered in bright patterns over the walls. There was no other sound. He found himself smiling, and looking across at Charlotte. Her face was full of expectancy. "Yes," he said with complete honesty. "I've never been in a better room in my life."

The day of the by-election was gusty with sudden showers and bars of brilliant sun. Jack was out as soon as he had finished his breakfast, and Emily could not remain in the house alone on tenterhooks, even though she knew she was of little assistance, and now even moral support was not enough to still the nerves.

Nigel Uttley was also out early. He was smiling confidently, chatting with friends and supporters, but watching him closely one might see that something of his former swagger was gone and there was an edge of anxiety visible in him now and again.

A few at a time those men entitled to vote went to the polling station and cast their ballots. They emerged looking at no one and hurried away.

The morning passed slowly. Emily moved from one place to another with Jack, trying to think of something to say that was encouraging without building his confidence when he could so easily lose. And yet as she watched the men coming and going, overheard snatches of their conversation, she could not help the surge of hope inside her that he would win.

And there was only winning and losing. Tomorrow either he would be a member of Parliament, with all the opportunity and responsibility, the work, the chance of fame which it afforded, or else he would be the loser, with no position, no profession. Uttley would be there smiling, confident, the winner. She would have to try to comfort Jack, to help him believe in himself, find something to look forward to, some other cause to build and care about and labor towards.

By a little after two o'clock she was emotionally drained, and the whole length of the afternoon still stretched ahead of her. By five she was beginning to believe that Jack really could win. Her spirits soared with hope, then plummeted with despair.

By the time the polls closed she was exhausted, untidy, and generally more footsore than she could ever remember. She and Jack went home in silence, sitting close together in a hansom. They did not speak. Neither of them knew what to say, now that the battle was over and only the news of victory or defeat lay ahead.

At home they had a late supper, too tense to enjoy it. Emily could not have said afterwards what it had been, except she thought she recalled the pink of salmon on the plate, but whether it had been poached or smoked she could not say. She kept glancing at the clock on the mantel, wondering when they would be finished counting and they would know.

"Do you think . . . ?" she began, just as Jack spoke also.

"I'm sorry," he said quickly. "What were you going to say?"

"Nothing! It was of no importance. You?"

"Nothing much, just that it could be a long time. You don't have to . . ."

She froze him with a look.

"All right," he said apologetically. "I just thought . . ."

"Well don't. It's ridiculous. Of course I'm going to wait until the last vote is counted and we know."

He rose from the table. It was quarter past nine.

"Well let us at least do it in the withdrawing room, where we can be as comfortable as possible."

She accepted with a smile and followed him into the hall. Almost as soon as they were out of the dining room door Harry, the youngest footman, appeared from the archway under the stairs, his fair hair untidy, his face flushed.

"They're still counting, sir!" he said breathlessly. "I just came back from the 'all, but I reckon as they done most of 'em, an both piles looks about the same to me. You could win, sir! Mr. Jenkins says as you will!"

"Thank you, Harry," Jack said with a voice very nearly level. "But I think perhaps Jenkins is speaking more from loyalty than knowledge."

"Oh no, sir," Harry said with unaccustomed assurance. "Everyone in the servants' 'all reckons as yer goin' ter win. That Mr. Uttley's not near as clever as 'e thinks. Cook says as 'e's overdone 'isself this time. An' 'e's not married neither, which Mrs. 'Edges says as makes 'im socially much sought after by rich ladies wif daughters, but they don't trust 'im the same as a man wot's got a family, like." His cheeks were pink with exertion and excitement, and he stood very straight, his shoulders back.

"Thank you," Jack said gravely. "I hope you are not going to be too disappointed if I don't win?"

"Oh no, sir," Harry said cheerfully. "But you will!" And with that he turned and went back through the green baize door to the servants' quarters.

"Oh dear," Jack sighed, resuming his way to the withdrawing room. "They are going to take it very hard."

"We all will," Emily agreed, going through the door as he opened it for her. "But it is hardly worth fighting for something if you don't want it enough to care if you win or lose."

He closed the door and they both sat down, close to each other, and tried to think of something else to talk about while the minutes ticked away and the hour hand on the gold-faced clock crept towards ten, and then eleven.

It was growing very late. There should have been a result. Both of them were acutely aware of it, and trying not to say anything. Their conversation grew more and more stilted and sporadic.

Finally at twenty past eleven the door burst open and Jenkins stood there, his face flushed, his tongue stumbling over his words in wildly uncharacteristic emotion.

"S-sir—Mr. Radley. There is a recount, sir! They are nearly finished. The carriage is ready, and James will t-take you to the hall now. Ma'am . . ."

Jack shot to his feet and took a step forward before even thinking of reaching back for Emily, but she had also risen. Her legs weak with tension, she was only a yard behind him.

"Thank you," Jack said a great deal less calmly than he had intended. "Yes, thank you. We'll go." He held out his hand towards Emily, then hurried to the front door without bothering to take his coat.

They rode in silence in the carriage, each craning forward as if they might see something, although there was nothing but the sweep of street lamps ahead of them and the moving lights of carriages as others hastened on this most tumultuous of nights.

At the hall where the ballots were being counted they alighted and with thumping hearts mounted the steps and went in the doors. Immediately a hush fell over at least half the assembled people. Faces turned, there was a buzz of excitement. Only the counters remained, heads bent, fingers flying through the sheaves of paper, stacks growing before them.

"Third time!" a little man hissed with unbearable tension in his voice.

Emily gripped Jack's arm so tightly he winced, but she did not let go.

Over at the far end of the hall Nigel Uttley stood glowering, his face pale and strained. He still expected to win, but he had not foreseen that it would be close. He had thought to have an easy victory. His supporters were standing in anxious groups, huddled together, shooting occasional glances at the tables and the piles of papers.

Jack's supporters also stood close, but they had not in honesty thought to win, and now the possibility was there and real. The die was cast, and they would know the verdict any moment.

Emily looked around to see how many people were here, and as her gaze passed from one group to another, she saw the light on coifs of gleaming silver hair on a proud head.

"Aunt Vespasia," she burst out with astonishment and pleasure. "Look, Jack!" She pulled violently at his sleeve. "Great-Aunt Vespasia is here!"

He turned in surprise, and then his face broke into a smile of intense delight. He made his way over to her, pushing through the crowd.

"Aunt Vespasia! How very nice of you to have come!"

She turned and surveyed him with calm, amused eyes, but there was a flush of excitement in her cheeks.

"Of course I came," she exclaimed. "Surely you did not think I would miss such an occasion?"

"Well it is . . . late," he said in sudden embarrassment. "And I may well . . . not win."

"Of course you may," she agreed. "But either way, you have given him an excellent battle. He will know he has seen a fight." She lifted her chin a little and there was a gleam of belligerence in her eyes.

Jack was about to add something when there was a sudden hush over the hall and everyone swung around to see the returning officer rise to his feet.

There followed a heart-lurching space while he went through all the formal preamble, waiting a moment, savoring all the drama and the power. Then he announced that by a margin of twelve votes, the member of Parliament for the constituency would be John Henry Augustus Radley.

Emily let out a squeal of sheer relief.

Jack gasped and then let out his breath in a long sigh.

Nigel Uttley stood stiff-lipped and unbelieving.

"Congratulations, my dear." Aunt Vespasia turned to Jack and, reaching forward very gently, kissed him on the cheek. "You will do excellently."

He blushed with self-conscious happiness and was too full of emotion to speak.

The party to celebrate the victory was held the following evening. It was a somewhat hasty affair since Emily had not prepared it with her usual care. She had not dared to believe it would be called for. Of course all those who had helped in the campaign were invited, with their wives, and those who had offered their support in his cause. Naturally his family were included, which was actually Emily's family. Charlotte and Pitt accepted immediately. There was a charming note of congratulation from Caroline, but no word as to whether she would attend or not.

It began early as people arrived breathless with the thrill of victory. Voices were raised, faces flushed, and everyone talked at once, full of ideas and hopes of change.

"It's only one new member," Jack said, trying to appear modest and keep some sort of perspective to things. "It doesn't change the government."

"Of course it doesn't," Emily agreed, standing very close to him and quite unable to take the enormous smile from her face. "But it is a beginning. It is a turning of the tide. Uttley is furious."

"He most certainly is," a large woman agreed cheerfully, balancing her glass of champagne in one hand, the enormous lace ruffles on her shoulders and sleeves endangering passersby. "Bertie says in spite of what the newspapers have been saying, he was taken completely by surprise. He really believed he was going to win."

Bertie, who had only been paying half attention, now turned towards Jack with a serious expression on his benign face.

"Actually, old boy, he really was very put out indeed." He bit into a petit four. "You have a nasty enemy there. I should be very careful of him if I were you."

For a moment their conversation was obliterated by the sound of chatter, clinking glasses, a swish of fabric and slither of leather soles upon the floor.

"Oh really, my dear," his wife responded as soon as she

could make herself heard. "He must have considered the possibility of losing, surely? No one enters any competition without knowing someone has to lose."

"Uttley did not believe it would be he." Bertie leaned towards them, growing even graver. "And it is not merely losing a seat he believed was his in all but name. He has lost a great deal more, so I hear."

His wife was confused. "What more? What are you talking about? Do explain yourself, my dear. You are not making sense."

Bertie disregarded her and kept his eyes on Jack.

"There's a great deal about it I don't understand, powerful forces at work, if you know what I mean." Bertie for once ignored his sparkling glass. "One hears whispers, if one is in the right place at the right time. There are people . . ." He hesitated, glancing at Emily, then back to Jack. "People behind the people one knows . . ."

Jack said nothing.

"Powerful forces?" Emily asked, then wished she had not. As a woman, she was not supposed to know about such things, still less at least half understand what he meant.

"Nonsense," Bertie's wife said briskly. "He lost because people preferred Jack. It's as simple as that. Really, you are making a secret where there is none."

"The people who voted obviously preferred Jack," Bertie said patiently, sipping at his glass again. "But they were not the ones who blackballed Uttley from his club." He looked at Jack meaningfully over his wife's head. "Be careful, old fellow, that's all. There's something going on a great deal more than meets the eye. And those with the real power are not always whom one supposes."

Jack nodded, his face grave, but the smile did not fade from his lips. "Now do have some more champagne. You surely deserve it as much as anyone."

When everyone had been welcomed, thanked and congratulated and the toasts drunk, Emily at last made her way over to Charlotte.

"How are you?" she said quietly. "I haven't even had time to ask you how everything went with the move. Is the new house comfortable? I know it's beautiful." She gave Charlotte's deep green gown an admiring glance. It had the new accented shoulders with a very fine sweep of feathers and was highly becoming. "Have you got everything sorted out and in its right place yet?" And before Charlotte could answer, her expression changed. "What about the Headsman? Is it true Thomas arrested someone and then had to let him go again? Or is that nonsense?"

"No, it's true," Charlotte replied, equally softly, moving a little to keep her back to a group of excited celebrants near her. "After the butler's murder he arrested Carvell, but one of his men found that Carvell could account for where he was when the omnibus conductor was killed, so he had to let him go."

Emily looked surprised. "What made him think it was Carvell? I mean, enough to arrest him this time? That butler was a swine." She said the word with uncharacteristic viciousness. "He could have had any number of enemies. If I had had to have anything to do with him I should have been sorely tempted myself."

"Don't exaggerate," Charlotte said dismissively. "He was rather bossy, and had a sneer built into his face."

"He dismissed that girl for singing," Emily protested with genuine anger. "That was brutal. He used his authority to humiliate other people, which is inexcusable. He was a bully. I wouldn't have wished beheading on him, but since it has happened, I cannot say I grieve for him in the slightest."

Pitt had joined them, carrying a plate of pastries and savories for Charlotte. He had obviously overheard the last remark. His face lit with a dry amusement.

"You are one person I had not suspected," he said quietly. Then his expression changed to one of seriousness. "Congratulations, Emily. I am delighted for you both. I hope it is the beginning of a fine career."

A burst of laughter drifted across the room, and someone called out with a loud cheer.

"Oh it will be," Emily said with not so much conviction as determination. "Whom do you suspect?" she went on without hesitating. "Do you suppose the omnibus conductor could have nothing to do with it after all?"

"And someone else killed him?" Pitt raised his eyebrows. "Why?"

Emily shrugged her slender shoulders. "I don't know."

Charlotte took the plate from Pitt. "Perhaps he was an offensive little swine, like the one who put me off the omnibus the other day," she said with sudden venom. "If someone had taken his head off I should not have grieved overmuch."

Emily looked at her curiously, her expression one of complete bewilderment. "What are you talking about?"

"Oh!" Charlotte pulled a face, hesitated whether to tell Emily or not, and realized the only way to deal with it was lightly. "The miserable little . . ." She could not think of a word sufficiently damning. The rage still boiled inside her, her memory scalding hot for its sheer humiliation.

Emily was waiting, even Pitt was looking at her with a sudden interest in his eyes, as if the story had taken on a new importance.

"Slug," Charlotte said with tight lips. "He wouldn't let me onto the omnibus because I had a bundle of cushions tied up in a sheet. He thought it was laundry!"

Emily burst into giggles. "I'm so sorry," she apologized happily. "But I really . . ." The rest was lost as she chortled with delight, picturing it in her mind.

Charlotte could not let it go. "He was so self-important," she said, still filled with indignation. "I would have given a great deal to have been able to squash him in some way or other." She shook herself. "He was so beastly to the man who stood up and came to the back to try to assist me. Can you imagine that?" She glanced at Pitt, and saw from his face that he was lost in thought. "You aren't listening, are you! You think it was ridiculous of me!"

A footman with a tray offered them savories and they each took one.

"No," Pitt said slowly. "I think it is probably the sort of reaction most people would have. And you did what most people do. . . ."

"I didn't do anything," she protested. "I wish now I had, but I couldn't think of anything."

"Exactly." He agreed. "You came home fuming, but you did nothing."

Emily was regarding him curiously.

"The omnibus conductor . . ." Charlotte said slowly, comprehension beginning to dawn. "Oh no—that's absurd! Nobody chops—" She stopped.

A large lady brushed past them, her sleeves barely missing the pastries. Someone else laughed exuberantly.

"Maybe not." Pitt frowned. "No, perhaps it is a foolish idea. I'm reaching after anything. There must be a better reason, something personal." He turned to Emily. "But this is your celebration. Let's talk about you and your victory. When does

Jack take his seat? What is his maiden speech to be about, has he decided? I hope it is not for some time, if it is still about the police!"

Emily pulled a face, but she laughed, and the conversation moved to politics, the future, and Jack's beliefs and hopes.

It was over an hour later when Charlotte was alone with Pitt for a few moments that she broached the subject of the Headsman again. In spite of her very real pleasure for Jack and Emily, she was beginning to realize just how serious the situation was for Pitt, and his new and now gravely threatened promotion.

"What are you going to do now?" she asked quietly, so the thin woman with the checked skirt and the enthusiastic voice a yard away could not hear her. Then as Pitt looked blank, she continued. "If it can't be Carvell, who can it be?"

"I don't know. Possibly Bart Mitchell. He certainly had every reason to kill Winthrop, and possibly Arledge, if he misunderstood his attention to Mina. But I can't think of any reason for the bus conductor or Scarborough, unless they knew something. . . . He must be a very violent man. His experiences in Africa, easy life and death . . ." He trailed off, leaving the idea unfinished.

"You don't really believe that, do you?" She screwed up her face.

"It doesn't seem very satisfactory," he replied. He nodded to an acquaintance and continued talking. "Actually we haven't found out his past movements, or the exact date of his return from Africa. Possibly he did not know of Winthrop's nature until very recently. Obviously Mina is desperately ashamed and does all she can to conceal it. She seems to feel it is somehow her fault." He frowned, his voice dropping and taking on a hard, angry edge. "I've seen women who have been beaten before. They all seem to take the blame on themselves. I can remember years ago, when I was a constable, being called in to fights, finding women bleeding and half dead, and still convinced it was their own fault and not the man's. They've lost all hope, all worth or belief, even every shred of dignity. Usually it was drink . . . whiskey more often than not."

She stared at him, visions of an unguessed and terrible world yawning open in front of her. She remembered Mina's overwhelming shame, her diffidence, and how she had blossomed since Winthrop's death. It seemed so obvious now, the only thing remarkable was why it had taken so long to reach its tragic climax.

"But it doesn't really explain why he killed Arledge," Pitt went on more thoughtfully. "Unless Mina knew he had killed Winthrop and somehow or other betrayed the fact to Arledge—unwittingly, of course."

"That would make sense," Charlotte said quickly. "Yes, that sounds as if it could have been. But then why the omnibus conductor and the butler? Or did the butler try his hand at blackmail of Carvell, thinking he killed Arledge, and so Carvell killed him to keep him quiet because he couldn't prove his innocence?"

Pitt smiled. "A trifle farfetched," he said ruefully. "But I've left poor Bailey looking into Carvell's story about being at the concert. I want better proof than we have, something absolutely irrefutable."

"Do you doubt it?"

"I don't know." He looked tired and confused. "Part of me does. My brain, I suppose."

A group of excited people next to them raised their glasses in a toast. A woman in peach-colored lace was so exuberant her voice was becoming shrill.

"But not your heart?" Charlotte asked quietly, looking at Pitt.

He smiled. "It's a trifle absurd to think with your heart. I should prefer instinct—which is probably just a collection of memories below the surface of recollection which form judgments for which we cannot readily produce a reason."

"Very logical," she agreed. "But it comes to the same thing. You don't believe he did it, but you can't be sure. Emily says that the butler, Scarborough, was an absolute pig. He dismissed that poor maid just because she was singing. The girl was beside herself. And what is so inexcusable is that he would know what losing a position would cost her. She may not be able to get another without a good character. She could starve!" Her voice was getting higher and higher with the distress of it, and her sense of outrage.

Pitt put his hand on her arm. "Didn't you say Emily was going to offer her a position as housemaid or something?"

"Yes, but that isn't the point." She was too outraged to be calm. "Scarborough couldn't know that. And if Emily hadn't happened to be there, then she wouldn't have. The man was still a total pig."

Pitt frowned, his face creased with thought. "He did it in public?"

She was obliged to move aside for a group of people laughing and talking.

"No—well, more or less," she answered. "The corner of the room, over by that chair where Victor Garrick was sitting with his cello, waiting to play."

"Oh. Yes, you are right," he agreed. "The man was vicious and arbitrary. It doesn't sound as if blackmail would be beyond him—"

They were interrupted by Emily in a swirl of apple-green silk embroidered with seed pearls.

"Mama still hasn't come," she said anxiously. "Do you suppose she is not going to? Really, it is too bad of her. She seems to think of no one but herself these days. I was so sure she would at least come to this, since Jack won." She waved her hand to decline any more champagne, and the footman moved on.

"There's time yet," Pitt said, but with a twisted smile, and no belief in his voice.

Emily gave him a long look but said nothing.

Pitt excused himself and went to talk to Landon Hurlwood, who had been a supporter of Jack's cause and had come to add his presence to the celebrations. He looked comfortable and relaxed, moving from group to group of people, full of vitality and optimism for the future. Under the chandeliers, the light gleamed on the pewter sheen of his hair.

"He's been such a help to us," Emily said, watching him greet Pitt with obvious pleasure. "A nice man. That is the happiest I have seen him look since his wife died, poor creature. She was ill for a long time, you know. Actually I never believed she was as ill as she must have been. She was one of those who made such a cause of it, it seemed she never spoke of anything else. Now it appears I wronged her, because she died of consumption, and I feel fearfully guilty."

"So you should," Charlotte agreed.

Emily glanced at her sharply. "You were not supposed to agree with me! Dead or not, she was still a most trying woman."

"I expect he was fond of her, and she may not have been so tedious before she was ill," Charlotte pointed out.

"You are being contrary," Emily criticized, then suddenly became serious again. "Are you worried about Thomas? Surely they cannot expect him to solve every crime. There are bound to be some that are beyond anyone."

"Of course." Charlotte became serious also. "But they don't see it like that. And I haven't been of any use this time." Her face tightened. "I don't even know where to begin to look. I have been trying to think who it could be, if it is not Mr. Carvell."

"So have I," Emily agreed, lowering her voice. "More especially, I have been trying to imagine why. Just to say it is madness is not in the least helpful."

Further discussion or conversation was prevented by a disturbance at the entrance to the room as people parted to allow the passage of an elderly person in black, leaning heavily on a stick.

"Grandmama!" Emily said in amazement. She looked immediately beyond her, expecting to see Caroline, but there was no one except a footman in livery holding someone's cloak.

Both of them went forward to greet the old lady, who looked formidable in an old-fashioned dress with a huge bustle and a bodice heavily decorated with jet beading. There were jet earrings at her ears and an expression on her face only relieved from total ill temper by a dominating curiosity.

"How delightful to see you, Grandmama," Emily said with as much enthusiasm as she could pretend. "I am so glad you were able to come."

"Of course I came," the old lady said instantly. "I must see what on earth you are doing now! A member of Parliament." She snorted. "I'm not sure whether to be pleased or not. I'm not entirely certain if government is something respectable people do." She looked around the room at the assembly, noting jewelry, the light glittering on the champagne glasses, the gleams of the silver trays and the number of footmen in livery. "A bit showy, isn't it? Putting yourself forward is not really the act of a gentleman."

"And whom should we be governed by?" Emily demanded, two spots of pink in her cheeks. "Men who are not gentlemen?"

"That is entirely different," the old lady said, brushing logic aside. "Real gentlemen of the class to whom government comes naturally do not have to seek election. They have seats in the House of Lords by birth, as they should. Standing on boxes at street corners asking people to vote for you is another matter altogether, and really rather vulgar, if you ask me."

Emily opened her mouth, then closed it again.

"You are a little old-fashioned, Grandmama," Charlotte said swiftly. "Mr. Disraeli was elected, and the Queen approved of him."

"And Mr. Gladstone was elected, and she didn't!" the old lady snapped with obvious pleasure.

"Which goes to show that being elected has nothing to do with it," Charlotte replied. "Mr. Disraeli was also very clever."

"And vulgar," the old lady said, staring at Charlotte, her eyes glittering. "He wore the most dreadful waistcoats and talked far too much, and too often. No refinement at all. I met him once, you know. No, you didn't know that, did you?"

"No."

"As I said. Vulgar. Never knew when to hold his tongue. Thought he was amusing."

"And wasn't he?"

"Well—yes, I suppose so. But what has that to do with anything?"

Charlotte shot a look at Emily, and they both gave up on the subject.

"Where is Mama?" Charlotte asked, then immediately wished she had not.

Grandmama's eyebrows shot up. "Good heavens, girl, how should I know? Tripping the light fantastic somewhere, no doubt. She is quite mad." She gazed at the whirl of color and chatter around them, the women with their more slender skirts and wide shoulders decorated with flounces, bows, frills or feathers, the heads with coils of hair, ornaments of diamante and pearl, plumes, pins, tiaras and flowers. "Who on earth are all these people?" she demanded of Emily. "I don't know any of them. You had better introduce me. I shall tell you whom I wish to meet."

She frowned. "And where is that husband of yours anyway? Why is he not by your side? I always said no good would come of marrying a man who is only after your money." She swept Emily up and down with a derisory glance. "It is not as if you were a proper heiress; then it would be quite different. Your father would pick someone for you with a good family background. No one has ever heard of Jack Radley, indeed!"

"Well they will now, Mrs. Ellison." Jack appeared from just beyond her field of vision, looking extraordinarily handsome and smiling at her as if he were delighted to see her.

She had the grace to blush, and grunted something inaudible. Then she glared at Charlotte. "You might have told me he was there, fool!" she hissed.

"I didn't know you were going to be so offensive, or I might have," Charlotte whispered back.

"What? Don't mumble, girl. I can't hear you. For Heaven's sake, speak clearly. Your mother paid enough to have you taught elocution and deportment when you were young. She should have kept her money." And with that she smiled at Jack. "Congratulations, young man. I hear you have won something."

"Thank you." He bowed, offering her his arm. "May I take you and introduce you to some interesting people who would no doubt like to meet you?"

"You may," she accepted, head high. Without a backward glance, she twitched her skirt around and sailed off, leaving Charlotte and Emily alone.

"If someone had taken her head off, I would understand it," Emily said under her breath.

"I don't think I should turn him in," Charlotte added. Then slowly she swiveled to face Emily just as the same thought was reflected in Emily's eyes.

"Do you really think . . ." Emily began. "No," she said, answering her own question, but without conviction. "Do you suppose there is someone who knows who it is? Would anyone protect . . ."

"I don't know," Charlotte replied slowly. "I suppose if it were someone you loved—a husband or father?" A haze of ugly and frightening thoughts filled her mind. "But how could you bear to believe that anyone you loved could do such things? It wouldn't be simply their guilt, you would feel as if it were part of yourself. You can't be separate, as if their acts or their nature in no way touched you. If they had done it, had lost their minds to madness, it would be as if you were touched with it too."

"No it wouldn't!" Emily contradicted her. "You couldn't blame—"

"It may not be fair," Charlotte went on, cutting across her, "but that is how you would feel. Weren't you embarrassed when your friends commented on Mama being seen with Joshua?"

"Yes. But that's—" Emily stopped, realization flooding her face. "Yes, of course," she said quickly. "And that's nothing, beside this. I see what you mean. One would feel as if one had

297

contributed to it, even if by sheer ignorance of something terribly, hideously wrong. One would fight against believing it to the very last, unarguable fact." Her face crumpled with pity. "How truly appalling."

"I suppose it could conceivably be Mina," Charlotte said slowly. "She might protect her brother, especially if he killed Winthrop to protect her."

"I can't think who else," Emily was thinking aloud. "Mr. Carvell hasn't a wife, and no one knows anything about the omnibus conductor."

"Do you suppose Mrs. Arledge might know anything?" Charlotte asked dubiously, half hating herself for speaking ill, even by suggestion, of Dulcie. Pitt so obviously admired her, and with excellent cause. It seemed small-minded to raise her name in this connection.

"Such as what?" Emily asked. "I doubt she has the faintest idea who killed Arledge, or she would have told Thomas, to get the matter cleared up and get the police out of her house. Then she could continue with her life discreetly."

Charlotte stared at her. "What do you mean, 'discreetly'? You sound as if you thought she had something to hide."

"Oh Charlotte, at times you are obtuse," Emily said with a patient smile. "Dulcie has an admirer, or maybe more than that. Haven't you seen?"

Charlotte was taken completely by surprise.

"No! Who is it? Are you sure? How could you know?"

"I don't know who it is, but I know he exists. It's obvious." Emily shook her head a little. "Haven't you looked at her, I mean really looked?"

"At what?"

"Oh for Heaven's sake, Charlotte!" Emily said exasperatedly. "At the way she dresses, the little touches, the dainty mourning brooch, the lace, the perfect fit of her gown around the waist and the fashionable sleeves set with the point at the shoulder. And she wears a beautiful perfume. She walks as if she knows people are watching her. And even when she is not speaking to anyone there is a . . ."—she shrugged—". . . a sort of composure about her, as if she knew something special and secret, and very delicious. Really, Charlotte, if you don't know a woman in love when you see one, you are a useless detective. In fact, even as a woman you are extraordinarily unintelligent."

"I thought it was . . ." Charlotte protested.

"What?"

"I don't know . . . courage?"

Emily smiled and nodded at an acquaintance who had campaigned for Jack, then continued urgently. "I don't doubt she has courage too, but that doesn't give anyone that inner satisfaction, it doesn't make you smile for no reason, and glance at yourself in mirrors, and always look your very best, just in case you run into him."

Charlotte stared at her. "How did you observe her so much? I only saw her at the Requiem."

"You don't need to see anyone very much to notice that. What were you thinking of that you didn't see?"

Charlotte blushed, remembering what her feelings had been. "I wonder if it matters," she said, changing the subject.

"Of course it doesn't matter," Emily replied, then stopped. "What are you talking about? Does what matter?"

"Who it is, of course!" She drew in her breath sharply. "Emily, do you think—I mean . . ."

"Yes," Emily said instantly, not even noticing an elderly man who was trying to attract her attention. He gave up and moved away. "We must find out," she continued. "I don't know how, but we must discover who it is."

"Do you suppose it could be Bart Mitchell? Maybe that is the connection Thomas is looking for."

"Tomorrow morning we shall begin," Emily promised. "I shall think about what to do, and so can you."

They were interrupted, before the quite unnecessary ending could be added, by Caroline and Joshua arriving, both dressed very formally and looking excited and happy.

"Oh thank goodness," Emily said with immense relief. "I really thought she was not going to come." She moved forward to welcome her mother, and Charlotte came immediately behind her.

"Congratulations, my dear," Caroline said ebulliently, kissing Emily on the cheek. "I am delighted for you. I am sure Jack will be magnificent, and there is certainly much to be done. Where is he?"

"Over there, talking to Sir Arnold Maybury," Emily replied. She looked at Joshua's charming, mobile face with its very slightly crooked nose and wry smile. "I'm glad you came too. Jack will be very pleased."

"Of course he came too," Caroline said with an odd little

smile. Then she turned and looked up at Joshua, her face flushed and suddenly self-conscious.

This time it was Charlotte who noticed, and Emily who was unaware.

"Mama?" Charlotte said slowly. "What do you mean?"

Emily looked at her, frowning. It sounded such a foolish question. She was about to make some impatient remark, then she realized she had missed a nuance, something far more important than the words. She waited, turning to Joshua, then Caroline.

Caroline took a deep breath and looked at neither of her daughters.

"Joshua and I have just been married," she replied very quietly, in little more than a whisper.

Emily was thunderstruck.

Charlotte opened her mouth to say something generous and congratulatory, and found her throat aching and her eyes ridiculously filling with tears.

Joshua put his arm around Caroline. He was still smiling, but there was a strength in his eyes, and a warning.

Jack returned with Grandmama still on his arm, a glass of champagne in her hand. He saw that he had entered a scene of high emotional tension. He turned to Joshua.

"Congratulations," Joshua said quietly, holding out his hand and taking Jack's. "It is a fine victory, and will bode well for all of us. I wish you a long and successful career." He smiled. "For our sakes as well as yours."

"Thank you." Jack let go his hand and reached for a glass from a passing footman. He held it up. "To the future."

Grandmama lifted her glass to her lips also.

"Everybody's future," Emily added, looking at Jack. "Mama and Joshua's too. We must also congratulate them and wish them every happiness."

Jack's eyes opened wide.

"They have just been married," Emily added.

Grandmama, halfway through a gulp of champagne, choked on it, blowing a mouthful over half the front of her dress. Her black eyes were furious, her face flushed with shock and outrage. However, it was impossible to be dignified while dribbling copiously. Emily reached for Jack's pocket handkerchief and, mopping her up, only made it considerably worse. Grandmama then took the only avenue of retreat open to her and sank in a faint to the floor, almost pulling Jack down with her.

300

Instantly she was the center of all attention. No one any longer looked at Joshua and Caroline, or even at Jack. People rushed from all surrounding groups.

"Oh dear! The poor lady," one man said, aghast at the sight of Grandmama in a heap on the floor. "We must help her. Somebody! Salts!"

"Has she been taken ill?" someone else asked anxiously. "Should we send for a doctor?"

"I'm sure that's not necessary," Emily reassured her. "I'll just burn a feather under her nose." She looked for a footman to fetch such an article.

"Poor creature." The woman looked at Grandmama's recumbent form with pity. "To be taken ill in public, and so far from one's own home."

"She's not ill," Emily contradicted her.

"She's drunk," Charlotte added with sudden, quite inexcusable, malice. She was furious with the old woman's utter selfishness in robbing Caroline of being the center of attention and happiness at this, of all moments. She glared down and saw the old lady click her teeth with rage, and felt acute satisfaction.

"Oh!" The other lady's sympathy vanished and she moved a step or two away, revulsion altering her face entirely.

"You'd better carry her out," Charlotte added to Jack. "One of the footmen will help you. Put her somewhere so she can recover, and then someone will take her home."

"Not I," Caroline said firmly. "Anyway, I'm not going home. This is my wedding night."

"Of course not you," Charlotte agreed immediately, then turned to Emily.

"Oh no!" Emily backed away, her face aghast.

The footman returned with a feather already smoldering, and offered it to Emily. She thanked him and took it with relish, holding it close under Grandmama's nose. She breathed in, coughed violently, and remained stubbornly on the floor with eyes closed.

Jack and the footman bent to pick up the still-recumbent form of the old lady. It was extremely awkward. She was short and heavy, and a dead weight. It took all their strength to get her up, with her skirts in order, and begin to move her through the crowd towards the doorway. Even so, as she passed Charlotte, she managed to lash out with her foot and very nearly land a swift kick on Charlotte's elbow.

"She won't stay under the same roof with me when I come home," Caroline said distinctly. "She has sworn never to abide with me if I disgrace myself and make myself a public laughingstock." She looked at Emily. "I'm sorry, my dear, but I think it is you who is going to have to offer her a home. Charlotte has no room."

"Even if I had," Charlotte replied. "If she weren't going to live with an actor, she certainly won't live with a policeman. Thank God!"

"I can see that winning the election is a very double-edged victory," Emily said gloomily. "I suppose Ashworth House is big enough to lose her—most of the time. Oh Mama! I wish you every happiness—but did you have to do this to me?"

Sammy Cates enjoyed getting up early. The first hours of the new day were clear and full of promise, and very often solitude as well. It was not that he disliked people, but he enjoyed his own company, and time to let his mind wander in any imagination or dream he fancied was the best entertainment he knew. Last night he had been to the music hall. It had been Marie Lloyd, outrageously dressed and singing marvelous songs. Even now he smiled at the memory of it.

He walked with a swing in his step along the quiet street where he lived in two rooms with his wife and children and his father-in-law, and out onto the main thoroughfare, which was already busy with carts and barrows going to market or delivering goods early to the large houses closer to the park. He passed this way every morning, and many people called out to him or waved a hand. He nodded or waved back, but his mind was still on yesterday evening.

He walked quickly, because he must be at the park gates in time to make sure all was well, there was no litter, no untidiness to offend the eye. And then he would begin his duties for the day. Sweeping, weeding, trimming were not especially enjoyable in themselves, but then on the other hand, neither were they particularly onerous. But it was being outside in the sun, and at this hour, the perfect solitude, which kept the smile on his face as he crossed Park Lane and entered the gates.

It was a bright day, but the dew was a heavy sheen over the grass and the leaves were wet on the bushes. There now. Some untidy person had left a bottle on the path. What a thoughtless thing to do. It could have got broken and then there would be shards of glass all over the place. Who knew what injury that would do? Especially to a child.

He walked over to it and bent to pick it up.

It was when he was thus contorted that he saw the foot sticking out of the undergrowth, and then the leg, and the sole of the other shoe where it lay at a different angle.

He let go of the bottle and moved over to the bushes. He gulped hard. Most probably it was someone who had drunk too much, but then there was always the other possibility. Ever since the first corpse had been found, he had been afraid of it, but still he had never really expected it to happen.

Gingerly, with his heart beating violently and his mouth dry, he grasped both the legs by the ankles and pulled.

The man was wearing dark trousers, navy or black, but they were damp from the dew and it was hard to tell. Then his body began to emerge, and Sammy was so appalled he dropped him and staggered back. He was a policeman! The uniform tunic and its silver buttons were unmistakable.

"Oh Gawd!" he moaned. This was no drunk. This was the Headsman's work again! "Oh Gawd!" he sobbed. Perhaps he should not have moved him. Maybe they would blame him for it.

He backed away and fell over the bottle, sitting down very hard on the stony ground, which knocked out of him what little breath he had left.

He looked at the awful object again. Yes, he was definitely a rozzer. He could see the gleam of buttons all the way up to his neck.

On his hands and knees, he crawled back to the body, and without any clear decision in his mind, began to pull it again. It emerged from the bushes slowly, waist, chest, neck—head! Head! He was whole!

Sammy fell backwards in a heap, his hands shaking, his stomach lurching with relief. Stupid man! He should not have let his imagination do that to him. Headsman indeed! Suppose a rozzer could get drunk like anyone else?

He got up and then bent over the man to see just how drunk he was. His face was terribly pale, in fact his skin was almost white. As though he were dead!

"Oh Gawd!" he said again, this time in a low moan. Reluctantly he touched the man's cheek with the back of his hand. It was cold. He felt his own stomach sick. He loosened the man's collar and slid his hand down inside his clothes. The flesh was warm! He was alive! Yes—please God he was alive!

He studied the face for a few moments, but he could see no sign of a flicker in the eyelids. If he was breathing, it was too shallow to see.

There was nothing to do but go and find help. The man needed a doctor. He rose to his feet and hurried off, starting at a fast walk, and then changing his mind and running.

"What?" Pitt looked up from his desk as Tellman stood in front of him, his face grim, and yet with a perverse glint of victory in his eyes.

"Bailey," Tellman repeated. "One of the park keepers found him this morning, about six o'clock. Been hit on the head and left under the bushes." His eyes met Pitt's unwaveringly.

Pitt felt ill. It was an agonizing mixture of pity and guilt.

"How badly is he hurt?" he said with dry lips.

"Hard to say," Tellman replied. "He's still senseless. Could be anything."

"Well, what injuries has he?" Pitt heard his voice, rough and with a note of panic undisguisable.

"Doesn't appear anything except hit on the head," Tellman answered.

"Anyone know what happened?"

"No. Except, of course, common sense says it was the Headsman. He wasn't on duty in the park, or anywhere near it. He was still chasing after Carvell's statement that he was at the concert, where you sent him." Still his eyes did not flicker from Pitt's. "Looks as though he may have found something after all."

There was no possible answer to that. Pitt rose to his feet. "Where is he?"

"They took him to the Samaritan Free Hospital, in Manchester Square. It's only half a mile or so from where he was found." He took a breath and let it out slowly. "Do you want me to arrest Carvell again?"

"Not until I have seen Bailey."

"He can't tell you anything."

Pitt did not bother to reply, but walked past Tellman without looking at him, and ignoring his hat and coat, went out of the door. He took the stairs two at a time, passed the desk without speaking and went out. It took him nearly five minutes to find a hansom and direct it to Manchester Square.

He felt wretched. There was now no longer any reasonable doubt that it was Carvell. It was Carvell's presence, or absence, at the concert Bailey had been checking. But the thought hurt. He had liked Carvell, felt an instinctive respect for him and a sympathy with his grief, which he still believed was real. And just as deep was his disillusion with himself, an awful sense of failure because he had been so deceived. His judgment had been fatally flawed.

He was guilty of Bailey's injury, and if he died, of his death.

How could he have been so stupid, so unaware? And even now, riding along in the hansom, he still could not see it plainly, only the evidence made it no longer escapable.

The hansom stopped and he alighted, telling the driver to wait for him. Inside he found the long ward where Bailey was lying stiff, white-faced and motionless. He was dressed in a rough calico nightshirt and covered with a sheet and a gray blanket. By the side of his cot stood a young doctor, frowning and pursing his lips.

"How is he?" Pitt asked, dreading the answer.

The doctor looked at him wearily. "Who are you?"

"Superintendent Pitt, Bow Street. How is he?"

"Hard to say." The doctor shook his head. "Hasn't stirred since they brought him in, but he's warmed up to a decent temperature at last. His breathing is near normal and his heart is beating quite strongly."

"He'll be all right?" It was more a hope than a belief.

"Can't say. Possibly."

"When might he be able to speak?"

The doctor shook his head, and looked up at Pitt at last. "I can't say, Superintendent. Can't even say for sure that he will. And even if he does, he may not remember anything. Could be in a very poor state of mind. You'll have to be prepared for that. I would go on with your investigation without relying on him, if I were you."

"I see. Do everything you can for him, won't you? Don't worry about the cost."

"Of course."

Pitt left feeling even more wretched and discouraged, and acutely guilty.

He arrived back at Bow Street to find Giles Farnsworth in his office, his face pale, his hands clenched by his sides.

"You let Carvell go again," he said between his teeth. "Now he has as near as dammit murdered one of your own men." He paced to the mantelpiece and turned. "I always feared this job was too big for you, but Drummond was adamant. Well, he was wrong. Worst misjudgment of his career. I'm sorry Pitt, but your incompetence is not acceptable."

He crossed the floor again and swung back.

"You are dismissed. You will complete the background work on this case, then return to your previous rank. You'd better move to another station. I'll think which one when I have time. Maybe somewhere on the outskirts." And without waiting for Pitt to reply, he went to the door. He hesitated with his hand on the knob. "I've told Tellman to arrest Carvell again. They should have him by now. You can start to arrange the evidence ready for the trial. When you have finished that, you can take a few days off. Good day." He went out, closing the door behind him, leaving Pitt alone, guilty and totally wretched.

11

CHARLOTTE WAS DEVASTATED when Pitt told her that he had been dismissed. Perhaps she should have realized more fully how real was the possibility, but her mind had been too filled with other things: the new house, and of course selling the old one, Jack's candidacy, Caroline's love affair, now her marriage. She had never really believed this would happen—it was so unjust!

Her heart sank for him, for his pain and humiliation, but she was furious for the unfairness of it. Then lastly she was afraid for herself and her children. What about the new house now? How would they afford it? And the old house was gone, they could not simply move back.

All these thoughts and emotions raged through her and she knew they must show in her face. She had never been good enough at concealing her feelings, but she did all she could to hide them, even as the blood drained from her cheeks and her stomach went sick and cold.

"We'll manage," was all she contrived to say, and her voice was rasping, her mouth was so dry.

Pitt looked at her, his own face pale, his eyes hurt and tired.

"Of course we will," he said gently, although he had no idea yet how. The thought of going back to work as an inspector again, in some other station miles away, was too bitter to do more than hear and turn away from until the reality of it forced itself upon him and he had to come to terms with it. Perhaps he would be able to persuade Farnsworth at least to make it at Central London station, so he could work in the area he knew and not spend half his time going backwards and forwards on omnibuses. He would not be able to afford a hansom.

For some time they both sat in silence, close together. Words would not help. There was nothing comforting to say except the banalities they had clearly both thought of, and dismissed.

At last Charlotte moved a little and sat more upright. She had lit the parlor fire, not because it was cold but because the flicker of the flames was comforting, creating briefly a little island from the rest of the world.

"Did Carvell finally admit it?" she asked.

"No." His mind was suddenly filled with the image of Carvell's wretched face, white and frightened, as he was taken down to the cells, his eyes meeting Pitt's in an abject plea. "No, he denied it passionately."

Charlotte stared at him.

"You believe him, don't you?" she said after a moment or two. "You still don't really think he did it!"

He sat still for several moments before replying. His face was crumpled with confusion, but there was no wavering in his voice when at last he answered.

"No. No, I can't believe he would willingly have hurt Aidan Arledge. And if he had killed him in a fit of blind passion and rage, I think he would be a broken man afterwards, and not even attempt to escape. In fact, I honestly believe if he had done it, he would accept, even welcome, punishment."

"Then you've got to find out who did do it, Thomas! You can't let him be hanged for it!" She knelt in front of him earnestly, her voice strong, full of entreaty. "There must be something. No matter how clever he is, the Headsman will have left something undone, some thread that if we pull at it, carefully, we'll unravel the truth."

"That's a nice thought," he said, smiling at her. "But I've racked my brains to think of what that could be, and I'm no further forward."

"You are too close to it," she said immediately. "You are looking at the details, instead of the overall picture. What have all the victims in common?"

"Nothing," he said simply.

"They must have! Winthrop and Scarborough were both bullies, and you said that the omnibus conductor was an officious little man. Perhaps he was a bully too."

"But Arledge wasn't. By every account he was a most courteous and gentle man."

308

"Are you sure?" She looked at him dubiously.

"Yes, I am sure. No one at all had anything ill to say of him."

She thought for a moment, and he waited in silence.

"Is it possible all but one were killed simply to hide the one that someone really wanted dead?" she said after several moments. "Maybe the others were random, and it didn't matter who they were."

"Doesn't make sense." He shook his head, putting out his hand to push away a stray strand of her hair which had fallen across her brow. "Scarborough was lured out of his own home to be killed. That's hardly random. Yeats was miles away in Shepherd's Bush, Arledge we don't know, and Winthrop was boating on the Serpentine, which in itself is ridiculous. Why would anyone go boating in the middle of the night? No one would do it with a stranger, and even with a friend it is hard to imagine."

"The Headsman wanted him there so he could kill him over the side," she answered.

"But how would he get him there? How would you persuade someone to get into a boat in the middle of the night?"

She drew in her breath. "Ah—I should—I should say I had dropped something in the water, off a bridge or something, and if I did not retrieve it, it would be lost," she said with satisfaction. "I should first have dropped in my hat, or whatever came to mind."

"Hat!" He sat upright, unintentionally knocking her sideways.

"What?" She scrambled to her feet. "What is it? Thomas?"

"Hat," he repeated. "There was a hat found when we dragged it! It wasn't Winthrop's. We didn't connect it, but that's what it could have been. Put there as a reason to lure him into the boat. You are brilliant! It's so simple, and so effective." He kissed her with enthusiasm, and then stood up and began to pace the floor. "It begins to make sense," he went on, his voice rising with excitement. "Winthrop was a naval man. It might be quite natural to appeal to him to assist in getting to the hat before it sank. The Headsman could quite easily affect to be useless with the oars. Many people are."

He waved his arms eloquently. "He would request Winthrop's assistance. Winthrop would naturally give it. They would both get into the boat—and the next thing the Headsman points to something in the water, Winthrop leans over the

309

side—and . . ." He brought down his arms with his hand stiff like a blade. "Winthrop is beheaded."

"What about the others?" she asked. "What about Arledge?"

"We don't know. We don't know where Arledge was killed."

"But Scarborough? And the omnibus conductor?" she persisted.

"Scarborough was killed on Rotten Row, right where he was found. The horse trough was full of blood."

"And Yeats?"

"Near Shepherd's Bush terminal. Then taken in a gig to Hyde Park."

She thought for a moment. "Makes it look as if Arledge was the one that was most important, doesn't it," she said at last. "Except that he wasn't first. Every time I think it makes sense"—she shrugged, sitting back again—"then it doesn't."

"I know." He stopped and held out his hand. "Enough for now. I'll start again tomorrow. Come to bed."

She took his hand and stood up slowly, but her face was still tight in concentration. Even when walking up the stairs her mind was working, turning over ideas, beginning plans. Only when she was in her nightgown and pulling the sheets up around her neck and snuggling closer to Pitt did she finally forget it and think of other things.

In the morning Pitt did not go to Bow Street; there was no point. His mind was whirling with ideas, uncertain, many of them half formed and depending upon facts and impressions he had yet to confirm. He could not serve his purpose by starting until the evening. He spent the day in trivial duties, checking and rechecking of details. Then at a quarter to eight he began. He wanted to see Victor Garrick, but did not have his address. He knew Mina Winthrop would know it, accordingly he took the omnibus to Curzon Street and alighted on the pavement in the clear spring dusk.

"Yes sir?" the parlormaid said inquiringly.

"May I please speak with Mrs. Winthrop?" he asked courteously.

"Yes sir. If you care to come this way, I shall see if she is at home."

It was the usual polite fiction, and he followed her in and waited obediently.

Mina came after less than five minutes, looking charming in

310

pale lavender muslin. As soon as she saw his surprise she blinked.

"Good evening, Superintendent. I am afraid you have caught me unexpectedly. I am not suitably dressed." It was an understatement. She looked years younger than when he had seen her immediately after her husband's death, dressed entirely in black and looking frightened and bewildered. Now her cheeks had color, her long, slender neck was bare but for a heavy bead necklace, and only because he knew it was there could he see the faintest purpling of bruises. To anyone else they would merely have seemed shadows. There was a spontaneity in her movement, as if she were full of purpose.

"I am sorry to have disturbed you at all, Mrs. Winthrop," he apologized in turn. "I came because I wished to call upon Victor Garrick and I do not know his address, except that it is close by here."

"Oh! Well it is fortunate you have come," she said quickly. "They are two doors away, but you would have had a wasted journey anyway. He is presently with us."

"Indeed. Would it be too much of an intrusion for me to speak with him? I will not detain him long."

"Of course not. I am sure if there is anything he can do to help he would be happy to." She frowned. "Although I understand from my brother that you have caught the man. What more can there be?"

"Some details to learn, so we are not taken unaware by a clever lawyer," he replied untruthfully.

"Then please come through to the garden room, Superintendent. Victor has been playing for us, and it will be a most pleasant place to sit."

He thanked her and accepted willingly, following her as she turned and led the way along the passage and into one of the most charming rooms he had ever seen. French windows opened straight into a small walled garden filled with plants with every shape of leaf. All the flowers were white: white roses, plantain lilies, carnations and pinks, alyssum, Solomon's seal, and many others of which he did not know the names.

Inside, the walls and curtains were green with a delicate white floral print, and a large bowl was filled with further white flowers. The last of the gentle evening light shone in, making the room warm and still giving the illusion of the freshness of a garden.

311

In the corner Victor Garrick sat with his cello. Bart Mitchell stood by the mantelpiece. There was no one else present.

"Victor, I am so sorry to interrupt," Mina began. "But Superintendent Pitt has actually come to see you. It seems there are some further details yet to clear up in this wretched business, and he thinks you may be able to help."

"Perhaps we should excuse ourselves." Bart moved as if to leave.

"Oh no," Pitt said hastily. "Please, Mr. Mitchell, I should be glad if you would both remain. It would save me having to ask you all separately." An idea was beginning to form in his mind, although still hazy and lacking many essential elements. "I am sorry to disturb your music on such a distressing matter, but I think we are really close to the end at last."

Bart moved back to the mantel shelf and resumed his position leaning against it, his expression cold. "If you wish, Superintendent, but I don't think any of us knows anything we have not already told you."

"It is a matter of what you may have seen." Pitt turned to Victor, who was watching him with his clear, very blue eyes wide and apparently more polite than interested.

"Yes?" he said, since the silence seemed to call for some remark.

"At the reception after the Requiem service for Aidan Arledge," Pitt began, "I believe you were sitting in the corner alcove near the doorway to the hall?"

"Yes. I didn't especially wish to wander around talking to people," Victor agreed. "And anyway, it is far more important to stay with my cello. Someone might accidentally bump it, or even knock it over." Unconsciously his arms tightened around the precious instrument, caressing its exquisite wood, which was smooth as satin and as bright. Pitt noticed the bruise and felt a stab of fury at the vandalism.

"Is that how that happened?" he asked.

Victor's face tightened and his skin went suddenly white. His eyes were hard and very bright, staring fixedly at some spot in the far distance, or perhaps within his own memory.

"No," he said between his teeth.

"What was it?" Pitt pressed, and found himself holding his own breath. He did not realize that the pain in the palms of his hands was his nails digging into the flesh.

"Some vile creature pushed me, and it knocked against the

312

handrail," Victor answered in a soft voice, his gaze still far away.

"The handrail?" Pitt questioned.

"Yes."

Bart Mitchell shifted his position away from the mantel and opened his mouth to interrupt, then changed his mind.

"Of an omnibus?" Pitt said, almost in a whisper.

"What?" Victor looked around at him. "Oh—yes. People like that have . . . nothing inside them—no feeling—no souls!"

"It's a senseless piece of vandalism," Pitt agreed, swallowing hard and stepping back a little. "What I wanted to ask you, Mr. Garrick, was if you saw the butler, Scarborough, when he was directing the other servants that afternoon?"

"Who?"

"The butler, Scarborough."

Victor still looked blank.

"A big man with a haughty face and arrogant manner."

Victor's eyes filled with comprehension and memory. "Oh yes. He was a bully, a contemptible man." He winced at Pitt as he said it. "It is beyond forgiveness to use one's power to abuse those who are in no position to defend themselves. I abhor it, and the people who do such things are . . ." He sighed. "I have no words for it. I search my mind and nothing comes which carries the weight of the anger I feel."

"Did he actually dismiss the girl for singing?" Pitt asked, trying to keep his voice casual.

Victor raised his eyes and stared at him.

Pitt waited.

"Yes," Victor said at length. "She was singing a little love song, quite softly, just a sad little thing about losing someone. He dismissed her without even listening to her explanation or apology." His face was even whiter as he spoke and his lips were bloodless. "She cannot have been more than sixteen." His whole body was tight, and he sat hunched, only his hands still gentle on the cello.

"Mrs. Radley heard it too," Pitt said, not as any part of his plan, but spontaneously, from pity. "She offered the girl a position. She won't be out on the street."

Slowly Victor turned to gaze at him, his eyes softened, very bright blue, and the anger drained out of him.

"Did she?"

"Yes. She is my sister-in-law, and I know it is true."

"And the man is dead," Victor added. "So that's all right."

"Was that all you wanted to ask?" Bart said, stepping forward. "I saw nothing, and to the best of my knowledge, neither did my sister."

"Oh, almost," Pitt replied, looking not at him but at Mina. "The other matter was concerning Mr. Arledge." He altered the tone of his voice to be deliberately harsher. "You told me before, Mrs. Winthrop, that your acquaintance with him was very slight, only a matter of a single kindness on one occasion when you were distressed over the death of a pet."

She swallowed and hesitated. "Yes?"

"I'm sorry, ma'am, but I do not believe you."

"We have told you what happened, Superintendent," Bart said grimly. "Whether you accept it or not, I am afraid that is all there is. You have the Headsman. There is no purpose whatever in your persisting in a matter which is peripheral at best."

Pitt ignored him.

"I think you knew him considerably better than that," he said to Mina. "And I do not believe the matter that distressed you was the death of a pet."

She looked pale, and distinctly uncomfortable.

"My brother has already told you what happened, Superintendent. I have nothing to add to that."

"I know Mr. Mitchell told me, ma'am. What I wonder is why you did not tell me yourself! Is it that you are not quite so quick with a lie? Or perhaps you did not think of one in time?"

"Sir, you are being gratuitously offensive." Bart moved closer to Pitt, as if he would offer him physical violence. His voice was low and dangerous. "I must ask you to leave this house. You are no longer welcome here."

"Whether I am welcome or not is a matter of complete indifference," Pitt answered, still facing, not Bart, but Mina. "Mrs. Winthrop, if I were to ask your servants, would they bear out your story of a domestic pet's death?"

Mina looked very white and her hands were shaking. She opened her mouth to speak, but found no words. Her lips were dry.

"Mrs. Winthrop," he said grimly, hating the necessity for this. "We know that your husband beat you—"

Her head jerked up, her face white with horror. "Oh no, no!" she said involuntarily. "It was ... accidental ... he ... it

314

was my own fault. If I were less clumsy, less stupid . . . I provoked him by . . ." She trailed off, staring at Bart.

Victor looked at Mina, his eyes wide and hard, waiting.

"It is not your fault!" Bart said between his teeth. "I don't care a damn how stupid or persistent or argumentative you were! Nothing justifies—"

"Bart!" Her voice rose close to a shriek, her hands flying to her mouth. "You're wrong! You're wrong! It was nothing! He never intended to hurt me! You misunderstand all of it. Oakley wasn't . . . cruel. It was the whiskey. He just . . ."

Victor looked at Mina's terror, and at Bart, white-faced and torn with indecision.

"Didn't it hurt?" he asked very gently.

"No, no Victor dear, it was all over very quickly," she assured him. "Bart is just a little"—she hesitated—"protective of me."

"That's not true!" Victor's voice was thick, almost choking. "It hurts—it frightens! It's in your face! You were terrified of him. And he made you feel ashamed all the time, and worthless . . ."

"No! No, that's not true. He didn't mean it. And I am all right, I promise you!"

"Because the swine is dead!" Bart spat. He was about to add something more, but he got no further. Mina burst into tears, her shoulders hunched over as dry sobs racked her and she sank onto the sofa. Bart strode forward, almost knocking Victor out of the way, and took Pitt roughly by the arm, propelling him towards the door. Victor remained immobile.

In the hallway Pitt made no protest, and a few moments later, feeling the bruises of Bart's fingers on his arm a trifle tenderly, he walked along the footpath towards the main thoroughfare. It was a clear evening, and still just light. He was not expecting anything to happen for some time.

He spent a tense fifteen minutes taking a glass of cider in a public house, then continued his way as the cloud cover grew heavier and the daylight dimmed. It was some time before he was sure he was being followed. At first it was only a sensation, a consciousness of a sound which echoed his footsteps, stopping when he did, resuming when he did.

By the time he reached Marylebone Road it was dark, and he had great difficulty in not increasing his speed. It was an odd, prickling feeling, and most unpleasant. If he were correct in his guesses, tenuous as they were, built on impressions and

315

a few threads of tangible, definite evidence, then it was the Headsman who was now behind him, watching, coming closer, waiting his chance. He would have the weapon with him. He would have taken it from its hiding place and left the house, hurrying to catch up.

In spite of his resolution to appear natural, he could not keep his step from hastening. He heard the rapid, slightly uneven tap, tap of his boots on the pavement, and behind him, closer now, the echoing feet, swift and light, of his follower.

Marylebone Road turned into the Euston Road. A landau passed him, carriage lamps yellow, horses' hooves loud on the cobbles. He was walking now as fast as he could without actually running. The lamplighter was passing, tipping his long pole to each wick and one by one they sprang to life, a row of brilliant isolated globes, between which stretched areas of darkness, hiding passersby, people on their way home, weary from the day or expectant of the evening. He saw the tall outline of a stovepipe hat against the light as a man hurried by.

Euston station was only a hundred yards ahead. He could feel the sweat of fear on his body and he was breathing hard, even though he still had not quite broken from a walk.

The steps were closer behind him.

He dare not force a confrontation here. Until he was actually attacked, there was no proof. All his bullying of Mina would have been to no purpose.

He turned into the entrance of the railway station. It was late and there were few people about. The chill air of evening after the warm day had turned misty. In the clatter of trains and the shout of porters, the whistles and hoots, the hiss of steam, he could no longer hear footsteps behind him.

On the platform he turned. There was a porter; an elderly gentleman with a document case; a woman with hair that looked black in the dim light, and a shawl around her shoulders; a young man half in the shadows, seemingly waiting for someone. Another, older woman came in, looking anxiously about her.

Pitt walked across the platform then turned and went along its length towards the bridge over the tracks. He climbed up; the steps were slippery. He heard his boots clattering on the metal edges of each rise. Clouds of steam billowed up into the gathering mist and slight drizzle. The platform lights were a jumble of harsh, gleaming globes, swimming in the closing night and the gray rain, the train headlights and the belching steam.

He walked across the bridge above the tracks. There was too much noise to hear anyone's footsteps, even his own. He could no longer see the platform.

Suddenly there was movement, a sense of violent danger, a hatred so scalding it was like a prickle at the back of his neck.

He swung around.

Victor Garrick was a yard away from him, the light from below catching his ashen face, his blazing eyes and the fair, almost silver gleam of his hair. Above him in his right hand was a naval cutlass, raised to strike, the arc of its blade shining.

"You're doing it too!" he sobbed, his lips stretched back over his teeth, his face twisted in tormenting, inner pain. "You're just the same!" he shouted above the roar. "You hurt people! You make them sick and frightened and ashamed, and I won't let you do it to her anymore!" He slashed the cutlass through the air and Pitt moved sideways just in time to avoid its blade on his shoulder. It would have been a crippling blow, all but severing his arm.

Pitt backed away sharply as Victor lunged forward, going past him and swinging around.

"You can't get away!" Victor's breath was hissing through his teeth and the tears streamed down his face. "Why do you lie to me?" The cry was torn from him in a terrible, wrenching sound, and he seemed to be looking not at Pitt, but somewhere beyond him. "Liar! Liar! You keep saying it doesn't hurt—but I know it does! It hurts right through till your whole body aches, and you lie awake all night, knotted up, sick and ashamed and guilty, thinking it's all your fault and waiting for the next time! I'm frightened! Nothing makes any sense! You lied to me all the time!" His voice was a scream and again the cutlass slashed through the air. "You're frightened too! I've seen your face, and the bruises, and the blood! I can smell your misery! I can taste it in my mouth all the time! I won't let it go on! I'll stop him!" Again he slashed wildly with the blade.

Pitt backed away desperately. He did not dare use his stick; that blade would have sliced it through and left him defenseless.

It was all very plain now: the bullying Winthrop, beating Mina; the bus conductor who had callously damaged the beloved cello; the arrogant Scarborough, who had dismissed the maid and threatened her with ruin; it was always the bruised and defenseless women. He must have attacked Bailey when he had been pursuing Bart's whereabouts at the time of the murders, and frightened Mina. She was haunted by the terror that Bart was guilty, at least of Winthrop's death.

"But why did you kill Arledge?" he shouted aloud, his voice hoarse.

Behind them a train belched out steam and blew its whistle. Victor looked blank.

"Why did you kill Arledge?" Pitt shouted again. "He didn't bully anyone!"

Victor was bending a little at the knees, adjusting his balance, one hand on the railing, the other clenched around the cutlass.

Pitt moved sideways again, and backwards, just beyond reach of the blade. "What did Arledge do?"

For a moment Victor was surprised. The sudden confusion showed in his face. The anger vanished and he stood motionless.

"No I didn't."

"Yes you did. You cut his head off and left him in the bandstand. Don't you remember?"

"No I didn't!" Victor's voice was a shriek above the hiss and rattle of the trains. He lunged forward, swinging the blade, his weight carrying him. Pitt leapt sideways and towards him, catching him on the shoulders as Victor's hand, clenched around the hilt, landed on his arm so hard he dropped the stick and heard it clatter on the bridge.

Pitt let out a yell of pain and fear, but it was swallowed up in the shriek of the train whistle. Now steam billowed around them. He charged forward, head down, and caught Victor in the chest. All his weight was on one foot as he reached to strike again. He lost his balance and fell backward. The railing caught him in the middle of his back and the weight of the cutlass carried him still farther. His foot slipped on the wet metal of the bridge.

Pitt scrambled after him, trying to grasp his arm, but it slipped out of his hands. His legs came up, catching Pitt and knocking him off balance.

With a scream of surprise, and then momentary terror, Victor toppled over and disappeared into the headlights of an oncoming train.

The sound of the impact was lost in the roar of the engine

and the shrill screech of the whistle. For a blazing second the engine driver's white face was imprinted on Pitt's mind, and then it was all over. He stood gripping the rail with shaking hands, his body cold and his mind illuminated with a harsh, clear understanding, and an undeniable pity.

Victor was gone. His rage and his pain were unreachable now.

Then as the steam cleared and he turned, he saw another figure behind where he had stood. She was moving forward, clasping the rail and pulling herself along like a blind person in the dark, her face ashen.

He stared at her in horror. Suddenly it was all clear. It was she Victor had been shouting at, not Pitt at all. That fearful emotion had been directed at her, and all the terror and pain of the past.

"I didn't know!" The words were torn out of her. "Not until tonight. I swear!"

"No," he answered, so overwhelmed with pity his voice was barely a whisper in his throat.

"It was his father, you see," she went on, desperate he should understand. "He beat me. He wasn't a wicked man, he just couldn't control his temper. I always used to tell Victor it was all right, that it didn't hurt. I thought it was the right thing to do!" A look of confusion and despair filled her, obliterating even grief for the moment. "I thought I was protecting him. I thought it would be all right, do you see? I didn't want him hating his father, and Samuel wasn't bad—just ..." An anguished pleading filled her. Her eyes searched his face, willing him to believe her. "He did love us, in his way, I know he did. He told me so ... often. It was my fault he got so angry. If I had been ..."

"It's over," he said, moving towards her. He could not bear any more. Down below them the train had stopped, billowing steam, and there were men running along the platform and shouting. She should not see this. Someone should take her away. Someone should try to do something for the terrible pain in her. "Come." He held her by the arm and half dragged her towards the steps. "There's nothing else here now."

That same morning Charlotte had gone straight from breakfast to see Emily. They were sipping lemonade together, sitting on the terrace in Emily's garden. It was a mild sunny day, and apart from that, they chose to be out of earshot of any possible hovering servant. The situation was desperate. Plans must be made which were better not overheard. Jack would disapprove intensely, he would be bound to, with his new responsibilities. But apart from the desire to know the solution to the problem, far more urgently than that, they must do everything possible to defend Pitt.

"How on earth can we find out the identity of someone's lover?" Charlotte said desperately, sipping her lemonade. "We can't follow her."

"That is impractical," Emily pointed out. "And anyway it would take far too long. It might be days before they see each other again. We must do something more rapid than that."

"But if she doesn't see him?" Charlotte said desperately.

"Then we must make her!" Emily had lost none of her resolution. One unexpected victory had filled her with confidence. "We must send her a letter, or something of that sort. An invitation, purporting to come from him."

"She will know it was not his handwriting," Charlotte pointed out. "Beside that, people who are in love usually have a special way of communicating with each other, some term of endearment, or pet name or the like."

Emily frowned at her.

"Apart from that," Charlotte went on. "Even if she answered it, that would not tell us who he is."

"Don't be obstructive," Emily said with a touch of asperity. "We should have to word it so that she would go to him, and then we should know who he was."

"And he would equally know who we were," Charlotte finished for her. "They would then know there was something very peculiar going on. It would look like the most vulgar of curiosity. We might do more harm than good." She set down her lemonade glass. "Don't forget that establishing who he is is only the beginning. To have an admirer is not a crime, in fact if you are discreet, it is not really even regarded as a sin."

Emily glared at her. "Do you want to solve this or not?"

Charlotte did not even bother to answer her.

"I don't think Dulcie will betray herself," she said thoughtfully, taking up her lemonade again. It really was delicious, and most refreshing. "But he might."

"But we don't know who he is," Emily retorted. "Before we know that, we have to trace him—through her."

"I am not sure that that is necessarily true."

Emily drew her brows together with suddenly sharpened concentration. "Do you have an idea?"

"Possibly. Let us consider what qualities he must possess."

"To be a lover?" Emily looked incredulous. "Don't be absurd. He must be virile—that's about all. Everything else is purely a matter of taste."

"You are being simplistic," Charlotte said acidly. "I mean what is it that makes sense of murdering Aidan Arledge now, instead of sooner, or later, or better still, not at all? Most people who are lovers don't murder a spouse. Why did it happen this time, and why now?"

Emily sat silent for several minutes, carefully eating a piece of fudge before she replied.

"Circumstances have changed," she answered at length. "That is the only thing that makes sense."

"Yes, I agree, but in what way?" Charlotte took a piece of the fudge also.

"Someone discovered her? No, that would mean they killed the discoverer, if he, or she, threatened blackmail. Her husband discovered, and was about to expose her to public shame? Even to throw her out for adultery?"

"When he was having a love affair with Jerome Carvell? Hardly!"

"She discovered him with Jerome Carvell and killed him in a fit of utter disgust," Emily offered.

"Thomas thought she didn't know about Jerome Carvell," Charlotte said. "She suspected he had a lover, but she thought it was a woman, as anyone would."

"But Thomas thinks she is a grieving widow," Emily responded, pulling a face. "He doesn't know she has a lover herself."

Charlotte conceded that point in silence. Pitt's opinion of Dulcie was not something she wished to dwell on.

"I love Thomas to distraction," Emily continued. "But he is not always the best judge of a woman. Very few men are," she added graciously. "Well, something made it imperative. Perhaps he was going away, because she couldn't marry him, and she had to make herself free to stop him leaving forever?"

"And maybe he was going to marry someone else?" Charlotte suggested.

"Which would mean he was free to marry," Emily said with rising eagerness. "That narrows down the field automatically.

321

There are not so many gentlemen of Dulcie Arledge's age who are unmarried, and respectable."

He did not have to be of her age, but that was a subject neither of them wished to pursue.

"Do you think he really intended to go away?" Charlotte was doubtful.

"No. All right then, if he is not about to become unavailable, perhaps he has suddenly become available? When there was no point in her being free before, because he was not, now he is, so she acted to become free also."

"That makes sense," Charlotte agreed. "Yes, indeed, that sounds quite possible. Or, of course, someone she has met only recently?"

"That too. Which could be Bart Mitchell, Mina Winthrop's brother."

"Thomas suspected him, I think, but not for that reason."

"What reason?"

"On account of Mina."

"What had Arledge to do with Mina?"

Charlotte explained the very little she knew.

Emily dismissed it. "Or else someone like Landon Hurlwood, who has been recently widowed. He is suddenly available, where he was not before. Now he is really most attractive." Her voice was touched with enthusiasm. "I could not blame any woman for being a little smitten with him. And I imagine if he cared for you, it would be very easy to lose your sense of proportion a trifle."

"Hitting your husband over the head and then decapitating him and leaving him in the park is not a trifle," Charlotte said swiftly. There was, however, a thread of enthusiasm in her too, and Emily disregarded the words in favor of the tone.

"But he fits the qualifications precisely, doesn't he?" Emily leaned forward, her elbows on the wrought iron table.

"Yes," Charlotte agreed with growing conviction. "Yes, he seems just the sort of person. But I imagine there must be many others. The difficulty is, how do we decide which one?"

"Do we need to?" Emily looked puzzled. "Surely you can see that this is almost certainly the right kind of answer?"

"Of course I can. But we need to prove it to be sure. Then we need to know if he killed Aidan Arledge, and of course, if Dulcie knew about it."

"Oh." Emily let out a long sigh. "Well, that is going to be

322

interesting. How can we do that? Especially since Thomas apparently could not . . ."

"He has never considered Dulcie," Charlotte said, biting her lip and feeling the twinge of guilt back again.

"Maybe she had no idea that he did it on her account."

This time it was Charlotte who gave the knowing, exasperated look.

"Yes, I suppose so," Emily agreed. "She is not naive at all. I'm sorry. What shall we do?"

"We must be certain." Charlotte was speaking as much to herself as to Emily. She relapsed into thought for a moment or two. "We must provoke a reaction," she said at last.

"In whom? Dulcie? How will that help? She won't betray him."

"Not in Dulcie, in him!"

"But we don't know who he is. It not only could be Landon Hurlwood. It could also be Bart Mitchell, or any of I don't know how many others!"

"Well let us start with Bart Mitchell and Landon Hurlwood." Charlotte bit her lip. "Although I confess I am not certain how to go about that."

Emily thought for a moment, then her face lit with a smile.

"I am. Obviously the affair is secret, and if it had anything whatever to do with Aidan Arledge's death, they will be desperate that it should be kept so for quite a while afterwards. It can only come to light as if they had fallen in love once she was a widow. If either you or I were to meet them, socially of course, so it will seem quite casual"—she leaned forward eagerly—"and make some remark, with a knowing look, then they would be sufficiently disconcerted that we should know immediately that we had the right person."

Charlotte opened her mouth to protest that she could not possibly do that, but her voice died away as she recalled Pitt's desperate situation, his dismissal, and even more than that the loss of the house, having to tell Mama, and having Grandmama's malicious satisfaction, but above all, the hurt to Pitt himself.

"Yes," she said, without the faintest idea how she would accomplish it. "Yes, that is an excellent idea. We had better begin immediately. I shall take Bart Mitchell, because I can call upon Mina. You must take Mr. Hurlwood." She rose to her feet. "How you will find him I haven't a notion, but that is your affair." And giving Emily a quick hug, without waiting to hear if there were any excuse or evasion, she swept in through the French doors and made for the hallway and the street.

She arrived at Mina's house within the hour, long before Pitt got there, and was greeted with pleasure and the sort of ease that usually exists only after considerable friendship. Ordinarily she would have felt guilt for using so generous an emotion in such a way, but today there was no room in her mind for anything but necessity.

"How delightful to see you Mrs. Pitt," Mina said enthusiastically. "How is your new house? Are you quite comfortable there now?"

"Indeed, thank you," Charlotte replied, seeing Bart Mitchell behind her with intense relief. "I like it extremely. Good morning, Mr. Mitchell."

"Good morning, Mrs. Pitt," he replied, not troubling to keep the surprise from his face. He took a step forward.

"Please do not leave on my account," she said in far too much haste. "I should feel most distressed." Then she could have kicked herself for overreaction. She sounded absurd. And yet if he left the whole journey would be abortive, and there was no time to lose. There were only a few days at most before Pitt would be off the case forever.

"Well—I . . ." He looked startled. It was not the reaction he could possibly have foreseen.

Then a wild idea occurred to Charlotte, desperate and ridiculous, but her own dignity was beside the point now. All she could think of was Thomas.

She had no difficulty in blushing. She certainly felt fool enough. She lowered her eyes modestly, as though to hide her emotions, and then looked up at him suddenly in the way she had seen countless women do. Emily did it to a devastating effect. She herself had only tried it a few times in her youth, and made a complete exhibition of herself.

Bart looked even more taken aback, but he did not leave, in fact he sat on the sofa as if fully intending to remain.

Good heavens. Could he possibly be attracted to her? Or was he merely flattered?

Mina was saying something and Charlotte had not heard a word of it. She must pay attention or she was going to compound the situation by even further idiocy.

"How kind of you," she murmured, hoping it fitted the circumstance.

Mina rang the bell and as soon as the maid appeared, ordered cool lemonade. That must have been what she had said.

Charlotte searched her wits for some intelligent topic of conversation. She knew nothing of current gossip in society, she had neither the means nor the inclination; it was not done for women to discuss politics; she was not up-to-date with fashion. She did not wish to go boldly into the subject of the Headsman. She had not been to the theater in months, nor to a concert.

"How is your arm? I hope the burn is healing," she said to fill the silence.

"Yes, indeed," Mina replied, raising her eyebrows as if she had not expected it. "Much more rapidly than I had thought it could. I believe your swift action may have saved me endless discomfort."

Charlotte breathed a sigh of relief. "I know cold water is merely an ease of the symptoms, which is very often nothing to do with treatment at all. But in the case of burns, the ease seems to last, and there is much less of a mark left. Do you agree, Mr. Mitchell?"

"I think I am obliged to, Mrs. Pitt," he replied with a smile. "Although I have little experience of domestic scalding."

"Of other burns, perhaps?" she pursued with far more desperation than her slightly shaking voice betrayed.

His smile broadened. "Oh yes. I have quite accidentally cured sunburn with cold water."

"Sunburn? How interesting." She gazed at him with rapture as if it were the most fascinating subject imaginable. He did have remarkable blue eyes.

He shifted his gaze discreetly and proceeded to tell her of his travels in Africa, of becoming sunburned and falling off his horse while crossing a wide river in spate, and in so doing, very quickly relieving the pain in his skin and the faintness he was beginning to feel as a result of the heat. It was an entertaining story and he told it with humor and animation. She did not have to affect to be interested.

The maid brought the lemonade, which was delicious, and Charlotte continued to ask him questions about his experiences, which he answered easily. Mina sat upright on the sofa, her hands folded in her lap, a small smile on her lips, completely at ease.

But time was slipping by. Charlotte had accomplished nothing decisive enough to prove her point. If Bart Mitchell were

Dulcie's lover then he was masking his feelings with consummate skill. But then the more she knew of him, the more did she believe that such a thing would be both natural and easy for him. He would not betray a woman he loved, either intentionally or by lack of thought or self-mastery.

She felt increasingly foolish with every passing moment. Please Heaven Emily was doing better. She must plunge in, whatever the cost. She must at least try!

"How long have you been returned from Africa, Mr. Mitchell?" she asked with wide eyes. Actually it was not proving as difficult to flirt with him as it might have. He was, on closer acquaintance, a most pleasing person, and most comely of appearance.

"Since the autumn of last year, Mrs. Pitt," he answered.

"Oh—some time." The words slipped out involuntarily. She swallowed, hoping the disappointment in them did not sound as clear to his ears as it did to hers. Still, perhaps that was not too long in which to fall in love—for some people. She could not imagine taking so long herself. And Bart Mitchell did not look like a man to take above half a year for his emotions to become engaged. "Do you enjoy London society, or does it seem very tame after all your adventures?" It was a clumsy question. It invited only a polite answer. "Oh—I beg your pardon!" She hurried on. "How can you say anything but that you do? But please give me a more honest reply, if you miss the sense of danger and something new each day." She was talking far too quickly, and yet she seemed unable to moderate herself. "The challenge to your imagination and courage, your ability to endure hardship, and to invent your way out of shortage or loss."

"My dear Mrs. Pitt." He smiled at her with what seemed to be quite genuine amusement. "I assure you, I had no intention of giving you an answer that was merely civil. I do not take you for a woman who passes her time in idle chatter. In fact, I think there is probably purpose to most of what you do."

She felt her face burn. That was far closer to the truth than, please Heaven, he had any idea!

"Oh," she said uselessly. "I—er . . ."

"To answer your question," he continued, "of course there is a great deal I miss about Africa, and times when London seems intolerably tame, but there are also many times when I look around at the greenness of gardens and the freshness of spring flowers, the gracious buildings, and know how much

326

permanent and civilized life there is behind the facades, how much beauty and invention, and I am excited to be here too."

She kept her eyes lowered. "Shall you be returning to Africa, Mr. Mitchell?"

"One day, I imagine," he replied quite casually.

"But you have no immediate plans?" She held her breath for his reply.

"None," he said with a lift of amusement in his voice.

"Of course," she said very gently. "Mrs. Arledge will be so glad. But then you would hardly have left her." She looked up swiftly to catch his expression.

There was not the faintest guilt in it, only complete incomprehension.

"I beg your pardon?" he said, frowning a trifle.

She had never felt more completely foolish in her life. She had flirted shamelessly with a thoroughly decent man, and wittered on as if her brain were stuffed with feathers, and now she could think of no graceful way whatever of extricating herself.

"Oh . . ." She struggled desperately. "I fear I have expressed myself very badly. I think I have misunderstood something that was said to me. Please forgive me." She did not dare to look at him, and she had temporarily entirely forgotten Mina's presence.

But he would not let her escape so easily.

"Mrs. Arledge?" he questioned.

"Yes—I . . ." She trailed off. There was nothing whatever which could explain her remark.

"She seems a woman of some dignity," he went on. "But not someone with whom I have any but the briefest and most formal acquaintance. In fact I think the Requiem service for her husband was the only occasion in which I have met her. Do you know her well?"

"No! I—I gathered the impression you were . . . but it must have been someone else. I daresay I was not listening properly, and misheard or misunderstood. I am so sorry." At last she looked up and met his eyes. "Please forget I spoke. It was most foolish of me."

"Of course, if you wish."

"Do have some more lemonade," Mina offered, speaking for the first time since the subject of Africa had been raised. She had been listening with attention and pleasure, but had not interrupted. Now she lifted the silver jug invitingly.

"No thank you. It is most kind, but I must be leaving."

Charlotte rose to her feet with rather more haste than grace. She was aching to escape. "I do not wish to outstay what has been a most delightful visit. Thank you so much for receiving me so generously when I called entirely without warning or invitation. I really only wished to tell you that your advice has been most successful, and I am truly obliged to you."

"It was a trifling thing," Mina said with a wave of her hand. "I am delighted if it worked out to your liking."

"Perhaps—in a little while, later on, you will be kind enough to call?" Charlotte invited her, offering one of her newly printed cards with the new address upon it. Only after Mina had taken it did she remember that in all probability she and Pitt would no longer be there. Not unless they were a great deal more successful than so far in solving the case.

"Perhaps you will call upon us again, Mrs. Pitt?" Bart asked with a smile that did not conceal a genuine wish.

"Thank you," she accepted, vowing to herself never to set foot in the place again. "I shall look forward to it!"

She fled out into the hall and out of the door as the maid opened it for her, and walked with indecent haste along the footpath towards the main thoroughfare and the first omnibus she could find.

Emily, on the other hand, had no trepidation whatever in finding Landon Hurlwood. It required a little more ingenuity to discover where he would be. Once that was accomplished she dressed in the height of fashion, in a white muslin with sprigs of Delft blue, pointed at the top of the shoulder, broad sleeved, and a marvelous hat with high crown and one ostrich feather over the brim, and called her carriage.

It necessitated the most precise timing in order to catch him. In fact she had to have her carriage stand still, causing some obstruction, for a full fifteen minutes, before she saw him leave his offices in Whitehall and head for Trafalgar Square. Fortunately it was the nicest of spring weather, and not at all a miserable day in which to walk.

She climbed down without the assistance of the somewhat startled coachman, and set off towards her quarry.

"Mr. Hurlwood!" she exclaimed with delight when she was within a dozen yards. "How pleasant to see you!"

He looked startled. Obviously his mind had been upon whatever matters of government and administration he had discussed last, or proposed to discuss next. Social acquaintances were not expected at this time in the afternoon, in the middle of the city.

"Good afternoon . . . Mrs. Radley," he said with surprise. He raised his hat and stopped, moving a little aside to allow others to pass. "How are you?"

She smiled charmingly. "In most excellent health, thank you. What a lovely day, isn't it? One feels filled with boundless optimism at such a time."

"Indeed," he agreed pleasantly. "You have every reason. It was an excellent victory, and the sweeter for having been unexpected, at least by some."

"Oh yes! I am afraid I did not even believe it myself at first. I should have had more confidence, shouldn't I?"

He smiled. "As events proved, yes, but I think it is far wiser to be modest beforehand, and then rejoice afterwards, than the other way around."

"Oh indeed. I am afraid poor Mr. Uttley did not take his defeat very well. One must learn to be discreet, do you not agree? Keeping one's emotions to oneself is a great part of success in public life, I think." She made it a question, and gazed at him with wide innocent eyes.

"I expect you are right," he said slowly, obviously uncertain quite what she was referring to in addition to Uttley, but he had realized she meant more than simple observation.

"What one knows about but has been conducted with the utmost discretion is quite another matter." She inclined her head with a knowing little smile. "Love affairs that are . . . quite private."

He looked a trifle uncomfortable, but she did not know if it was guilt or merely embarrassment at a rather tasteless remark.

"I think Mrs. Arledge is bearing up very well after such a wretched bereavement, don't you?" she went on. "Such a difficult time for it to have happened. But I am sure you will be of the utmost comfort to her, and the soul of good judgment and discretion."

He blushed deeply and his hand on his cane was clenched. His voice was a little husky when he replied.

"Yes—quite. One does what one can." It was a meaningless remark, and they both knew it. His hot, uncomfortable eyes gave her the answer she was seeking. An admission in words was unnecessary.

"I will not keep you, Mr. Hurlwood," she said graciously. "I am sure you have some business of importance to attend, and you have been so courteous to me already. I wish you a good day. It was most agreeable to have met you." And with a charming smile, all innocent pleasure, she swept away and crossed the street back towards her waiting carriage and a footman who knew better than to wonder what his mistress was about.

"What do we do now?" Emily said eagerly, but with a faintly puckered brow. She and Charlotte were sitting in Emily's boudoir in Ashworth House. It was a better place than the withdrawing room, because although Jack was supposed to be at the House of Commons, it was just possible he might return, and this was a conversation it would be a great deal better he did not overhear, even in part.

Similarly, Charlotte had left instructions with Gracie that she did not know what time she would return, so Gracie should give the children their evening meal and see them to bed, and if the master came home, she was to inform him that the mistress was visiting with Emily and might even stay the night. It was not a time when she would normally have been absent, but there was no help for it. Of course the difference was that Charlotte would tell Gracie the reasons, whereas Emily would very much rather not have her servants know anything about it. They were all very impressed with Jack's victory, and their loyalties were acutely divided.

"We must find proof, if there is any," Charlotte replied.

"There's bound to be, isn't there?"

"Only if one of them did it. If they are innocent there won't be."

Emily waved her hand. "Let's not even think of that. How do you suppose it happened? I mean, how could she have done it, if it were her?"

Charlotte thought for several moments.

"Well it's not very difficult to hit someone on the head, if they trust you and are not expecting anything of the sort. Obviously you are very pleasant to them . . ."

"You'd have to lure them to where you wanted." Emily took up the thread. "A grown man, even a thinnish one, would be terribly difficult to move once he was insensible. How on earth did she get him to the bandstand in the park?"

"One thing at a time," Charlotte reproved. "So far we haven't even hit him on the head."

"Well get on with it! What are you waiting for?"

"To get him to the right place, of course. It takes some planning. It must be the right time, too. We don't want him lying around for hours!"

"Why not?" Emily asked immediately. "Does it matter?"

"Of course it does! There are servants. How can you explain your—"

"All right," Emily interrupted. "Yes. I see. Then it has to be after the servants have retired, or in a place where they will not go. What about the garden somewhere? After dark you can be certain the gardener will not be working. A greenhouse or potting shed?"

"Excellent," Charlotte agreed. "How does one persuade him to go to the greenhouse after dark?"

"To show him something. . . ."

"What about if one had heard a sound?"

"Send the footman," Emily answered.

"Oh yes, of course. I don't have a footman."

"You don't have a greenhouse either."

Charlotte sighed with a brief second of regret. If they had been able to keep the new house, she might have had one. She might even have had a male servant in time. But that was all unimportant now.

"Then one lures him into the greenhouse," she reasoned, "by saying that there is something special to see. A flower which blooms at night and has a remarkable perfume."

"Is one on blossoming terms with a husband one is about to murder?" Emily grimaced.

"Then something else. I don't know . . . something amiss that the gardener has done? Something extravagant you need to speak to the man about, or his permission to dismiss him and employ someone else?"

"All right. You get him to the greenhouse, have him bend over to look at whatever it is, and hit him on the head as hard as you can with whatever comes to hand. At least in the greenhouse there will be plenty of tools one could use. Then what?"

"Leave him," Charlotte thought aloud. "Until the middle of the night, when you can return, to take off his head. . . ."

"Suitably dressed," Emily interposed.

"Dressed?"

"In something that will not show the blood!"

"Oh." Charlotte wrinkled her nose with distaste, but she realized it was an extremely practical remark. "Yes, of course. It would have to be either something she could dispose of entirely, or else something that was waterproof and from which it would wash off."

"Like—what? What can you wash blood off without leaving a stain?"

"Oilskins?" Emily asked dubiously. "But why would she have oilskins? It's not the sort of thing one keeps. I don't have anything remotely like that."

"Gardener's?" Charlotte thought aloud. "And then she could pass as a gardener going across the park." Her voice rose in excitement as memory returned. "And there was a gardener seen in the park, wheeling a barrow! Emily! Maybe that was the murderer—wheeling Aidan Arledge's body from his house to the bandstand?"

"Then was it Dulcie, or Landon Hurlwood?" Emily asked.

"It doesn't matter!" Charlotte replied urgently. "If it was Hurlwood, he can't have done it without her knowledge. She's guilty either way. Arledge must have been killed in his own greenhouse and taken to the park in his own wheelbarrow!"

"Then we must prove it." Emily stood up. "Knowing it is no use if we don't prove it."

"We don't know it. It's only a guess," Charlotte argued, rising to her feet also. "We have to prove it to ourselves first of all. We'll have to see it—find the place. There must be some stain of blood still there, if we know where to look."

"Well she's hardly going to give us a tour of her greenhouse, if she's cut her husband's head off there, is she!" Emily responded.

"No, of course not." Charlotte took a deep breath and plunged on. "We'll have to go at night, when she won't know."

"Break in?" Emily was incredulous, her voice rising to a squeak. Then as quickly the horror vanished from her face and a look of daring and enthusiasm replaced it. "Just the two of us? We'll have to go tonight. There's no time to lose."

Charlotte gulped. "Yes, tonight. We'll—we'll go from here, as soon as . . . well, about midnight, I suppose?" She looked at Emily questioningly.

"Midnight is far too early," Emily said. "She could still be up at that hour. I often am."

"You are not in mourning. She'll hardly be out dining or dancing."

"We should still leave it until one o'clock at the earliest."

"Oh—well I dare not return home. Thomas would . . ."

"Of course not," Emily agreed. "We'll have to leave from here. That's obvious. I could hardly explain it to Jack either. He'd take a fit! We'll have to leave here and wait somewhere else until one o'clock."

"Where? How should we dress? It must be practical. We shan't need to break in literally. All we need should be in the greenhouse or the gardener's shed. But we must have a lamp of some sort. I wish I had a policeman's bull's-eye lamp."

"No time," Emily dismissed it with regret. "I'll take a carriage lamp, that should do."

"How are we getting there? We can hardly expect your coachman to take us."

"We'll have to have him take us somewhere close by. That's simple. I know someone just 'round the corner. I'll say I'm calling there."

"At one o'clock in the morning, and dressed fit to burgle," Charlotte said with an involuntary giggle.

"Oh—yes." Emily bit her lip. "Well perhaps not. I'll say she was taken ill. I'll dress to burgle underneath, and put a good shawl on the top. You will have to do the same." And before Charlotte could protest, she added, "I'll find you something. We'll borrow from one of my maids. They wear plain stuff, dark colors. That will do excellently. Come. We have a great deal to see about." She shot Charlotte a look of fear and trembling excitement.

With her heart in her mouth, Charlotte followed her.

At five minutes past one o'clock Charlotte and Emily, dressed in dark stuff gowns and with shawls tied over their heads (Emily most particularly to hide the pale gleam of her hair), crept along the pavement towards the garden entrance of Dulcie Arledge's house. The carriage lamp was not lit; the streetlights were sufficient, and anyway, they wished intensely not to be noticed.

"Next one," Charlotte whispered. "I've got a knife and a skewer in case it is locked."

"A skewer?" Emily questioned.

"A kitchen skewer. You know—to test if things are cooked."

"No, I don't know. I don't cook. Can you use it?"

"Of course I can. All you have to do is poke it in."

"And the door opens?" Emily said with surprise.

"No of course not, fool! You know if the meat or the cake is cooked."

Emily giggled, and immediately in front of her Charlotte gave a little hiccough of excitement, and giggled as well.

When they reached the gate it was indeed padlocked, and Emily was obliged to light the lamp and hold it, with her back to Charlotte and her eyes fearfully watching the road, while Charlotte twiddled the skewer around carefully and at last managed to move the very simple latch. Emily doused the lamp instantly, and they undid the lock, took it off its chain and opened the door.

They slipped inside with a gasp of relief and pushed the gate closed again, being careful to take the chain and padlock with them, in case its open state should be noticed and cause suspicion.

Charlotte looked around her. It was extremely dark. The wall was high enough to block off almost all the light from the streetlamps beyond, and the sky was too overcast to allow much of the pale, three-quarter moon to shed more than a faint luminescence.

"I can't see," Emily whispered. "We aren't even going to find the greenhouse in this, never mind a bloodstain."

"We can find the greenhouse," Charlotte replied. "We'll light the lamp again when we are inside it."

"Do you really think anyone in the house would be awake at this hour?"

"No, but it isn't worth the risk. We would be turned out before we could find anything, and how on earth would we explain ourselves?"

The argument silenced Emily. The thought of being found was too hideous even to contemplate. They had no imaginable excuse whatever.

Charlotte leading the way, they crept forward along a narrow cobbled path, slimy with moss and dew, Emily clinging onto Charlotte's skirt to make sure they did not lose each other in the dark. To do that, and then come face to face, would be enough to break their nerve entirely. One shriek, however involuntary, would waken the neighborhood.

The huge mass of the house rose to their left, black against the pale clouds, and ahead of them was a broken roofline and the serrated edge of the spine of a lower roof, an elegant finial pointing a sharp finger upwards at the end.

"Greenhouse?" Emily asked softly.

"Conservatory," Charlotte replied.

"How do you know?"

334

"Final," Charlotte whispered back. "Don't have a finial on a greenhouse. It must be beyond, 'round the corner."

"Are you even sure they've got one?"

"They must have. Every house this size has a greenhouse or a potting shed. Greenhouse would be better."

"Why?"

"Easier to lure him to. How would you lure your husband to the potting shed in the middle of the night?"

Emily giggled nervously. "Don't be ridiculous. Conservatory, maybe. A romantic tryst? Put on your best peignoir and languish among the lilies?"

"Hardly. If you've been married twenty years—and he preferred men anyway. Damnation!" This last was added as Charlotte tripped and stubbed her foot against a large, decorative stone.

"What is it?" Emily demanded.

"A stone. It's all right." And gingerly she resumed her very slow forward pace.

It was five minutes before either of them spoke again. By this time they were around the back of the conservatory and creeping across an open terrace towards a further dense shadow ahead.

"That must be the greenhouse," Emily said hopefully.

"Or a summerhouse," Charlotte added. "Maybe that would be as good. Oh—no, of course it wouldn't. Nothing in a summerhouse to cover stains."

"I can't see any glass," Emily said with a note of desperation.

"I can't see anything at all!" Charlotte responded.

"If it were glass we should see some gleam of light on it!" Emily hissed. "It's not that dark!"

Charlotte stopped and turned around slowly, and Emily, not having noticed, bumped into her.

"Say something!" she snapped. "Don't do that without telling me."

"Sorry. Look! There's a gleam. There's glass over there. That must be the greenhouse." And without waiting for comment she set off in the new direction. Within moments they were outside a small building where dim panes of glass reflected the fitful gleam of the moon in a watery pattern like dull satin.

"Is it locked?" Emily asked.

Charlotte put her hand to the door and tried it. It swung

open under her touch, giving a painful squeak of unoiled hinges.

Emily let out a gasp, and immediately stifled it with her hand.

"Lamp!" she ordered.

As soon as they were inside Charlotte held it up and Emily lit it again. In its warm radiance the inside of the greenhouse sprang to vision. It was a small place set aside for forcing early flowers and vegetables. Trays of lettuce and marigold, delphinium, and larkspur seedlings sat on benches. Several geraniums were in pots on another shelf.

"Floor!" Emily whispered sharply. "Never mind about the shelves."

Charlotte held the lamp down about two feet above the wooden planks on which they were standing.

"I can't see anything," Emily said with acute disappointment. "It looks like hard-packed earth to me. Move it a bit." This last instruction was directed at the light.

Charlotte inched farther along, holding the lamp carefully. The corner of her skirt caught a flowerpot and sent it over with a dull thud.

"Ah!" Emily drew in her breath with a suffocated cry.

"Ssh!" Charlotte moved the light again. Then she saw it: a long dark stain on the ground near the far wall. "Oh . . ."

Emily bent down and peered at it. "It could be anything," she said with sharp disappointment. "Look." Above it was a shelf with various tins and bottles containing all sorts of chemicals and mixtures of fertilizer, creosote, and poison for wasps' and ants' nests.

"It's probably creosote," Charlotte said guardedly. "But not necessarily. If I had blood all over the place I should mask it by adding something strong like that. Here, pass me that trowel."

"What are you going to do?" Emily passed it immediately. "Dig."

For several moments Charlotte scratched at the hard earth, painstakingly removing the ground soaked with creosote and exposing under it a further layer whose odor, when she lifted it gingerly to her nose, was quite different. There was nothing sharp or pungent about it; it was stale and a little sweet.

"Blood?" Emily said with a catch in her voice.

"I think so." Slowly Charlotte rose from her knees, her face pale. "Now we've got to find the barrow. Come on. It's probably outside somewhere at this time of year."

Very carefully, the lamp held low and half covered by a shawl, they tiptoed out of the greenhouse, pulling the door closed behind them, and into the garden again.

"You'll have to hold the light up," Emily said anxiously. "We'll never see it otherwise."

Charlotte held it up obediently.

"Where does one keep a barrow?" she said thoughtfully, her voice so low Emily barely heard it. "And the oilskins. I wonder where they are?"

"Maybe she burnt them?" Emily suggested. "I would."

"Only if you've got an incinerator, and the servants wouldn't notice. Oilskins would make a terrible smell. Anyway, I don't suppose they are hers. They probably belong to the gardener. He'd miss them. No, she'd wash them off thoroughly and put them back. There must be a shed somewhere, for spades and forks and so on." She turned around slowly, holding the light higher.

"There!" Emily said hastily, just at the same moment as Charlotte saw it. "Put the light down! Someone'll see it! Come on, hurry up!"

At a rapid shuffle, so as not to trip or bump into anything, they moved towards the shed, which mercifully was not locked either. Once inside, the light was set on the bench, although it was hardly necessary. The wheelbarrow was immediately apparent, and the oilskins were hung on a peg above it.

Emily gave a little squeak of fear, and Charlotte shivered with a sudden consciousness of horror, knowing what it was she saw. Very carefully, her heart beating so violently it seemed as if her whole body shook with it, she put out her hand and ran her finger over the wooden surface of the wheelbarrow.

"Is it wet?" Emily asked.

"No, of course not," Charlotte replied. "But it is stained pretty badly. I think it's creosote again." She moved over to the oilskins and held the lamp close up to them. "There's something in the seams here. I'm sure that's blood."

"Then come on!" Emily whispered urgently. "We've got enough! Let's leave before someone catches us!"

Gratefully Charlotte turned around and retreated, snagging her shawl on the barrow handle and yanking it in sudden fear.

Outside, they were about to douse the light and try to make

their way back around the conservatory towards the wall when they saw another light about ten yards ahead of them, in the garden.

They both froze.

"Who goes there?" a loud masculine voice demanded. "Stop, or it'll be the worse for yer!"

"Oh God!" Emily sobbed. "It's the police!"

"We'll tell them what we found!" Charlotte said boldly, but her legs were shaking and her stomach felt decidedly sick. For a moment or two her feet would not obey her.

Emily tried to speak, but no coherent sound came.

The constable was almost upon them. His cape and gleaming buttons were clearly visible. He held up his bull's-eye lantern and stared at them incredulously.

"Well now then, what 'ave we 'ere? Two servant girls out to steal the lettuces, eh?"

"Most certainly not," Charlotte said with as much dignity as she could muster, which was very little. "We are—"

Emily suddenly came to life and gave her a resounding kick. Charlotte shrieked and swore involuntarily.

"Now then!" the constable said calmly. "There's no need for bad language, miss. Who are yer, and wot are yer doing 'ere? I'll 'ave ter take yer in charge. Yer don't live 'ere. I know all Mrs. Arledge's servants, and yer ain't one of 'em, or two of 'em I should say."

There was no evading the issue.

"No we are not!" Charlotte said, finding her voice at last. "My husband is Superintendent Thomas Pitt, of Bow Street station. And this is my—my maid." There was no need to incriminate Emily, at least not yet. She felt rather than heard Emily's sigh of relief.

"Now then, miss, that's a silly story that will just get you nowhere," the constable said with some surprise.

"This is the scene of a murder!" Charlotte said fiercely. "There are bloodstains in that greenhouse, and if you don't call Superintendent Pitt you will never be excused for it!"

" 'E'll be at 'ome in 'is bed," the constable said firmly.

"Of course he will. He lives at number twelve, Gordon Square, Bloomsbury. Send for him!" Charlotte ordered imperiously. "And there's a telephone."

"Well, I don't know if . . ."

He was saved from further argument or excuse by a light in the house going on and the scullery door opening.

"What's going on?" a man's voice called out peremptorily. "Who's there?"

"Police, sir," the constable replied confidently. "Constable Woodrow, sir. I just caught two burglars in your garden."

"We are not burglars!" Charlotte hissed.

"You be quiet!" Constable Woodrow was becoming unhappy; he was placed in a ridiculous situation. "No need to worry, sir. Everything is in 'and, you tell Mrs. Arledge not to disturb 'erself. I'll take care of this."

"It is nothing of the sort," Charlotte said with sudden desperation. "We are not burglars. Send for Superintendent Pitt immediately." She gulped. It was now or never. Everything was in the balance, Pitt's career, their home. "This is the—the scene of a murder!"

"Murder?" The butler, dressed in his nightshirt, came out of the doorway at last, the lantern still in his hand. "Who is dead?"

"Mr. Arledge, you fool!" Charlotte said exasperatedly. "He was killed in his own greenhouse, and taken to the park in a wheelbarrow. Now send for the police! Have you one of the new telephone instruments?"

"Yes, ma'am."

"Then use it. Call Bloomsbury one-two-seven and fetch Superintendent Pitt."

"Now, just a minute ..." Woodrow began, but the butler had already turned and gone back into the house. A decisive command was better than standing in his nightshirt on the steps in the cold, arguing with a constable. He knew Pitt's name, and the mistress had welcomed him in the house. He would sort out this fearful situation.

"Yer shouldn't 'ave done that!" Woodrow said angrily.

A light sprang on upstairs in the house.

"Now look what you've done!" he went on. "Woke up poor Mrs. Arledge. As if she 'adn't enough to bear, what with 'er 'usband's death an' all."

Charlotte ignored him, pulling her shawl tighter around her. Now that they were no longer absorbed in what they were doing, she was growing cold.

Emily stood beside her shivering. She did not even wish to imagine what Jack might say when this came to his knowledge. There was just a faint hope Charlotte's lie would hold.

That was ruined by more lights from the house and footsteps across the kitchen, and after a moment more, Dulcie Arledge

339

herself appearing in the scullery doorway, dressed in a gorgeous sky-blue wrap and with her brown hair falling gently over her shoulders.

"What is going on here?" she asked with polite surprise. "Have you found intruders, Constable? Did I understand correctly?"

"That's right, ma'am." Woodrow stepped forward, dragging Charlotte and Emily with him.

Emily cowered, but surely Dulcie would not recognize her in this dress, in the uncertain light of the bull's-eye lamp.

"Women?" Dulcie said incredulously. "They look like women."

"They are women, ma'am," Woodrow agreed. "After vegetables, likely. Don't worry about it, ma'am. I'll take 'em in and likely as not, you won't 'ave ter do anything about it except agree ter the charge. Now come on." He yanked at Charlotte a good deal less gently than before. Apparently his patience had snapped and he had changed his mind. Dulcie's quiet authority had been enough to dispel any doubts.

"Charlotte!" There was panic rising in Emily's voice. "Think of something! Not only will Thomas be ruined, Jack will be too!"

Such desperate times called for extreme measures. Charlotte opened her mouth and let out an earsplitting scream.

"Gawd!" Constable Woodrow leapt into the air and dropped the lantern. It rolled on the ground without breaking, ending up almost at the stone edge of the path. Charlotte did it again, and was rewarded by blinds shooting up in the house and more sounds of obvious activity.

"What did you do that for?" Emily hissed furiously.

"Witnesses," Charlotte replied, and screamed again.

Woodrow swore vehemently and dived for the lantern.

"For Heaven's sake stop it!" Dulcie commanded. "You'll disturb the entire neighborhood. What on earth is the matter with you? Be quiet at once!"

Emily hesitated on the edge of trying to run away, and abandoned it.

Charlotte moved towards Dulcie, and into the radius of the light from the back door, just as Landon Hurlwood, hair disheveled, nightshirt showing above and below his dressing robe, appeared behind Dulcie, his face filled with alarm.

"Are you hurt?" he asked her, his voice husky with anxiety.

340

She froze, the blood draining from her face, leaving her suddenly ashen.

He looked beyond her at Charlotte, but there was no shred of recognition in his eyes. Then he turned to the constable. "What's going on? What's this? How serious is it?"

"No one's hurt, sir," Woodrow said, for the first time total uncertainty in his voice. He understood a scandal when he saw one, but to find it in Mrs. Arledge's house destroyed his composure entirely. "This woman"—he indicated Charlotte—"this woman screamed, but no one has touched 'er, I swear."

Hurlwood peered at her, and saw a young woman in a maid's dress and with her hair wild and her skin stained with creosote and dust. Then his eyes went beyond her to Emily, now also in the light.

"Mrs. Radley . . ." Then he blanched, realizing at last what Dulcie had seen from the first.

"I can't imagine, Mrs. Radley, what persuaded you to break into my garden in the middle of the night," Dulcie said with a cold, shaking voice. "But there is nothing I can do to assist you. I think you must be mad. Perhaps the strain of childbirth, and then the political campaign, has broken your health. Your husband—"

"The police are coming," Charlotte interrupted firmly.

"The police are already here!" Dulcie pointed out.

"I mean Superintendent Pitt." Charlotte pushed her hair out of her eyes. "We have found the place where Mr. Arledge was murdered. There is still blood on the ground, in spite of the creosote you've poured over it. And also the wheelbarrow in which you took him to the park, after you had cut his head off."

Dulcie opened her mouth to protest, but her voice died in a gasp.

Behind her, Landon Hurlwood was so white his eyes looked like holes sunken into his skull.

"And the oilskins," Charlotte continued relentlessly. It must be finished. "Which you used to protect yourself from the blood."

"That's stupid!" Woodrow said with a strangled gasp. "Why would Mrs. Arledge ever think of such a dreadful thing? That's wicked."

"To be free to marry Mr. Hurlwood, now his wife is dead too; to escape from a dead marriage and revenge herself for twenty years' betrayal," Charlotte said, her voice strangely level in the awful silence. "She took advantage of the Headsman's crimes to kill him and open the way for her."

Woodrow turned to Dulcie. Landon Hurlwood had moved a step away from her, a terrible comprehension filling his face, like the knowledge of death.

Dulcie shot a look of hatred at Charlotte so intense Emily stepped backwards away from her, and Charlotte felt the cold run right through her body. Then Dulcie turned to Hurlwood.

"Landon!" She let out a single cry, then saw his expression—the horror, the tearing bruising guilt, and the revulsion—and knew that everything was lost.

It was impossible to say what she might have done next, because the garden doors had opened without their hearing them and Pitt stood wild-haired and ill-dressed not a yard from them.

Dulcie turned to him, opened her mouth, but no sound came.

Pitt's face was filled with a disillusion that carried all the pain of every awakening from a sweet and gentle dream into a bitter reality. Then even as Charlotte watched him, she saw the admiration and tenderness bleed away until there was only an agonizing remnant left, that small shred of pity that never left him, no matter for whom or what the wound or the guilt. And with a coldness that ran right through her, leaving her shaking, she realized how deeply he had been moved by Dulcie, and how close she herself had come to losing a part of him which she could never have regained.

"Constable, take Mrs. Arledge to the Bow Street station. She is under arrest for the murder of Aidan Arledge," he said very quietly.

Woodrow gulped. "Yes sir. Yes sir!" And he moved forward to obey.

Landon Hurlwood stood rooted to the spot like a man already passed beyond the world of ordinary exchange and the small businesses of life.

Pitt turned to Charlotte and Emily.

"Your own husband can take care of you," he said to Emily. "You, thank God, are not my problem." He turned to Charlotte. "You have some explaining to do, madam. You deserve to be taken in charge for breaking and entering!"

"You've got her." Charlotte disregarded his words completely. "Will you be restored to your position now?"

For several seconds he struggled manfully to retain his anger, and lost. In spite of his best efforts his face broke into a smile of overwhelming relief. "Yes. I got the Headsman today, too."

"You did?" She did not even care who he was, or why. She launched herself forward and threw herself into his arms. "You are brilliant! I always knew you were brilliant!"

He clasped her as closely as he could and kissed her cheek, her hair, her eyes, and then her mouth. Then he put out his other arm and took hold of Emily as well.

"Shall you tell Jack?" Emily asked in a very small voice.

"No," Pitt replied with a muffled laugh. "But you will!"

Coming soon from

ANNE PERRY

featuring Charlotte and Thomas Pitt

TRAITORS GATE

Secret information is being passed to a foreign power, and Pitt knows that the traitor can only be one of a half dozen distinguished public servants. At the same time, in defiance of his superior in the police, Pitt is looking into the tragic death of his childhood mentor from an overdose of laudanum called at best an accident, at worst—a suicide. Then, when the strangled body of a beautiful young society woman is found floating near the Tower of London, Pitt begins to suspect that the cases are all connected, and with Charlotte's help he begins to untangle the threads....

Published by Fawcett Books.

Available in your local bookstore in March 1995.

Bestselling novels by
ANNE PERRY
Available in your local bookstore.